W9-CCV-104

Dear Reader,

Is finding true love a matter for fate to decide? Is it always "meant to be"? Can destiny bring two lovers together, even when life seems determined to pull them apart?

We think so, and we're excited to offer two brand-new stories that dare to test the boundaries of destiny's reach and ask the question, "What if?"

Follow the heartache and joy of one man's redemption in Crystal Green's "First Love," when a wealthy businessman's brush with death convinces him to reunite with his high school sweetheart. And in "Second Chance," Judy Duarte spins a delightful tale of a woman who faces her past, only to find that the man of her dreams may be the one she left behind.

We hope you enjoy this entrancing beginning to *Montana Mavericks: The Kingsleys*, where we return to the little town of Rumor for a new miniseries chock-full of twists, turns and tons of true love. This year, nothing is as it seems beneath the big skies of Montana.

Enjoy your brush with destiny!

The Editors
Silhouette Books

Be sure to catch the continuing story of Rumor, Montana's ruling family, The Kingsleys, available only from Silhouette Special Edition:

MOON OVER MONTANA by Jackie Merritt (SE #1550)
Available now!
MARRY ME...AGAIN by Cheryl St.John (SE #1558)
Available August 2003
BIG SKY BABY by Judy Duarte (SE #1563)
Available September 2003
THE RANCHER'S DAUGHTER by Jodi O'Donnell (SE #1568)
Available October 2003
HER MONTANA MILLIONAIRE by Crystal Green (SE #1574)
Available November 2003
SWEET TALK by Jackie Merritt (SE #1580)
Available December 2003

CRYSTAL GREEN

lives in San Diego, California, where she writes full-time and occasionally teaches. When she isn't penning romances, she enjoys reading, wasting precious time on the Internet, overanalyzing movies, risking her life on police ride-alongs, petting her parents' Maltese dogs and fantasizing about being a really great cook.

Whenever possible, Crystal loves to travel. Her favorite souvenirs include journals—the pages reflecting everything from taking tea in London's Leicester Square to backpacking up endless mountain roads leading to the castles of Sintra, Portugal.

She'd love to hear from her readers at: 8895 Towne Centre Drive, Suite 105-178 San Diego, CA 92122-5542.

JUDY DUARTE

is an avid reader who enjoys a happy ending, and she always wanted to write books of her own. One day, she decided to make that dream come true. Five years and six manuscripts later, she sold her first book to Silhouette Special Edition.

Her unpublished stories have won the Emily and the Orange Rose, and in 2001, she became a double Golden Heart finalist. Judy credits her success to Romance Writers of America and two wonderful critique partners, Sheri WhiteFeather and Crystal Green, both of whom write for Silhouette.

At times, when a stubborn hero and a headstrong heroine claim her undivided attention, she and her family are thankful for fast food, pizza delivery and video games. When she's not at the keyboard or in a Walter Mitty–type world, she enjoys traveling, romantic evenings with her personal hero and playing board games with her kids.

Judy lives in Southern California and loves to hear from her readers. You may write to her at: P.O. Box 498, San Luis Rey, CA 92068-0498. You can also visit her Web site at: www.judyduarte.com.

MONTANA MAVERICKS

DOUBLE DESTINY

CRYSTAL GREEN
JUDY DUARTE

Silhouette Books

Published by Silhouette Books
America's Publisher of Contemporary Romance

Special thanks and acknowledgment are given to
Crystal Green and Judy Duarte for their contributions
to the *Montana Mavericks: The Kingsleys* series.

 SILHOUETTE BOOKS

DOUBLE DESTINY

Copyright © 2003 by Harlequin Books S.A.

ISBN 0-373-21859-1

The publisher acknowledges the copyright holders
of the individual works as follows:

FIRST LOVE
Copyright © 2003 by Harlequin Books S.A.

SECOND CHANCE
Copyright © 2003 by Harlequin Books S.A.

Visit Silhouette at www.eHarlequin.com

Printed in U.S.A.

CONTENTS

FIRST LOVE
Crystal Green

To Kim Nadelson:
I couldn't have custom-ordered a greater editor!
Thank you from the bottom of my heart.

Chapter 1

The night Russell Kingsley crashed his vintage 1949 Mercury into the guardrail on a lone Montana highway, he'd been thinking of only one thing.

Suzy.

Suzy McCord.

Even as glass from the windshield shattered and fell like tears from the impact of his head bulleting against it, even as his knees hit the dashboard with such force that the denim of his faded jeans split over his kneecaps like bruised frowns, his thoughts were mired in a single groove.

Suzy's back. Back in Rumor.

Something sticky, wet and red filtered over Russell's vision as he opened his eyes. Steam hissed in his ears, sounding more like accusations than the last wheezes of a decimated engine.

After what you did to Suzy, how can you face her again?

"Dear Lord," said a panicked voice he didn't recognize.

Russell barely had the strength to glance at a face peeking through the jagged glass of his driver's side window. The man was just a shape, a stranger framed by the blue void of a late-November sky.

"I'm so sorry," he said, his breath coming out in a cloud, his voice riding the edge of hysteria. He continued apologizing, saying something about needing sleep but not being able to get it if he wanted to deliver the frozen goods packed into his eighteen-wheeler to MonMart on time.

Russell tuned out, darkness rising behind his gaze. He was dizzy, so damned dizzy. So damned sorry, too.

Something scratched against his right hand, and he grasped at the solid sensation—the snapshot. The one he'd been staring at just as he'd rounded a corner and swerved to avoid hitting the semi that had drifted into his lane.

The image burned into the backs of his eyelids.

Prom night, May, 1986. Suzy in her lacy, pink dress, her blue eyes sparkling as a tuxedoed Russell held her gloved hand, her chin-length red hair shining under the photographer's lights.

Seventeen years ago. It had been that long since he and his family had ostracized her from their circle, causing her to leave Rumor.

The flash of red-and-blue lights jarred him out of his stupor.

"Sir?" said a different voice.

Strange. How much time had passed?

"We're gonna get you right outta here. Just sit still and don't worry about a thing. Got it?"

As the sound of steel yawned and creaked around Russell, he held on to his picture, held on to Suzy, seeing her laughing as head cheerleader for the Rumor High School Rangers. Seeing the emotion pooling in her gaze as she said yes to his prom-night marriage proposal. Seeing an altogether different sheen of tears as he told her goodbye.

When he opened his eyes again, he realized more time must have escaped him. The white streak of fluorescent hospital lights bolted over him while he lay on a gurney, wheeled down a sterile hallway.

"The OR better be ready—STAT!" yelled the woman hovering above him. She wore blue scrubs and a worried gaze. ''This one's in bad shape, so don't mess around!''

Bad shape, huh? Were they talking about him? The guy who was way too busy creating a multi-million dollar empire to worry about anything?

He felt the photo, crinkled in his hand. Good. Still there.

He didn't want to lose Suzy again.

As his gurney flew around a corner and skidded to a stop in front of a bank of elevators, Russell allowed his head to flop onto its side.

Through a space in the bodies surrounding him, he saw a girl. A redheaded, ponytailed teenager dressed in a pink-and-white candy striper uniform and clutching a vase of flowers. Though her eyes were as wide and full as summer moons, she tried to smile at him. But her gesture failed, crumbled, falling into a tremulous frown.

Damn, he must be a bloody mess. But how bad off could he be if he was still conscious, still thinking of…

A blinding pain rushed his body. The pain of emptiness. Darkness took over from there, welling up, swallowing him whole, blacking out the candy striper, the white-flare hospital walls and the rising tide of panicked shouting.

Then there was nothing at all.

* * *

"Got him!" said a familiar female voice.

Russell's eyelids fluttered open, only to close again when a blast of lamplight hit him.

"Mr. Kingsley?" Same voice, different tone. More relaxed, tinged with something like triumph. "I'm Dr. Fisk. Welcome back to the world."

He could barely talk around the sore dryness cottoning his mouth. "Where the hell did I go?"

He wedged open his eyes a bit more, enough to see the lady doctor from the hallway, in addition to several more medical personnel, pulling down their half masks to smile at him. They floated around his vision, kaleidoscope swoops of color, circling, winging over him with bleary grace. In fact, the entire room seemed fuzzy at the edges, the hazy shade of lost dreams, but when his gaze finally locked into place, he could see with enough detail to discern that sweat soaked the necks of the medical teams' scrubs.

"We thought you were heading toward a coma," she said.

A coma?

A burst of memory, of twisted metal and a warm, bloody numbness across his forehead, consumed Russell, bringing back the moment when he'd glanced up from Suzy's picture to see the semi's headlights heading toward him. Then there'd been that split second when he'd overcompensated with the steering wheel, the yelp of tires on the highway as he'd swerved, then the lightning-crash image of a windshield coming toward his face. The breath left his lungs.

He could've died tonight.

Russell clenched his right hand, noting the absence of Suzy's picture. A fist of panic squeezed his insides. "Where's...?"

"Don't worry, Mr. Kinglsey. We'll return your personal effects soon. Let's get you settled first."

And they did, situating him in a private, nondescript room where he could rest and repeat, over and over, I'm alive.

I'm alive.

He had no idea how much time had passed when a nurse entered and asked if he felt strong enough for visitors.

"Your family's outside," she said. "And Dr. Fisk okayed guests."

Russell nodded, leaning against the hard pillows tucked behind his back. He'd caught a smudged glimpse of himself in a mirror on the wall—yup, except for the damage he saw the same intense green eyes and black hair, the same driven fool, all right—and he wondered if the swelling and cuts would make his family crazy.

They'd have no idea that the real agony was inside, where Suzy rested in his heart.

The Kingsley brood crept into the room, headed by his father, Stratton. "Well, son. Looks like Whitehorn Memorial has its hands full now that you've taken up residence."

It was his father's best attempt at humor, so Russell did his darnedest to smile. Damn, it hurt to do even that. But it'd taken years for him and Stratton to come to this point, to offer uncomfortable jokes, to forget that Stratton had been the one who'd forced Russell to make the choice between Suzy—his first and only love—and the family.

Carolyn Forsythe Kingsley, his mother, stepped forward, typically dressed to the nines in a crisp, tweed suit that complemented her auburn hair. The only indications that her East Coast polish had cracked were the lines of pink that trailed down her face. She ran a tender hand down Russell's arm, then kissed him on the cheek, expertly avoiding his injuries. "Thank the Lord you're alive. We were so very worried about you."

Behind her, his younger brothers, Taggert and Reed, lingered. Tag had his arm around the shoulders of his petite sister, Maura, whose tear streaks matched her mother's. The only person missing from the Kingsley welcome-back-from-the-near-dead committee was his cousin, Jeff Forsythe, who'd lived with them until joining the U.S. Forest Service.

"I'm sorry," Russell said. "I didn't mean to cause so much consternation."

"What were you doing?" asked Carolyn. "There's a storm warning. You know better than to be out at such times, even if the weather did pass us over."

Storm. He almost laughed. The only storm warning he'd been paying attention to was the turmoil he'd felt when Tag had told him about Suzy.

She continued. "And driving one of your collectible cars, without an airbag, besides?"

Russell shouldered the brunt of her anger. "It was a good time to take the Mercury out for some exercise."

"Oh, Russell—"

"It's over and done with, Mom. Okay?" He grabbed her hand from his arm, squeezing her fingers. "I'm fine."

The nurse popped back into the room. "Folks, the doctor says ten more minutes, then he rests."

The family nodded, and she left. His father gave them a meaningful glance—what meaning it had,

Russell wasn't sure—and his brothers and sisters fussed over him before filtering out of the room. Taggert was the last sibling to leave, following his mother out the door before turning around at the last minute.

"Did this happen because of Suzy? Because if it did…"

"Don't take this on yourself, Tag." Russell watched his father, who stared at him with an unreadable expression in his green eyes. Like father, like son, thought Russell, wondering if he resembled his father in more than just eye color.

Tag gazed at them both, then shook his head and left the room.

Pure silence, laced with the lingering smells of Phisoderm and bitter medicine. Eau de hospital.

Stratton dug into his pocket, unearthing the crumpled, bloodstained prom picture. He held it out to his son.

"What is this?" asked Russell. "Some warped peace offering?"

"Let's not start up again." His father's shoulders slumped as he walked nearer the bed, taking a seat. He placed the picture on the table, propping it against one of many filled flower vases. "We've been through too much to resurrect old hurts."

Russell wanted to forgive the older man, and he

thought he'd done so, before today. "She's back. I'm sure Tag told you."

"And you just had to go hunting through your mom's memory boxes for a sentimental relic, reliving something that ended seventeen years ago. Haven't you moved past Suzy McCord?"

"Obviously I haven't."

"What did you do, Russell? Carry that picture around town with you all day, staring at it as if it would bring her back to you?"

He didn't say a word, embarrassed because he'd been caught in a weak moment. Embarrassed because his dad knew him so well. Too well.

Stratton continued, his face growing ruddier with each question. "Has she consumed you so much that you couldn't drive a damned car?"

"I just needed to clear my mind."

"You almost had more than your mind cleared." Stratton stopped, took a deep breath.

"Don't get worked up," said Russell. He wanted his father to leave now, to go away and let him sleep off the past few head-spinning hours. To allow him to wallow in the stunning fact that he was alive for a reason.

Good God, that was it. He was being given a second chance, wasn't he? Another opportunity to ask for Suzy's forgiveness, to make up for sending her out of town with a look so heartbroken that it pained Russell to recall it.

"I'm not worked up," said Stratton. Then, quietly, "We almost lost you, son. I deserve to blow some steam out my ears."

Russell gathered his energy. "You've done a pretty fair job of not sticking your nose into my business lately. Now I'm wondering if you're so bored with pseudoretirement that the temptation to do it again is overwhelming."

"Your accident put some spit and fire into you, didn't it?"

Russell settled back a moment, the memory of his face hitting the windshield rushing up to blind him. He shut his eyes, trying to block out the image.

"I can't believe I almost died tonight."

Stratton gruffly patted Russell's hand. "You just rest up. The family's worried. Besides, MonMart's waiting for you, and I know you can't spend more than a precious minute away from your brainchild."

MonMart. The superstore that had turned the Kingsley's ranching finances into a fortune. The development of MonMart—opening stores across the state, the plan to cultivate other sites across the country—had taken over his life. It had nursed him through the loss of Suzy. It had been his consolation, his savior.

But now it didn't mean quite as much, without a special someone to help him enjoy its success. Someone like the woman he'd let go.

"I don't think you understand," said Russell. "For some reason, I'm still here among the living."

Stratton nodded his graying head. "I know all too well what you're talking about. I felt the same after I beat my lung cancer."

The reminder of Stratton's illness slammed between Russell and his father like an invisible, unbreachable wall.

Russell said, "Then you know how important it is to live each day to its fullest."

"I know what's coming, and I don't like the sound of it. Listen, I regret what happened with little Suzy McCord, but it's over. You're both adults now, with different lives. There's no changing that."

"*Carpe diem.* Do you know what that means?"

"It's Latin for 'forget it.'"

Every minute convinced Russell that he was losing time. Suzy was waiting.

"Fate's telling me to see her again." Russell smiled, really smiled, reopening a cut on his lip. The tang of blood in his mouth only made him feel more vital. "I'm alive because I need to correct the mistake I made with her all those years ago."

Stratton stared at him, and Russell knew his father was thinking about how he'd had one lung removed, how he'd suffered through chemotherapy and radiation just to get his own second chance.

He nodded, and Russell could tell his father was clean out of arguments.

"I hope Suzy has enough grace in her soul to forgive the both of us. Best of luck."

Russell closed his eyes, feeling Stratton pat his hand and murmur, "Love you, son," before he left.

Seize the day.

And he would, once they let him out of this stinking place.

Soothed by the thought, Russell fell asleep, darkness covering him like a heavy comforter, embracing him.

After several days of "observation," a time in which Russell had nearly gone stir-crazy with all the tests, prodding and rest, Dr. Fisk finally allowed him to return home.

"With the family to aid you," said the good doc, a knowing scold to her tone.

Maura, baby sister extraordinaire, had decided to step in at this point, taking over Russell's life, fluffing his pillows, cooking his meals, generally dictating his existence.

She didn't seem to understand that he needed to see Suzy. *Now.*

The urge was even stronger now that his brother Reed had told Russell that Suzy had been hired at MonMart as a cashier.

Fate. God bless it.

In the meantime, Maura held him against his will in his own home. Even if she was petite and cute, she was still the one in charge, efficiently tucking a blanket around him as he rested in a wide leather TV chair.

"How am I supposed to switch channels like this?" While he was at it, how was he supposed to sneak out to contact Suzy, held captive by this cocoon of wool?

Maura grinned. "This'll ward off the chill."

"Here in the twenty-first century, we've got a central heating unit, Miss Bedpans. Besides, I've got things to do. I need to get to MonMart."

His sister merely gave him an exasperated look.

"Would you lay off your mission? Jeez, I rue the day Reed told you that Suzy is working there. It's given you twice as much impatience. She's not going anywhere, okay? And you need to rest."

A knock sounded on the door, sending Maura through the maze of get-well stuffed animals, flowers and joke gifts that brightened up his dark-wooded abode.

"Nurse Ratched," he muttered as she disappeared.

"I heard that. And I hope you didn't phone anyone to come visit you. You've had enough guests today."

Russell tried to tamp down his grumpiness. He'd give anything to get out of here, have a beer at Joe's Bar with the boys. After, of course, he saw Suzy again.

Dammit, he needed to find her. This waiting around was useless.

But...

No, he didn't want to think about that.

Shoot. Great. He couldn't help it.

What if Suzy didn't want to see *him?* What if coming face-to-face with her again only stirred up old, agonizing memories?

Russell shrugged off his blanket, risking Maura's wrath. He was talking himself out of a reunion with the woman he'd loved more than anything.

Hell. He'd created MonMart, a monster among businesses, selling everything from clothing to groceries to household goods at a discount. It was an unqualified success.

So why did the thought of seeing one, gentle ex-girlfriend concern him so much?

His vision blurred for a moment and Russell shut his eyes, clearing the smeared colors of his sight. Every once in a while, he'd get like this—disoriented. Maybe he did need a good rest after all.

Maura slowly walked back into the room. "Russell?"

He thought she was going to yell at him for taking off the blanket, leaving only a cable-knit sweater and jeans to warm him.

"Don't start," he said.

He should've caught the furrowing of her brow, should've read something into it.

But before he could process the change in his sister, Suzy McCord walked into the room, holding a vase of orchids in front of her as if it were a shield.

His heart jumped right to his throat, and he felt it pounding there, the pulse spreading through his veins to throb through every inch of his skin.

She just stood in place, flushed against the pink of her heavy coat and long, wool skirt. God, she was the same. Just the same as he remembered.

She still wore her red hair to her chin, still was as slender and delicate as a reed that swayed and bent—but never broke—in a harsh wind. This was his prom picture come to life.

He couldn't form words, couldn't bring himself to be the Russell Kingsley who forged hard deals, who broke business egos on a daily basis.

Suzy spoke first, her voice floating around his head, whipping up his senses until they flared with heat.

Was it his imagination, or was she just as stunned to see *him* again?

"I heard about your accident, Russell."

He wondered if, when he stood, she would still reach to just below his shoulder. Wondered if she would still fit against him perfectly during a slow dance.

He finally found his voice. Unfortunately, it broke on his first word. "It's good to see you."

Maura backed out of the room, then disappeared.

Suzy cleared her throat, pushed the flowers in front of her, as if she just wanted to get rid of them and be done with all this awkwardness. He could see the wariness in her blue eyes, in the way they swept over his body as if he was about to pounce on her.

Well, hell. Wasn't he?

"I brought you these," she said. "Orchids. But I see you've got a full house."

As she set the vase on a gift-choked end table, he watched her take in the home he'd built on his family's ranch estate. Watched her gaze skim over the high ceiling with its crossbeams, the stone chimney with its roaring fire, the tacky deer-antler lamp his brother Reed had given him as a house-warming joke.

He wished she seemed more at home. "Thanks, Suzy." Pause. "It's good to see you."

Understatement.

"Likewise. Even if you do have a few more fresh scars than usual."

Several beats of silence separated them. He couldn't believe there wasn't anything to say. Actually, there was *too much* to say, wasn't there? Too many hurtful phrases she could throw at him, too many accusations he didn't want to hear.

Hold it. He'd already beaten himself up over the years. He'd done his time.

"I hear you're working the registers at Mon-Mart," he said, rising from his chair. His limbs protested, but at least his head didn't swim. Not from his injuries, anyway.

"No, don't." She held out her pink-gloved hands. "Don't."

He stopped at the blunt command.

Instead of showing his singed feelings on the outside, he rested his hands on his hips instead. "Not even a welcome-home hug between old friends?"

They'd never been just that. Friends. They'd been so much more.

Now that he was standing, he noticed that her gaze lingered over the length of him, the visual caress at odds with her casually cold words.

"I came over to wish you well. Trying to win over the boss and all that, you know." She blinked, girding herself once more, then she backed away a couple of steps, as if preparing to leave.

"Stop," he said. He reached out, probably moving too quickly. "I haven't seen you for years."

Her eyes darkened. "You made sure that was the case."

"Suzy—"

She laughed, and the sound needled under his skin.

"I shouldn't have come here."

Was this really happening? Russell couldn't believe his reunion was souring at such breakneck speed.

Before he could recover from her last words, she turned around, walking toward the front hallway as she said over her shoulder, "Have a speedy recovery, Russell. And, please, don't think I came here because I want to start things up again. I truly wish you well. I—''

She stopped, bit her lip, then opened the door and stepped outside. A blast of bracing air flew against him, ghostlike.

The door slammed, cutting off the cold, bringing Maura out of the kitchen where she'd been hiding.

''Was it all you'd been hoping for?'' she asked, patting Russell's arm in apparent pity.

Surely Fate hadn't brought him back from the edge of death to kick him in the face like this. He'd be damned if he gave up that easily.

''At least she knows I'm still alive.'' He smiled, his lips weighted just the slightest bit by a melancholy ache.

''Well, you've got one thing going for you. She came to see you first.'' Maura walked away.

Hell, she was right. Suzy had made first contact, held out the olive branch. That had to mean *something*.

This time when he grinned, it didn't even hurt.

Chapter 2

Finally. Back in the saddle.

As Russell checked his watch—yes, it was definitely four o'clock—and sauntered out of his upstairs office at MonMart, he hoped Suzy hadn't called in sick today.

He'd waited two days from the time she'd brought him flowers. Two dismal, long days filled with drumming fingers and endless ministrations from Maura. It was enough time to allow Suzy to think he wasn't going to put pressure on her, to think maybe Russell would respect her obvious desire to steer clear of him.

She'd been nervous the other day, sure, but he couldn't help feeling there'd been something *there*. A lone spark, a subtle sigh, an indication that Suzy still might harbor a feeling or two for him.

You didn't just forget your first love.

Russell passed his administrative assistant's desk, setting a wrapped truffle on the corner of it. "Almost quitting time, Mahnita."

She spied the chocolate, glowed at him. "Good to have you back, Mr. Kingsley."

As he disappeared around the corner by the stairs, he grinned and said, "Yup. Back in the saddle, all right."

His stomach jumped. Butterflies. You had to be kidding. Grown men didn't get winged creatures brushing around their stomachs. Or did they?

Hell, he thought, buttoning his heavy sports jacket over his jeans. He hadn't been seriously interested in a woman in ages. MonMart had been his main focus, leaving no room for long-term dalliances.

After opening the Employees Only door, a whir of hustle and bustle assaulted him: shoppers steering their carts through aisles of produce, meat, fresh-baked goods, toys, clothes—everything a body needed, and then some. Russell made his way to the front of the store, greeting the townsfolk, thanking them for their concern when they remarked on his accident.

Dee Dee Reingard, one of Rumor's sweetest, most luckless citizens, cornered him in front of the registers, barring his way with her cart.

"Land sakes, Russell. You look fit as a fiddle already."

He scanned the cashiers, disappointed when he couldn't find Suzy. "A little mishap can't keep a Kingsley down," he said absently, smiling at Dee Dee.

After a minute or two of small talk, he sensed Suzy more than saw her. She'd relieved the employee at register number two.

Russell had a hard time keeping his feet in place. "I won't keep you from your shopping, Mrs. Reingard. You have a good night now."

He clasped one of the older woman's hands in his, causing her to sigh.

"You charming guy," she said, shaking her head. "You make a woman forget her troubles, even for a minute or two."

She smiled, then left him. As Russell watched her shuffle away, he couldn't help feeling sorry for Dee Dee. Her husband was in jail, charged with killing the woman he'd had an affair with.

Poor lady. A victim of idle talk. Just as Suzy had

been after Russell had broken off their short-lived engagement and she'd left town.

He adjusted his jacket again, as if testing his shining white armor. Or was it rusted armor?

Get it together, Russell, he thought. This is your second and last chance. Don't blow it.

Suzy had a short checkout line, so he decided to grab a couple magazines and a few packs of gum then wait in her aisle. He even opened up one periodical, pretending to be so engrossed that the pages hid his face.

As Suzy efficiently took care of the customers, he stepped in front of her, grinning.

She shook her head. "Not you."

"I'm in dire need of reading material."

"Right." The conveyor belt hummed, sweeping the magazines into her hand. "*Cosmopolitan. Glamour. YM.* Are you looking for a sassy shade of lipstick to go with your Christmas party outfit?"

Thank goodness, she still had that sense of humor. Suzy had perfected a bubbly delivery, one that often covered a pointed wit.

The challenge of it spiked his heart rate to a dangerous speed. He strained against his jeans, encouraged by her liveliness, her vivid beauty only slightly blurred by the soft pink of her work smock.

"I'm just doing my research," he said, leaning

against the counter, crossing one booted ankle over the other. "A man needs to labor hard in order to understand women."

"We're not so tough to solve." Suzy's gaze went wary, warm dark blue chilled by a few flecks of protective steel.

The reflection of his betrayal almost chased him out of her line, but Russell stood firm. Suzy, with the way she'd been raised, with all the disappointments of her life, wasn't going to be an easy woman to win back.

"From what I remember," he said, "you weren't tough at all."

She looked away, seized the magazines, scanned them into the register.

He lowered his voice, leaning in closer. "That night, in the back of my granddad's Chevy, by Lake Monet... You had no rough spots, Suzy. Not when I touched you—"

"That'll be thirteen seventy-two."

She was eyeing the build-up of her line. He could see that, behind the counter, she was tapping her foot.

He got out his wallet, handing her a twenty. "I didn't mean to shake you up."

Thunk, thunk. She punched at the register keys,

but the only response she received was a long, wailing *beeeeep*.

"Shoot," she said from between clenched teeth.

She jabbed at a few more keys.

"Maybe if you just..." He gestured toward the machine.

"I know how to work this darned thing." She shot him a deadly glare.

Finally, after a few seconds more of the excruciating mechanical scream, Suzy hit the right buttons, and the register drawer flew open. She coolly counted out his change, then bagged his merchandise.

"Thank you very much, Mr. Kingsley. Come to your own store again soon, now, y'hear?"

He inclined his head toward Suzy, acknowledging his obvious ploy just to talk to her.

But was that all she had to say? A polite brush-off, as if he was a stranger who didn't know how soft her skin was under that smock?

Her perfume—an exotic springtime-in-Paris scent that had haunted him for years—wandered over to him, warming his lower stomach, making him want to reach out and hold her. To cup her jaw in his hands and feel the angles of her face. To brush his lips over hers, upending the lines of her frown.

"Suzy—" he said.

But she'd already started on the next customer, one who was watching Russell as if he'd lost his mind.

Well, maybe he had. Maybe that car crash had knocked thousands of brain cells out of his body and he just hadn't been aware of it.

Maybe Suzy had the right idea about ignoring each other.

Why wasn't Fate helping him out here?

Yeah, right. Fate required too much hope, too much suspension of reality. He'd survived his accident only because he'd lucked out. It had nothing to do with winning back Suzy. Nothing at all.

As he started to walk away from her line, she turned to him, red hair fluttering along the shape of her jaw as she bagged the purchases.

"Don't you dare think I'm shaken up, Russell Kingsley. Not by a reminder of *that* night."

The fact that she was still dwelling on it heartened him. "We can discuss this over dinner. What do you say?"

"Well, let me think." She returned to the customer and closed out the transaction. Then, with a swift, lethal glance over her shoulder, she said, "No."

"Ouch. Arrow to the heart."

The customer brushed past him, eyebrow cocked. Russell smiled, nodded, then looked at Suzy again. "You didn't say no with much conviction."

As the last shopper in her line stepped forward, Suzy stared at Russell. Then, she picked up the phone by her register, pressed a button and spoke into the mouthpiece.

"No," she said, the word echoing throughout MonMart.

She patently pasted a bittersweet smile onto her face and hung up the phone. "Convincing enough for you?"

With haste, she waited on the last customer. Russell motioned to the manager, and he opened another line, allowing Russell to get back into Suzy's lane.

When it was his turn again, she groaned. "This is too much."

"Listen," he said. "I can't blame you for putting me at arm's length. But, darlin', it's not far enough to make me forget about a time when you were only too willing to be my wife."

She bit her lower lip, her façade crumbling. God, he hoped he wasn't making her cry. Soft, gentle Suzy...the one who existed in the bloodstained colors of his prom photo. The last thing he wanted to do was hurt her.

He took a chance, reached out a finger, ran it under her chin. She jerked away, as if stung by his touch.

"Suzy, the one night we had together wasn't enough. For years, I've wanted to explain why I broke off our engagement, but I want you to know that—"

He cut himself off. He couldn't tell her something so nakedly vulnerable. Couldn't tell her that he'd always been married to her in his heart.

She waved him off, voice trembling. "Excuses. I've lived a lifetime of excuses."

"Come with me somewhere…anywhere…and we'll get this all worked out," he said. "I need to tell you things. About how I was pushed into a corner by my father, about how I had to choose family over the one woman…"

He trailed off at her wide-eyed glance.

Stupid. Why was he baring years of regret and heartache to her all at once?

He needed to gentle her, make her trust him again, before he revealed his feelings.

Frankly, his emotions even scared the tar out of him.

Suzy still stared, and he could only guess at how pride and curiosity were battling it out in her mind.

Did she want him as much as he wanted her? Even after the passage of all those years?

"Come on, Suzy," he said, grinning.

She blinked, seemed to snap out of it. "I don't think so. I'll please the boss to the best of my ability here at the register, but don't expect anything more, Mr. Kingsley."

The formality of her statement whipped him across the face, sharp as a well-aimed slap.

But the friction had flared that spark between them, stoking a smoldering flicker in her eyes.

As he left, he held her gaze. "You can change your answer anytime."

"Not likely." She turned around, staring at the empty space in front of her as if she wished a customer would come to fill up the awkwardness.

Russell chuckled, then walked away.

A few days later, on a Saturday morning, the Rumor High School football team held a fund-raising pancake breakfast in the mammoth MonMart parking lot. The lingering Indian summer sun stabbed through a layer of coolness, reminding everyone that they hadn't seen much rain or snow for this time of year. Some gossiped about the drought conditions, some took the weather for what it was worth and enjoyed the reprieve.

But on this particular day, most of the town had followed the sunshine outside, including Suzy.

Russell sat back in a lawn chair, his booted foot resting on a knee as he watched her flip pancakes on one of the griddles. High school kids served their patrons, balancing loaded plates on the sleeves of letter jackets while an acoustic band played on a makeshift stage.

His brother, Reed, wandered over, mouth full of food. He sat in the chair next to Russell's while swallowing.

"Hey, Fire Chief," said Russell.

Reed washed down his food with some coffee. "Maura decided to lay off the nursemaid bit for a while?"

"She's writing equipment grants for the community garden, which means it's my day off. Bless her baby-sister heart, but I'm feeling stifled. A man can only stand so much coddling."

"Stop your bellyaching." Reed ran a hand over his dark buzz cut. "And stop staring at Suzy. She'll think you're comatose or something."

"Damn. That obvious, huh?"

"Just keep your tongue in your mouth, and you'll do better."

A girl's voice, laced with a singsong hint of

amusement, broke into their conversation. "Mr. Kingsley? I mean Reed?"

His brother stood. "Hey, Isabelle."

"Hi." She was a redhead, her hair pulled into a springy ponytail. Dimples lined her smile. "They're running out of pancake syrup."

Reed, an ex-star athlete, had taken it upon himself to head up this year's fund-raiser. He gestured toward MonMart, looming in back of him. "I'll just step into the family pantry to replenish our supply."

He took off, leaving Russell with the young girl. Isabelle.

"How about some more food, Mr. Kingsley?"

Russell couldn't help taking a second, no, a third glance at the girl. There was something familiar about her. "I was just about to walk over to the tent to get some myself."

"Oh, no. You sit right on down, sir. I'm here to help you, okay? Don't you exert yourself." She grinned, then scuttled off to the food tent.

As Russell waited, his gaze caught on Suzy again. She was staring at him, her brow furrowed. When Isabelle held out a plate for the pancakes, Suzy said something to the girl, causing her to shake her head and send her ponytail swishing through the air.

Isabelle approached Russell again, rolling her eyes. "Here you go."

Something wasn't sitting well with him. "Is Ms. McCord all right?"

Isabelle innocently shrugged one shoulder. "She told me that you aren't an invalid. That there're other people who need food just as much as you do. But I said we need to be mindful of your accident."

"I'm over it." Except for the times when his sight went misty and he felt...well, as if he wasn't altogether out of that windshield yet. Yeah, it was ridiculous, but his brush with death still hovered over him, whispering in his ear every so often.

The girl's dimples drew him back to the moment. "Don't fret about the extra attention. A lot of people in Rumor are worried about you."

Ironic. People he hadn't known before today—like Isabelle here—seemed to care more for him than Suzy did.

Again, he reminded himself. *Give her time.*

He looked up once more to find his ex-girlfriend watching him, spatula in the air as smoke rose up to greet her. She started, waved a hand in front of her face, then seemed to mutter to herself as she returned her attention to the griddle.

Russell tamed a grin. Not interested in him, his foot.

Someone stepped into his line of vision, blocking Suzy. A willowy figure with short, wavy blond hair.

"I see you've met the irrepressible Isabelle."

Russell stood, taking the woman's hand in the grip of the one that wasn't holding a plate. "Donna Mason. How's life treating you?"

"Fair to middling. You've obviously gained some fading bruises and cuts since we last met." Her intense blue eyes softened. "I'm happy that you're healthy."

Isabelle *hmphed*. "See, plenty of people care. Now you rest well, Mr. Kingsley, and I'll check on you soon. You sure can put away those flapjacks."

She winked and left, causing Russell to wonder....

Donna sat down. "Cute kid."

"Yup."

He sat, too, coming face-to-face with Donna's speculative gaze.

"What?" he asked.

"I don't know." Donna leaned forward. "I'm just noticing some tension around here. And, you know what? It zips in a straight line, right from your eyes to Suzy."

Damn, he needed to cool it with the hot glances, didn't he?

"I'm surprised she's back. That's all," he said.

"I talked her into it."

He glanced at her.

"It's true," she said. "We've been best friends since high school, kept in contact since. That's why I know how miserable she was out in California."

Something twisted in Russell's gut. Shame. Regret.

Donna continued. "She had a job in a department store. A manager. Even though she'd been promoted, she was still relieved when she was laid off a few months ago. I convinced her to come back to Rumor. To get a fresh start."

"Even though she knew she'd return to gossip?" To *him?*

"Well, she was hesitant at first, but then I guess she came to terms with it. You know, sometimes people have to confront their problems before they move on."

He deserved Donna's blunt words. "So I fall under the category of 'problem,' do I?"

"I wouldn't exactly call you a joyful memory, Russell. Suzy's been struggling to make a good life for herself. And for her daughter."

It was as if he'd gone headfirst into that windshield again, smashing against it, stunning him senseless.

"A daughter?"

Donna widened her eyes. "I thought you knew."

He could only shake his head.

"Oh, boy."

His eyes sought Isabelle, her perky red hair, so much like Suzy's. Her sparkling blue eyes, as bright as a prom-night sky.

Could Isabelle be…?

He did the math. Lake Monet. Seventeen years ago.

"Isabelle's her daughter?" he asked, just to be sure.

Donna nodded.

"How old is she?"

A heavy sigh. "Sixteen. But don't assume anything, Russell."

Frustration thrashed through him. "What the hell do you mean?"

"I mean Suzy loved you with all her heart, but you did a real number on her. I'm sure she doesn't tell me everything, but…"

"But what? Was she with another man?"

Donna held out her hands. "You'll need to ask her."

His gaze returned to Suzy, who was brushing

back a stray hair from Isabelle's face, smiling, *mothering* her.

Her daughter.

His daughter?

How could he ask her? All he knew was this wasn't the time, not with the way Suzy still watched him with disappointment in her eyes.

Not long ago, he'd almost lost his life. Now it was possible that another had been added to his care.

A child.

He smiled, unable to stop the emotion, the surge of hope. MonMart hadn't filled the emptiness inside him.

He'd been searching for contentment for years, and here it was. There was no way on earth he would turn his back on this possibility.

He just prayed Isabelle was his.

The thought of her having another father almost made him double up. God, please have her be his. His and Suzy's.

"Donna?"

It was Suzy. She must have seen his startled expression, his physical reaction, and rushed right over to see what Donna was telling him.

"Hi, Suz." Donna stood, motioning to the chair. "I'm going to split, okay?"

Suzy didn't move, didn't look at Russell. She merely dug her fingernails into her palm.

"Suz?"

"I'll stand, thank you."

Donna hugged her friend goodbye and, as she left, shot Russell a warning look. Great. He didn't need Donna's ill will, too.

He got to his feet, cutting through the tense silence that remained. Odd. The citizens of Rumor were buzzing all around them but, between him and Suzy, there was a space, a nothingness, filled only by those damned imaginary sparks.

"She didn't reveal a whole lot," he said. "So don't jump to conclusions."

He pushed back the urge to ask about Isabelle.

Suzy flexed her hands, and Russell caught a glimpse of the red marks she'd left with the pressure of her nails. He wanted to erase the pain of them, wanted to smooth his fingers over the temporary scars and tell her that she could talk to him about anything.

"Here it is, Russell." She looked around, seemingly lost, wanting something to cling to for safety. "I'm still livid with you for what happened between us, and it made me think long and hard about coming back to Rumor. But I'm here, and the last thing I expected was for you to get into a life-threatening accident and for me to feel sorry for you.''

"I didn't crash on purpose," he said, trying to lighten up the mood. He hated seeing her sad, angry.

"Of course not," she said, hardly taking the hint to soften her hard emotions. "Years ago, I loved you so deeply that it hurt—but in a good way. I know, that doesn't make sense, but I used to think you could understand what I'm talking about.''

He grinned. "Love like that doesn't just disappear.''

"No, it has to be murdered. And you took care of that the night you turned me away.''

He must've looked devastated, because she suddenly reached out to him, her fingers flitting over his biceps, burning his skin, before she pulled them away, as if she hadn't any idea what her body was doing before her brain caught up.

He lightly gripped her hand, felt her stiffen up. "Do any of those feelings remain, Suzy?''

Her gaze locked on their connected skin. "I was horrified when I heard about your accident. That's what's making me so emotional, so stupid.''

"Do you still have feelings for me?''

Her lips parted—those soft lips that he'd kissed

under the shade of the bleachers, in the cool of his granddad's car—but no sound came out.

He could wait forever for her answer. He wouldn't go anywhere, especially since her pause spoke volumes.

"Suzy."

She shook her head, yanked her hand away from his touch. "You know there's no future here, right? Because I can't bring myself to forgive you, Russell. I just can't."

Tears brimmed in her eyes, her cheeks flaming. All he wanted to do was stroke her fiery hair, to tell her everything was going to be okay. That he'd make up for every second of agony he'd caused her.

Instead, the sound of brass instruments—trumpets, trombones, tubas—hit the air, accompanied by the sonic explosions of a drum corps. The steady beat of the school song pulsed in his ears while high school kids cheered, jumping up and down, whipping themselves into a frenzy in an impromptu football rally.

Suzy shook her head, and if he read her expression correctly, he'd guess that she hated herself. Hated that she'd shown her tender side. Hated him for bringing it out.

She charged away from him, weaving through

the letter jackets and the discarded paper plates littering the blacktop.

Weaving through all the questions he still wanted answered.

Chapter 3

The next day, Mahnita stood in Russell's office doorway, hands on hips.

"You're pushing it, mister."

"What?" He went back to reviewing a proposal. "I'm only in for a half day, just as the doctor ordered."

"A half day. Let's see if we can tell time here. You came in at noon, and it's now 9:00 p.m. That's not half a day, Mr. Kingsley. You're working as if the devil were after you."

And maybe that was true, he thought, trying to block out his assistant. Maybe the devil was trying to drag him back to the wreckage of his collectible car, right where he belonged. He'd cheated death, and now it was time to pay up.

"I hate to be a hypocrite," continued Mahnita, "but work shouldn't be your life. Go home, okay?"

The papers fluttered from his fingers to the desk.

Work shouldn't be your life.

Isn't that what he'd decided right after the accident? As he'd reclined in his hospital bed, his skin pounding from the bruises and blood-crusted scars, hadn't he told himself that he needed to change his priorities?

He stood, grabbed his coat from the stand in the corner. "Thanks. Why don't you mosey on back to the homestead, as well?"

She laughed. "I will, just to set a positive example for you. Good night."

He lingered in the office, hesitating as Mahnita doused the lights in her room.

What was he going to do now? Go back to his home, where nothing waited for him except for that blasted deer-antler lamp?

He finally dragged himself down the stairs, through the quiet store where employees were closing up shop. As he walked through the front doors, the bleak expanse of the parking lot hit him. A few leftover vehicles, parked and empty, speckled the blacktop, emphasizing the loneliness.

This was his life, wasn't it? A big gaping space, dotted by a few points of color—just like those faint dots you got on the backs of your eyelids right before you fell asleep.

He peered closer at one of the cars. Suzy hovered over it, kicking a tire. The hood was propped open, but it slammed shut with the force of her anger, causing her to jump back.

Last time he'd seen Suzy, she'd run away from him. Run away from the questions she thought he'd probably ask about Isabelle.

Even if she never wanted to see him again, he couldn't just go to his own car, ignoring her.

He walked toward her, his boots thudding with an even cadence against the blacktop, echoing against the cold, night air. "Need some help?" he asked.

She whipped around, her breath forming clouds. "Well, isn't this the cherry on the top of my problems."

Hell, at least she hadn't called him something far less appetizing. "I'm just your basic, friendly Rumor neighbor, offering my aid. What's wrong with the car?"

As he got closer, he could see the faded paint job, the rust chipping the seams of the body.

A wave of pity washed over him. Suzy worked as a MonMart cashier. She had a vehicle that was all but falling apart.

Had he set her on this path?

Suzy lightly kicked the tire another time, but now it seemed more of a way for her to avoid looking at him. "This darned thing won't start again. I peeked at the engine, but…" She laughed. "Actually, I hate cars. Nothing about them interests me, and the thought of knowing about how much oil they take or how many cylinders they run on makes me want to scream."

Russell thought about his collection of vintage classics housed in a custom garage next to his home. He didn't want to admit that maybe their interests had gone in opposite directions over the years.

He propped open the car's hood, peered at the engine. "Let me get my jumper cables."

"I hate being such trouble."

"You're not."

She bit her lip, brushed a strand of hair behind an ear. "All right."

It didn't take long for him to wheel his Range Rover—his everyday wear-and-tear vehicle—in front of her car. Soon, he had the cables connected from his battery to hers.

They attempted to start the engine, but to no avail, causing him to take out a flashlight and further inspect the guts of it.

"Bad news, Suzy."

"Is there any other kind?" She laughed a little, a nervous sound.

He detached his equipment and secured her hood. "Your battery's cables are corroded and you'll need to get them fixed if you plan to drive this thing again. Jumping you isn't working."

She shot him a sidelong glance, and a second passed before he realized what he'd said.

He grinned. "Unless…"

"Don't even think about it."

But he could tell that *she* was thinking about it. A hot early-summer night, the windows down in his granddad's Chevy, a slow song from the radio blending with the scent of night-cooled grass, water from the lake lapping on the shore, the satin of her prom dress pooled on the back seat floorboards as he slid into her for the first—and last—time.

What if Russell could fit his hand into the curve of her waist right now? What if he could stroke his thumb over her flat belly, summoning the memory of sweating skin and breathy promises?

She interrupted his moment. "I mean it. Nothing can ever happen with us."

He stepped toward her. "Why not?"

"Because you're the only man I've ever loved, and you hurt me too much, Russell."

The only man, huh? "I'll apologize until I'm blue in the face."

"It's not enough."

"I can make it up to you and—"

He almost said *Isabelle,* but she must've sensed the direction of his words. She got into her car, preparing to slam the door. "No."

"Suzy, come on. You can't go anywhere in that hunk of junk."

Her shoulders slumped. "I'll manage."

Didn't she know that he could give her ten cars? That he could send Isabelle to any college she wanted?

"From what I hear," he said, "you've been managing a long time. Alone."

"And doing a great job." She clenched her jaw, and Russell could see the muscles flexing, dancing.

"Yeah." He bent down to the window, close enough to smell that orchid-laced perfume she'd worn since the night of their first kiss in his parents' dressing room. So long ago....

"You're my hero, Suzy. A single mother who's raised a hell of a kid."

Silence yawned, and it was all he could do to refrain from filling it by asking about the identity of Isabelle's father. He couldn't shatter this temporary truce. Not now, when she wasn't running from him or watching him with that aching caution.

God, he felt guilty about Isabelle. If she was his, he didn't know how he'd be able to forgive himself for not being there.

"How do you plan to get home?" he asked.

Her lips quirked in apparent defeat. "I suppose that's your way of asking if I need a ride."

"It's the subtle method."

A shower of fluorescent light from a lot lamp smoothed over her skin, made her eyes as blue as the days he'd lived without her.

"Okay," she said, holding up her hands. "But straight to my placc."

"Actually, I was thinking we could stop by the Calico Diner for a bite to eat. I'm famished."

She paused.

"My treat," he added.

"That's not the issue, and you know it."

"Still, it's an incentive. Come on, Suzy. Remember those milk shakes, the Elvis jukebox music?"

"I *have* missed those French fries. And I haven't eaten dinner."

He recognized justifications when he heard them. "Just a casual pit stop, all right? Then straight home."

Was there a sparkle in her eyes? He hadn't seen a gleam like that since she'd come back to Rumor.

"Just don't entertain any ideas," she said, getting out of the car and shutting the door.

"Who me?"

As she walked to Russell's Range Rover, his heart skidded to his stomach, doing hot-rod laps and kicking up the dust of old memories.

He had ideas all right. And Suzy was in the midst of every single one of them.

Years ago, someone had transformed a long mobile home into a fifties-inspired eating establishment known as the Calico Diner. Pictures of Elvis, Marilyn Monroe, James Dean and Chubby Checker lined the walls, mixing with old 45 records. Waitresses wore poodle skirts and ponytails ribboned by sheer scarves while sashaying across the checkered floor in their saddle shoes.

As Russell waited for Suzy to return from a phone call she was making, he settled into the booth's tacky, retro red-glitter upholstery, hoping their Big Bopper Burger plates would appear soon.

In a few minutes, Suzy sat across from him, handing him his cell phone.

"How's Isabelle?" he asked, clipping it to his belt. "Is she shocked that her mother isn't home by curfew?"

Suzy smiled at him—a tentative upward sweep of the lips, as if she was testing the feel. "She couldn't be happier. I'm wondering if she's throwing a party and doesn't want me to return."

"She's got her mom's spirit, huh?"

"No, she's not that airheaded." Suzy lifted her eyebrows. "This move back to Rumor has been wonderful for Isabelle. She's so sensitive, and I was afraid she wouldn't make friends right off the bat, but she's surprised me."

"Good. Anyone would be lucky to count her as a pal."

Suzy shifted in her seat, watched for the waitress. "I noticed you and Isabelle were getting along pretty well at the pancake breakfast."

Was this his opening, a good time to ask about…?

Suzy added, "She's good around adults. Better than I am, I think."

His heart sank at the false opportunity. "You

used to be the life of the party. Even the first time I saw you, at the post-football-game bonfire during the playoffs, I knew you were one in a million.''

She'd been dressed in her cheerleading uniform, colored with the Big Sky blue and gold of the Rumor High School Rangers. With her pompoms and a shiny, red ponytail, he couldn't have missed her. Their first awareness had been almost like a song, one in which boy and girl lock gazes over the flames of a fire, smile, look away, then can't help but to look back again.

''I only knew of you,'' Suzy said, resting her chin on the palm of one hand, her eyes gone melancholy.

As he watched her, something in his chest wrenched, twisted, groaned. She hadn't changed at all—not in seventeen years.

She continued, ''You were the rich boy on campus, the one the girls chased. How many cheerleaders, or otherwise, had you dated before I came along?''

Damn, he couldn't even remember. Nothing had existed before—or after—Suzy. ''And how about you, Ms. McCord? You had a résumé, too.''

The waitress brought their shakes—hers, strawberry, his, a bland vanilla—then left.

Suzy delicately sipped at her drink, maybe buying time. Finally, she said, "I have to say this. If anything, you made me feel so good about myself while we were in love. Before, I'd dated guys because I wanted them to complete me in some way. I started to absorb their tastes in music, their hobbies, their philosophies. But with you… On our first date, you asked me what *I* liked to do, and I couldn't answer, because I didn't believe you cared. No one else had."

Russell pushed back his shake. "You mattered more than anything to me. Hell—" he grinned "—I never would've known about that band Oingo Boingo if you hadn't brought one of their cassettes back from that California Christmas trip to your aunt's."

She threw back her head, laughed. "You thought I was wild for listening to what the other kids thought was 'crazy music.'"

"No," he said. "Never crazy. Montana just seemed so odd for you, almost like everyone else was running in slow-motion black-and-white while you sped by in a blur of Fourth of July fireworks."

"How things have changed." She poked at her beverage with her long straw.

The waitress returned with their food. Suzy immediately began to nibble at her fries and burger while Russell merely stirred ketchup over his own greasy grub.

Things hadn't changed *that* much. Couldn't she see? He was still head over heels for her, and he suspected that she felt the same, in the depths of her heart.

"Do you think so?" he asked, just as if there hadn't been a long, strained pause between her last comment and this question.

"Think what?" She worked on a French fry.

"That so much time has passed that it's changed everything."

She swallowed. "You're persistent."

"I remember a night," he said, leaning forward, "when we sneaked into my parents' dressing room, and you sat at my mom's vanity table, sniffing her perfumes."

"Russell…"

He took a chance, reached out and, when she didn't flinch, ran a finger over her cheekbone. Her eyelids fluttered closed, then opened again.

He said, "You tried a scent she'd placed at the back of the tray because she never wore it. Then you ran the stopper over your throat. And when I kissed you for the first time, you smelled like flowers, just like you do now."

"It's not the same."

Yet she still hadn't pulled away. So Russell took a breath, lightly brushed his thumb over her lower lip. God, soft as a fading memory.

This time, she did scoot back in her seat, her face flushed, her gaze lowered. "I told myself I wouldn't ask, but I can't help it."

Russell's hand thumped to the table, fisting, wishing he could punch away what he knew was coming.

She looked up, her eyes welling with tears. "Why wasn't I good enough for you?"

Whoosh. The air left his lungs, deflating his hopes. He couldn't blame her for not being able to forgive him.

"You really want to hear this?" he asked.

She slowly nodded.

Here it was. "My family's always expected certain things from me," he said. "I was the heir apparent to the Kingsley business, the ranch, and from day one, my father brought me up to take control of it. In high school, I thought it would be years until I had to be the adult around the household. But my time came sooner than expected."

Suzy traced the edge of her plate, and Russell couldn't drag his gaze away from her pink-frosted fingertip, wishing she would sketch her nail over *him*.

He said, "Dad became concerned when we got serious."

"I know. Never being invited to family meals was an obvious clue. I always thought he didn't like me because I never knew who my father was. Because I was illegitimate."

Shame coated Russell's face with heat. "My father's changed over the years, Suzy."

"That doesn't really affect your explanation, now, does it?"

"I know." How was he going to get through this? "Dad thought that a Kingsley needed to marry someone of our own status, someone—"

"Who wasn't a gold digger?"

She'd said it, and Russell couldn't contradict her. Echoes of Stratton's voice filled his mind: *Suzy McCord is a bastard, Russell. The heir to our family's hard work shouldn't be focused on a girl like her anyway; you need to devote yourself to the Kingsleys.*

"You were never after my money. I know that."

She didn't say anything.

He sighed. "You might not believe me at this point, but I told him that I was going to marry you, no matter what. That I had already proposed to you. And that's when he dropped the bomb on me."

I'm dying, son.

Under the table, Russell clenched one hand into a fist. "He'd been diagnosed with lung cancer, and he was afraid he was going to be useless to us soon."

She sat up straight. "Russell. Oh, God. I'm so sorry."

He recovered, relaxed his grip, swept a crumb from the table. The gesture soothed him somehow. "It's okay. He went through treatment and eventually recovered, but we didn't know what would happen at the time. Because of my dad's health, my mom was going through a severe depression. I was the only one equipped to take over, so I did what I thought I had to do. I pleased my dad by breaking up with you in what I believed were the last days of his life."

A tear trickled down Suzy's cheek. "Why didn't you tell me about him?"

"Reveal a weakness in the man?" Russell clipped out a bitter laugh. "Strictly off-limits."

"I would've understood."

"Would you have?" He met her gaze. "He gave me an ultimatum. Drop Suzy McCord for the sake of the family or be disowned. You know the rest."

She shook her head, and Russell wondered if she was denying the entire story.

"I loved you," she said. "I would've—"

She stopped, pressing her lips together.

"What?" Russell leaned forward again. She would've stayed in Rumor, given birth to Isabelle and made the girl an obvious bastard, too?

What would he have done if he'd known about a baby?

He wanted to ask her. Was Isabelle his? Was that the reason she couldn't finish her sentence?

"All these years," she said. "Such a waste."

He could only stare at her in silent pain, wishing he could erase every single moment of anguish.

"I know what it did to you," he said. "After you left for California, I even tried to get ahold of you, but your aunt Hazel—"

"You tried to call?"

"Yeah." Wariness crept over his skin, shivering it.

She tilted her head, her face a mask of frustration. "Aunt Hazel never told me."

Dammit. Maybe Fate had been working against him all along, and now it was trying to make amends.

Was that it? Well, damn Fate.

He said, "When I called I was having second, third, fourth thoughts about letting you go. I don't know how it would've changed anything. Maybe it would've opened the door for the day when my father recovered. Maybe I would've gotten in touch with you then... But Hazel cut off every hope of that.''

"What did she say?'' Suzy's voice shook.

The words were as harsh as if he'd heard them a moment ago. *Haven't you done enough damage to Suzy already? She's recovered from you. If you want her to heal, you'll just leave her alone.*

He repeated the conversation, ending with, "She was trying to protect you.''

Suzy wiped another tear from her cheek. "She died without telling me. I can't believe it. All this time I thought you were to blame.''

"I didn't want to hurt you any more than I already had. So I stayed away, aching every day, throwing myself into my work just to forget about what I'd done to you.''

"You did that for me?''

"Hey. Don't make me into the good guy.''

She palmed a hand over her chest, squeezing her fingers together. "Funny. My heart's in pain. Literally. I feel sick.''

"I'm sorry.''

"Don't apologize, please.''

"Does this mean you forgive me?'' He grinned hopefully.

"Not quite.'' She smiled, as if trying to soften

the blow. "I hated California, you know. Never felt like I belonged there. Somehow, even though I never fit in to Rumor's landscape, either, I missed my friends, the down-home comfort of this town."

He touched her hand, and she grasped his. Then, deciding to press his advantage, he cupped his other hand over the both of them, warming her skin under his own.

She said, "I lived with Aunt Hazel until she died a few years ago, raised Isabelle the best I could. I worked at a department store, dreading every minute, but made ends meet by slogging away. When I had the chance to come back to Rumor, I took it."

He wanted to tell her how much he wished he could've helped with Isabelle, how much he wished he could've welcomed Suzy into his arms night after night. But, still, even after clearing the air, asking for more didn't seem wise.

He'd just have to be patient where Isabelle was concerned. Hell, he'd already waited seventeen years. What was a little more time?

"I'm glad we could talk," he said.

A tear wavered on the line of her jaw, trembling before its fall. Russell thumbed it away, rubbing the wetness onto his skin, welcoming even this small part of her into his body, where she belonged.

''Me, too.'' She stiffened, then pulled her hand away from Russell's. ''But I have to be honest.''

Here it comes, he thought, preparing himself for the worst.

Her gaze reminded him of the moment before he'd broken their engagement, when they'd sat on the steps of her run-down home on State Street and he'd told her that he didn't have a choice.

She exhaled. ''Even if you made the only decision possible and remained loyal to your family, I still wasn't good enough for them. For you. And I can't forget that.''

She reached for her battered purse, stood. ''Not right now.''

As she headed for the door, Russell sat still for a moment, just to pull himself together.

If the truth hadn't changed Suzy's mind, what would?

He settled the bill, feeling as if he'd be paying up for the rest of his life.

Chapter 4

The drive to Suzy's old house was laced with tension, thick as thunderclouds shuddering the air.

Russell was almost relieved when they pulled up to her ramshackle white-clapboard home. Suzy and Isabelle had obviously tried to dress up the paint-chipped walls—the trim boasted green wisps of new color—but the job was half done, speaking, even silently, of defeat.

A buttery light suffused one window shade, hinting that Isabelle was probably waiting up for her mother.

Russell drove his vehicle onto the weed-lined

drive, where any attempts to dress the place up with plants would have to wait until the sun chased winter back to the other side of the world.

He idled the engine while Suzy opened the passenger side. As she started to climb out, she looked back at him, hanging on to the door, ushering in the frigid air.

"Just so you know, I'm going to stop thinking about you."

He cocked a brow. "Huh?"

She smiled, as if talking sense to him was no easier than explaining physics to a three-year-old child. "It shouldn't be as hard to move on, now that we've got everything settled."

"Darlin'," he said, "this is just the beginning."

They stared at each other, his statement burning a line between them. Her lips parted, but there was no comeback, no lighthearted scolding.

"Hey, you two!"

Suzy gasped, then turned to Isabelle, who'd opened the door and was shivering on the slanted porch. A stretched-out sweater hung down to her jeaned knees and, as she propped her hands on slim hips, the sleeves flopped like numbed wings.

"Isabelle," said her mother, "isn't tomorrow a school day?"

"How can I sleep when my nearest and dearest

is running wild in Rumor?'' Isabelle waved a wool-flapped hand. "Hello, Mr. Kingsley.''

Russell held up a palm, then turned to Suzy. "You'd better get inside before you get grounded.''

"I think Isabelle will have mercy on me. I'm not too worried.''

He gazed back up to the porch, drawn to the shape of the girl who might be his daughter. For a second, he saw Suzy's mother standing in Isabelle's place, a cigarette hanging out of her mouth as she wore a low-cut dress and high boots. *Suzy, you get your sorry rear end in here before I whack it.*

The car door shut, slapping the image from his thoughts. As Suzy met Isabelle with a hug, the girl pulled back, talking to her mother. Suzy shook her head, but Isabelle was obviously not listening.

The teen summoned Russell with a gesture, and he couldn't ignore the invitation to climb on the porch with them.

He cut the engine, slid out of his vehicle.

When he mounted the stairs, a spiderweb veiled his face, silking over his skin like the touch of a woman's fingers. "You called, Miss Isabelle?''

Her ponytail wagged back and forth as she shook a finger at him, a dimpled smile on her face. "So you were the reason my mom was out late.''

"Guilty as charged.''

"Just make sure your intentions are honorable, okay, Mr. Kingsley?"

Suzy rolled her eyes, mussed her daughter's hair while she started walking into the house. "For heaven's sake, Isabelle."

His gaze followed her as she swayed by them, slipping past the door and shutting it until merely a wink of light poured out. Isabelle definitely noticed his interest.

She grabbed his wrist and pulled him inside, too. "Standing around in the cold isn't going to do your health any good. Come on and sit. I'll get you something to drink."

Before he could object, she had him in the warm house. The smell of mothballs hovered over a trace of perfume—Suzy's mother's scent. A cheap designer knockoff that had probably worked itself into the threads of the ratty carpet.

Isabelle led him to the Naugahyde couch he used to sit on while Suzy got ready for their dates. She'd always scheduled his presence in the house to avoid her mother, to avoid her catty comments about rich boys and how it was beyond her that Suzy had ever snagged one.

Isabelle gently sat him down. "What would you like? Milk? Water?"

"Nothing, really. I'll just wait for Suzy and say a definite good-night."

The girl gave him a sideswipe grin, shaking Russell to the core. It was *his* grin.

"You need to rest," she said. "We want you to get better."

I thought I was better.

His pulse pounded in his ears, covering her words with a sense of panic. No, maybe not panic. Anxiety? Fear that Suzy would never allow him to be a father to Isabelle?

It's just a smile, he thought. Not a blood test. She might not even be yours.

Still, he searched her face for any other hints of himself.

That's when Suzy walked into the room. "Still here?" she asked, the epitome of the antiwelcome committee.

He cleared his throat, hoping it would buy time, slow down his heartbeat. "Your daughter's convinced that I'm going to collapse if I get to my feet again. I'm not sure she's going to let me out of this room."

Suzy came over, wound Isabelle's ponytail gently around her hand, then lightly tugged. "You leave the poor man alone."

"But..."

"Come on." Suzy unwrapped her hand, rested it on Isabelle's shoulder, then turned her daughter toward Russell again.

They were almost mirror images of each other, a reflection of everything he couldn't control, couldn't redeem.

"All right," said Isabelle. "Poof. I'm gone."

She backed away, winking at him, then disappeared from the room, leaving him with Suzy.

"So she lured you in here, huh?" Suzy walked toward the door, a clear indication that she wanted to lure him *out.*

Russell got to his feet. "The trap wasn't half-bad."

He stood before the entry, towering over Suzy. It'd be so easy to press her against him, fitting her curves into his grooves, filling him completely once again.

But he didn't. Couldn't. Chasing Suzy to the other side of the room wasn't the plan.

"Good night, Russell," she said, opening the door, ushering him into the night.

He nodded, flicking his gaze to the shadows of the hallway, just to see if he could catch one more glimpse of Isabelle. No such luck. She was gone.

But Suzy had seen the tacit inquiry. The quiet fear in her blue eyes told him so.

"I'm not going to hurt you again," he said softly. "No matter what you need to tell me."

There. It couldn't be any clearer without stepping over the line she'd drawn in the dirt.

Tell me about Isabelle, Suzy.

She glanced away and, for a second, he thought she was going to come out with it, to relieve them both of this tense charade.

She exhaled. "Have a safe drive."

He hesitated, part of him wanting to pursue the matter, part of him clinging to common sense. Finally, he crossed the threshold.

And when he did, he felt as if he'd left his real home. One decorated with a loving wife and child.

One mired in what could have been.

Yesterday had thrown him for a loop.

He could feel Suzy's confusion, could feel her desire to let him know about Isabelle. Last night, she'd come close to telling him. He just knew it.

He'd been so consumed with frustration that today's MonMart effort had been fruitless. All he'd done from noon until four o'clock was daydream, plot to buy Suzy a new car, worry.

Good God. Him. Russell Kingsley. Worrying about a woman. This was one for *The Rumor Mill* headlines.

He'd come home from work only to pace the floors. Finally, long after darkness had fallen over the Montana sky, he'd decided to "exercise" one of his babies—his vintage cars.

But it would be a careful drive, this time. No gazing at Suzy's prom picture then crashing into a guardrail. Nope. He'd stick to safe roads tonight. It was the only way he knew to calm his mind.

He hopped into his 1957 T-Bird, with its shiny white paint job and red interior, cruising out of town through the shade of pine copses and fenced-off stretches of ranch land.

Oh, yeah, this felt right, almost like a time machine carrying him back to the days when he'd fully trusted his family, when he'd loved without caution.

Speaking of which… He approached Rumor limits again, slowing the car as he came upon State Street, where Suzy lived. What was she doing right now? Would it hurt just to drop by, say hello, tell her that while she'd had the day off he'd bought her a new car—a Saturn—by the way?

What the hell.

He parked around the corner, tightened his coat collar around his neck, warding off the below-freezing chill. As he approached the house, the same depressing façade greeted him, yet something was different.

The lights weren't on, but a slight burst of yellow poured into the backyard, revealing skeletal clotheslines and a toolshed. It was from this tiny structure that the light shone.

Okay. No one was in the house, most likely. How about knocking on the toolshed door?

He stepped over the crisped grass of the yard, then stopped short.

Through the window, he could see Suzy, holding on to a slender, horizontal barre, bending backward with one arm curved over her head.

The breath left his body, beaten out by the sight of her lithe figure encased in a thin pink leotard, her hair slicked back into a spritely ponytail.

Years ago, he'd watched her practice ballet while he did his homework after school. She'd plié and stretch, balance on the tips of her toes, practice so she could be a dancer one day.

Now, her hips were rounded, her breasts swollen from the aftermath of childbirth—all indications that she'd given up her dreams to raise Isabelle.

Had he killed her hopes by getting her pregnant?

Damn, Russell, he thought. Stop standing out here like an obsessed fool and knock on the door.

He did. Once. Twice. On the lawn, the light from the window showcased Suzy's shadow, and it froze, her arms spread in front of her in a graceful arch.

The image disappeared as Suzy answered the door, peeking around the side of it to hide her body.

"Russell?" she said on the edge of a breath.

He shrugged into his coat. "I saw the light on back here."

She watched him expectantly, probably needing a better explanation than that.

"Damn." He chuckled. "I feel pretty lame right now."

The door opened wider. "I suppose you can come in. I'm feeling sorry for you again."

He accepted her invitation, stepping into the toasty room. A barre lined one wall. On the other was a makeshift long mirror, pieced together from smaller ones. A workbench and tools still haunted the other two walls, contrasting sharply with the jaunty piano music flitting over the air.

"You still dance?" he asked.

Duh. But, hell, it was an opening.

"I try." Suzy walked over to the boom box and popped it off. "I have to tell you, though, an arabesque doesn't feel the same when I'm staring at a handsaw."

When she stood up, she double whammied Russell, making his belly clutch with tight heat. Sweat misted her leotard, making it obvious that she wasn't wearing a bra. The dark of her nipples pushed against the near-sheer material, and he could imagine running his palms over the firm curves of her breasts, the tautness of her stomach.

She must have realized—too late—that she was hardly dressed for company. She covered her chest with her arms. "I should get my sweater."

"Don't." A command. He couldn't help it. Depriving him of all that he'd been longing to see was cruel, unthinkable.

Surprisingly, she didn't move to hide herself any more than she already had. Russell was grateful for the favor.

"Um, so." Suzy swooped up on her toes, back down, marking the seconds. "Are we just going to stare at each other all night?"

"Fine by me." He grinned, trying not to seem as aggressive as he wanted to be. If she could see into his fantasies—the way he wanted to bend her back over his arm, nuzzling her neck, tasting her sweat, rocking his body against hers—she'd be warier than ever.

"Seriously, Russell. Is there a reason you're here?"

Business, then. "I need to arrange a time for your new car to be delivered."

Her eyes widened, bluer than the deep of a flame against her flushed cheeks. "Excuse me?"

''Your bucket of bolts is done for. So I—''

''Oh, no, you don't.'' Her arms relaxed from her chest, offering Russell a peek of skin against wet material. ''I'm not a charity case.''

''I never called you one. But let's be honest. How're you going to keep a job without reliable transportation?''

He could sense her mind whirring with options. Rumor had no public transit, no taxis. And MonMart was too far of a walk.

''Russell…''

''Just accept gracefully. It's a homecoming gift. Okay?''

''Don't you know how to spend your money?'' She shook her head, sighed. ''I'm not an investment.''

''I beg to differ.'' He stepped forward, hardly thinking of the consequences. All he could concern himself with right now was her slim body, the way it was giving off heat, drawing him closer, driving him crazy. ''When you dance, you remind me of a butterfly resting on a branch. You know how its wings just float up and down?''

She chuffed. ''How poetic. You and the resident Shakespeare, Isabelle, really need to get together.''

But a heavy sigh told him her sarcasm covered more than it revealed. How had it felt when she realized that she'd never dance professionally, that she'd, instead, spend her life ringing up customers as they trooped through her line, day by day?

"Hey," he said. Slowly, he brought his hand up, pausing in midair, letting her know that he wanted to touch her.

She didn't move, merely watched him, her chest rising and falling, her arms slipping lower until he could see the outline of her breasts again.

Damn, he couldn't contain himself much longer. He sketched his fingers over the throbbing veins of her neck, rubbing a thumb against the base of her throat.

She closed her eyes, swaying a little to the rhythm of his touch. "I almost feel like my mom's going to catch us out here, then give me a good whooping."

Rage flashed through him. "I wish I'd known she laid a hand on you, Suzy. I would've protected you."

"It wasn't anything I couldn't handle. Her put-downs were the worst, though. I was the scapegoat for everything: our financial troubles, her man struggles... She used to accuse me of trying to seduce her boyfriends. Can you believe that?"

Yeah, Ms. McCord had been a real winner, all right. "Don't worry. She's not here anymore. I heard the news—that she passed away up in Alaska.''

Suzy nodded, and Russell could feel the tightening of her throat as he traced a finger over it.

''She followed one of her men up there, but that's all I know. We'd been estranged for years, not that I had much of a choice after she abandoned me. She never even met Isabelle.''

''I'm sorry to hear that.'' He pulled her to him, enfolding her in his arms, closing her over with safety, comfort. ''I know I didn't do much to help your situation.''

She melted into him, slowly, like wax flowing down the stem of a candle. This was right, having her in his arms again. Pure peace. Serenity.

Her breasts pressed into his ribs, nubbing through his button-down shirt. She shimmied against him, maybe to seek warmth, or...

God, he hoped she wanted something more.

''Actually,'' she said, her breath hot, steaming the material over his heart, ''you were my saving grace. Every time trouble hit me—whether it was during high school or after—I thought of you. You're the only person who made me feel adequate, even if it was only temporary. I used to remember the way you'd grin at me, the way you'd brag to your friends about my dancing or my A on a tough test. Even with all the boys I dated, I never found one who made me feel like my own person, Russell. Not until you.''

He leaned a cheek against her hair—so soft, so sweet—and ran his lips over the strands. He murmured, ''Something tells me you haven't outgrown the skin of that doubtful girl. The one who was always hiding under a bright smile.''

She angled her face upward, light catching the pert tilt of her nose, the thickness of her lashes. ''And if you're right?''

''I aim to make you believe that you're the most beautiful…''

He slowly kissed her forehead. ''Talented…''

Then her nose. ''Desirable…''

Then the spot just below her eye, so that her lashes swept against his skin, stirring the hunger within him. ''Woman on earth.''

She rested against him, and he wondered what she was feeling. The same restlessness? The same aching fever?

She shifted, and he grew hard, then distanced himself, not wanting to scare her.

But she pressed her hips to him, testing the bulge between his legs, arching upward on a deep shudder he could feel throughout her entire body.

Light flooded the backyard, hitting them with reality. A door shut.

"Isabelle," said Suzy, pulling away so quickly that she knocked against a shelf, spilling paperback books to the floor.

As she slipped into her sweater, Russell steadied himself, breathed deeply to banish the sharp reminder of what-might-have-been in his groin and bent to replace the books.

Suzy opened the door, greeting Isabelle with a fake cheerleader voice. Hell, Isabelle was going to know what was what in about two seconds flat, when she saw him in here grinning like an idiot.

He shook his head, flipped through a couple of novels.

True crime. Suzy had been addicted to the genre, tearing through a few stories per week. She used to joke that if she couldn't be a dancer, she'd be a lawyer.

But she'd never wanted to be a cashier.

He finished cleaning up, preparing himself to greet Isabelle, the lovable, flesh-and-blood reason Suzy had never reached her dreams.

The reason he needed to make everything up to her.

Chapter 5

That weekend, Donna Mason threw a surprise welcome-home party, and all Suzy's high school friends were invited.

Including Russell, whom many had judged to be less than a friend.

"Dang," said Wally Sampler, class president and Beta Club treasurer, as he and Russell grabbed beers from the ice cooler resting on the floor of Donna's game room. Wally set his beverage on a card table amongst the chips, dip and lipstick-lined wineglasses. "I never would've predicted you'd show up at a party for Suzy McCord."

"Why's that?" Russell jarred off the bottle cap, flicked it into a trash can.

"Well, gee, Russ. With the way you just sorta dumped her, it doesn't compute."

Neither did the fact that Wally had ended up being the toy department manager for MonMart, not that the position was a bad thing. Everyone had just expected more from the class valedictorian.

But Wally was right. "Who says I'm not trying to make up for it?" Russell asked.

"Heck. As far as women are concerned, men are a species that's always trying to make up for something." Wally picked up his beer and saluted his wife, who was watching him from across the room. "I'm up the creek without a paddle as we speak, myself."

One of Suzy's fellow ex-cheerleaders, Nancy Baranski, bounded down the stairs. "She's here!"

Suzy. Russell rested the iced beer bottle against his mouth, remembering back to a few nights ago. His lips against her face. That see-through leotard.

Maybe he needed to ice his jeans, too.

He thought seriously about the option as the lights went out. Then two shapes bumped down the steps. Suzy and Donna.

Light flooded the room again as Donna whipped off Suzy's blindfold.

"Surprise!"

Russell settled against a paneled wall, watching Suzy's genuine astonishment as her old friends crowded around, hugging and kissing her.

He wished he could bring himself to do the same, without causing a scene. Because he knew that's what would happen. People would step back from them, whisper, wonder.

Instead, he waited while Suzy caught up with school chums.

His classmates stared at him anyway.

Ah, who gave a tinker's damn. Let them speculate.

He turned to face the minibar situated in a corner, a TV mounted against the wall. He'd watch tonight's football game, act like he belonged in the room.

"Fancy seeing you here," said the one voice he wanted to hear. She was behind him, her mere presence tickling desire down his spine.

He turned around to face Suzy, her skin flushed against the deep pink of her sweater and long skirt.

"They couldn't keep me out. Not for the world." He leaned against the bar, grinning.

She tilted her head, her eyes going dreamy for a moment. Was she thinking about the other night, too?

Quick as white lightning, she zapped out of it, straightening as if perfect posture would guard her from his intentions.

"The Saturn was delivered today," she said.

"*Your* Saturn. I'm not into modern cars, remember?"

She put her hands on her hips. "I can't accept such an expensive gift, Russell."

"Why not? Haven't you earned it?"

He wished he could take back that last sentence. It'd do no good to air his guilt over Suzy raising Isabelle all alone, over the way he and his family had treated her.

"Are you expecting me to earn it?" she asked, her tone cut with ice.

"God, Suzy, no, that's not what I meant."

She crossed her arms over her chest, reminding Russell of how she'd protected herself when he'd caught her dancing, how she'd covered herself from his hungry gaze—one that had probably scared her senseless.

She shrugged. "People don't normally go around giving other people cars, you know?"

"Would you call our situation normal?" He laughed, trying to smooth over the escalating tension.

"I'll pay you back. Every penny. I promise."

"Don't you dare."

"Russell—"

"You're being proud. Now, you can go ahead and punish me all you want for what happened in the past, but don't hurt yourself in the process." He took a forceful swig from his beer, then clapped it to the bar. "I don't want to hear any more about that car."

She opened her mouth again, but Donna stepped between them, slipping an arm around Suzy's shoulders.

"Hey, you two. Do you enjoy being the entertainment for tonight?" Donna nodded her blond head toward the rest of the room.

Their classmates stood, gazes locked on to them. Anger blasted through Russell's chest, burning him.

"I'm glad we're amusing," he muttered.

Suzy turned around, parting the crowd as she headed toward the stairs.

Russell cursed to himself, then followed her. He could hear Donna behind him, chiding everyone to mind their own business.

As they reached the top, someone in the game room had the presence of mind to throw on some CDs. Eighties tunes, simpleminded technopop with upbeat melodies and throwaway lyrics.

The nostalgia of the music made Suzy's doleful expression all the more heartbreaking.

She'd already flopped onto a couch in the family room, pushing a hand to her forehead as if she was holding back the world's hugest headache.

"Why did I think returning to Rumor wouldn't be a big deal?" she asked no one in particular.

Russell stood away from the couch, wondering if he should go ahead and sit. Donna, however, pushed him forward until he gave in and perched on the edge of a cushion. He shot her a glare that he hoped was half spiteful, half thankful.

"Listen," she said. "You both obviously have issues to work out. Now, while I return to this Rumor High School reunion, why don't you take a few seconds to air your problems. Then maybe—just maybe—you can have some fun."

Suzy glanced at Donna as if she was about to ask what the word fun meant.

Hell. She used to know, back when she could walk into a room and make it sparkle just by being there. Back before he'd...

Donna flapped her hands at them, a true "whatever" gesture, and backtracked down the stairway, descending into the bouncy music and spurts of laughter.

Suzy leaned her elbows on her knees. "She always was the peacemaker between us."

"Did we really fight that much?"

"Maybe once or twice."

They listened as songs from the movie *Footloose* bopped through the room.

"Why should our arguing be the scandal of the day anyway?" asked Suzy, chin on fist. "I'm sure there's a lot of juicy gossip circulating around Rumor. Enough to please everyone."

"I don't pay that stuff much mind."

All he concerned himself with was Suzy, her flowery scent wrapping around him, snuggling up to him just as *she* used to do in front of those football victory bonfires.

Suzy said, "It's odd, really. I haven't kept in contact with anyone but Donna. I'm not sure if I have anything in common with these people anymore."

"I know what you mean." Russell settled back into the couch, relieved that she hadn't brought up the car for the last few minutes. Not arguing was nice. "Even when I see Wally or any of my old friends in town, I'm not sure what to say sometimes. Most of them are married, with kids. I can't relate to that."

The words froze between them.

Isabelle.

Could he relate to the other parents in town, after all?

God, he wanted to. Wanted to go down to Joe's Bar and say, "Hey, guys. You know what my girl did today?" He wanted to glow with pride, watching her grow up, get married, have her own children.

The uncertainty of her parentage left him empty, lacking.

Suzy stared straight ahead. "I don't think we have much in common, besides going to the same high school. We haven't moved beyond that."

Was she referring to their relationship, as well?

He sat there, stunned. What *did* they have to talk about? Homecoming, Friday nights cruising Main Street, French fries at the Calico Diner?

Or maybe what they had in common was far too painful to mention.

He took her hand in his.

At first she didn't say or do anything. They listened to the song "Almost Paradise," knowing that it wasn't.

Finally, she whispered, "Russell?"

"Yeah?"

"The other night? I, um…"

She took her hand out of his, leaving him with nothing.

Then she settled against the couch. "I wasn't thinking straight, you know, right before Isabelle came home."

Uh-huh. Right when she pressed into him, feeling the extent of his need for her.

"I'm not sure anyone has their thoughts in order at such times, Suzy."

"But that's it. Ever since I came back home, I've been walking around like a brainless idiot, almost like I haven't told myself a million times that being with you is a terrible idea."

"Why?" He leaned back into the cushions, face-to-face with the woman who'd haunted him for years. "Why is it such a bad thing to be with me?"

Her breath shook as she drew it in, then out. It bathed Russell in warmth, longing.

"We've gone over this," she said.

"Then let's *get* over it."

He moved closer, his mouth so close to hers. So close he could feel a buzz between them.

"There's no chance of this." Her voice was a whisper, almost a plea for him to stop.

"No chance at all?"

"Mmm." She sort of shook her head as she watched his mouth.

A few beats of music passed, another slow song. As the lyrics faded away, Suzy rested a hand against Russell's chest, no doubt feeling the skip of his heart.

She nudged him back, just an inch or two.

"I forgot to thank you for the car," she said.

And that made him retreat a few inches more. Enough to leave a space between them that was too large to cross.

At least for the moment.

When they came back downstairs, the party was in full swing, people having imbibed enough beer and wine to loosen them up. Hopefully, they were too busy dealing with their own personal soap operas to pay any more attention to Suzy and Russell or to ask where they'd disappeared to for the past hour.

At least, that's what Russell had been hoping.

Wally Sampler stumbled over to him. Russell wasn't even sure his friend was sober enough to know that he was stepping in time to the heavy downbeat of "Big in Japan" from an Alphaville CD.

"Hey, boss!" he said, reaching out to pat Russell on a shoulder. "We's all planning to play a round of Spin the Bottle! What do ya say?"

Next to him, Suzy groaned. "He must be joking."

Wally pulled back, eyes comically wide. "Not good?"

"No."

Wally continued his mission to drum up support for the game, and Russell led Suzy to the bar, where he asked her what she wanted.

"Just soda," she said. "Can you believe that? Spin the Bottle? First of all, that's so junior high. Second of all, yuck."

He filled a plastic cup with ice and pop. "You didn't seem to mind at Steven Ford's birthday party our senior year."

"Oh." Suzy took the drink. *"That."*

"Yeah. And the time we locked ourselves in the closet at Joy Scott's? Silly games didn't put you off then."

"You would have to dredge up those embarrassing moments."

When she laughed, he knew she didn't mind. In fact, her blue eyes glowed, perhaps banked by memory. Russell wished he could travel into her brain, share the comfort and good times with her.

One of the partygoers dimmed the lights as another switched songs on the CD. Alphaville's "Forever Young" played.

No one in the room said anything while the music flowed, while the singer expressed his yearning to stay locked in a time of innocence.

Suzy leaned over to him. "John Hanson," she whispered, and he could detect the threat of tears in her voice.

The song had been popular when a classmate had been killed by a drunk driver while riding his bike home one night. "Forever Young" had become his shrine, and the Homecoming Dance Committee had chosen it to be that year's theme.

It was the year Suzy and Russell had been elected king and queen.

He felt her hair brush against his neck as she snuggled against his shoulder and, automatically, he faced her, wrapped his arms around her. She wedged into him, resting her hands in the crook of his arms, nestling against him while keeping a bit of distance.

They moved to the music, and Russell barely noticed the other couples doing the same. All he cared about was surviving, being alive to hold Suzy, to feel her breathing in time to the song's wistful beat, to feel the curve of her back underneath his palm.

Time seemed to stop, reverse itself, fly by in a blur of sepia flashback.

Past his first sight of the grown-up Suzy holding

get-well orchids for him, past the accident, past the long blasé years that stretched between a shattered windshield and a time when she'd been his.

They'd been royalty then, Russell Kingsley with his ranch fortune and granddaddy's 1957 Chevy, Suzy McCord with the secondhand clothes that she somehow turned into a fashion statement. Nothing was ever going to come between them. Nothing.

Except for his father's ultimatum.

Russell snapped back to reality, realizing that Suzy was staring up at him, her eyes wide with apparent concern.

"Are you okay?"

"Fine."

Why did he have to be so brusque? You'd think that just about losing your life would convince a guy to be less stingy with his feelings, to take a chance when every chance had almost been taken away.

He caught his breath, then said, "This is how it should be, Suzy. Me holding you."

Her body wilted. "Can we just not say anything right now?"

"No. I'm tired of keeping my tongue. Especially since there's so much to be talked about."

"Oh, so now that it's convenient for you, we're going to lay it all on the line?"

Her voice had risen, so he tenderly touched a finger to her lips, tracing their fullness, the tilt of her chin.

"You're right," he said. "Normally, I'd agree to being far more cautious. But I almost died. I can't be sure that there'll be a tomorrow to wait for."

She looked at him in that I'm-so-darned-lovable manner of hers: the heavily lashed, brilliant eyes, the pinked cheeks. "I'm sorry for your pain. I really am."

"I don't need apologies. I need to know—"

She'd anticipated what he wanted to ask; it was obvious from the way she froze in his arms. "Don't say it."

"Dammit, Suzy."

Did she think that admitting Isabelle's parentage would commit them? And that, if she bound herself to him again, he'd break her heart a second time?

That had to be it.

"I told you before. I won't hurt you again."

"You didn't mean to the first time. I understand everything about Stratton's cancer and the choice you had to make. But you might not be able to help it. *Again.*"

Loads of bitterness in that last word.

He stopped their dancing, pressed her against

him, maybe too roughly. But he couldn't help himself.

Her head bent back to meet his gaze; her lips parted.

"You have to believe me," he said, his whisper harsh. "We're meant to be together. People don't walk away from the sort of accident I had unless there's a damned good reason."

"And I'm that reason?" She pulled away slightly, glancing around the room.

Nobody was watching, or at least they were pretending not to. They swayed on, dreamlike, blurring against the dark-paneled walls, almost as if Russell and Suzy stood inside their own bubble of existence.

Russell took both her hands in his, locked gazes with her. "Think of all we've been through together."

He paused, hoping she'd say something about Isabelle.

Didn't happen.

He played another card. "Back in high school, didn't you feel it? I know you did. We were perfect together, and just because some time has passed that doesn't mean it's still not true."

Suzy smiled sadly. "I loved you so much that it consumed me."

The breath caught in his throat, stinging there, rendering him wordless.

"But," she said, disengaging herself, "that was then, this is now."

He almost felt like she was testing him. "I've reassessed my life, and I've decided that you're the most important person in it."

I'd do anything for you, Suzy.

The thought echoed back from the past, when he'd proposed to her by the night-shrouded shore of Lake Monet.

When she'd said yes.

Her eyes misted over. "It took a tragedy for you to want me again?"

He couldn't say anything. He'd never stopped wanting her, but…

But what? Fate had worked against him, first through Stratton, then Aunt Hazel. He hadn't wanted to hurt Suzy again, though here he was now, doing it.

She shook her head, pulled away then disappeared into the throng of slow dancers, hardly disturbing them in her wake.

The lights seemed to dim even more, casting him in his own, private darkness.

Chapter 6

It took a few days for Russell to come out of his brooding funk.

Ultimately, he decided that shooting hoops in his backyard during the cool, crisp sunshiny days and chaining himself to his MonMart desk the rest of the time weren't half as exciting as being with Suzy. Even when she was rejecting him.

So, with that in mind, he emerged from his office one afternoon to stand in her checkout line again. Just for old times' sake.

The early December Christmas rush had started, filling the poinsettia-strewn store with customers toting loads of merchandise out MonMart's doors. Holiday music sang over the harried metallic clash of carts bumping into each other. The constantly ringing registers should've made Russell ecstatic, but it didn't much matter. Not without Suzy.

This time, as he waited in her line, he varied his products. Now he absently tossed a *National Enquirer,* Lifesavers and a miniflashlight onto the conveyor belt.

His turn.

"Oh, brother," she said when she saw him standing there with what had to be a goofy grin on his face.

"Happy Holidays."

She blew a lock of red hair from her eyes. She'd swept her short, gleaming strands into a barrette at the back of her neck, but the frazzled style reflected a stressful day.

"Why don't you just take the merchandise from the store?" she asked. "You've already paid for the darned stuff."

"I wanted to see my favorite cashier. What's the harm in that?"

The customer in back of Russell bumped his thigh with her cart. He smiled at her, earning an impatient frown in return.

Suzy rang up the merchandise with the efficiency

of a heartless automaton. She was obviously still smarting from the last time they'd seen each other, when they'd danced.

Why was it that, when all was said and done, Suzy always ended up disappointed in him?

"Ten twenty-two," she said, busying herself by bagging his merchandise.

"You know, I crashed into that guardrail because I was looking at our prom picture."

She stopped and stared at the plastic bag she was stuffing the magazine into. "Do we need to have this conversation right now?"

"No. We can go out tonight, talk about it over a nice candlelight dinner."

"Jeez, Russell. You never stop."

"Damned straight. Not when something is left unfinished."

She thrust the bag forward, finally looking him in the eye. There was a certain softness in the cool of her iris, a wistfulness buried beneath the icy surface. "Ten twenty-two."

Patience, he told himself. That top layer of frost will wear off with some extra effort.

The woman in back of him sighed dramatically. Other customers had lined up behind her, all with rushed holiday expressions on their faces.

Russell paid Suzy, and she gave him change.

''Thank you, Mr. Kingsley,'' she said, slamming shut the cash drawer.

''So what about it, Suz?''

''Not a good idea.''

He had visions of her announcing her rejection over the store's speaker again. God, he loved her spunk.

''Sure it is. Listen, we're starting with a clean slate, accident or no accident. Two people out to enjoy each other's company. We can do that, can't we?''

Suzy's gaze locked on to the woman in back of him, almost as if she was asking the elderly lady for help.

The woman nudged Russell with her cart again, then said to Suzy, ''You might as well get a free dinner out of it.''

The two customers behind her, both men, chuckled. ''Give the poor guy a chance,'' said one.

By this time, Suzy had gone completely red in the face. When she glanced at Russell, the loose hair had wiggled its way over her eyes again, causing her to seem lost, in need of rescuing.

Great. Rescuing from *him*.

Russell shrugged, reached out to smooth the hair back. ''The customer is always right, you know.''

He didn't think it was possible, but she flushed

an even deeper shade of crimson. "This is unbelievable."

Two teenagers in line started a low, giggling chant. "Say yes. Say yes. Say yes...."

Hands started to clap in rhythm to the words and, suddenly, Suzy's line was atwitter with deck-the-halls cheer, smiling faces.

"Oh, for heaven's sake," said Suzy, giving him the evil eye. "Yes. Okay? Does that end this pretty little scene?"

The staccato claps turned into applause. The customer in back of Russell said, "Hallelujah. Let's get back to business."

He moved out of the way so Suzy could take care of the woman. The teenagers gave him the thumbs-up sign, goading Russell to give a slight nod of thanks for their good cheer.

Russell bagged the woman's purchases when Suzy finished ringing her up. She absently turned to help him.

"Still here?" she asked, her voice edged with weary amusement.

"Remember when we were young, and you always wanted to go to that place in Billings? That swing club?"

Suzy's head shot up, her eyes alight. "The Fedora?"

Call off the dogs. He'd hit the mark. "Yeah. We were underage, but you always said that, someday, you were going to dance there. How about to-night?"

A smile widened that kissable mouth, though he could see she was trying her best to hold it back. "I think that might be fine."

"Great." He'd always imagined Suzy in a gauzy forties dress with her hair twisted back from her face, her legs encased in those stockings that had lines down the back.

Damn. He was already getting way too excited about this.

Her smile crumbled. "But I don't have anything to wear."

Russell cocked a brow, running a slow gaze over her body. "You've got clothes, right?"

"Not the right ones. I don't know. I just always wanted to do The Fedora right, with my skirt flying around me, with the right lipstick and shoes...." Suzy smiled sadly. "Maybe another time."

"Don't worry about the clothes. I've got it covered."

His mind was already whirring. One of his gardening department employees went to The Fedora regularly. If he took a walk over to her area, he wondered if she'd be able to tell him where to buy the right wardrobe.

"What time do you get off?" he asked Suzy.

"Five, but—"

Russell held up a finger, grinning. "Trust me. I'll make sure you're suited up right and proper for The Fedora. Don't get dressed until I bring your dancing duds, okay?"

She looked doubtful, but finished bagging and thanked the customer, who managed to squeeze her cart by Russell without banging into him this time.

"I'll pick you up at eight," he said.

Suzy merely shook her head at him as he walked away backward, unable to take his gaze off her.

Isn't that the reason he'd gotten into the accident? Because he'd been staring at that damned picture and hadn't been paying enough attention?

While Suzy went back to work, Russell made his way to the gardening department, his attention fogged by thoughts of Suzy's lengthy dancer's legs darkened by sheer stockings.

So he was a bit early, thought Russell as he pulled his turquoise 1957 Chevy Belair hardtop into Suzy's driveway.

Twenty minutes early. Would Suzy think that his inability to sit at home, tapping his booted foot while watching the clock, marked him a pathetic man?

He grabbed a couple of brown-paper-wrapped clothing packages on his way out of the car, adjusting his Stetson over his brow. Just because Suzy would fit the forties mold tonight didn't mean he had to change.

He'd always be the mogul cowboy who adored Suzy McCord.

He knocked on the door, trying not to seem too eager. But when Isabelle answered, all Russell's coolness flew into the night wind.

"Well," said the dimpled teen, "hello again, Mr. Kingsley."

He touched the rim of his hat and nodded. "Evenin', Isabelle. I suppose your mom's still getting ready."

"Isn't she always." Isabelle ushered him inside the cheaply furnished house with no apparent embarrassment regarding her surroundings. Most folks thought they had to provide tea service or a string quartet when a Kingsley visited. He liked Isabelle's ease with him.

She sat on the couch, right next to a spot where the seams had split, revealing a belch of stuffing. He followed, removing his hat.

"Where are you taking her?" she asked.

Russell leaned his forearms on his denim-clad thighs, hulked over, trying not to seem as nervous as his fluttery stomach indicated.

You'd think Isabelle was Suzy's mom, with her lullaby-low voice and maternal concern.

He said, "We're going to The Fedora in Billings. Suzy…your mother always talked about going there when we were younger. Now we've got the IDs to get us past the bouncer."

Isabelle folded prim hands together on her lap, cocking her head as she listened, making Russell feel like he was on the spot.

"But," he added dryly, "I'll make sure she doesn't have too much fun."

The redhead laughed. "I'm not here to give you the third-degree, you know. I'm just interested in what adults do on dates. Do you get all nervous around each other when you walk her to the door? Do you make out in cars?"

"In answer to your first question, yes, I'm sure most adults still get anxious about the end of the night, but I haven't gone out in years."

"Really?" Isabelle looked stumped. "You don't have a lot of girlfriends?"

Called out by a mere girl. Russell had to chuckle. "With MonMart, I haven't had the most active of social lives, no."

"Mom doesn't, either."

His heart jolted with the cocky hope that Suzy hadn't dated because she'd still been in love with *him*. "A knockout like your mother?"

"She was busy working. And working."

Sounded familiar. He'd used toil to avoid relationships, as well.

Isabelle said, "She had a hard time raising me, being a single mom and all, but she never complained. I got lucky in the parent department."

Parents. Her father.

He could see himself sitting on this same couch with Isabelle, giving *her* the pre-date talk instead of the other way around. The possibility of being a father was so near that his chest tightened with the image.

At the same time, if this wasn't the perfect opportunity to dig for information about her father, Russell didn't know what would be. "Tell me about your dad. Why isn't he still around?"

His blood raced through his veins, waiting for her answer.

Isabelle pursed her lips, then glanced at her folded hands. "I never met my dad."

"Oh." Did he really want to hear this? Did he want to go behind Suzy's back to wheedle a confession out of her daughter?

"Say no more," he murmured, staring at his hat as he turned it in his hands.

"It's okay. Mom said that Dad left us when I was newly born, that we'd done fine without him."

It was as if Fate had kicked him in the stomach, robbing him of breath. If Isabelle was telling him the truth, then maybe he wasn't her father. Maybe that's the reason Suzy was reluctant to talk about her daughter's parentage.

The revelation squeezed his throat, choking him.

He slid a finger along the inside of his collar as Isabelle continued.

"I can't help being a little angry with my dad, this random man who's roaming the earth. But Mom tells me she's got enough love for two parents. Sometimes that's sufficient."

Russell wanted to reach out, comfort her, but he felt frozen, unable to move.

He wished he could take the place of the man who left her. Wished that Suzy had been lying to Isabelle in the hopes her daughter would never find out the truth once they returned to Rumor.

His voice scratched out of him. "Any man would be lucky to have you for a child, Isabelle."

She smiled brightly. "You think?"

"Yeah." Hell, yeah.

"Well, I've had reason to be optimistic lately."

Russell blinked. He opened his mouth to tell Isabelle that her mother had just about the opposite idea when it came to falling in love with him again, much less becoming a family.

But before he could say anything, a pink-robed, barefoot Suzy swayed past them down the hall, her hair just as he imagined: parted in the middle, the sides twisted back in rolls, ending in a free fall of red shimmering locks that fell to her nape.

"Oh," she said, clutching the terry cloth around her. "You're earlier than I expected."

Russell offered up the two boxes. "I promised that I'd bring your wardrobe. Remember?"

"Yeah, but... Oh, brother. Really, Russell. You're generous, but..."

Isabelle watched them, patently amused.

He stood, just as a flash of headlights cut across the front window. The glare flooded Russell's eyes, blinding him for the slightest moment.

The teen rushed to him, resting a hand on his arm. "You okay, Mr. Kingsley?"

"I'm fine, thanks." He was a little dizzy, but...

"Good." Isabelle relieved him of the packages, officially becoming the go-between for him and her mother.

She handed the boxes to Suzy. "Have fun, Mom."

Suzy paused, then with a look of entertained resignation, took the parcels and went into her bedroom.

A sharp *beep* sounded from the street.

Isabelle fluttered to the window, waving. "That's my ride," she said to Russell. "We're just hanging out, watching movies tonight. But don't think I won't be waiting up for Mom. I'll be keeping my eye on you."

"Yes, drill sergeant."

She grabbed her purse, which waited for her at the foot of the couch. Then she faced him, suddenly serious. "I've never seen her so excited before, especially about a man. I know she's been hurt in the past, otherwise she'd date more, I think. You get my meaning?"

"I'll treat her well, Isabelle. And don't get too worked up. She's just going out with me tonight to stop me from asking again."

"Give me a break." She tossed up her hands, her jaunty red purse swinging from her sweatered arm. "Wake up, Mr. Kingsley. Would you please? Just wake up!"

Another beep, and she was out the door, waving to him as she left. He listened to a car door thump shut, heard the roar of an engine as the vehicle pulled away.

He didn't know why he'd said what he did about a pity date. Maybe it was because, deep down, he wasn't as confident about Suzy as he let on.

But he wouldn't allow the woman of his dreams to know that. In front of her, he needed to be Russell, the golden boy of the Kingsley family, the heir apparent, the confident one.

But what if this *was* a pity date?

A trace of Suzy's flowery perfume teased him, beckoned him down the hall, toward the sleepy slit of light coming from the crack of the not-quite-closed door.

They were alone in the house. No one to keep tabs on them.

He stood in front of her door, resting his fingers against the wood's flaked, white paint. Inside the room, he could hear Suzy rustling about, could see a flash of darkness as she walked by.

The pressure of his touch pushed in the door slightly, expanding the view.

Suzy had unwrapped the boxes and was holding up the dress he'd purchased for her. Actually, he'd sent his garden department employee away from work early, paying her to shop for him at a vintage clothing store in Billings where she got her own Fedora wardrobe. Before leaving MonMart, she'd stopped by Suzy's cashier station to do some spy work, to estimate her sizes. Russell could only hope that his employee was successful.

As he watched, Suzy held the wispy material to her face, rubbing it against her skin. The dress suited her with its full pink, flower-printed skirt that would flare from her body when she twirled on the dance floor, its tight bodice that would cling to her breasts like petal-beaded water, its short sleeves.

With her hair rolled into that forties style and lips painted flame red, he wanted her to complete the fantasy he'd conjured this afternoon. He wanted to watch her slip into the dress.

"Suzy?" he said, voice low as a rumble of storm-gray air.

She dropped the material, and it pooled on her quilted bedspread, forgotten. "Russell? I'm not dressed yet."

He pushed open the door with his fingertips, allowing it to float away from him on protesting hinges. "Is it going to fit?"

She wore a cautious expression, one telling him that she knew he wasn't here to ask about dress sizes. "It should be fine. You even got the shoe size right."

She indicated a pair of black strappy, World War II era pumps.

"And...?"

He wanted her to show him the stockings. Wanted to see the sheer silk drape over her hands with a soft whisper as it settled against her skin.

As if reading his mind, she obliged him, holding up a thigh-high stocking with the seam running down the back, the motion causing it to catch a breath of breeze, making it billow in the air with the grace of a falling spiderweb.

"I think," she said, "you're asking for more than I can give, Russell."

"I'm not asking you to do anything you don't want to."

She hesitated, carefully laying the stocking back on the bed.

"You said earlier that you were looking at our prom picture when you crashed."

He leaned against the door frame, willing to stand here all night and just *be* with Suzy, if that's what she wanted.

Patience.

"I recall words to that effect."

She touched her hair, the dress. "Sometimes I think that, for you, a day hasn't gone by since I left."

"My feelings are just as strong."

"That's what scares me."

His gut twisted. "I told you before. Don't worry. Don't be afraid."

"It's just that…" She sighed, her eyes soft with pain. "I am afraid. I'm scared to death that I'll fall for you as hard as I did the first time, and it'll hurt worse, because I know better."

"So you'd rather serve away the hours at a cashier stand, pushing your feelings back into a place where you can't get at them?" He tossed his hat on the bed, right next to the shoes. "I've tried that and, frankly, it stinks. Life is too short to be afraid of it."

Her gaze smoothed over the fading cuts on his face. The sensation was almost tangible, like the touch of anxious fingertips soothing his heated skin.

He could've sworn that she was looking at him as she used to, with her heart in her eyes, exploding there because she couldn't contain all her love for him.

"Put on the dress," he said softly.

Her chest rose on a startled breath, then fell. After a pause—one in which he wondered if she was going to tell him to go to hell—she undid the sash of her robe, letting the terry cloth wither around her shoulders, revealing sin-black bra straps. The bra of a bad girl. The type of lingerie she'd secretly worn under her cheerleading uniform, teasing him about it until he'd just about groan with longing. She'd been such a good girl, hiding more than her insecurity under her clothing.

The rest of the material dropped to the carpet, leaving Suzy in matching panties.

Russell could feel a pulsing in his lower stomach, his groin. Blood surged, heating up, boiling.

First, she stepped into the dress, sliding the pink material up her long, lean-muscled legs, slipping into the sleeves, leaving the bodice unbuttoned. It took all the strength Russell had to keep himself in check, to hold back from palming the curves of her breasts as they peeked at him from the sexy garb.

He fisted his hands while Suzy dipped into her black garter belt. As she worked it up the same path the dress had taken, the tops of her breasts spilled out of her bra, making Russell almost choke on his own breath.

She stood straight again. "How're you doing?" she asked, an almost-hidden smile on her lips.

Damn her. She knew how he was doing.

"Keep going," he said, kicking a boot over one ankle, crossing his arms in an attempt to stay calm, outwardly in control.

She sat on the bed, watching him the entire time, even when she fetched the stocking. With an endless tease, she gathered the silk, fitting it over one red-painted toe, running it up a long leg—over a trim ankle, a toned calf, a dainty knee....

She tugged up the skirt, resting a pointed toe on the floor, and ghosted the stocking up a smooth thigh.

Russell's mouth went dry.

She elegantly clipped the silk to the garter belt.

Smiled at him.

He thought he might explode if he didn't get out of the room. That would really impress her.

"You know what you're doing, don't you?"

She shrugged, tracing her fingertips over her sleek thigh, drawing his eyes there.

This was Suzy's way of composing herself, her way of letting him know that she wasn't going to be a puppet.

Well, hell. He wasn't about to embarrass either of them by giving in to his desire.

Using his thumb, he indicated the hallway. "I'm gonna wait outside."

"Oh. Okay." The smile was still in place, innocent as springtime.

Just as she lifted the next stocking, Russell left the room, blowing out a pent-up breath, realizing that he'd left his damned hat on the bed in his haste to remain a gentleman.

Patience, he reminded himself.

He had the rest of his life to convince her to take him seriously.

Problem was, he wanted to start his life with Suzy right now.

He glanced back at her room, the light peeking from the space between the doorway and wall.

Let her turn the tables again, testing him, he thought, grinning.

Next time, he wouldn't walk away.

Chapter 7

The slap-happy beat of swing music jumped out of The Fedora and into the street, too joyful to be contained by one mere brick-and-stone building.

Russell didn't know if Suzy realized it or not, but she'd grabbed on to his hand, leaning against his arm in her excitement.

"You don't get out much, do you?" he asked.

The neon light from the marquee washed over her face, casting a blue glow over her smooth skin. No wrinkles, no scars, no marks of years passing.

Forever young.

"I've been concentrating on work," she said. "You know that."

Guilt sucker punched him once again, leading him to thoughts of Isabelle's dad. He wanted to ask for the truth.

Too late. Suzy was already pulling him to the door, past the bouncer and into the burst of music and energy known as The Fedora.

Cigar smoke mingled with sweat and heavy cologne as dancers flew past them on the dance floor, jumping, jiving, flipping through the air with boundless energy. The band members stepped in sync to the rhythm of chatty trumpets, saxophones, basses and drums, pouncing every once in a while to the heavy-headed microphones to weave their voices into the tune. Dim lighting shadowed the brick walls, soaking the room in a brandy-tinged hue.

The beat filled Russell's head like a pinging heartbeat, making Suzy's beaming smile the only possible form of communication. She pulled him to a booth in the corner, slightly away from the bustle, where they ditched their coats and settled into the mahogany-dark damask upholstery.

He leaned toward her. "This isn't the most intimate of settings."

Nodding, she smiled even wider. No wonder she'd agreed to come to The Fedora. He'd had no idea that conversation—or was that *confrontation*—would be next to impossible.

"Look at that!" She pointed toward a T-shirted man in suspenders who whirled a woman over the wood-planked dance floor with such speed that her gartered stockings were a blur.

The song ended with a rim-shot explosion of notes, encouraging enthusiastic applause. Suzy joined in, practically bouncing up and down in her seat. The band climbed off the stage—break time—allowing Russell the opportunity to say something in a normal tone of voice.

"I knew you'd love it here."

She leaned her elbows on the table, fixing a long look on him. A look he couldn't decipher. "I'm glad to be back so I could enjoy this."

Then she glanced away, grabbing a menu and studying it with intense concentration.

He did the same, or at least, pretended to. Food had nothing to do with the hunger ripping through his body.

Instead, he watched the low light as it wavered through Suzy's hair, turning it a rich shade of crimson.

As vivid as blood pooled over the faded colors of a photograph.

He shook himself out of it. Suzy was his lifeline,

his reason for living. Falling into a stormy mood wasn't going to help him win her again.

Tentatively, he reached out, combed his fingers over the crest of her hand. "If it isn't obvious, I'm glad to have you back, Suzy."

Who knew what ran through her mind in the few seconds it took for her to slip out of his grip? All Russell understood was that the loss of her burned him. Her withdrawal was like ice scraping over his skin, cutting it to slices, wounding him.

She set down the menu, clearing her throat. "Let me correct the assumption that you have me back. Because you don't. I didn't return to Rumor for you."

The waiter popped up to their table, asking for their orders before Russell could think up an answer clever enough to cover the damage her words had wrought. Good thing, too. He couldn't think of a damned thing to say.

They sat in shredded silence as the waiter left and the band struck up a lively tune again. Suzy bolted up in her seat once more, gazing hopefully at Russell.

"I've got to go out there!"

He made a be-my-guest gesture, causing Suzy to pout her lips at him.

Nice. He'd always been a sucker for her kiss-me-now mouth.

She slanted toward him, tickling his ear with her words. "You know how to make your way around a dance floor."

He leaned his mouth near her cheek, the movement brushing her lips against his neck. He felt her mouth widen against his skin, probably in surprise or…

Right, he thought. You can't possibly be hopeful after her last verbal volley.

"Hey," he murmured, while enjoying the feel of her breath fanning into the gape of his shirt collar, "just because you went through a swing phase our senior year and dragged me to your room for secret dance lessons doesn't mean I remember any smooth moves."

She nudged her nose against his jugular, sending a bolt of lightning through his belly. "I know. You hated it. Can't you indulge me, though?"

God, he'd do anything for Suzy. Didn't she know that by now?

"I'm all left feet," he said. "Don't expect too much of me."

With a certain amount of resignation, he tugged her out of their booth, toward the throng of slick-haired men with their bowling shirts and natty vests, toward the black sea of swirling skirts, toward the sounds of a fast-talking sax that coaxed him into the sway of bodies. The *tchaaa-tcha-tcha-tchaaa* of drumsticks teasing a symbol was a harsh, demanding whisper, much like the thrum of adrenaline pounding through his veins.

He faced Suzy for a moment, noting how she stood out against all the darkness—a smiling, flushed-cheeked angel with pink-tipped wings.

At first, he felt frozen, unable to move. Then Suzy, with her natural grace, led him into the dance, willing him into motion. Spinning, stepping, melding together until even the slight pulse of his muscle was enough to signal the next sway, the next dip.

He almost wished they could be like this forever, trouble-free, holding each other on a dance floor without a thought of consequences.

He loved seeing her so happy, so…Suzy.

She'd always contained sunshine, a life force that drew him to her. And here it was, blasting through with her joy of dancing.

Dancing with him.

God help him. He really had never fallen out of love with her, had he?

The fast song ended, chased by applause. Suzy stood in front of him, her chest rising and falling with every breath, her gaze so blue, so steeped in fear.

He pulled her against him, running a hand down her hair. "Don't look at me that way," he murmured in her ear, before the next number kicked in.

A trumpet strolled to a sinuous be-bop cadence, trailed by the heavy drag of bass strings and the rattle of a snare drum. For a sweet moment, she grooved against him, their bodies fitted together, made for each other.

"I'm not sure what else to do," she said. "I don't want things to go too far."

Her hair smelled so good, just like the orchids that had framed his hospital bed such a short time ago. Just like a stroll along the Seine River, where vendors sold exotic flowers, where love songs rode the Paris wind.

He nuzzled against her tresses, breathing them in, making her scent a part of him. "Things will go as far as you want them to, Suzy. I'm open to all suggestions."

"What if I think we should just be friends?"

He swallowed away his disappointment. "Then that's how it'll be."

For now.

"Well." Suzy glanced up at him, the gem-soft lighting bathing her skin. "You're very cavalier."

''Not really, darlin'. If you could read my mind, you'd run clear to Wyoming to get away from me. I'm taking things slow, because that's how I think you want it.''

The suggestive overtones of that final statement obviously didn't escape her notice. Her gaze flamed up by several degrees, stroking over his chest, his neck, his face with an easy, heated pace.

''Slow sounds nice,'' she said.

Damn, did it ever. Slow caresses, slow thrusts. The slow arching of her body beneath his own as he...

Russell grew hard. He couldn't stop it.

Suzy leaned her forehead against his chest, and he felt her shudder. His own body was playing the same tricks, whipping up a nest of teenage tingles in his stomach. The kind of tingles that started low in the belly, then consumed the rest of you.

Uncontrollable. Out of character for a guy who was used to handling the reins.

This time, he was the one who pulled away from her.

''I think our food's got to be on the table,'' he said, taking her hand and leading her back to the booth.

The slow song ended, making Suzy's voice too loud in the sudden vacuum.

"Russell?"

He sat down to a plate of ribs, grilled corn on the cob, grated carrots and thick sourdough bread, but couldn't eat a damned thing. She didn't talk during the pantomime, either.

After all, what could he say now?

He'd just discovered that the force of his love jarred him, too.

Even when the clock struck twelve, she hadn't wanted the night to end.

When they'd finally left The Fedora, Russell's eyes had gone bleary, his head closing in on itself with an oncoming headache.

But Suzy had looked at him with stars in her eyes, brilliant and glimmering. He would've been a fool to take her home, especially when she'd said, "I haven't had this much fun in... I don't know. Forever!" then smiled at him, twisting his heart around her little finger.

They drove through the crisp, moonlit landscape, past gnarled cottonwoods and winter-browned grass. He took the scenic route, toward his family's estate and vast cattle ranch.

As they drove through the impressive iron gates marking the entrance, Suzy exhaled. "Wow. The

Kingsley place. Seems like just yesterday when Stratton wouldn't invite me to dinner.''

"The folks are on vacation now. You don't need to worry about my dad."

A sassy grin lit over her mouth as he wheeled the car down the endless Douglas-fir-lined driveway. The trees dwarfed them, crowning the skyline with thickly needled branches.

"Who's worried? I've run into Stratton a couple times at MonMart recently. He's always got this sheepish expression, as if he could apologize enough times for what he did, he would."

Russell pulled the Chevy in front of the door, then cut the engine. "My dad regrets what he put you through. He's probably choking on the words right now, but he'll come through. The man really is a softy when it comes right down to it."

Suzy smiled at him, then peered out the window toward the mansion. Was she intimidated by their obvious wealth?

His mother, from East Coast privilege, had decorated this châteaulike log structure, adding a tasteful beige-and-cream motif throughout the many rooms. The building stood three stories high, the logs bolstered by stones, the rooftops boasting steeples. They even had an indoor pool and minitheater among the meal nooks, parlors and solariums.

Suzy shook her head. "How did you turn out to be a fairly normal guy?"

He laughed. "That's arguable."

"Really. But tell me. What exactly are we doing here?"

"I don't know. I thought maybe a dip in the pool?"

She cocked an eyebrow. "Unless you had someone buy a bathing suit at that vintage clothes store, I'd say dream on, buddy."

He tried to smile, but the darkness pounding at his temples made him grimace instead. He lifted a hand to his forehead, rubbing it.

"What's wrong?" she asked.

"Ah. Nothing."

"Russell. For heaven's sake. Don't be so macho."

She scooted over, brushed away his hand, pressed a thumb to the beginning of his eyebrow. The pain slowly vanished, the black waves of discomfort receding.

Her voice was low, comforting. "There. I took a massage class once, hoping to meet people, I guess."

He could live with this. "Did you? Meet anyone, I mean."

"No. But at least I give a killer back rub now."

Before he could open his mouth to comment, she'd released the pressure and opened her car door. "Don't even ask."

He got out of the Chevy, too. "Suz. I thought you didn't want to go for a moonlight swim."

She shut her door, and he followed. "Right. But that doesn't mean I don't want to be naughty and explore. Your dad never did let me past the foyer— not unless you were sneaking me in when they weren't home. I suppose it was because I'd bring a touch of bastard to the furnishings."

"Don't talk about yourself like that."

Suzy grinned. "I'm joking."

But Russell wasn't laughing.

Nonetheless, he unlocked the front door. Whispering, he said, "The house employees have got to be snug in their beds by now, but even if they're in the cottages out back, we can't make too much of a racket."

"Oooh. This responsible streak of yours is quite sexy, Russell."

Had she sensed his sudden skittishness back at The Fedora? Did she feel safe, now that he'd backed off a little?

Give him time to recover, he thought, and he'd be right back in pursuit.

Soon.

He still had to get over the shaking that had consumed his body, his emotions.

They sneaked up the dim entryway, up the open-arm staircase.

"Where're we going?" Suzy whispered.

He wasn't sure. But something was leading him to the most private sanctuary of his father's house, to the place he'd first kissed Suzy.

His parents' bedroom.

The choice of destination was pretty symbolic, taking Suzy back to the place where she'd be least welcomed. But, this time, it was different. This time, his father wouldn't refer to her as "that illegitimate kid" who was good enough for Russell to fool around with, but never to marry.

They crept through the empty halls, down to the massive bedroom, dominated by a wall-length window that overlooked an expanse of Kingsley land and sky. A stone fireplace covered another wall. On yet another, a door led to a massive walk-in closet attached to the granite-studded bathroom.

He could hear Suzy's quick gasp, as if being in this room again had flooded her with old insecurities. Hell, those inadequacies had never gone away, had they?

Russell turned on a stained-glass Tiffany lamp,

the dim light barely suffusing the room with faded colors, all bleeding together on the walls.

He followed Suzy, who had shed her heavy coat on the king-size bed and wandered through a door, to his mother's vanity room. A marble table laden with expensive lotions and perfumes lined the wall, and it seemed to draw her.

It always had.

She sat gingerly, floating her palm over the cut-glass atomizers and jars. "Nothing's changed."

Moonlight filtered through the Belgian lace curtains, lending more light than the multihued trickle from the other room afforded. Russell moved to stand behind Suzy, meeting her gaze in the mirror.

She said, "When I was young, I used to dream of growing up, living with you in this mansion, wearing creamy lotions and silks that would drive you wild."

His throat tightened, closing off a response.

Suzy opened a jar, dipped in a finger, dabbed some white, frothy substance on an elbow. With her forties garb, she almost seemed like a ghost from the past, haunting him.

She continued. "I had a lot of goofy dreams, didn't I? Ballet. Marriage. It's funny how one little moment in life can change everything."

"Which moment?"

He was hoping she'd answer with a reference to prom night, in the back seat of a car, when they made love. Made Isabelle.

Again, she met his eyes in the mirror. "The moment on my porch, when you let me down."

If he'd been hoping she'd gotten over that, he'd been wasting his time. But he knew it would take more than a few days and a new car for her to forgive him.

Capping the lotion jar and lifting up an atomizer, sniffing at the nozzle, she laughed a little. A delicate, pained laugh.

"I wish I'd known about Stratton's cancer. Do you know why I thought you'd broken up with me?"

He shook his head.

"I thought you'd seen through me. That you'd realized I wasn't this bubbly cheerleader who made the honor roll every semester. That I was ultimately as stupid and uninteresting as I'd feared."

He reached out, flitted a hand over her nape, under her hair. He felt her shiver.

"You were—are—the most fascinating woman I've ever known. Fascinating enough to cause a car crash."

"I'm sorry," she said. "We've both got a lot to recover from."

She put down the atomizer, reached to the back of all the jars, picked up another capped bottle. She took out the stopper, sniffed, froze.

He knew which perfume she'd come across. One that his mother never wore. An orchid scent. For Christmas that year, he'd contacted his mother's perfumer, asking him to create the same concoction for Suzy.

She'd worn it the last time he'd seen her.

Slowly, she dotted the stopper in the cove between her collarbones.

Years ago, on the night he'd first kissed her, she'd done the same. He'd placed his hand over hers, leading the stopper over the pulse of a neck vein, behind an ear. Then he'd kissed her—innocent, sweet, light, with a hint of desperation. The embrace of two teens who'd fallen in love despite the wishes of his father.

Now, he repeated the moment, capturing her hand, sketching the stopper over the same warm places. Their gazes met in the mirror again, and he knew that she knew.

He was going to kiss her.

Her hand fell from the object, lingering at the base of her throat, where her heartbeat fluttered just under the skin. He could feel it echoing there as he moved his other hand to cover the area, to slip under her fingers, skimming over that dip at the top of her chest.

With his other hand, he traced the stopper from her ear to the point where her neck met her shoulder, that fragile, smooth curve of skin, barely covered by her sheer dress. He slipped under the material, and Suzy trembled, angling her face away.

He should've been ecstatic that she wasn't backing away from him again. Should've felt a surge of triumph. But a sense of protectiveness shrouded him instead, a need to shield Suzy from himself.

Don't stop, he thought. If you do, she'll think you're leaving her again.

He removed the stopper and pressed his lips to the slope of her neck and shoulder, his other hand slipping down, trailing over one breast.

She shifted, moaning low in her throat, her hand covering his as he palmed her, rubbing the firmness of her flesh, the slight fullness of it.

''Russell.''

She turned her head toward him, her lips meeting his temple. He slid his mouth upward, dragging his lower lip up the throbbing, orchid-fresh scent of her neck, her hair flirting over his jaw.

Their mouths met, hot and hungry, urgently sipping at each other. This wasn't a teenage kiss, a blushing flutter of lashes and pucker. This was now, seventeen years later, full of hidden desires and second chances.

Suzy pressed her chest against his hand, coaxing him to circle his thumb around the center of her breast. Her nipple crested under his touch, pebbling under the sheerness of her bra and dress.

With her free hand, she feverishly pressed his mouth to her lips with renewed force, increasing the heat, the rawness of their need.

It wasn't enough. He wanted to lay her down on the floor, bunch up all that gauzy, pink material, slip her panties down her legs and enter her, spill himself into her.

But she wasn't ready for it. Her body was, yeah. But not any other part of her.

He'd be a jerk to take advantage.

He must have stiffened or given some indication of his damned chivalry, because Suzy evidently felt it, breaking off their kiss on a heavy intake of breath.

She stood from the chair, straightening the bottles, the glass clinking as her hands shook.

"I can imagine your mom walking in, scolding me for using her perfume."

Russell paused. "Are you always afraid of getting caught?"

"For a good son, you're awfully rebellious, bringing me in here like this."

Suzy stopped her fussing, smiled at him. The gesture trembled her mouth, and he ran a finger over the swoop of her lips, straightening them.

"You're welcome here, Suzy. I'm going to make you see that."

She backed away once again, causing Russell to wonder why she was always leaving just when he'd gotten ahold of her.

"It's time to go back," she said softly.

She walked away, leaving him to stare in the mirror. He reached out, touching his fingertips to a man who didn't quite exist.

Chapter 8

That night, when he dropped Suzy off, Isabelle hadn't been waiting on the porch, as he'd expected. Instead, Suzy had crept in the front door, dousing the porch light, casting him into the emptiness of night.

It almost seemed like he'd stayed there—in darkness—for the next few days, probably because she had time off from her MonMart cashiering duties, and he didn't have the opportunity to stand in her checkout line to needle her.

But, when he did see her next, she came to him. He was chatting with some young female employees, complimenting them on their innovative displays for the teen clothing department, when Suzy appeared next to him, glowing in her pink smock.

"Howdy, stranger."

He grinned at the ladies, who giggled and returned to work. Then he paid full attention to Suzy. "You're chipper."

"I'm brimming with holiday cheer, even if we're only at the start of December."

"Well, 'tis the season, I guess."

"It's more than that. Life is good. I've got my health, a beautiful daughter and a steady job."

And he could give her so much more—if she'd just take it.

"Is that what you came here to tell me?" he asked.

She blushed a little. "Actually, I've got something of yours."

Yeah, Isabelle. Maybe.

Shivers ran through Russell's skin, sharp as needles slipping under the surface. There it was again—that scary devotion, those overwhelming feelings for her.

Suzy glanced sidelong at him, probably wondering why he seemed so uncomfortable, so impatient.

"Your hat," she said. "I didn't want to bring it

to work. It was bad enough that Isabelle found it on the bed when she came home that night.''

"Ah." He bent closer to Suzy, lips near her ear, his words low and scratchy with remembrance. "Little does she know that a mattress wasn't even remotely involved."

Suzy didn't even flinch, much to Russell's satisfaction.

"I had to make up a silly story to please Isabelle. She's a strict guardian."

A herd of customers maneuvered their metal carts around Russell and Suzy, the wheels clicking over the floor in time to "Jingle Bells." He placed his palm in the small of her back—that slope of spine and skin that had been draped by a sexy forties dress only a few nights ago—and led her to a vacant spot between the Wrangler rack and the boot display.

Russell couldn't help the sideswipe smile that pulled at his lips. "Did you tell Isabelle you were dressing and not *un*dressing?"

"Russell." Suzy glanced around, wide-eyed.

"Darlin', if you're worried about the denim spreading gossip, I wouldn't pay it another thought."

"Ha, ha, confident man. You think you're pretty collected, don't you?"

She ran her blue gaze over the length of him, like a fever spreading over his body, burning it.

Lowering her voice, she continued. "I recall that you forgot your cowboy hat because you weren't as cool as you'd like to believe."

Pink dress, wispy stockings, black bra…

"That obvious, huh?" he asked.

"Terribly." She laughed. "Isabelle actually wondered if we'd even left the room."

Her candor surprised him. "And you said…?"

"I said that I'd forgotten my coat on the bed and you, playing the gentleman, went to retrieve it for me." Suzy fixed one of those quasi-innocent smiles on her mouth. "She seemed disappointed."

Russell paused. Had the other night's kiss brought out the flirt in Suzy? Lord knew, she was back to the bright-eyed girl he'd known all those years ago.

He said, "Isabelle's got some ideas about me and you dating. I think she wants you to go out and have some fun. But not too much, of course."

Over the loudspeaker, a stressed-out voice interrupted the holiday carols. "All cashiers report to checkout. All cashiers report to checkout."

Suzy leaned her head back, shut her eyes. "That's my cue."

"And my curse."

She shot him a saucy glance. "So do you want your headgear back or not?"

If it meant he had another excuse to be with Suzy and Isabelle, yeah, he did.

"I've got a history with that Stetson, got a certain fondness for it."

She nodded, raising an eyebrow. "Come by at five tonight, and I just might give it to you."

"I'll take anything you care to dish out."

"Down, boy." Suzy bit her lower lip, seeming as if she might have more teasing barbs to jam his way. But after a few beats, she grinned, then headed toward the checkout stands.

Russell watched her go, already counting the seconds as they took him closer to seeing her again.

Hat on head and heat on full blast, Russell drove down State Street, past the general store, past *The Rumor Mill* newspaper office and toward Lake Monet, with Suzy in the passenger seat of his granddad's Chevy.

She wore a fuzzy pink sweater and a slim skirt, her hair loose, the ends clipping her chin. "Thanks for giving in to my whim, Russell. With Isabelle studying at the library, I couldn't stand to be alone in that house. Not again."

As if he would complain about Suzy's request to

"go cruising" with him. This was paradise—controlling a sleek, purring machine with a beautiful woman on the seat next to him.

"Bad memories in the house?" he asked.

He was driving one-handed, his other arm propped on the top of the seat, hovering near Suzy. As she shrugged, her soft sweater brushed his fingertips.

"It's almost like she's still there sometimes. My mom. Yelling at me, cutting me down. If I could afford to live anywhere else, I would. But, surprisingly, she left me the house when she passed away. It's all I have right now."

"You know I can help you with that."

She sighed. "The car you bought me was generous, you know that, but it cost me a lot of pride to accept it. A house is out of the question."

"Dammit, Suzy."

"Hey, listen. I'm not ungrateful. Not at all. But I'm going to succeed on my own, okay?"

She paused as Rumor grew tinier behind them, miniaturized by an endless sky swept with fast-moving clouds and purple-orange streaks of twilight.

"Besides," she said, "when my daughter's with me, I don't think about my mother as much." She sniffed. "Isabelle's my saving grace."

Russell glanced over at her, noting how Suzy was wiping her face. "Don't cry. Come on."

He thumbed some moisture from a cheek, all the while mindful of the road ahead of him. A semitruck appeared in the near distance, looming and growing like a rushing, black storm cloud.

Eerie. This was almost like a replay of his accident, one in which he had the chance to correct his mistakes.

Russell put both hands on the steering wheel, his jaw tight, knuckles white, while the semi roared into range.

With a shaking whoosh, the vehicle zoomed past, shuddering the Chevy in its wake.

He mentally prodded himself to reality, glancing at the seat next to him. Suzy was still there. Not a prom picture he grasped on to for dear life. Suzy.

You okay, Mr. Kingsley?

Russell glanced at Suzy. "What?"

"Are you okay? You got intense for a minute there."

He exhaled, hoping the gesture would still the blood rushing through his veins, right to his head. "I don't know if I'll ever feel the same about driving on an open road."

"Of course not." Suzy played with the hair at

his temple, soothing him. "You've been through a traumatic experience."

A sign for Lake Monet speared out of the ground, just ahead. His jittery heartbeat had spread to his hands, shaking them. Damn, why couldn't he calm down?

"Let's pull off here," said Suzy.

Was she making the request because she'd seen what the truck had done to him? Or was it because this was where they'd consummated their love on prom night? Where he'd proposed to her, hoping she'd be his wife with every hopeful teenage speck of naiveté he'd possessed?

He obliged her request, steering the Chevy to a pine-shaded, secluded spot overlooking the lake. He turned the ignition just enough to keep the heat going.

"Look at it," said Suzy. She still toyed with his hair, almost as if she didn't realize what she was doing, how she was so innocently revving his engine.

She continued. "It's the same, but different, like most things in Rumor. Same sky, same shore… same spot."

Silence.

Russell took up the awkward slack. "Because of the weather, there's a low water table this year.

That's why the lake really isn't the same. But—"
he pointed toward the cloud-mirrored water "—you
can always see why our legendary town romantic
named this place after Monet."

The surface did resemble a painting by the im-
pressionistic artist. But the colors were dim, like a
rust-tinged mockery of "Water Lilies."

Suzy laughed, leaning forward, toward the windshield. "You know how you can peer into a fun-
house mirror and glimpse a warped rendition of the
truth? Well, see that? Those clouds look just like
little Maltese dogs, scampering across a shiny table."

"That was creative." Russell rested his head
against Suzy's hand.

"That? You should hear what Isabelle comes up
with."

Pride rang through Suzy's voice, causing Russell
to gaze at her. He wondered if he had any part in
Isabelle's accomplishments. If success was in the
genes or in the raising.

She watched him for several heartbeats, and he
could sense the doubt in her gaze. Her hand drifted
downward to rest on his shoulder.

She said, "I didn't ask you to stop at the lake in
order to recreate what happened in the past."

Disappointment fisted inside him. Deep down,

he'd been hoping that she'd allow him to make love to her again and not necessarily in the back of his granddad's car, either. The thought of holding her on the banks of Lake Monet had been ideal, romantic, too good to be true.

Suzy snared his gaze with her own. "It's time to move on, Russell. I want to clear the air of these hard feelings that make talking to you so tense. I want you to be a part of—"

She stopped herself, clasping a hand to her mouth.

"Part of what, Suzy?"

Was she going to tell him about Isabelle?

A tear swerved down her cheek, wild as the skids of a careening car. She covered her face with her hands, her fingers long and pale. Fingers that had soothed him to comfort only moments before.

He took her hands in his and kissed the tears from her fingertips. He tasted the salty moisture; the bittersweet tang made him feel ten times more alive.

"Tell me something about Isabelle," he said. "Anything."

Suzy swallowed, a great gulp of anguish, then smiled through her tears. "When she was ten, she wrote a poem about clowns and how they scared her to death. Her teacher made sure it was published in a children's magazine, and I carried a clipping of it in my purse, wherever I went. She had autographed it, you know, in that ten-year-old happy-face squiggle that little girls use. But a year ago, when I was working in the department store, that purse was stolen, and I was never able to replace that piece of her youth.''

''I'm sure it hurt to have it taken away.'' Just as much as it hurt to have nothing, as far as Isabelle was concerned.

''Yeah, it did. But she's so optimistic. She said, 'Mom, that's how authors gain name recognition. One more person had the chance to read my poem. Word of mouth is where it's at.'''

Russell laughed. ''She's quite a girl.''

Come on, Suzy. Tell me.

Her hands trembled in his. ''Isabelle's so sensitive, so kind. Once, she found a bird with a broken wing. She didn't tell me about it, thought she could nurse it back to health on her own. But it ended up dying, and it broke Isabelle's heart. Every night she'd pray for forgiveness, and I'd tell her it wasn't her fault. She seems to take responsibility for everything. Just like I used to.''

''You still do. Too much sometimes.''

''Oh, God.'' She leaned her head against his

shoulder, and he stroked her hair, pressing his lips against her forehead. "This is so hard."

Could he make it easier for her?

"Suzy?"

"Yeah?"

"The other night, Isabelle told me what you said about her real father. That he left when she was newly born."

More tears, wetting his shirt, causing him to stroke her hair to calm her.

He could feel her shaking her head against his chest. "Isabelle," she chided.

Dammit, he had to know. "Is it true? Did her father leave?"

She sniffled, blew out a long breath. "No. That's not quite the way it went."

Relief deflated him, choking him up, racing his pulse in anticipation of her confession. The rhythm of his heart pinged in his ears, making his head swim.

It wasn't true.

He waited, hoping she'd elaborate, but she didn't. She merely huddled against him, as if hiding from the need to come clean with him.

Damn. He wanted to pound at the steering wheel, wanted to take out his frustration on the nearest punching bag.

But that didn't change the fact that she probably wasn't ready for this conversation, wouldn't be ready for a long time.

He sighed in defeat. "Whenever you want to talk, my ears are open. Just know that."

Her nails softly scratched down the front of his shirt. Then she picked at his buttons, marking the passing seconds.

She said, "I guess wounded people just need time to heal. You know that better than most."

Russell chuffed. "Hell. I'm the one who hurt you in the first place." He owed her some time.

"Russell?"

He made a low sound of acknowledgment.

"If I asked you to just hold me, would it offend your testosterone?"

Great. He'd become a damned Galahad.

But even Russell had to admit that her faith in him remaining a gentleman felt pretty decent.

"I'll roll up a newspaper and give my hormones a good thump if they get out of hand." He snuggled closer to her.

Suzy. His Suzy.

She tilted her face up to give him an enigmatic glance, then pulled away, slipping out the door before a protest could even form in his mouth. She reappeared in the back seat after slamming the door.

He stared at her. She stared at him.

"Well?" she asked. *What's the problem, slow-poke?*

Calmly, he left the front seat and joined her in the back. When he settled into the vinyl upholstery, he tried not to seem like a kid who was shocked to be in a compromising place with a...gulp...girl.

Immediately, she resumed her position, nestled against his chest, his chin resting on her head. They stayed like that until the stars came out, erasing the pictures from the lake's surface.

This had to be some kind of male record: Most Time Snuggling with a Girl in the Back Seat of a Guaranteed Make-Out Machine When You Could Be Shaking the Chevy.

But it was okay. Suzy trusted him enough to ask him to just hold her. And he was actually doing it. Liking it.

She stirred against him. "We remembered the heat, but forgot to turn on the radio."

"I can—"

"No. I sort of enjoy the quiet."

They both listened, and Russell discovered that he could hear something. A soft voice in the back of his mind, whispering in cadence. Poetry, sweet and true, vibrant with conviction and hope.

He closed his eyes, basking in the rhythm, in Suzy's touch.

His hand lazily slipped to her waist—that girlish, slender waist—and rested there, his fingertips splayed over her toned stomach. The force of her breathing moved his hand up and down, and pretty soon, he was stroking her with the motion, rubbing her belly until she moaned against his chest.

She rocked toward him, turning to press her body against his in one fluid motion, locking her mouth to his, insinuating her hand under his shirt, scratching his chest with her nails.

"Do you still feel the same about me?" she whispered, dragging her lower lip between both of his, then over his jaw.

"I've never stopped."

He pushed up her skirt, over those sleekly lined thighs, up to her hips. A peek of black, lacy underwear invited him to run his thumbs along her inner legs, to reach the apex of her thighs.

She grabbed his hands, halting them, before he got there. "What would you have done if I'd changed? If I hadn't been the same Suzy?"

He circled his thumbs over her hot skin. "I'd still want you."

She cocked her head, as if deciding whether or not he was stretching the truth. Then, as he slipped his hands under her skirt to cup her derriere, to pull her against his hardness, she closed her eyes, arching back, her mouth parting in a groan.

Shifting against him, Suzy brought his ache to the point of bursting, her lace panties rubbing, wisping against the denim of his jeans. He moved with her, guiding her hips against him, rolling her, churning her until she braced her hands against his shoulders, biting her lip, trying to hold back a soft cry.

Gently, he lay her down on the white vinyl, cradling her head in the crook of his arm, kissing her neck, taking her ear between his teeth to tenderly nibble the lobe. She wiggled underneath him, undoing his shirt, rendering him bare chested.

He did the same, drawing her sweater over her head, watching as her gleaming hair trailed out of the collar. Tossing the fuzzy material aside, he bent to take a lace-covered nipple into his mouth, laving it through the material while Suzy ran her fingers through his hair, encouraging him.

When he came up for air, he stroked a forefinger into the other bra cup, teasing the flesh to hardness.

"I missed this in my life," he said, his breath short, scarce. "Missed having you, missed feeling your breasts against my skin. Damn, that's my favorite part of it all, feeling you hot and excited, rubbing against me.''

He undid the front clasp of her bra, watching as her breasts settled into flat, full mounds that would fill his hands, fill his hunger.

''I was under the assumption…'' Suzy gasped as he ran his thumbs over both nipples. ''That men only liked the intercourse part.''

He grazed his teeth under a breast, backtracking with his tongue, finding the center of her chest, tracing the line traveling down to her belly button, ending the trip with a slow kiss.

''Oh, guys do like it. That's a given.''

She swayed her hips again, moving her body to a near-sitting position in the cramped back seat, skimming her panties against his breastbone. He pushed up her skirt farther, licking her flat belly, easing his thumbs under the pink material once again.

Her knees clenched upward, and he slid her undies over her long, booted legs, looping her limbs over his shoulders.

When he glanced up at Suzy, her eyes had gone wide, excited, fearful.

''No one's ever done this with you.'' It was a statement, not a question.

''No. Russell, I don't—''

He bent down, kissed her there. She convulsed, fisting his hair.

He loved her with his mouth, gently, conveying every emotion he couldn't say out loud. As she sobbed, reaching the peak of her excitement, Russell smoothed back up her body with his lips, kissing her with the demanding urgency of one who, for the moment, couldn't communicate any other way.

He held her in his arms when she trembled afterward. Held her, even though he was about to explode, himself.

Taking a deep breath, he rubbed Suzy's back, worked her skirt back down her legs.

For a fleeting second, he remembered another pink skirt—a prom dress—spread across the back seat of this car. Remembered how he'd taken the promises of that night and torn them apart.

"I'm going to make up for all those lost years," he said, feeling her hair curl around the corners of his mouth as he spoke into its softness.

And, when she didn't say anything in return, he took that as a good sign.

Chapter 9

He did make it up to her, just as he promised, without any more nights like the one at Lake Monet.

Yeah, the lack of physicality was killing him, but Russell knew that, in order to win Suzy's trust completely, he needed to go after her heart. Not her libido.

The following days were filled with long, leisurely dinners at the Rooftop Café. Energetic, lighthearted lunches at the Calico Diner. Work-hardened, soul-cleansing weekends repairing Suzy's house. More swing dancing at The Fedora.

Last, but not least, Russell found himself abandoning his own lonely cabin on the Kingsley ranch for TV nights at Suzy's place. Nights when he could chat with Isabelle and sit with the woman he loved, feeling like part of her family.

Tonight, Isabelle had brought home a slew of what she called "old-timer" movies: *Better Off Dead, Peggy Sue Got Married, Pretty In Pink.* Problem was, Isabelle wasn't here to watch them.

Suzy sat next to Russell on the bloated couch, setting two cups of hot cocoa on the end table before them. She'd concocted a pizza from scratch, both of them playfully mixing the dough and flicking the flour at each other before it had been covered with tomato sauce, vegetables and pepperoni, then shoveled into the oven. The oregano-laced aroma floated into the family room.

"Isabelle told me she'd be home by seven," Suzy said. "Usually she's on time, but after school she went out with one of the football players. You know, superjock."

Russell picked up his steaming cup of cocoa. "Hey, not all athletes are evil. My brother Reed was an honorable superjock."

"Sure. You're right." Suzy sat back, watched him sip the beverage. "This particular stud's just a boy who's taking out my little girl. I guess that's what makes it scary.''

They'd talked more about Isabelle these past few days—what she liked to eat, her college dreams, her crush on that actor Josh Hartnett—but Suzy hadn't volunteered more than that. Nevertheless, he felt closer to the youngster who might be his daughter, having had the opportunity to spend more time with her.

"Listen," he said, putting down the drink and turning to Suzy, resting a hand on her knee, "Isabelle's a big girl with a good head on her shoulders. Has she ever let you down before?"

Suzy shook her head. "But she's usually on time."

A flare of paternal concern lit through him, but he tamped it down. "Let's wait for a half hour. Then we'll get worried. She's only twenty minutes late. Okay?"

With her head tucked against the couch, Suzy seemed so vulnerable, so open to anguish. The wrinkle between her eyebrows only emphasized the fragile angle of her chin, the pale tint of her skin.

"Half an hour?" she asked.

"Give her some leeway."

He chucked Suzy under her jaw, making her smile. Almost.

She jiggled her ankle, directed her attention to the television, which featured some kind of silly reality show. Soon, she was on her feet again, heading toward the kitchen.

"I'll check the pizza," she said.

"Relax. It's not done."

"I need something to keep myself occupied."

Russell stared at the clock above the TV, entranced by the digital readout, the flashing colons that pounded out each passing second. Before he realized it, he'd floated into a light sleep, broken only by the feel of a hand slipping into his own.

Soft, warm, safe.

"Suzy," he mumbled.

A moment passed. He squeezed his fingers together, only to find emptiness.

Russell opened his eyes, squinting at the digital clock. Suzy walked out of the kitchen, standing before him, frowning.

"Another headache?" she asked.

"Nah." He flexed his fingers again. "Just sleepy. Dreaming."

She pressed her lips to his forehead, leaning her hands on his thighs. Desire buzzed through him, flooding his head with a hive of voices, all mingling into one, numbing drone.

God, what she did to his body.

Not now, he thought. He wanted to court Suzy, to woo her. Not to overwhelm her with his frustrated passion.

Russell opened his arms to her, and she fell into them, sighing as she grooved against his body as if it were a well-used security blanket.

"You're cozy," she whispered.

"Just what every man wants to hear." Russell chuckled, bouncing her head on his chest with the mirth.

She peered up at him, her lids heavy over her eyes. "A real man knows how to make a woman feel safe. That's how I feel when you hold me."

The genuine compliment stunned him, lit a fire in his gut. Made him glow from the inside out.

He drew her further into his embrace, loving how she clutched his arm, how she breathed against him.

A car door slammed outside, hopefully signaling Isabelle's return.

"Thank goodness." Suzy extricated herself from Russell, standing. "Should I be angry with her?"

What? Was she asking for his advice? "Well, what do you usually do when she breaks the rules?"

"I don't know." She shot him a panicked glance. "She's always obeyed me. Isabelle's never even talked back before."

Damn. The closest experience he had to dealing with kids concerned his brother Tag's young daughter, Samantha. Needless to say, he had nothing to do with his niece's discipline.

My God. Was he about to play father with Isabelle? Was Suzy asking him to?

Russell stood, as well, waiting for the teen to come through the door.

When she did, her face was tearstained, and he didn't have the heart to come off as an authority figure.

Suzy must have felt the same. She held out her arms, all anger at Isabelle's tardiness evidently forgotten. "Oh, sweetheart. What's the matter?"

Isabelle braved a smile but it trembled, melting into more tears. She wilted into her mother's arms.

Okay. What was his part in this? Should he make it a group hug? Or maybe standing here, awkward as all get out, was a better option.

He stuck his hands in his jeans' pockets, waiting.

Suzy brushed back Isabelle's red hair, gazing at her with a mother's knowing eye. "You're never late, but I'm not going to cause a big fuss about that. Obviously, something else is wrong."

Isabelle wiped her cheeks against her sweater, eyes widening when she saw Russell. "Hello, Mr. Kingsley. How're you today?"

Polite to the end.

He offered his most gentle smile. "I'm great, thanks."

To Suzy, he said, "Listen, I'm going to duck into the kitchen—"

"No," said Isabelle, sinking to the couch. "Don't bother. The news will be all over Rumor by tomorrow morning."

Suzy's face paled. "News?"

Was she thinking of a worst-case scenario? That Isabelle had pulled a prom-night Suzy and slept with a guy who'd told her that he loved her?

Because that's what Russell was thinking. Dreading.

He hunkered down on the couch next to Isabelle, leaving an I-might-be-your-dad-but-maybe-not space.

The sixteen-year-old held up her hands in apparent dismay. "He dumped me."

Why he'd throttle the kid. "Who?"

"Brady Coffey. You know. The quarterback." Isabelle laughed a little. "Boy, was I blind. I kind of thought he looked like Josh Hartnett and all, but when he told me that he wanted to date Allison Cantwell, too, I realized that he looks more like Frankenstein's monster."

Russell laughed, eased that she had a sense of

humor about it. "Too many hits to the head on the football field, I suppose."

Suzy sat next to Isabelle also, trading understanding glances with Russell. Her shoulders had relaxed, indicating relief. Obviously, she'd raised her daughter to avoid the mistakes she herself had made with Russell, to be a good girl. And while the thought hurt, he knew it was the right thing to have done.

"Isabelle, you know what they say." Suzy slipped an arm around the girl. "There're too many fish in the sea."

"And most of them are slippery," added Russell. "So you're smart to be careful."

"I just wish…" Isabelle's sweet voice trailed off, leaving a wistful sheen in her eyes.

"Wish what, honey?" asked Suzy.

"I don't know." Isabelle absently used her finger to draw circles on her knee. "I mean, I'm sixteen and I haven't found the love of my life yet."

Suzy smiled, but as she locked gazes with Russell, her happiness faded.

He'd found *his* first love, his only love, as a teen. Was Suzy thinking the same thing?

Suzy cocked her head, turned Isabelle to face her. "You've got so much time. Just do me a favor, okay? Don't rush it. Don't try to be an adult before you have to be.''

He imagined her changing Isabelle's diapers. Imagined her staying home to rock her daughter to sleep while her friends flirted at dance clubs or watched movies with flickering dreams shining over their unlined faces.

Isabelle kissed Suzy on the cheek. "Thanks, Mom."

Then she faced Russell. "And you, too, Mr. Kingsley. This is almost like having a dad around."

Russell about keeled over, and when he glanced at Suzy, he knew that she was blindsided by mortification, also.

Isabelle stood, fresh-faced, just as if she hadn't rocked the room with her last comment. "What are you cooking? Pizza? It smells great! When're we eating?"

Suzy's voice winced. "In a few minutes."

"Cool." Isabelle scampered off in the direction of her room. "I want to get comfy for the movies. Be right back."

Left alone, Russell and Suzy merely glanced at each other, then away.

After Isabelle's offhand comment, he wished he could get comfy also.

* * *

A couple days later, Russell had fully recovered from movie night.

Suzy had ignored Isabelle's comment, maneuvering the seating arrangement so that her daughter sat between her and Russell during the cinematic marathon.

But he had volleyed, inviting mother and daughter to his place for a brisk Sunday barbecue with his siblings. After all, he wasn't about to let something like discomfort hold her back from falling in love with him again.

Now, as he stood under his covered back porch, coat bundled around his body, watching the sun cool itself in the blue sky, Russell flipped burgers on the grill, surrounded by family and space heaters.

This was perfect, with his brothers Reed and Tag talking football while kicking back in Russell's wooden chairs. With Suzy and his sister Maura encouraging Tag's daughter, Samantha, as the little girl jumped rope on the black-topped basketball court. With Isabelle bundled in a heavy sweater and coat, knees tucked to her body while sitting under the protection of a fir, thumping a pen against a scarf-covered mouth as she pored through a battered journal.

Before the car accident, his life had been all

MonMart and toil. Since Suzy had come back into his life, his existence had pulsed, growing into something much more colorful, simple and pure.

He scooped the burgers onto a plate, then called, "Chow's on!"

Everyone, save Isabelle, charged the food table: the beef, beans, salads, corn and buns. When Russell called to the teen, she merely pulled down the scarf and said she'd eat later then proceeded to shift her attention back to her work.

He'd leave her alone, wouldn't be pushy.

Suzy took a seat next to him, as if the position was natural. As if they were a couple who sat together at every function. His siblings noticed right away, judging from the we-knew-it-all-along expressions they wore.

Reed, his buzz cut spiking as if in reaction to the cool weather, spoke first. "I doubt Mom and Dad are eating this well, even in Europe."

Five-year-old Samantha piped up, inspecting her hamburger with big, sad hazel eyes. "I miss Grandpa's candy."

Stratton hid goodies in his desk for his granddaughter, betraying a once-steely image. Russell only wished the older man would give Suzy her version of a treat: to apologize for what they'd done to her all those years ago.

Much to Suzy's credit, she remained bubbly, even at the mention of Stratton. She bent toward Samantha, smoothing back the girl's light brown hair. Echoes of her loving relationship with Isabelle reverberated through Russell's chest.

She said, "Your grandpa will be back soon. And I'll bet he brings back fancy candy from overseas, too."

The little girl's eyebrows shot up, her mouth forming a big O. "Lollipops? Chocolate bars? Taffy?"

Tag hauled his daughter to his lap with carpenter-rough hands. "Don't get so excited that you can't eat real food. Here." He put the burger back in Samantha's hands. "Protein."

The child diligently complied, taking dainty bites.

"Suzy," asked Maura, pulling her thick coat around her, "how's life in Rumor treating you so far?"

That was his baby sister, all right. Subtly trying to wheedle information about his and Suzy's relationship. Why didn't Maura just come right out and ask if they were seeing each other?

He shot her a look that contained the question. She smiled back, hardly flustered.

Suzy finished swallowing a bite of her salad. "I

made the right decision, moving back here. Everyone's been incredibly helpful and caring. But I'd really be happy if it'd snow at Christmas. We didn't get that kind of weather in Oceanside.''

Maura leaned forward in her chair. ''I love that name. Did you go to the beach a lot?''

A shadow passed over Suzy's face. ''No, actually. I didn't have much time for sunbathing. But—'' she pointed to her fair skin ''—it's a good thing. I'd need a sunblock so strong that they haven't invented it yet.''

When she glanced at Russell, he gave an encouraging grin. She was probably nervous about being with his family, even with the absence of Stratton.

Did she realize how well she fit in with the Kingsleys? How easily she made conversation and became one of them?

Reed interrupted Russell's musings by jovially saying, ''In your honor, Suzy McCord, I predict a white Christmas. Even if the weather hasn't been going that direction.''

''Well,'' said Suzy. ''That's an amazing welcome-home gift, Reed.''

He nodded. ''Why not put our family's power and fortune to good use, I say.''

The chatter skidded to a halt.

Damn, they were all thinking about what he'd done to Suzy, weren't they? From the pained look on her face, he knew she definitely was.

Time to stop beating around the bush. Russell said, "Suz, I told you my father's changed. When he comes back into town, you'll see that."

Tag got out of his chair, Samantha in tow. With the little girl curiously glancing over her shoulder, he walked her back to the jump rope.

"Congratulations," Maura said to Reed. "You really know how to conjure up an awkward moment."

Reed frowned. "Sorry about that, Suzy."

"No." Suzy waved away the apology. "Please, don't walk on eggshells around me. I know why Stratton didn't want me around."

Russell said, "I told her about the cancer, about everything."

"Great," said Reed. "Dad's going to bask in his kinder, gentler reputation."

"Dad can take care of himself just fine." Maura addressed Suzy. "We're all sorry about what happened. And we're well aware that there're several loose ends. One of which is the need for Dad to tell you he's sorry. Because he really is."

Suzy fidgeted with her hands, then stopped, as if suddenly becoming aware that it made her appear vulnerable. "You all have been supportive, and I appreciate that. But, no matter what you say, I'm afraid that winning over your father isn't going to be as easy. I remember a hardheaded man who protected his family with fangs and claws bared."

Russell said, "That's in the past. Just sit back and enjoy your burger. I'm telling you, it doesn't get much better than my cooking."

Reed made a choking noise, lightening the moment.

As everyone laughed, Russell spared a glance for Isabelle, who was still working away at her journal, pen scribbling furiously on the paper.

The adults' conversation settled into a safe topic: local gossip. Without a word, Russell stood, trailing a hand over Suzy's shoulder as he left the family circle.

He caught her gaze, her relieved smile, as he sauntered away toward his maybe-daughter.

The postbreakup Isabelle seemed so contemplative, so alone out here, sitting against the fir. Yet, thinking back to the days after he'd called it off with Suzy, he'd felt the same way. Hadn't he?

Almost as if he'd gnawed his own heart out of his chest because of the trap it'd been caught in.

She must have sensed his presence, because she

peered up at him, whisking the scarf from her face. "Hi, again, Mr. Kingsley."

"Hey. Why aren't you under the porch with us and the heat?"

She indicated the journal, its brown leather cover worn with usage, the pages dog-eared. "The weather's invigorating. It's helping me to write poetry for English class."

"Oh? Sunsets and puppies dogs?" He sat on the ground. "Pinafores and pansies?"

"Wouldn't that be nice. You know, to be so carefree."

"What? Are you saying you have a dark side? Shoot. Not with those cute dimples."

She flashed them. "I suppose I'm taking my frustration with Brady Coffey out on the pages. It's more constructive than letting the air out of his tires or toilet papering his house."

That's my girl, he thought. Maybe even literally.

"Pain makes great art," he said, lying on his side.

"Did you hear the news?" she asked, a wicked glint in her blue eyes. A glint like her mama used to have when she'd stand on the sidelines and cheer, working the crowd.

He thought a moment. "Can't say that I'm up on the latest."

"Allison Cantwell already dumped him. Said he was a scumbucket." She cocked a brow. "He called me last night, contrite as you please. 'Oh, take me back, Isabelle. I was a bad boy.'"

Little piece of slime. "And what did you say?"

Dimples again. "I was kind, but still took great satisfaction in hearing him beg."

Russell must have seemed worried, because she laughed and said, "I told him to take a dive into a bottomless lake. Yeesh, don't you have any faith in my common sense?"

"Yeah, Isabelle," he said. "I do."

Something passed between them, an understanding, making Russell wonder if she suspected that he might be her father, if she was too polite or afraid to ask for confirmation.

"So," she said. "You want to hear a poem about the experience? It's full of bitterness and smug victory."

He grinned, rolling to his back, folding his arms under his head to prop it up, kicking a heel over the other boot. "Emote away."

And she did, her voice lilting, soft as the down of an angel's wing. He closed his eyes, listening to the words flow together, images swirling like floating feathers through his consciousness.

The poetry faded away. In its place, a lone wind blew, lulling him, drawing him into sleep.

"Mr. Kingsley?" The voice tickled his perception.

Isabelle.

"Mr. Kingsley? Wake up."

He opened his eyes, seeing Isabelle above him, shaking his arm.

"You fell asleep on me. It must've been pretty awful stuff. I'll get an F for sure."

"No, it was great. You've got a way with words." He sat up. "Your mom used to write poetry, too. Great stuff. Sweet and gentle."

"I had no idea."

"It's true," he said. "That's one of the reasons I was—" he grinned, knowing he shouldn't insult Isabelle's intelligence "—*am* nuts about her. She's good, through and through."

She tilted her head, smiling at him as if he'd created the world with its flower petals and snowflakes.

So what if she didn't turn out to be his biological daughter? It'd be easy to love Isabelle anyway.

The girl pushed up her sweater cuff and peeked at her watch. "Know what? I've got a study date. A monstrous essay due in chemistry. Yuck. Science sucks the creativity right out of me."

"Go." Russell playfully swatted at her pants leg as she stood and started walking away. "Make your mother proud."

She halted, turned back to him, opened her mouth as if to say something, but stopped.

You'll make your dad proud, too, he thought. Wherever he is.

Then, as if she'd heard him, she nodded and left.

Chapter 10

After Maura, Reed, Tag and Samantha called it a night and left Russell's home, Suzy lingered, helping him clean.

"Isabelle took the car," she said, rinsing the plates and organizing them in the dishwasher. "I hate when she does that."

Russell closed his industrial-size refrigerator and wiped his hands on a dish towel. "Why?"

"Because it's unnatural, seeing your baby cruise away from you. Not that she isn't a safe driver. She's better than I am. It's just…"

He came to stand behind her. "She's all grown up."

"Right."

Suzy turned around, front to front with him, her sweater brushing against his shirt, her skirted thighs skimming his jeans.

It had been days since they'd kissed, touched, rocked against each other.

He was dying inside.

Suzy's voice lowered, obviously aware of how close his body was to hers, aware of how his proximity was no careless accident.

He wanted her until it pained him.

"I wish you could've seen her when she was tiny," she said. "She looked like the Gerber baby—chubby cheeks, wide eyes and all. She was always giggling."

"I would give anything to have been there."

A pause stretched between them.

Suzy ducked under one of his arms, escaping him, adjusting the toaster, the blender. "Isabelle really likes you, Russell. I don't know how you managed, but she can't stop talking about you."

There was that warm glow inside him again. "I'm honored. Really."

She stopped her busywork, studying him. "I believe you are."

Once again, no confession, no more information. Okay. What had he told Suzy to do with Isabelle when the teen had stayed out late, disappointed her, even for a short time? He'd suggested some leeway for the girl to come through. And she had.

Now, he was going to follow his own advice, giving Suzy two more days before he forced the issue. A two-day deadline to come clean with him, no matter the consequences.

His patience was running out.

And maybe she sensed his frustration, too.

With a backward glance, she left through the door frame and into the family room, with its wide-screen TV and stereo-surround system, its burning stone-chimney fire, its pool table complete with a spray of balls covering the green felt surface.

Suzy sauntered over to the table, leaned against it and rolled a striped ball under her palm, back and forth, back and forth. Russell busied himself at the DVD player, playing a Dwight Yokum CD. The singer's lazy twang reminded him of open prairies and low fires, of Suzy's slim curves lit by twilight.

"You up for some pool?" she asked.

"I didn't think you played." He came to hover near the table, retrieving two sticks from the mahogany holder on the wall.

She started racking the balls. "I dabbled here and there. Aunt Hazel had a liking for pool. She was one of those women who spent a lot of time in the neighborhood bar, cracking balls with the locals. She tried to teach me, but I never got the hang of it.''

''You're good at anything you try.''

She shot him a miffed glance, as if he'd been attempting a double entendre. But he hadn't. It was true. Suzy had gotten good grades, was a graceful ice skater, rode horses with ease. She'd been a natural at everything.

She'd always tried so hard to please others.

The table set, Russell gestured to the triangle of striped and solid balls. ''You break.''

A confident grin cast her in a devilish light. ''I lied before. You know I'm going to beat the pants off you, right?''

''Promise?''

She bent over the rim of the table, cue stick positioned between the fingers of her left hand, right hand on the butt of the stick. Was she pressing her chest against the table, rubbing against the polished wood like a cat, for strategy's sake?

Or was she trying to drive him out of his mind?

With a sure stroke, she drew back the stick, deftly hitting the cue ball so that it fractured the formation. Two striped balls dove into the end pockets.

''Well, look at that,'' she said.

"What do you know?"

She lined up her next shot. Russell decided to have some fun, standing behind her, urging the front of his thigh against the firm curve of her derriere. He adjusted her stick.

"You're off a little."

She put it back where it was in the first place.

He grinned, the expression widening when she scattered the balls over the felt without any results.

"Cheater," she said, walking away from him, running a hand up and down the cue stick.

He ignored the sensual suggestion, watching her with what he hoped was detached amusement.

When he finally took his shots, he sank three solids in a row, performing a mock yawn as he lined up his next feat.

Suzy nestled next to him, her sweater rubbing against his arm. That orchid perfume teased him, and she damned well had to know it.

"Let's make this interesting," she said.

"I'm all ears. And more."

She grinned. "For every shot we sink, the other player has to answer a question."

He almost dropped his stick, thinking of the possibilities. You mean she actually wanted to know something about him? "Truth or dare?"

"But without the dare." She pushed off from the table. "I'm not brave enough for that yet."

His gaze followed her, dwelling on the sway of her bottom underneath the cling of her pink skirt.

Was she, in a roundabout way, inviting him to ask about Isabelle?

And did he really want to shatter this playful, sexy interlude by taking her up on it?

She was strolling around the table, catching his eye, circling him, challenging him. He hunkered down again, concentrating on his shot.

Lining it up.

Drawing back his stick.

Waiting....

Just as he was about to push forward, Suzy's finger brushed his ear, throwing off his aim.

He missed the cue ball altogether.

"What did you say about cheating?" he asked, giving her a sidelong glance.

"Now we're even."

She used her hip to nudge him away from the table, then proceeded to sink a ball.

"Oh." She smiled innocently. "That means I get to ask a question."

He backed against the table, leaning on his stick. "Bombs away."

"Hmm." She bit her lower lip and squinched her

eyes, thinking way too hard to be convincing. "I know. Tell me about your last girlfriend."

Hell. This was a sure ticket to breaking the flirtatious moment. "I'm a monk. A slave to MonMart. The store is a demanding mistress."

He grinned. She shook her head, eyebrow raised.

"You have to tell the truth," she said.

"Or what?"

"Or…" A considering gaze. "I get to scratch dirty words into the paint job of your beloved Chevy."

Russell put his hand to his heart. "Ouch."

"That's right. Now out with the truth."

Great. "Last girlfriend, huh?"

"What, do you have so many that you need time to sort through your files?"

She actually seemed ticked off, with her hand cocked on her hip and her blue eyes blazing.

"Hey, calm down. It's been a while."

"Right."

"No, really." He reached out, laid a hand on her cue stick, pulled her a step closer. "I haven't had what you'd call a 'girlfriend' for a good span of time. Sure, I've dated, but…"

She swallowed, her voice cracking. "But…?"

How could he tell her that she'd been the only woman he'd loved? That she'd been the only one to survive in his memory without the taint of a one-night-stand sense of regret?

She cleared her throat. "It was a stupid question. None of my business."

"I want it to be your business."

From the way she stared at him, he thought he was in for another disappointment. Thought she'd stiff-arm him again, saying, "I can't trust you, Russell. Not after what you did to me."

But she surprised him, reaching up to touch her fingertips to his lips. He closed his eyes, opened them, just to see if this was real.

Yes.

A flush pinked her cheeks. "You've been so patient."

He kissed her fingers, causing her to lean into him.

Suzy. So warm, so soft…

So his.

But only momentarily. After a beat, she pulled back, smiling, straightening the collar of his shirt, once again flirty and inaccessible.

"I've had enough pool for the night," she said, stepping away, walking toward the fire.

He watched her settle in front of it, not knowing what to say now.

Instead, he got his coat and went outside. Maybe

she'd be there when he got back, maybe she wouldn't. All he wanted to do was walk, spend his energy, forget the urgency that was battering against his groin.

He had to work off the hunger or he'd explode.

Thank God she was there when he returned an hour later.

After he'd shed his coat and shrugged off the nighttime chill, he'd found her sleeping in front of the fire, her stylish boots discarded to the side. She'd grabbed a couple of large pillows from a couch, slumbering against them with a sheen of heartbreaking serenity smoothing her face.

He bent to a knee, watching her. If he'd played his cards right as a senior, he could have woken up to Suzy every morning, breathing in her dream-warmed scent, teasing her awake with caresses.

But he knew better by now than to play "what if" with himself. He needed to work out the present, not the past.

He rose to his feet, got a few fluffy comforters from a hall closet, then returned to tuck them around Suzy. He laid another blanket on the ground and climbed on top of it, kicking off his own boots.

The fire crackled and winked, stroking his face

with fingers of heat, while he reclined next to Suzy, spooning her from the back, holding her to him.

Soon, he fell asleep. A deep, empty abyss where nothing bothered him.

Not until he felt someone touching him.

Jerking awake, he found Suzy, her chin resting on a forearm as she rubbed his bare chest with her other hand. Somehow, without him awakening, she'd unbuttoned his shirt, slipped her hand inside.

When she saw that he'd come back to the land of the living, she tugged back her hand, bit her bottom lip then said, "I didn't mean to startle you."

"No harm done." He stretched his arms over his head, turning to face her.

She said, "You left the cabin. Is it something I did?"

He laughed tightly. "I'm a red-blooded male, Suz. After that pool game, I was ready to rumble."

"Oh."

"Don't worry, I'm over it. But sometimes a guy needs to cool off."

"Yeah. I get it."

Firelight gleamed in her hair, flitting over the red strands. She was so beautiful, so unchanged from the woman he'd always loved.

"Shouldn't you be home?" he asked.

"Not tonight. Isabelle's study date was a combination academic retreat and sleepover party. She'll be fine without me.''

Hope jumped in his chest, trying to bust through the hazy aftermath of slumber. Even the edges of his sight seemed to blur around Suzy, rendering her in soft-focus, pink-tinted beauty.

He grasped her hand again, putting it right back where it had been, massaging his chest. ''Don't let me interrupt you.''

''I…'' She blushed ten shades of red.

''No apologies necessary. Damn, Suzy, staying away from you has been driving me to distraction. I haven't wanted to rush things.''

''I've missed you, too. I thought maybe…well, maybe you were disappointed in me when we went to Lake Monet. That I didn't measure up to your seventeen-year-long fantasies or the other girl-friends you'd had after me—'' She cut herself off. ''Isn't that pathetic?''

The insecure, browbeaten girl who used to shoulder constant cut downs from her mother reappeared.

He ran a hand up her arm, inside her baggy sweater sleeve. ''Believe me, Suzy. There's no woman I want more than you. I need you so bad that I ache.''

He could see the questions forming the shape of

her mouth, the part of her lips, and he answered them before she could ask.

"I'd give up everything for you." He shifted forward, his voice low. "Forget the money. It's nothing."

"I'm not asking you to turn your back on your family, Russell."

"I know. But they'll accept you. My brothers and sisters have already welcomed you. Don't worry about anyone else."

"But—"

"Trust me."

He withdrew his hand from the warmth of her sweater, resting his fingers on her hip. An intimate gesture.

She locked a gaze on the touch, then on him. "I trust you. You've managed to win me over, damn you."

A smile softened the words, but he knew that she was still at war with her lack of confidence. It was his job to bolster her, to make her love herself as much as he loved her.

She sat up, pulling her sweater over her head, revealing another lacy, black bra. Next, she shed her skirt and stockings, leaving her in nothing but her lingerie.

Damn, that walk had done him no good whatsoever. He hadn't let off any sexual steam. It was all still contained in his lower belly, pounding there, whistling through his veins.

Suzy settled back with a sigh as he bent over her, trailing his fingertips over her cheek, neck, the swell of a breast, lingering, tracing, watching the nipple pucker under the lace.

"You're still perfect after all these years," he said, traveling downward to her rib cage, where the reflection of flames danced over her skin. "No marks, no scars."

"Only on the inside."

She smiled, then swanned her neck back as he continued his exploration of her skin, palming her flat stomach, over her panties, thumbing between her legs, teasing the nub between the folds of flesh there.

Moving with the motion of his fingers, she groaned, resting a hand against her forehead, shutting her eyes.

He needed more. Needed to be inside her, sheltered by heat.

With a surge of desire driving him onward, he lengthened himself over her body, pressing his denim-contained erection to the center of her legs, straining against her as she grasped at him, discarding his shirt, his belt.

Their lips met, tongues plunging in time to the grind of their hips.

"Let me be inside you," he whispered.

Panting, she wiggled out of her bra, her distended nipples dragging over the skin of his chest, his own nipples. The sensation spiked through him with a rush, blinding him with agitation.

With greedy strokes, he bent to take a breast into his mouth, laving it, tasting her scent—the tangy sweat, the flower-sweet perfume of her. He kissed downward, turning her onto her stomach, mouth tracing a slender bone in her rib cage, the bump of her spine. He used a hand to ease up the front of her thigh, to feel the moisture beading the inside of it.

The murmured words came before he could stop them. "I love you, Suzy. Damn, I've always loved you."

She gasped. He didn't know if it was because of what he'd said, or what he'd done: plunged his fingers into her underwear, slid them inside of her, thrusting in and out.

"Russell." Almost a sob.

He cupped a breast, lightly bit her earlobe, swirled his tongue around the delicate shell of her ear.

"Tell me what you want," he whispered.

"I don't know."

"Bull." He pulled her derriere against his hardness. "Tell me, Suzy."

Her smooth back stuck to his chest, slicked by sweat. The feel of her wet skin slipping against him sent more blood pounding to his groin.

Unbelievable, this insistent surge of emotion and hunger. He hadn't felt so out of control since prom night.

But he'd been a kid then, losing his innocence to the girl he thought would be his wife for the rest of his days.

"Suzy...."

He felt a shudder rip through her body, travel to the tips of her fingers, which she dug into his arms, leaving stinging marks.

She fought for breath, then turned her face into his neck. "I want you inside me."

Inside her. Just as she was inside *him*.

He turned her around. With infinite care, he coaxed his knuckles over her cheekbone, wanting to touch every angle, every curve.

"I'll always love you," he said.

A pained expression crossed her face. Sadness?

Maybe she'd never come to love him again. He buried his face in her neck.

That would be the deepest pain of all. Living without Suzy's love.

She stirred underneath him, pushing his jeans off his body, stripping out of her panties until they were skin to skin, drops of his sweat mingling with hers.

She opened herself to him, searching him out until he prodded the damp opening between her legs.

With a slow thrust, he eased inside her, surrounded by fire and the slick of burning ice. He moved in a rhythm dictated by memory—the lazy May lapping of water upon a shore, the rustle of pine needles, the disembodied whispers of a radio DJ.

His pace quickened, punctuated by her gasps.

In…out.…

Coasting…driving into her.…

Grinding, build-up of heat, aching to the point of bursting.…

A whir of colors flashed over his sight, spinning, clouding, leaving him almost breathless.

Then, it happened. With the force of glass splintering around his body, he spent himself inside of her, holding her to him as if no one—no thing—could tear her from his arms again.

He used his fingers to urge her to a peak, also, her body soaring against him, digging her nails into the skin of his back, cutting into him with the sharpness of splinters.

"Russell, I..." She didn't complete the sentence, just trembled, moaned, quaked to a panting stillness.

Soon, she nestled against him, hiding her face against his chest, sobbing and trembling as if he'd broken her heart.

Russell's arms stiffened around her.

And he'd hoped that making love would make things so much better.

Chapter 11

Later that night, as they lay in bed with Suzy's back resting against Russell's chest, he had to ask her about the crying.

He brushed a lock of hair away from her neck, kissed the vein there. "Suz?"

"Mmm?"

"Is everything okay?"

She laughed a little, and he could feel her breasts move against the arm he had wrapped around her front.

"Just like a man. It's not enough that we've made love three times since the beginning of the night. Now he wants to know if everything is okay?" She turned her face in profile, revealing her cute, tilted nose, her saucy chin. "Everything's wonderful."

Was it? After their first encounter, he'd wanted to comfort her, to ask why she was weeping. But instead, she'd led him to the bedroom, where she'd distracted him with more lovemaking—fast and raw, slow and passionate.

"Why do you ask?" she said.

"Earlier..." What if it was nothing? Ah, damn. "Earlier, after the first time, you were upset, and I just wondered..."

She leaned back against him. "It's nothing. Hormones. Years of stress and emotion overcoming me."

His ego wanted to buy that explanation. Common sense told him to leave it there. But he couldn't.

"Was it because I told you that I love you?"

The breath whooshed out of her on a long sigh. "I'm not going to hold you to that, Russell. You said it in the heat of the moment."

"Twice, as I remember."

"Still."

He rested his hand on her belly, trailing his fingers around and around. She'd carried Isabelle down here, a swollen, miraculous event that he wished he could've been a part of.

He said, "If you don't love me, I'll wait."

"Your confidence astounds me." She laughed, leaning over to plant a kiss on his biceps.

His skin beneath her lips tingled, jarring other parts of him awake. *Again.*

"Hey," he said, "we're meant to be together. Don't mess with Fate."

During the following silence, moonlight burst through the window, covered the sheets with a luminous, pale glare. It bathed the outline of their bodies—her legs entwined with his, her hips buried under his, the expanse of his hand on her stomach.

Holding her in the moonlight was so natural.

Destined to be.

She shifted, and the slight rise of her belly moved his hand, making him wish he could feel a child growing there, inside her womb.

She murmured, "We didn't use a condom."

A sly sense of satisfaction forced a grin. "So?"

"So?" Suzy sat up, turned to face him, the moonlight masking half her face. The visible side revealed panic in the widening of her eyes, the gape of her lips. "We have no business being so careless."

"We did the same thing years ago."

She stiffened, and Russell knew that she didn't want to talk about this again, didn't want to tell him about Isabelle.

He'd promised that he'd wait two days to force the issue, know the truth.

Screw two days.

"I've had enough of these games."

Milky light brushed her skin, her breasts creamy and firm. She grabbed the sheet, covering herself, depriving him of the sight.

"Not now," she said.

"Then when?" He cupped the back of her neck, stroking her throat with his thumb. "Tell me."

"Please. Don't do this."

"Suzy. Am I Isabelle's father?"

As she sat in silence, biting her lip, his heartbeat thudded, growing louder, an approaching monster with earth-shaking footsteps pounding in his ears.

She tucked a strand of red hair behind her ear, gaze downcast. She closed her eyes.

"Yes," she said.

So many emotions attacked at once: pure joy, stretching his mouth into a smile. Sharp agony, ripping his chest in two. Futile hope, dividing his heart with its razor of uncertainty.

"God, Suzy." He took her into his arms. "I'm really a dad."

She sobbed, then clung to him, heaving against him with…relief? Shame? Happiness?

"Don't cry," he said, caressing her. "Why're you so sad? We're parents."

Her breathing was ragged, serrated with more tears. "How can you be so good to me right now? How can you sit there and act like I didn't rob you of Isabelle's early life?"

A bite of anger shocked him, but he shoved it to the back of his mind. "I suppose I earned it. If I hadn't betrayed you, I could've seen Isabelle in diapers, could've seen her take those first steps, say her first words."

He stopped the "could've" stream of consciousness. Each one hurt a little more as he added to the list.

"Well." Suzy looked up at him, sniffling. "Aren't you the cool-headed one."

He wouldn't rise to this bait, wouldn't play into her insecurities by shifting the subject to something she could control.

Besides, his father had always told him that men shouldn't show their emotions. And they *never* wept, even if they were about to burst with happiness.

He was still the Kingsley heir—collected and capable.

"Don't fault me for my reaction. Just know that I love you and Isabelle, and I want us to be a family. Even if we're starting off with a sixteen-year-old."

Okay. Maybe he sounded more enthusiastic than he'd meant to. But what else could a guy do?

He was a father.

Isabelle's father.

He thought of her poetry, Suzy's inherited red hair, his own sidelong grin. Isabelle was the best of both of them.

His daughter.

He folded his arms behind his head, staring at the ceiling in thought. "I've got so many extra rooms in this place that it'll be no problem. Isabelle can have her pick, but I think she'll like the one overlooking the pine forest."

"Oh, wait. Wait, wait, wait." She wrapped the sheet around her body, stood from the bed. "See, this is what I was afraid of."

"What?"

She paused, ran a gaze over his naked body, swayed toward him, then retreated a couple of steps into the corner.

"You're jumping to conclusions. I mean, yes, Isabelle is your daughter, but that doesn't mean I'm going to clap my hands and jump up and down, hoping to move into your beautiful house with her.''

''Why not?''

''Russell.'' She shook her head as she leaned against the wall, all but fading into the white paint. ''This confession doesn't change a thing. Stratton won't want me around. I've already been tarred with the brush of illegitimacy, and Isabelle, through no fault of her own, followed in my footsteps.''

''Is that what you're afraid of?'' He wiped a hand down his face. ''Dammit, Suzy. I thought you'd come to terms with reality. My father *will* accept you both into the family.''

''Don't make promises you can't keep.''

Dormant anger stirred again, flaring from the depths of his soul, where he'd packed it away.

''I'm not a slave to my family.''

Yeah, Russell, he thought. Keep telling yourself that. Maybe you'll come to believe it.

Would he truly turn his back on his fortune, the parents and siblings who loved him?

The money. Yes. Hell, yes.

But his parents? Reed, Tag and Samantha, Maura, his cousin Jeff, who was like a brother to him?

Dammit. How could he possibly answer that?

A muscle jumped in his jaw. ''Are you giving an

ultimatum, forcing me to choose between you and the Kingsleys?''

She merely stood there. Finally, just when he thought she'd have nothing to say, she pushed off from the wall.

''Ultimatums are for Stratton. He's better at them than I could ever hope to be.''

''I'll tell you what. If my dad took out a full-page ad in *The Rumor Mill,* accepting you into the fold, would that help?''

She shoved a hand under her eye, probably wiping away more tears. But, this time, she smiled a bit. Even that tiny gesture offered hope.

''Actually,'' she said, ''I think a brass band with a grandstand speech would be more appropriate. I'm worth nothing less.''

''You're worth all the brass all the gold, as a matter of fact—in creation.'' He lifted an arm, hoping she'd take the hint to come back to him. ''We should be celebrating, not arguing.''

She hesitated, then walked back to the bed, the sheet gaping to reveal the curve of one breast. His body froze with sudden fire, just at the sight of her.

The mattress dipped as she sat on it. Then, with the softest of touches, she traced a finger up his arm. ''You're tense.''

''No kidding.''

"Turn over."

He quirked a grin at her, then complied, lying facedown on the bed, arms supporting his chin.

She began to massage him, hands kneading his back, his hips, lower.

"Don't say anything to Isabelle," she whispered.

Russell was so relaxed—so *relieved* that she wasn't going to run away from him anymore—that he could barely talk. "She really has no clue?"

"She's a smart girl, and she knows that something's up between the two of us. But I've never gone into great detail about her father."

"When can we tell her?"

Suzy paused in her motion, sighed, resumed the circling pressure on the small of his back. "I need to think about this."

"You still don't trust me, do you?"

Would she ever?

"I trust you more than I did when I first came back to Rumor."

"That's not saying much."

"We can talk about this later." She laughed lightly. "Would you just loosen up? There you go."

He felt her fingertips brush between his legs, and he was instantly hard.

She said, "I've been stretching your patience to

the limit. I know that. But I'm asking for a little more time."

She cupped him, making him groan.

"I'm not going to leave you," he said, reaching backward, tugging at the sheet until it draped down her skin, freeing her breasts. "Never again."

"Shh." She nudged his hand, his face, making him turn away from her.

He felt her nipples comb over his back, the down between her legs coast over his hip.

Even as she started kissing his neck, he still wasn't sure that she believed his promise.

But Russell was damned certain. He wouldn't leave Suzy for anything.

During the next couple of days, Russell managed to keep his trap shut around Isabelle.

Throughout their movie night, even during dinner at a swanky restaurant in Billings, he'd allowed Suzy to set the pace, catching the warning glances she'd shoot at him whenever he smiled too much at Isabelle or patted her shoulder with fatherly affection.

It was driving him nuts to keep the secret.

Today he'd invited Suzy and Isabelle over to his place for dinner. Suzy had wanted to take his large, well-equipped kitchen for a "test drive."

Have at it, he'd told her, thinking that he'd basically used the microwave for his bachelor meals and that's about it.

She'd decided on pot roast—real home cookin'. Family food. The aroma of beef and potatoes filled his cabin with comfort, with fantasies of Suzy and Isabelle living in the same space.

Outside, the weather had grown even cooler, abandoning the pretense of its extended Indian summer conditions. He and Isabelle were on the blacktop, shooting hoops, waiting for dinner, trying their best to manipulate the ball without their coats and gloves getting in the way.

Maybe it would be a white Christmas, after all, he thought as he passed the basketball to Isabelle. If not, he'd do his best to make it one.

For Suzy.

"She shoots..." said Isabelle, jarring him back to their friendly sparring.

The ball swished through the hoop, all net.

"She scores!"

Russell opened his mouth to make a flip comment. Something like, "Hey, you must've gotten your athletic talent from my side of the family."

But he caught himself just in time.

"Impressive," he said, dribbling the ball, faking

her out with a swift feint to the left. "But can you do this?"

He executed a Kareem Abdul-Jabar sky hook, curving the ball over his head with a flick of his wrist.

Oh, yeah. All net.

Isabelle, hands on hips, smirked. "Not bad for the old school. But…" She faced backward, shot the ball over her head without looking. Missed.

"I'll give you points for gumption," said Russell, retrieving the ball.

They both laughed. He could get used to this. Spending all his time with a daughter who brought sunshine into his life, even when the Montana chill was at its worst.

Isabelle peeked past him, then wiggled her fingers. Russell turned to find Suzy watching them from the kitchen window, waving.

He bounced the ball to his daughter.

Yeah. *His daughter.* If only he could say it out loud, tell the whole world.

Tell his father when he returned from Europe in a few days.

"Practice that fancy shot," he said, winking at Isabelle, "and I'll run inside to see what kind of damage your mom's doing to my house."

"You know, Mom's made a couple of meals on her own before." Isabelle offered a cheeky grin.

Russell started to walk away. "You're much too clever for your own good."

Behind him, he heard the ball smack the blacktop with its wincing bounce, then a metallic clang as it hit the backboard.

His daughter.

Damn. He'd have to keep repeating it until the extended shock and pride wore off. If it ever did.

Even when he entered the kitchen, Suzy still stared out the window at Isabelle. Russell stood behind the woman he loved, slipping his arms around her middle.

"Doesn't this feel right?" he asked. "With Isabelle in the backyard, you in the kitchen?"

She elbowed him gently. "Haven't you heard of women's lib? I belong in more places than just a steaming den of female drudgery."

"Forgive me, darlin'."

"I'm giving you a hard time. Cooking soothes the soul."

"And the stomach."

They watched their daughter shoot baskets. Watched the graceful determination she'd inherited from her mother, the sports ability she'd gotten from her father.

"She does more than write poetry," he said. "Isabelle's just like you. She's good at everything. Isn't she?"

"She tries."

He paused. "I'm going to see my father when he and my mom get home."

Suzy's back straightened, as if pride had shot up her spine. "They're coming back already?"

"It had to happen someday." He bent toward her ear, brushing the hair around it with his whisper. "Don't worry. Everything will work out."

She unlocked his hands from around her waist, pulled away from him. "You're so stubborn. How do you think Stratton's going to react when you spill the good news? Do you think he'll roar with joy? Or do you think his face will fall in disappointment?"

Russell couldn't answer, because he wasn't entirely sure, himself. "Don't assume anything. That cancer changed his outlook on life."

"You don't sound too certain about that." Her fingers worried the pocket hem of her skirt as she paced away from him. "What are you going to do if he asks you to stay away from me? If he tells you that claiming Isabelle, your illegitimate child by way of an illegitimate mother, will taint the good Kingsley name?"

"I can't believe you're asking me this."

"Why? Because it might happen?" She stood in front of him, her eyes soft, worried. "We need to be realistic about this. Thinking like moonstruck kids in love won't prepare us for Stratton's possible reaction."

"He wouldn't make me choose. Not again. He'd be afraid of my answer."

She looked at him as if asking, "And what would that be?"

Guilt weighed down his words. "I'd live like a church mouse if it meant winning your love, Suzy. But don't ask me to turn my back on my family. I have loyalty toward them, too. That's why I believe they won't make me decide between being with you and remaining true to them."

Her shoulders slumped and, after a pause, she gestured toward the pot roast in the oven. "It should be ready in thirty minutes and—"

He tenderly grabbed her hand. "Tell me you're not going anywhere. Tell me you're not afraid of what I need to say to my father."

"Russell." She started to back away from him, slipping out of his grasp. "Maybe I was wrong to think we could get past all the mistakes that piled up around us. I was being too optimistic, I mean, I don't deserve—"

"That's your mother talking."

She closed her eyes. "I wish I didn't believe what she always told me. 'Suzy, you look too cheap to be with a rich boy like Russell Kingsley.' 'Suzy, what makes you think you deserve his kind of life? I'm the one who's suffered for you, sacrificed everything just to bring you up right.'"

"And she was wrong." He wanted so badly to touch her, to stroke away the worry lines that had gathered around her eyes. "I love you. That's all that matters."

While she hesitated, he felt as if he were skidding toward that guardrail once again, knowing that anything he did to save himself would be fruitless, knowing that the end was near.

"It should be that way, shouldn't it?" she asked. "Love should conquer all. But it doesn't. Years ago, it didn't overcome your father's sense of family dignity. It didn't overcome my shame."

"But we're adults now. Things are different."

She gazed at him, her heart breaking, shattering into the splinters of her irises. "I guess I am different. Ever since I came back to Rumor, I've felt better about myself. I think I've earned your love and, really, it's a noble feeling. And that's why I'm about to save you from the hardest choice you might ever have to make."

Fear froze him solid. "Don't."

She shook her head sadly. "I'm not your kind. Look how I handled things with Isabelle. She hasn't had a father for sixteen years, all because I couldn't love myself enough to stand up to the Kingsleys sooner."

He took her by the shoulders, his fingers firmly making it clear that he wouldn't let her go. "Marry me, Suzy McCord. Forget all your doubts and make me the happiest man in the world by giving me a family. By being my wife."

Her faint smile, heavy with regret, was answer enough.

He loosened his fingers. "You're the one I want. The one I've *always* wanted. I survived for you."

The smile disappeared. "The thing of it is, I love you too much to put you through more turmoil. I've loved you ever since you looked at me across that bonfire in high school."

She clasped his hands between hers, kissing his fingertips. "I love you too much to make you choose again."

Just as he was about to argue, she pressed a finger to his lips, silencing him.

"You can still see Isabelle. We'll work something out for visitation. But I can't be your wife."

And, with that, she left him staring out the window, watching her collect Isabelle, then drive down his long driveway, out of his life.

He sat at the table in the kitchen until the pot roast burned in his oven, dousing him in dark, bitter smoke.

You might have to sit in the truck for a few
minutes while I deal with...

"She pointed at the house, and the woman
waved from the porch, and she told her to
stay.

Chapter 12

The following days were a bleak stretch for Russell—empty and black, soundless as holding your breath underwater with your eyes shut.

Suzy wouldn't answer his calls. She'd phoned in sick to work for two days in a row. He didn't dare step foot on her porch, because he knew that his presence might cause a scene in front of Isabelle. And that's the last thing he wanted.

No, he had to play this smart. Had to convince her that she was *too* good for him.

This is what brought him before his father on a rainy Montana day, here in the grand Kingsley estate's reception room.

His mother had decorated the area with the flair of a Great American log lodge, with a mammoth tumblestone fireplace, a vaulted ceiling and cast-iron light works highlighted by cream-and-beige upholstery.

Stratton reclined on one of the overstuffed chairs, green eyes sparkling from his relaxing vacation overseas. "Russell, you should've seen Florence. Now, I'm no art flake, but that statue of David, buck naked or not, was a sight to behold. The food was stupendous, with so many courses that I gain ten pounds every time I think about it."

Russell took in the sight of his father: the dark hair taken over by heavy drifts of gray, the long-legged splay of a sixty-five-year-old who'd finally begun to enjoy his wealth and good fortune.

"You brought nasty weather with you," Russell said. "Too bad the rain's not heavy enough to fill up Lake Monet."

"Yup. I've heard Rumor has had a run of dry skies while your mother and I have been gone."

Russell kicked back in his chair. Would there be a perfect moment for him to mention Suzy? Or had Stratton already heard about them through the light-ning-quick Rumor grapevine? After all, it wasn't as if he and Suzy had taken great pains to hide their relationship.

His mother sashayed into the room, encased in a teal silk suit. Even on a day when she wasn't taking care of her charity efforts, she was polished to a shine.

She stood beside Russell's chair, inspected his face, angling it back and forth with her hand. "You're much less brutish without those cuts and bruises. Thank goodness you healed well."

"Glad you approve, Mom."

"Stratton." Carolyn straightened again, patting her auburn hair and turning toward her husband. "I've got an appointment at The Getaway. Just to wind down."

The older man chuffed. "You didn't get your fill of spas in Europe?"

"Oh, don't act as if you didn't enjoy the pampering." She bent to give Russell a kiss on the cheek, then did the same to Stratton. "We scheduled enough business dinners for you to avoid guilt."

With a smile, she left the room, Stratton's gaze trailing after her.

Grinning, Russell cleared his throat, bringing his father back to their conversation.

"Isn't she a heart stopper?" asked the older man.

"She is. For a mom."

"The best wife there is." Stratton stopped himself, took a sip of his favorite brand of gourmet coffee that waited for him on a dark oak end table. "I hate to think that I put her through so much when I was dealing with my cancer. The shadows under her eyes, the way she wouldn't eat her food because she was so upset. Frankly, I worried about her more than I worried about me."

"Those were hard times." His father's cancer, his mother's severe depression, Suzy and the ultimatum...

Stratton set down the beverage, then peered straight at Russell. "So you and Suzy McCord have taken up where you left off, eh?"

"Someone must've whispered the news in your ear as you stepped off the plane." His father could be so hard to read, his eyes hooded with business-sharp blankness. "Actually, Dad, I didn't come here today to ask your approval. I'm seeing her whether you like it or not."

Stratton grunted. "How serious is it?"

"Very. I never stopped loving Suzy, and I'm going to marry her."

Even if Russell had seemed incredibly confident about Stratton's reaction, he half expected his father to sink down in his chair, white as a hospital sheet. Maybe he even thought the older man would grow as red as lava bursting out of a volcano.

But he was relieved to see that his dad didn't blink an eye.

At least it wasn't outright anger.

Russell chuckled, determined to retain the upper hand here. "No temper? I'm impressed."

"I've learned several things over the years, son, one of which is that I can't control what I can't control." Stratton closed his eyes, nodded, blinked open. "My sickness humbled me, changed how I see life. You've realized that for years."

Russell knew a thing or two about events changing a life outlook. "Does that mean you'll welcome Suzy into the family?"

During the ensuing pause, the fire popped, mingling with the taps of soft rain on the room's windows.

"Well," said Stratton, "I can't tell you who to love."

"So you're still the same head-in-the-sand control freak, aren't you?" Russell stood, taking position next to the fireplace, leaning against the stones and staring into the flames.

In the flashing light, he saw Suzy's skin, warmed by another fire. Warmed by his body covering hers.

"I didn't say I'd stop you from marrying her, now did I?"

Russell shot a glare toward his father, softening

it as the words sank in. "That's a backhanded blessing, if I've ever heard one."

Still, he realized that the older man was trying his damnedest to rummage some pride. Even cancer couldn't change Stratton *that* much, robbing him of his innate dignity.

He turned toward the older man. "Dad, you never knew her very well, never took the time to see that her smile can make your day. You never even sat down to talk with her. She's as smart as she is beautiful, and she's got class, in spite of where she lives or who her parents are."

"I never thought one of my kids would marry a woman who lived with a needy mother and didn't have a father to speak of."

His mellow voice belied the harsh words. Russell had the feeling that his father was putting on a show, unwilling to give in too easily.

The soft-hearted side was winning.

He tried not to smile. The gesture would fluster Stratton, no doubt.

"Hell, Dad. Maybe Reed, Tag, Maura or Jeff will hook up with royalty or something. But I guarantee that they'll never be as happy as I am when I'm with Suzy."

"Good Heavens. Suzy McCord, a Kingsley."

A grin lingered around Stratton's mouth, and Russell pretended not to see it.

He continued. ''That girl always did know how to hold her head up high, didn't she? She never flinched when I treated her like she wasn't good enough to grace our doorway. I always did admire that about her.''

This time, Russell did smile, staring at the floor.

Stratton would support them. The thought tightened his chest.

The older man sighed. ''I suppose I've got some apologizing to do. You know, I tried to make amends a couple of times when I saw her at MonMart. But you don't just erase the past with one weak stroke.''

He was right. Suzy was going to need a whole lot of persuading if he was going to have the honor of marrying her.

An idea took shape in Russell's mind. But first...

''I need to tell you more, Dad.''

Stratton cursed under his breath.

''Suzy's got a sixteen-year-old daughter, Isabelle. Sweet as maple syrup, and sharp, too. She looks like Suzy.'' Russell paused. ''And she's got my smile.''

This time Stratton did turn pale. ''I think I'm

going to hell for what I did to Suzy McCord. Was she pregnant when...?''

"Yeah. And you're not going anywhere—especially hell. Europe was obviously enough of a journey for you.'' Russell stood by his father's chair, bending to eye level with him. "You're making up for lost time by accepting Suzy. Do the same with Isabelle, your grandchild.''

"This is enough to give a man ulcers.'' Nonetheless, Stratton patted Russell on the shoulder. "Congratulations. Fatherhood's quite a test, but you've proven yourself worthy.''

"Speaking of which, I need your help.''

The older man perked up. This was his forte, his reason for living. Russell was glad to see he could make the man chipper again.

"Dad, believe it or not, Suzy doesn't believe that you'll want her in the family. I have to show her that she's wrong.''

Stratton chuckled. "I sense a scheme. I tell you, after you dreamed up MonMart, I knew the sky was the limit for you, Russell.''

It was all falling together in Russell's mind— logistics, numbers, images all crashing, swirling, fitting together amidst a whirlwind of inspiration.

He said, "All I need from you is the promise that

you'll keep Isabelle's parentage a secret for now. She still doesn't know.''

''Easy enough.''

But the way Stratton drummed his fingertips on top of the arm rest told Russell that the older man was eager to meet his granddaughter, to dote on her as much as he did Samantha, Tag's child.

''And,'' he held up a forefinger, stressing the importance, ''I need you to capitalize on your ability to eat crow.''

Stratton lifted an eyebrow. ''Don't tell me....''

''Yeah. Public speaking.''

His father ran a hand over his more-salt-than-pepper hair. ''If this is my penance for what I did to Suzy, then I'll accept with Kingsley stoicism. Dammit.''

Russell relaxed, knowing that Stratton—his biggest barrier—was on his side. Now he just had to tell the rest of his family about his plans, then talk Donna Mason and Isabelle into performing a bit of sly work.

Mere days ago, Suzy had said she'd like to see a big, brass band ushering in Stratton's apology.

Russell was about to make sure she got it.

It seemed the entire town of Rumor turned out for the Friday night football rally.

The team hadn't enjoyed the greatest of seasons this year. Brady Coffey, the quarterback, had concentrated on trying to date as many girls as possible and, thus, his performance had suffered. In more than one way, too. And several of the defensive players had been plagued by injuries, allowing the less-experienced junior varsity substitutes time to play, time to give up points to the other team.

But the town loved its high school sports. As the fans crowded into the Rumor High School gymnasium, the coach, wearing a cap and jacket of Big Sky blue and gold, held a microphone, introducing the players, drawing cheers from the crowd. Voices choked the room, overcoming the stench of locker-room sweat and lemon floor polish. The marching band sat in metal folding chairs, blasting out the school song.

Russell perched on the bottom edge of the bleachers, next to his entire family.

During a pause in the festivities, Maura leaned over, looking every bit as nervous as Russell felt. "Did Suzy come with Donna and Isabelle?"

He peeked a few rows up and over, seeing Donna's wavy, blond hair along with the two redheads he loved more than life itself.

"Looks that way."

"Russell, how can you be so calm when I'm about to fall apart?"

He gave Maura's cheek a pat. She rolled her eyes, probably getting ready to chide him for treating her like a baby sister.

"How can I be afraid of the best thing that's ever happened to me?"

Reed and Tag glanced over at him, grinning at each other.

On the other side of Russell, his mother clutched at his arm. She'd told him earlier that she was excited about officially meeting Isabelle, welcoming her as a grandchild. "Everything will go splendidly. Don't give in to nerves."

"You fussbudgets are making *me* nervous," said Stratton. "Russell, you promised that we'd keep our pride during this presentation of yours. Right?"

"Of course, Dad. This is nothing." Russell tried to convince his thumping heartbeat of the same sentiment.

No go. His blood thundered through his veins.

He was about to take the biggest chance of his life. In front of all Rumor, no less.

The varsity cheerleading squad flipped onto the basketball court, ripping into one pom-pom explosion of a cheer.

This was it, his cue. He'd arranged the timing with the rally's coordinator.

He stood, tugging at his sports coat, adjusting his Stetson, making sure he seemed presentable enough for a lovelorn suiter.

Tag calmly looked him up and down. "I'm proud of you, Russ."

He grinned sidelong at his little brother. "Thanks. Just trying to live up to the Kingsley name."

Tag's gaze darkened as he slid an arm around his daughter's shoulders. Samantha beamed up at him, her hazel eyes capturing the excitement.

Russell winked, then walked to the coach, who handed him the microphone then stood to the side.

"Good evenin', Rumor," he said, his voice a strange echo, bouncing back to him from every corner of the gym.

The crowd cheered, probably because of MonMart. It was no secret that the store had given a healthy boost to Rumor's economy, thus making the Kingsleys a favorite family in the community.

But as much as Russell was thankful for their admiration, it didn't measure up to the approval of one person in the audience. A redhead who'd withstood too many Russell Kingsley-administered fissures to her heart over the years.

He rested his gaze on Suzy, saw how her skin seemed drawn and pale, how her eyes carried a sad light while she watched him.

His belly heated, boiling his blood, the resulting warmth surrounding his heart until it nearly kicked out of his chest.

"This isn't your average football celebration tonight. We've all supported our Rangers this season. Through thick and thin, we've taken great pride in this town's honorable athletes. Now, in light of all that heartfelt community spirit, I'm here to ask a favor of you."

Whistles from the younger people in the crowd. From the rest, polite attention paid in silence.

"I'm going to ask you to forgive me for something I did a long time ago to one of you."

He saw Suzy put her hands over her mouth, saw Isabelle and Donna hold her, making her stay in place while comforting her.

Russell took a deep breath, exhaled. "This is tough."

Some male laughter bolstered him.

"Years ago, many of you know that I fell in love with Suzy McCord. A lot of you, being great believers in the grapevine, also heard that she left town, that she was driven out in embarrassment.

Well, I'm here to tell you that you've got the wrong story.''

A cell phone rang softly in the silence, but nobody answered it.

"It's really no one's business as to what the details are. But I will tell you that I was the one who made the mistake, the one who takes every ounce of blame for making her leave. You all know that car accident I had?''

Nods from the audience.

Amongst them, Suzy just sat there, staring at him as if he'd lost his marbles.

"Well, when people who've teetered on the edge of death tell you that your life flashes before your eyes, they're not exaggerating. The thing is, it's a slow flash, like an atomic explosion, where it comes in waves. It's drawn out, giving you time to think about everything you regret while, at the same time, giving you no time to do anything about it.''

A woman in the front row bent her head while her husband rubbed her back, gazing at her with an apologetic frown.

Isabelle laid her head on her mother's shoulder, watching him.

"Hey, I don't want to get preachy here, but I do believe in righting the wrongs of the past. I've come to humble myself in front of the woman I love, because she thinks that she doesn't fit in the Kingsley family." Russell took a step closer to the audience. "I'm here to tell the entire town that she's the best thing that's ever happened to us."

God, he couldn't believe he was doing this, making a complete idiot out of himself for love. But he was being a good kind of idiot. Fate supported that theory.

As three women sitting in front of Suzy turned around and patted her leg, she shook her head at Russell, patently on the edge of tears.

He got down on one bended knee, sweeping off his hat. "Suzy, don't ever think I'm ashamed to love you. I'm asking you again—be my wife."

A few sobs marked the passage of seconds, one in which Russell was pretty sure that the microphone was picking up the accelerated pings of his heartbeat.

He was never going to live this down. His buddies were going to rib him until kingdom come.

But judging from the loving sheen in Suzy's eyes, it would be worth every joke, every poke at his ego.

Stratton Kingsley knew when to take a cue, so Russell wasn't surprised when he led the family onto the court, coming to flank their eldest son. The marching band rose from their chairs, horns at the ready.

His father grabbed the microphone. He cleared his throat. In a rehearsed, monotone voice, he said, "Most people know me as a hard man. My friends know a different sort of guy from the past few years."

His tone became more relaxed, more emotional as he made eye contact with Suzy. "I'm here to ask your forgiveness for giving my boy something that really wasn't a choice at all. I was selfish and myopic in my dreams for the family, and it drove you away in the process."

Russell glanced up at his father, and the man just looked at him like, "Do I have to go through with this?"

Reed gently pushed Stratton to a position that echoed Russell's. The audience chuckled, then listened intently.

"Suzy McCord, speaking on behalf of the Kingsleys, I'd like to invite you to join our family."

Applause filled the room, filled Russell's ears. But he barely heard a sound. Every sense was locked on Suzy, her tear-blushed face. On Isabelle, who kissed her mother's cheek and whispered in her ear.

The band played their song, "Forever Young,"

as Donna and Isabelle got to their feet, bringing Suzy with them, escorting her to the floor. The crowd made a path for them, touching Suzy in encouragement as she passed.

First, she helped Stratton to his feet. Russell could hardly hear what his father said to her, but it looked like the words, "Welcome to the family. If you'll have us."

She smiled at him, taking the microphone from his clutches. Then he hugged her.

As Suzy disengaged herself, Stratton took Isabelle's hand. That's all Russell saw before he rose in front of Suzy.

Here she was again. Springtime-in-Paris, creamy skin, bright blue-star eyes. Suzy.

She switched off the microphone while the crowd calmed down. "A brass band, huh?"

"You asked for it."

"I didn't think you'd be so literal."

Russell realized that the people of Rumor were watching them. "See, this is what you get when you don't answer my calls, darlin'."

Suzy obviously noted everyone's silence, as well. "You're really out there. You know that?"

This banter was killing him. "You realize that I proposed to you, in front of all these people, too."

Chuckles. An "Attaboy, Russ" from four rows up.

"I..." She pursed her lips together.

"Suzy." He held her against him, and she cozied in to his embrace.

"Hey," he whispered. "I mean what I said. I'm never going to leave you. You can always count on me."

She hiccuped, peering up at him. "Darn you, Russell Kingsley. You can't be so charming and flippant one moment, then so loving the next. What am I going to do with you?"

"Marry me."

She gazed at him, sending those butterflies through his stomach, just like doves at a wedding.

Damn, he was *really* in love if she had him thinking that kind of silliness.

But, deep down, he guessed he didn't mind so much.

"I'll marry you," she said.

Isabelle shot over to them, hugging them both. "Was that a yes?"

Suzy hiccuped again, then smiled at Russell, blazing his heart with her own brand of sunshine. "Yes."

Isabelle spun around to everyone. "Yes!"

Rumor cheered. Gossip-crazy hounds. Always on the tail of a good story.

As the rest of his family circled around Isabelle, Russell took his hat and shielded him and Suzy from the onlookers.

Under its security, he kissed her softly.

"I'm all yours," he said. "Now, let's talk to Isabelle at home."

They touched foreheads. Together again.

Chapter 13

Russell, Suzy and Isabelle finally broke away from the crowd and drove straight to his cabin.

As Suzy and Isabelle nestled against the couch, laughing together, Russell suddenly realized that the hardest part of the night wasn't over yet.

Isabelle still thought her real father had left her when she was just weeks old. What would she think of him?

"How about some drinks?" he asked, walking toward the kitchen, needing time to recover from delayed stage fright and this new possibility of rejection.

Suzy must have sensed his restlessness, because she popped up from the couch. "Isabelle? How about some tea?" The teen nodded, watching her mother and future stepfather leave the room together, no doubt thinking up romantic poems in her mind.

In the kitchen, Suzy cornered him. "It just hit you, didn't it?"

"What? About the story you told Isabelle so she wouldn't know about me? Yeah. With all the energy I put into winning you back, this didn't seem as pressing."

"We knew it'd come up sooner or later."

Russell smoothed a strand of red away from her cheek. "Isabelle and I get along well together. Maybe it won't be a big scene."

"She doesn't know you're her father. That changes the situation."

"Damn." He clinked around his pans, trying to find a tea kettle.

Suzy, though it wasn't her kitchen, found it before he did. She filled the implement with water, then set it on the large steel stove to boil. "I can't believe what you did tonight."

"I had to win you back. At any cost."

She swayed over to him, wrapping her arms around his waist. "I'm going to marry you," she said dreamily. "Do you know how many times I fantasized about this? I never thought it'd happen. And I still can't believe it will."

"The sooner the better." He kissed her temple, breathing in her scent.

She talked against his neck, her lips against his skin. "I thought staying away from you, not answering your calls and the like, would solve everything. Thought it'd chase the love right out of me. But it did no good. Especially when you walked onto the gym floor, handsome as can be in your cowboy hat and boots. It was all I could do to stay seated, pretending like I didn't want to run right on down there and tell you how much I love you."

They embraced, and Russell could have sworn that the tempo of her pulse became a part of his body, beating in time to his blood, his thoughts.

The kettle whistled its readiness, and Suzy gathered the filled cups, saucers, tea bags, sugar and cream on a tray.

She walked ahead of him, then peered back over her shoulder. "Ready?"

"As ever."

He took a deep breath, then followed her out of the room.

Isabelle perked up from her seat on the couch.

"There you two are. I thought maybe you'd run off somewhere to elope."

Russell took the opening, sitting on one side of his daughter while Suzy sat on the other, preparing the tea.

"You're too important to us," he said. "We'd never do something like that without you at our sides."

"That's sweet, Mr. Kingsley. I can't wait to be your daughter."

As Suzy handed the hot beverage to Isabelle, the cup clanged against the saucer.

"I'm glad to hear that," he said, intercepting the china and placing it on the coffee table. "Because you're not far from the mark."

Isabelle stared at him, then at Suzy, who smiled and nodded, obviously concerned about her daughter's reaction.

Maybe he'd been wrong in thinking that Isabelle suspected her parentage, because when she gazed back at him again, questions swam in her blue eyes.

"I'm not sure I take your meaning," she said softly.

"Honey," said Suzy, "I wasn't entirely truthful when I told you that your father left shortly after you were born."

"You lied to me?"

"Only because…" Suzy looked to Russell for help.

And he'd been hoping for Isabelle to do back flips at the news. Welcome to reality.

He said, "Your mom and I loved each other when we were young. You were conceived the night I proposed to her. But then my father found out that he had lung cancer, and I had to be with my family."

Isabelle's eyebrows knitted together as her face fell.

Suzy took over. "He didn't know I was pregnant. *I* didn't even know until I moved in with Aunt Hazel when I got to California. To make a long story short, we got caught up in more lies until it became too hurtful to contact each other again."

"But you were in love," said Isabelle.

Russell smiled to soften her bruised words. "You make it sound so easy."

"The thing is," said Suzy, touching Isabelle's hair, "you're the light of my life. Russell and I had a rough start when you and I moved back here to Rumor, but we've worked through it. We want to be a family, to forgive what happened in the past and move on from there."

Isabelle covered her face with her hands, and Russell thought the battle was lost. She wasn't going to accept him, wasn't going to understand that he'd beaten himself up over the mistakes he'd made with her and Suzy.

"Isabelle?" asked Suzy.

The teen sighed. "This is a heavy trip," she said through her fingers.

Russell and Suzy exchanged worried glances.

When their daughter revealed her face again, a smile had taken the place of the frown.

"I have a dad," she said, her voice wavering.

"Oh, God." Russell pulled her into a hug, wrapping Suzy in the embrace at the same time. She wept, probably with the relief that he felt, too.

Muffled by the hug, Isabelle said, "But don't think I'm not miffed about this. I still have to sort through this tale of yours."

As they all laughed, Russell felt their tears soaking his shirt.

His family.

There was nothing more precious to him than this. How had he existed throughout the years, fed merely by MonMart and boredom?

"Take your time to do the sorting, Isabelle," he said. "We've got forever."

He drew back, giving the women some breathing room.

"Whoo," said Isabelle, swiping at her eyes. "It's

hitting me now. All the things I can do with a dad. Let's see, there's parent night, fishing trips and, well, maybe one day, if I don't date guys like that dork Brady Coffey, you'll dance at my wedding.''

Emotion jabbed at him. "Hey, don't move too quickly. I just got you, remember?''

Suzy watched them as she cuddled in the corner of the couch, hugging knees that were tucked underneath her pink skirt. A content smile glowed over her lips—all sunshine and love.

The exact smile caught in their prom picture.

He grasped her hand, squeezed it. Then she leaned forward, pressing an innocent kiss to his mouth.

Between them, Isabelle sighed. "I can't believe it. A dad. Road trips with the family to Disneyland. Nightly dinners around the table…''

Russell's heartbeat pinged in his ears, sounding more like a beep than a pulse. He bent his forehead to Suzy's. "Just remember, I'll always love you.''

He felt her mouth smile against his cheek. Finally, she said, "I love you, too, Russell. Always. Forever.''

Isabelle laughed, clearly delighted by their feelings for each other. She launched into a poem about love and roses, longing and fire.

His daughter. The flesh-and-blood proof that he and Suzy were meant to be together.

Russell shut his eyes, wanting to hold this moment for all eternity—the feel of Suzy against him, the sound of Isabelle's poetry, the flashes of color blinding the darkness of his mind, mingling with the smell of a thousand flowers flooding his senses.

The beeping throb of his pulse grew louder, increasing in volume with the cadence of Isabelle's poetry.

An odd tightness needled one arm.

He couldn't feel Suzy anymore. Couldn't hear her breathing against him, couldn't hear the rasp of her sweater brushing against his shirt.

Couldn't feel her hand in his.

Forever, she said, her voice fading, echoing, disappearing.

He flexed his fingers, grasping air.

The reds, yellows and blues on the backs of his eyelids blinded him, making him stir, squint.

"Suzy?" he mumbled, interrupting Isabelle's poetry.

The girl's voice stopped, then faltered. "Mr. Kingsley?"

"Isabelle." It was okay. His daughter was here. All he had to do was open his eyes to see Suzy again.

He did.

He was lying prone in a white-sheeted bed, needles sticking out of his arm, tubes taped to his skin. A girl with a red ponytail and a candy striper uniform sat next to the mattress, holding a book, her mouth and eyes wide.

"Mr. Kingsley?" she asked again, sounding panicked. "Are you awake? Are you actually awake?"

What was this? Where was Suzy? Isabelle was here, but why weren't they in his cabin continuing their family reunion?

Russell tried to close his eyes again, but the skin around his eyes felt bruised. Next to his bed, he heard the pinging acceleration of a heart monitor.

Beep, beep, beep, beep.

The girl dropped her journal, backed away toward the door. From the flower-shrouded corner of the room there came a muttered curse, then a splash and muted crash. Taggert, his haggard, unshaven, sleepy-eyed brother, came into view, coffee dripping down his shirt.

"Good God, Russell." His hazel eyes lit up. "Sheree, go get Dr. Fisk. Hurry!"

The candy striper ran from the room.

Dizzy. He felt so dizzy, disoriented.

"Where's Isabelle going?" he mumbled. Damn,

it felt as if he hadn't used his mouth in days, rendering his voice rusty and tight.

"Who the hell's...?" Tag hovered over him, his brow furrowed, his voice choked. "Thank God you're out of it. Everyone was worried."

A commotion in the hall, footsteps, harried tones.

A female doctor, the one Russell remembered from his car accident, rushed into the room with her staff, all of them circling his bed. Tag faded to the corner again, giving them space.

"Mr. Kingsley?" asked the doctor.

"What's happening?" Too much cottonlike dryness in his mouth, making it hard to talk. "Where's Suzy?"

The doctor smiled down at him while hands busied themselves with his body, tending to him, smoothing his forehead, just as Suzy's fingers had so many times. "We'll get everything cleared up in a moment, Mr. Kingsley. Right now I want to check you over."

She turned to Tag. "Would you like to call your family?"

His brother said yes, then left the room with the girl Russell knew as Isabelle. He felt like his last link to sanity had deserted him.

"I want my fiancée. My daughter."

The doctor nodded. "Your family's coming. But

first, stay calm and let us do our job. You've been
in a coma for three days. I'm sure it's a bit con-
fusing for you."

Coma?

The word blasted through him, leaving him
numb.

As the medical staff worked on him, he wondered when the hell he'd lost consciousness.

Wondered where the hell his future wife and
daughter were.

After the doctors and nurses left him, they allowed Tag back in the room.

His brother sat by Russell's bedside, his eyes red
and weary. "We thought we'd lost you."

Russell felt better, less thirsty, but still bruised,
cut and frustrated. "Where did Isabelle go? And
why was she dressed like a candy striper?"

Tag glanced around the room, then said, "Oh.
The girl who was reading poetry to you? That's
Sheree Henry, and she volunteers here. She's been
great about being with you. Dr. Fisk said that, even
if you were in a coma, you could still hear and feel,
could still be stimulated and encouraged to return
to consciousness, so she let Sheree in here every
day after she got out of school."

"I don't—"

An image hit Russell with the force of a crash. Hospital lights over his head, doctors' faces above him as they wheeled his gurney beneath the blinking numbers of an elevator. A candy striper standing against the wall, staring at him.

She'd been one of the last things he'd seen before slipping into the coma. Was that it?

Tag cleared his throat. "As for Suzy, she's meeting with Dad at MonMart right now."

Chaos still whipped around in his mind. That's right. Stratton had already welcomed Suzy into the family. "Is the old guy promoting her?" He laughed, then sucked in a breath of pain from his ribs, his cut-crusted mouth. "She wasn't meant to be a cashier."

"Ah, actually, Suzy's been hired as a consultant for…" Tag frowned. "Russell, what's going through your head? You keep calling that candy striper Isabelle and asking for Suzy. You don't know what's what, do you?"

Russell had a bad feeling about this. "There's no way. No way it couldn't have been real."

"What?"

He related the past few weeks to Tag: Suzy's return, Isabelle, the brass-band proposal as Stratton apologized.

Tag looked at him with a trace of pity. "It's all

been whipped up by your brain, Russ. Look, Isabelle doesn't exist. And Suzy is a different woman than the one in your head. Be prepared for that.''

He didn't want to hear that Suzy—his sweet, forever-young Suzy—was different.

''It all seemed so real.''

He could still feel her skin against his, still smell the orchid perfume....

Russell glanced at the flowers next to the bed. Orchids. Rich, sweet, intoxicating as the scent of Suzy's hair.

Every time his heart beat it hurt physically. Heavy, aching, discordant throbs of unresolved longing.

He clenched his fingers. ''Where's the picture of me and Suzy?''

Tag turned to a chest of drawers, opening the lower one, sifting through clothing and bags. He held up the prom photo, blood-printed and wrinkled. ''This? They packed it away with your clothes, or at least, what's left of them.''

Russell took the picture, running his thumb over it. Suzy. Her red hair falling to the line of her chin, her smile like the one she'd shined on him when Isabelle had accepted him into their family, her eyes blue-bright with love.

Her prom dress pink, just like all the dresses she'd worn in his dream.

Because there was no other way about it. His guilty conscience had created a dream to comfort him, to solve his problems, to bring him back to a world where Suzy was still waiting for him.

"I owe her so much," he said, lowering the picture to the bedsheets, grasping it like a lifeline. "Brass bands, apologies... I guess my mind created Isabelle as a bond between us."

A bond that he longed for, even though none of it was true.

What if he and Suzy were meant to have a daughter? Someone just like Isabelle? A girl with red hair, blue eyes, his grin?

Hope lifted the heaviness in his chest.

"What're you smiling about?" asked Tag. "You having another fantasy?"

"Hey, if it'd been a fantasy, Suzy wouldn't have kept running away from me. She would've jumped in my arms the first time I saw her. This was a dream, a way for Fate to help me work things out."

Tag laid a hand on Russell's arm. "I'm glad you're optimistic again."

Did he have reason to be?

He still felt the darkness lapping at him, still felt

a keen sense of loss, knowing that Isabelle had only been a figment of his imagination.

He turned his head. Outside, it had begun to snow. Light, cheery crusts of ice, each flake someone's lost dream.

Hadn't Suzy wanted a white Christmas?

"Tag?"

"Yeah."

He looked at his brother again. "Can you find that girl, Sheree? I want to thank her."

"Sure. The family should be here soon, too."

"Thanks. For everything." For telling him that Suzy was back, for setting the dream into motion.

Tag nodded. Russell's gaze was caught by an object to his right side, just in back of his sibling's dark head, something hiding among the flowers spread around his bed like gentle poetry, welcoming him back.

In one vase, isolated from the others, an orchid withered, bending its head as if burdened by secrets. Suzy had brought him orchids in his dream, the petals as exotic and vivid as this plant.

Tag plucked a small card from the petals. "They're from Suzy."

So she *was* here, with him, even in a small way.

See? All hope wasn't lost. She'd given him flowers in real life, too. That had to mean something.

He grinned, knowing he could still win her over, get busy making Isabelle a reality.

Russell took the card from Tag and read it.

Best wishes for a speedy recovery.
Sincerely,
Susannah

Susannah?

"I told you," said Tag. "She's changed. And it starts right there with her name."

Russell turned the impersonal message face down on the sheets, obliterating the words, then looked at Suzy's—that's right, Suzy's, not Susannah's—gift once again.

Even though the orchid was exhausted, drooping with fatigue, it would survive. He would make sure of it.

And as soon as he got out of this stinking bed, he was going to win back Suzy McCord. Just as he had in his dream.

"Did you hear a word I said?" asked Tag. "The dream's over."

"I don't think so." Russell chuckled, ignoring the throb of his wounds, the ache of his beaten skin. "This is just the beginning."

He settled back in his bed, nodding to himself. ''Rest assured, Tag. You can make sure that it's not over yet.''

* * * * *

Turn the page
to follow Russell Kingsley's story in

SECOND CHANCE

by Judy Duarte

SECOND CHANCE
Judy Duarte

To my husband, Sal, a veteran bachelor who didn't let a single mom with four young children chase him away. You've not only been a steady, loving force in all of our lives, but you've encouraged me to chase my dream. Thank you for giving us both a second chance at love.

There will always be a little bit of you in all my heroes....

Chapter 1

A heck of a lot had changed in the past seventeen years.

Susannah McCord was no longer the teenage girl who wasn't good enough for Russell Kingsley.

The Suzy everyone remembered had left Rumor with her tail between her legs, but she'd made her mark on corporate America and returned with her head held high. And this morning's business meeting with Stratton Kingsley validated her success.

Susannah sat across the polished mahogany desk from Russell's father and studied the patriarch of the wealthy Kingsley clan. He wasn't nearly as gruff or ominous as she remembered. With a full head of hair that had turned mostly gray and intelligent green eyes, Stratton had a grandfatherly way about him. But he also had an uncanny head for business.

Not to mention, a way of dredging up old memories, disappointments and pain.

"It's nice to have you back in Rumor," Stratton said.

Was it? In a business sense, she supposed that was true. Was the man sorry for thinking she hadn't been good enough for his firstborn son? Or merely realizing a mistake in judgment? She supposed it really didn't matter anymore. "It's good to be back. Thank you."

"I heard you plan a remodel of your mother's house. Sounds like a major undertaking. Have you hired a contractor?"

"Actually, I plan to roll up my sleeves and do most of the work myself." The home Susannah remembered had always been dark and dreary, which was one reason she hadn't rushed back to take possession after her mother's death four years ago.

But on her thirty-fifth birthday, she'd faced a day of reckoning, acquiring both a change of heart and a new attitude. And now she was back in Rumor, intending to make the little house on State Street a home.

Her first effort would be to put in new bay windows to allow in more sunlight. Then she would convert the back bedroom into a nursery. Of course, that was none of Stratton Kingsley's business.

He placed his elbows on the desk and leaned forward in a gesture of intimacy and cooperation. "You've done very well for yourself."

She had, although she didn't particularly like the subtle reminder of where she'd been, particularly since she'd tried hard to shake a shabby beginning and lousy home-life. But maybe he was merely referring to her achievements after fleeing Rumor.

After a slew of academic accomplishments and a law degree, Susannah had become a well-respected business consultant—so successful and respected that Stratton Kingsley had offered her a lucrative consulting job once he learned she was in town.

The fact that Stratton could still stir up old insecurities didn't sit right with her, so she put on her best hard-nosed consultant demeanor. "Let's discuss the agribusiness acquisition."

Stratton cleared his throat, then leaned back in his leather seat. "As you know, MonMart has become very successful here in Rumor, as well as the other five locations we've opened. And our produce department is a large part of that success.''

He was right. MonMart, a superstore that sold groceries, clothing and household goods at a discount, had the entire produce section laid out like a farmer's market, offering the best fruits and vegetables available at a reasonable price. The innovative idea, she'd been told, had been Russell's.

''Right now,'' Stratton continued, ''the MonMart chain has spread throughout Montana, and within the next few years, we plan to open stores all over the western United States.''

''From what I've seen, the plan is very realistic.''

''I'm glad you agree. That brings me back to the business at hand. We want to purchase a large farming operation and produce brokerage firm so we can secure a much higher profit margin. Did you get a chance to look over the possible ventures?''

''Yes, I did. Eden Garden Farms in California appears to be a good choice, at least on paper. Of course, we'll need to fly out to Monterey and see for ourselves.''

''I'd hoped to wait until…'' The gray-haired man paused, then blew out a ragged sigh.

She sensed his thoughts had drifted to the son who continued to hover in comatose limbo at

Whitehorn Memorial Hospital, and she felt sorry for the man. Both men, actually.

Russell might have once broken her heart, but that didn't mean she didn't care, didn't feel compassion. But there wasn't much she could do. She'd sent flowers— or rather an orchid, something classy and simple.

Stratton looked at her with grief-stricken eyes. "It should be my son talking to you, not me. Hell, I'm semiretired. My wife and I were supposed to be in Europe. Instead—"

"I'm sorry," she said, although the words seemed terribly inadequate.

"This deal means a great deal to my son, and helping him put it together seems like the right thing to do." The gray-haired man waved his hand at the files spread out on his desk. "The produce merger is Russell's baby."

Russell's baby. In spite of her efforts to forget, Susannah was momentarily swept back to the day she left town carrying Russell's child. She could still recall the shock of discovering she was pregnant, the wretched nausea, the excruciating pain that sent her to the hospital late at night. The loss of the baby, the surgery to correct the damage a tubal pregnancy had caused.

She struggled to shove the memories back in

place and tried to rally her thoughts to the present. "I was sorry to hear of your son's accident."

"It's been a strain on all of us, not knowing when or *if* he'll recover from the coma."

Russell's condition concerned Susannah, too. At one time, she'd loved the firstborn Kingsley son. And he'd rejected her. Tossed her aside, choosing his wealthy family over her. Their romance, like their baby, hadn't been destined to thrive.

She'd gotten over her disappointment years ago, yet memories tugged at her heart, as they had when she'd first hit city limits. Donna Mason, her old high school friend, had told her about Russell's accident. The tragic news had struck like a shot of adrenaline, although she'd blamed the reaction on the fact that she and Russell had once been high school sweethearts.

The concern she felt for Russell muscled back to the forefront. "How is he doing? Is there any change?"

"Depends on who you ask. A candy striper noticed him responding to her voice. She said his eyes flickered, and he squeezed her hand." Stratton blew out a ragged sigh. "As much as the family would like to believe that, the doctors are skeptical. I suppose we'll have to chalk it up to a teenage girl's fantasy."

As a girl, Susannah had a few fantasies of her own—fantasies that had dissipated in the wind like the seeds of a dandelion. But she couldn't hold Russell or his father to blame. A certain amount of the responsibility fell on her own shoulders.

People created their reality, as well as their futures. White knights mounted on horseback—or rather rich golden boys in their granddad's vintage cars—didn't rescue damsels in distress. And hopes and dreams didn't do anyone a bit of good unless a person was willing to wake up and make those dreams come true.

As she had.

Determined to rebound, the former Rumor High cheerleader had thrown herself into her studies and won several scholarships and internships. From law school, she took a top job at a corporate, big city consulting firm.

It was Susannah's success and reputation that granted her respect in Stratton's eye.

And placed her in the seat across from his.

"So, tell me," Stratton said. "Are the principals of Eden Garden Farms willing to negotiate?"

"I believe so." Before Susannah could comment further, the intercom buzzed.

Stratton wrinkled his brow and jabbed at a flashing red button on the shiny, black phone system.

"Mahnita, I told you not to interrupt me. I'm in a conference."

"I know, sir. But the hospital is on line three."

Susannah nearly stood, ready to offer Stratton a ride into Whitehorn, but she remained seated and gripped the polished mahogany armrests until her knuckles ached.

Upon first learning of the accident, she'd had an urge to rush to Russell's bedside at the hospital, but she didn't. It wasn't her place.

And it never had been.

She forced herself to appear only briefly interested in the news Stratton would hear.

He snatched the telephone and quickly pressed the lighted button. "This is Stratton Kingsley."

Susannah had no idea who was on the other line, who relayed the news to the bereft patriarch, but he leaned back in his seat, his eyes closing as though in prayer. Her heart thudded in her chest, and her palms grew moist. *Speak up, Stratton. Give me a clue.*

"Thank God," the older man said. "I'll be right there."

He hung up the phone and looked at Susannah, but she'd already assumed the gist of the conversation.

Russell Kingsley had come to.

* * *

Nearly a week after he'd awakened from a three-day coma, Russell stood before the window of his hospital room, scanning the grounds down below. The cottonwoods surrounded the hospital like a stark, barren fortress.

Winter had descended upon Rumor, and also on his heart. It had shocked him to learn that he and Suzy McCord hadn't reconciled, that they hadn't fallen in love all over again. That they'd never had a sixteen-year-old daughter named Isabelle.

It was only a coma-enhanced dream, he'd realized. But the heartfelt reunion he'd had with his high school sweetheart was more than a dream. It was Destiny peering out of the dim recesses of his mind, poking him and prodding him to find Suzy, the woman he'd always loved.

Russell glanced at the clock on the wall, a clock he'd grown weary of looking at over the past week. Where was his brother? Tag was supposed to be here by ten-thirty, and it was now nearing eleven.

The doctors had insisted they keep him for observation, but there was no need for him to stay any longer, imprisoned. He was in damn good physical shape. A little bump on the head couldn't keep him down. Nor could a few lacerations and bruises.

He was a lucky man. Damn lucky he didn't die

when his car slammed into the guardrail and his head shattered the windshield. But the accident had been a blessing in disguise. A reminder of what was important in life.

Again, he glanced at the clock on the wall. Where the hell was his brother?

All he wanted to do was go home, get one of his vintage cars out of the showroom garage and head to MonMart.

His Range Rover had been running rough, which was one reason he'd been driving the 1949 Mercury and hadn't had the protection of an airbag. The Mercury, he'd been told, had been totaled.

The door to his room creaked open, and Russell turned slowly, expecting to see Tag or one of the starkly dressed nurses who'd poked and fussed over him for the past week or so.

Instead, he saw a ray of sunshine in his bleak existence. The pretty, redheaded candy striper who resembled Isabelle in his dream. Somehow, he supposed, her face and voice had superimposed themselves in his mind.

She carried a tray laden with paper cups. "Hello, Mr. Kingsley. I brought you some juice."

"Thanks, Sheree." Russell didn't want anything to drink, but he smiled and took the cup she offered.

He couldn't help but stare at the vivacious young

woman. Even her voice, soft and melodious, was the same as Isabelle's had been.

Maybe it was because she'd read to him while he was in the coma, going so far as to share the poems she'd written.

"Have they said when you get to go home?" Sheree asked.

"As soon as my brother gets here, I'm history." He struggled not to call her Isabelle, even though her name was blatantly pinned to her pink-and-white-striped uniform. "Sheree, I want to thank you for coming in to read to me while I was out of it. You went above and beyond the call of volunteer duty."

She offered him a crooked smile that dimpled her cheeks. "My brother was in a coma a few years ago—after a skateboarding accident. I read to him, too. I thought it would help."

"Did it?"

Her smile disappeared, and the light in her eyes dimmed. "No. He never regained consciousness. His death was a real blow to my mother and me."

As, he imagined, it should have been. He noticed she didn't mention a father. "What about your dad?"

"He died when I was a baby. I never really knew him."

Russell wanted to go to the girl, offer comfort. Maybe give her a fatherly hug, but he wasn't sure what was appropriate. He was a patient, and she was a teenaged hospital volunteer. Still, he felt a strong paternal urge, but not only toward Sheree.

It was more than that. He was actually having fatherly urges. It was time for him to have a family of his own.

But the only woman he wanted to bear his children was Suzy McCord. And the sooner he found her, the better. He could still feel the soft womanly curves that leaned into him, still savor the orchid-laced springtime-in-Paris scent she'd worn in his dream.

As Sheree turned to go, her leg bumped the corner of the hospital bed, jarring the tray from her hands and sending cups and juice flying across the room.

"Oh, dear. I'm *so* sorry." She quickly hurried to snag paper towels from the bathroom.

"Hey, it's no big deal." Russell figured she was embarrassed about being clumsy, but those things happened. "Let me help."

"Oh, no," Sheree said. "I'll get it."

She scurried to wipe the floor, her head bent. Her hair was a dazzling shade of red, much like the color of Suzy's.

This girl wasn't his daughter, but she still held a subtle resemblance to a young, redheaded Suzy McCord. Or maybe, subconsciously, he just wanted to hang on to Suzy's memory.

Either way, Sheree was a great girl.

"What made you decide to be a hospital volunteer?" He stooped to pick up the scattered cups. "You've played a big part in my recovery."

"I'm glad," she said, her head still bent, ponytail bobbing with her movements. "I like helping people and want to work in a field where I can do that. I'm not sure what I want to be when I get out of school." She grinned, revealing her dimples. "It may seem weird, but at Rumor High, I belong to the Future Teachers *and* the Health Careers clubs. I thought it might help me decide on a major."

"I don't think it's weird at all," Russell said. "But I'd suggest you stick with the medical field. You've got a great bedside manner."

"Even if I spill things?" She carried the soiled paper towels back into the bathroom.

"Accidents happen." When she returned, Russell noticed tears in her eyes. "What's the matter?"

"I've just got the weepies. That's all." She swiped a hand across her cheek, snagging a tear. "Just feeling sorry for myself. No big deal."

Russell didn't believe her. "For some reason, I think it's important to you."

"I've got to give up being a candy striper. Like I said, it's not a big deal. My mom had an accident on the way to work the other day. She's going to be on disability for a while, and I've got to find a job that pays." She sniffled, then garnered a smile. "Really, I don't mind helping out. My mom works two jobs to make ends meet. I probably should have been working before. And thank God her disability won't be permanent. It could have been much worse. I don't know what I would have done if my mom had died."

In spite of his resolve to keep his distance, Russell placed an arm around the candy striper's shoulder. "Hey, don't cry, Sheree. I just happen to know that MonMart is in need of a cashier. If you want the job, it's yours."

She glanced up at him, her eyes watery but bright. "Really? Do you mean it? I don't have to actually comb the want ads and fill out tons of applications?"

"You can start any time you want. Just let me know what kind of schedule you need, and I'll work it out with the manager. Why don't you stop by my office tomorrow after school?"

"Thanks, Mr. Kingsley." She sniffled then

snatched her empty tray from the bed and headed for the door. She'd no more than stepped into the hall when Tag walked in.

"You ready to go?" his brother asked.

He'd been ready a week ago. Russell blew out a sigh. Why wasn't anyone else concerned about him getting back to work, getting his life back on track? He'd wasted seventeen years, so to speak, and now all he wanted to do was make things right with Suzy, tell her about the little redheaded girl they were destined to have.

"You're thirty minutes late, Tag. What kept you so long?"

"Take it easy, big brother. There was a lot of paperwork to take care of."

"Well, let's get out of here." Russell grabbed the white plastic bag that held his belongings and the drooping orchid Suzy had sent, the plant he was determined to revive.

She'd brought him an orchid in his dream. And the fact she'd sent the same type of plant in reality only validated his belief that Destiny had a hand in all of this.

The dark-haired, quiet-spoken man remained in the doorway, arms crossed. "Not so fast, Russ. The business office says we've got to wait for a wheel-chair."

"You gotta be kidding. I'm walking out of here."

A smile tugged at his little brother's lips. "It's hospital policy."

"Well, it's not my policy. What are they gonna do, tackle me in the lobby and put me in that damned chair?"

"You're more feisty than usual," Tag said.

"I just want to go home."

Home. The house Russell had built on a hilltop overlooking the Kingsley ranch had always been a place of refuge for him. And in his dream, Suzy had brought a feeling of warmth and love to his otherwise manly abode. It was a feeling he was determined to restore.

Tag placed a work-roughened hand on Russell's shoulder. "Then let's get out of here before the nurse arrives with the wheelchair."

They walked briskly down the hallway and toward the elevator.

"You'll never guess who's working for Mon-Mart," Tag said.

Russell wasn't in any mood to play guessing games. He'd watched too many game shows on TV while waiting for some medical power structure to discharge him. "Who?"

"Suzy McCord."

Suzy. His dream suddenly felt more like a pre-monition. A revelation of what was to come. "Well, I'll be damned. That makes my job easier."

"What do you mean?" his younger brother asked.

"I don't have to look far to find her."

"I know you woke up thinking that you and the Suzy from your high school-tainted fantasy got married and that you'd had a daughter. But Russell, she's changed. Big time."

"Maybe so. But I've got to talk to her."

"Okay, but don't call her Suzy. I did, and she let me know in no uncertain terms that she goes by Susannah now." Tag jabbed at the elevator button.

Russell couldn't help holding on to his fantasy. It had been too real, too eye-opening and heart-stirring. "Is she working as one of the cashiers?"

"Nope. Dad just hired her as a consultant about a week ago, just before you gained consciousness."

"What kind of consultant?"

"She's with the agribusiness division, helping to put together that new purchase you were working on before the accident." The elevator doors opened, and Tag stepped inside.

Russell stood motionless, his hand holding the elevator door open. "Why didn't someone tell me about this?"

"You were in a coma for three days. And during your recovery, no one wanted to cause you any additional stress."

"Keeping secrets from me causes a great deal of stress. What else is going on that I don't know about?"

"That's about it."

Russell joined his brother in the elevator and pushed the button that said Lobby. The doors closed, and they began the descent, taking the first step in his search for Suzy. "How does she look, Tag?"

"She's a knockout, if you like coolheaded women in business suits."

Okay. So Suzy had changed. Russell had changed, too. That didn't mean they couldn't start over, couldn't learn to love each other again. Couldn't have a baby who would have Suzy's red hair and a poet's heart and soul.

Russell never had a problem getting what he wanted. And now that his dream had opened his eyes, he knew exactly what was missing in his life. And he had every intention of filling the void.

How much could Suzy have changed?

Maybe all she needed was a little stroll down memory lane. And he knew just the guy to take her there.

* * *

Russell knew that Tag hadn't been happy about him not sticking close to home on the day he was discharged from the hospital, but his brother had known better than to argue. Russell didn't like being challenged. He knew what he wanted and went after it. That's what had made him a successful businessman.

He entered MonMart through the front door, then spoke to the manager and told him about Sheree Henry.

"Make a position for her, if you have to," Russell told the man. "And make sure her schedule doesn't conflict with her schooling."

If the man wanted to object, he knew better.

Russell took the stairs to the second floor offices of the MonMart executives. It felt good to be back. Back on his feet. Back in charge.

Mahnita, the administrative assistant, sat at her desk working diligently at the computer keyboard. She glanced up when Russell entered. "It's good to have you back. We've all been worried about you."

"Thanks. I'm looking for Suzy McCord."

"You mean Susannah?" Mahnita asked, arching a dark brow.

Obviously, Tag wasn't the only one to learn Suzy

preferred to be called Susannah. Well, that was fine with Russell. He didn't care what name she went by. She'd always be Suzy to him. "Has Ms. McCord arrived yet?"

"Your father gave her a master key. She's beat me to work every day this week."

Everyone in the Kingsley family, as well as the MonMart employees, knew Mahnita prided herself on being the first one to arrive at work each day. "Which office is hers?"

"Third one down the hall. Right next door to yours. Mr. Kingsley said you'd be working closely together."

They had that right. "Thanks, Mahnita."

Russell stopped at his own office long enough to peel off his down-lined jacket and deposit it in the closet. He took a quick scan of his desk and furnishings, noting that things looked the same as he'd left them. Then he headed to the office next to his and knocked lightly.

"Come in."

The sound of her voice, even behind a closed door, caused his pulse to kick into overdrive. And he felt like a nervous adolescent all over again, waiting to see the girl of his dreams.

When he stepped inside, Suzy looked up from her desk. He wasn't prepared for the sight of her.

She was dressed in a cream-colored business suit, elegant and rich. Her hair had been swept into a twist, but he suspected it was much longer than it used to be.

She wasn't at all like the cheerleader he remembered, or the cashier he'd dreamed about. Sure, she was every bit as pretty, he realized, with the same striking red hair and vibrant blue eyes. Her body screamed femininity, but her demeanor was cool and professional.

"Russell," was all she said. Then she paused and added, "I'm glad you recovered. I know how worried your family was."

Had she been worried, too? he wondered. He couldn't be sure. She seemed so different.

The sound of her voice was deeper than he remembered. Formal, but with a sultry edge that made his blood pump. She stood and stepped away from her desk. In his memory, she'd worn pink, like her prom dress. And she'd been maternal and down-to-earth.

For a man who'd always been sure of himself and confident, he couldn't seem to find his voice. He studied her a moment longer, then uttered the only word that had been haunting his dreams and his waking hours. "Suzy."

"I've gone by Susannah since law school. I'd prefer you didn't call me Suzy."

Russell nodded, his senses and memories swirling. "Sure, but will you forgive me if I forget? You'll always be Suzy to me."

She crossed her arms and rested a hip against the mahogany desk. "The Suzy you once knew doesn't exist anymore."

That's what he was afraid of. The sweet, loving girl he'd known was a business-minded stranger, but that didn't soften his desire to renew their friendship, tap into what they'd once felt for each other.

People didn't change. Not really. And Russell had every intention of reminding Suzy that they'd once had something special, something they could recreate. "Maybe Suzy's still somewhere deep inside."

She offered him a wry smile. "I doubt it, Russell. Time has a funny way of changing things."

"And so does a life-threatening accident." Russell had always been smart and driven, a businessman through and through. But his brush with death had caused him to reevaluate his life. And the dream he'd had during his coma had convinced him what he was missing: kids, a wife. Suzy McCord.

He'd always placed business and family first, but

now he was determined to seize the day, find his destiny and make things right.

All he needed to do was convince the beautiful lady standing before him that she needed him, too. That they had a future together—a child waiting to be born.

But when he glanced at the strangely familiar woman who called herself Susannah, he realized the task might be a lot tougher than he'd anticipated.

Still, Russell had no qualms about going after what he wanted.

And he wanted Suzy McCord.

Chapter 2

Susannah wasn't prepared for the heart-soaring re-action she'd felt when Russell walked into her of-fice. The air grew heavy, laden with memories and desires she'd once thought buried too deep to be resurrected, and she struggled to catch her breath.

In spite of a yellowed bruise and a pink scar over his left brow, the years had been good to the captain of the high school debate team. His black hair still glistened like a raven's wing, and his lanky form had filled out.

Even in boots, black jeans and a white shirt, Rus-sell Kingsley had power and money written all over him. A man like him didn't need a three-piece suit to look the role of an executive.

And in spite of the accident that had marred his brow and knocked him unconscious for days, he appeared strong, healthy. Vital. Most likely, work-outs and physical fitness were a critical part of his daily routine.

Did he still shoot hoops in the backyard, still run along the banks of Lake Monet each morning?

Susannah tried to shake off the curiosity, yet it took every bit of her concentration not to fawn over him like a lovesick teenager.

Or a star-struck business consultant.

In an effort to protect herself, she donned an aloof, businesslike stance. Her relationship with and interest in Russell Kingsley was strictly profes-sional, and she had every intention of keeping it that way.

She brushed a hand over the files spread atop her desk. "I've been studying the Eden Garden Farms financial reports. They look good, but I'm sure some changes in their corporate and managerial structure are needed."

"It's not a good idea to buy out a company and immediately make changes in management."

"Nevertheless," Susannah said, "some changes will need to be made."

Russell bristled. "I don't think you heard me. It isn't a wise executive decision to purchase a functioning business and instantly make sweeping changes."

That had usually been Susannah's opinion. But Russell didn't have all the facts. "The only reason the stockholders are considering a sale is because of their labor problems. And I believe those issues are a direct result of mismanagement. Major changes will need to be made."

Russell crossed his arms. "I'll make that decision."

He'd always been strong-willed and opinionated. Apparently, that hadn't changed. Or maybe he didn't like being crossed by a woman. Either way, he'd better get used to Susannah speaking her mind. Besides, she'd honed a few debating skills of her own in law school. "Maybe you'd better take time to look over the files before voicing your opinion. And I'd suggest a trip to California to look over operations."

His jaw tensed, and his green eyes narrowed. If he thought an attempt at intimidation would work on her, he was sadly mistaken. Then, as if having second thoughts, he leaned against the doorjamb, reminding her of the way he used to lean against his locker and wait for her to come out of fourth period chemistry.

"Maybe we got off on the wrong foot," he said. "Can we start over?"

In a business sense, they could begin again. But Susannah had no intention of starting over, romantically speaking. Too much murky water had passed under the bridge. "I'm sorry, Russell. I get a bit intense when I'm working on a merger or acquisition. We jumped right into a business discussion before you had a chance to prepare for it."

He didn't respond right away, didn't smile. He merely watched her with those perceptive green eyes. "Tag was right."

"About what?"

"You've changed."

"We all have." She supposed it would take a little time for Russell to get used to the new Suzy. And to learn to accept some professional guidance. Most likely, he was accustomed to being surrounded by eager yes-men. The only time Susannah agreed to anything was when she'd given every option a great deal of consideration.

"How about a cup of coffee?" he asked.

"Sounds good."

He continued to stand there, as though expecting her to make the first move. She hoped he didn't think she'd serve him. A grin tugged at her lips, and she reached over and pressed the intercom button. "Mahnita?"

"Yes, Ms. McCord."

"Can you please bring Mr. Kingsley and I two cups of coffee?"

"Certainly."

Susannah took her seat and pointed toward the chair in front of her desk. "Why don't you sit down?"

He seemed to ponder her words for a moment, then slowly sauntered forward and took a seat.

His legs were long and lean, and he sat in the chair as though he'd be more comfortable on horseback. "You look good, Suzy."

"Susannah," she corrected. "And so do you."

There was no denying it. Russell Kingsley still made her blood race, her heart soar. She might not like it, but there was no getting around it. Some things, unfortunately, hadn't changed at all.

Russell eyed the pretty woman carefully, the fiery red hair she'd carefully swept into a neatly contained businesslike coiffure, vivid blue eyes that challenged his. He noted the slender neck, the silver-and-gold necklace that adorned her suit.

She was a beautiful force to be reckoned with, he supposed. But she seemed to know her stuff and wasn't a bit shy about stating her opinion or arguing. In a way, he had to admire her for that.

Mahnita carried in two cups of coffee, placed them on the desktop, then quietly slipped away.

His coffee was black, rich and strong—the way he liked it.

Susannah's had been lightened with cream. He nodded at her cup. "Do you use sugar?"

"Yes."

"Sweet. And creamy." He smiled. Suzy—or rather Susannah—was softer than she admitted. Or so he hoped.

"Your father hired me as a consultant, Russell. I'm not trying to challenge you. I'm just doing my job. I call it as I see it."

He cracked a crooked smile, one meant to show her he was in charge. "And I've got my own way of doing things. I hope you'll forgive me if we don't see eye to eye."

"I'm sure this won't be the last time. But if you'll look over the Eden Garden Farm reports, I think you'll find I'm right."

It grated upon him to admit he was wrong. *To anyone.* And he especially disliked taking advice from a clever, upstart woman he used to love, a woman who was determined to act as if their high school romance never existed. "I'll look over the reports and the files."

She smiled, offering him a brief glimpse of the Suzy he remembered, the bright-eyed vibrancy of the cheerleader he had once loved. The woman he believed lived somewhere deep inside this business-minded consultant sitting across from him.

Could he somehow reach the old Suzy, make her remember the love they once shared, the memories he would never forget?

"How about dinner tonight?" he asked.

She arched an auburn brow. "A business dinner?"

"Sure," he said, although a business discussion would be the last thing on his mind.

She slowly shook her head. "Not tonight."

He stiffened. "Why not?"

"You need time to go over these reports and files. Otherwise, we won't have anything to talk about." She leaned back in her chair and crossed her arms. "Besides, I already have dinner plans this evening."

A pang of jealousy sneaked up on him, jabbing him in the chest. There was so much he didn't know about her. So much he wanted to learn. "Anyone I know?"

She studied him a moment, as though trying to

decide whether to answer or not. "Just an old high school friend."

Donna Mason, he supposed. And probably at the Rooftop Café. It had always been Suzy's favorite. The one-story restaurant was fancy on the inside, but had a festive, more casual setting on the roof. Of course, in mid-December, no one would be eating up there, out in the open. Montana winters were too damn rugged for a couple of butane heaters, even if this winter was expected to be unseasonably mild.

The Rooftop was one of the nicest restaurants in Rumor, with an eclectic menu offering a variety of fine food that would please even the fussiest food connoisseur.

In fact, Russell just might drop in at the Rooftop himself tonight. He had a hankering for the Chef's Special, whatever that might be.

Susannah entered the Rooftop Café, where she planned to meet Donna, and struggled out of her full-length coat. She'd forgotten how cold Rumor could be in December, but was still glad to be home.

She scanned the dining room, searching for her old high school friend.

Time and mileage had done little to wear down

the bonds of their friendship. And Susannah had a ton of long-distance telephone charges over the years to prove it.

"Suzy!" Donna Mason wiggled her hand in a little wave.

Donna was the only one allowed to call her Suzy, although Susannah wasn't entirely sure why. Maybe it was because theirs was the only friendship that had survived the teen years and continued to develop through adulthood. They had a history, she supposed, a closeness that superseded formality.

Other than the usual maturation and a new hairstyle, Donna hadn't changed much in seventeen years. At five-eight, she was tall and willowy, with bright blue eyes and blond hair that she wore short and wavy.

Ambitious and used to getting her way, Donna had done well for herself. She owned The Getaway, a spa that provided a place for the locals to unwind and relax. Susannah planned to schedule a deep body massage soon. She could feel the tension building in her neck, particularly after today's stressful meeting—or rather, confrontation—with Russell.

Susannah made her way to the bar where her old friend waited with what looked like a martini in front of her. "Sorry I'm late. But sometimes when

I get elbow-deep in my work, I forget to look at the clock.''

"No problem. I haven't been here very long. But I did give them my name. It should only be ten minutes or so. Want something to drink?''

"Sure. I'll have a glass of Merlot.''

Donna motioned for a waitress, while Susannah took one of the two empty chairs at the small linen-covered table near the fireplace that lit the room with warmth and charm.

"Last time we ate here, it was in June, and we sat on the roof,'' Susannah said. It had been her last night in Rumor.

Donna smiled. "I don't recall what we ate, but you broke down in tears, and we left before dessert.''

Susannah remembered the evening all too well. The Rooftop Café was gossip central, and she'd nearly blabbed her painful secret to her best friend.

Suzy McCord, head cheerleader and honor student, feared she was pregnant. And the father of her baby had made it all too clear he wouldn't marry her.

Not that Russell knew they'd conceived a baby in the back seat of his grandfather's 1957 Chevy. Suzy had planned to share the news the night he'd told her their relationship was over. She hadn't had the chance.

His words had blindsided her, slicing open her heart. "I can't get involved with anyone right now," he'd said. "It's not you, Suzy."

But it *was* her. Stratton Kingsley had made no secret of the fact he thought Suzy McCord wasn't good enough for his firstborn son. And obviously, Russell agreed.

"I care about you," Russell had said. "But we're both too young to think of anything crazy like marriage."

She hadn't mentioned anything about the baby after that. The problem she'd wanted to share with the guy she loved had become hers alone.

And when Russell had driven away from her house that night, she decided to get out of town before her pregnancy became public knowledge. Three days later, she packed her bags, walked to the bus station and hopped on the Old Grey Dog, as some folks called it, then went to California to live with Aunt Hazel.

The rest was history.

"So, how's the job going?" Donna plucked the olive from her martini and popped it in her mouth. "Must be weird working for the Kingsleys."

"It's just a job," Susannah said, although she

had to admit it was strange. And working with Russell was the strangest of all. The old attraction was still there, not to mention a stirring of unwelcome desire. But the years had undoubtedly changed them both.

They were strangers now—strangers with a past.

"How's the remodel coming? With all that time you spend at MonMart, maybe you should hire someone to help."

"This job with MonMart won't last forever. Once we close the agribusiness deal, I'll have plenty of time to work on my house."

"Tag Kingsley is one of the best carpenters around," Donna said. "You might want him to do some of the more difficult work. Those bay windows are going to be a major remodel."

"You're right. I'll have him give me an estimate." Susannah settled into her seat and fought the urge to kick off her heels. The day had been long and emotionally draining, to say the least.

"But the nursery should be fun to work on." Donna smiled and leaned forward. "How does it feel to know you'll be a mother soon?"

A mother. Her. Susannah McCord. Warmth settled in her heart, and excitement fluttered. "It feels wonderful."

"I've gotta tell you," Donna said, tucking a

short, wavy strand of hair behind her ear and leaning forward. "Your decision to adopt shocked me.
You've become so success-driven that it seemed
kind of...well, you know..."

"Inconsistent?"

Donna nodded. "I guess. When are you going to
find time to join playgroups and bake cookies?"

"I'll make time," Susannah said. "And believe
it or not, I'm looking forward to it. That's why I've
moved back to Rumor. I'm going to start my own
business, one that will allow me to spend plenty of
quality time with my baby."

"It sounds like a good plan to me. Have you
heard any news yet?"

Susannah had started the long process of adopting a baby girl from China. She'd filled out all the
forms and had been preapproved as a single parent
through a new but reputable agency. "I'm in the
third and last phase—the wait."

"And you're sure about this?" Donna's intense
blue eyes locked on Susannah's. "Motherhood is a
big step."

"I've never been more sure about anything in my
life." Susannah's early years hadn't been pleasant,
and as a child, she'd felt unloved, unappreciated.
But that only made her more resolved to be a
mother, to welcome a child into her home, to cher-

ish a little girl who hadn't been loved and appreciated. She placed a hand upon her friend's arm. "Six months ago, at my thirty-fifth birthday, one of my colleagues commented about the decision I'd made to be a career woman and put family and children aside."

"And?" Donna asked.

"I hadn't made a decision to do anything of the kind. It just sort of happened." The waitress placed a glass of red wine in front of Susannah, and she took a slow sip. "It was like an epiphany."

"What was?"

"I'd been so busy working, I forgot to have kids."

"You *forgot* to have kids?"

Susannah fingered the stem of her wineglass. "Given my age, and the fact I've already lost one ovary and a fallopian tube, and the absence of a husband or even a lover who shows long-term promise, my chances of having a baby have nearly passed me by."

"So, you've decided to make a family happen."

"In a way, I suppose. But a good friend in California adopted a baby girl from China, a little girl who'd been abandoned. I can't think of a more worthwhile and rewarding venture than providing an unwanted child with a heart full of love, a home, a wealth of opportunities.''

''A kid would be lucky to have you for a mom,'' Donna said. ''I'm impressed with the way you make things happen in your life. Any decision on the new business venture?''

Susannah's consulting fees had provided well for her over the years. She had a hefty amount of cash built up in stocks, money market funds and bonds, enough to start her own business and have plenty to spare.

''No. I haven't decided yet. It's not just a matter of starting a business that will be successful and rewarding; I want to be able to have time with my daughter. I'm not about to put her in day care from morning until dark.'' Susannah could still remember being the first child dropped off at the sitter's and the last one picked up at night. Her daughter wasn't going to have that same experience.

Donna glanced at the doorway and waved to an attractive young woman with long blond hair. ''That's the new art teacher at Rumor High. Gorgeous, isn't she?''

The teacher smiled in greeting, then spotted two friends at a corner table. The other women, both young and stylishly dressed, welcomed her.

''The other two work at the high school, too.''

Donna chuckled softly. "Remember when our teachers seemed old and out-of-date?"

There were a lot of things Susannah remembered about her teen years. And some she'd rather forget. "Time has a way of changing our perspectives."

"Ever wish you could go back in time? Do things differently?"

Yes, she did, when she allowed herself to contemplate the past. The biggest mistake of her life had been falling in love with Russell Kingsley and believing in the Cinderella myth. "I probably wouldn't have ever dated Russell."

"Oh, yeah?" Donna said. "Surely there were some good memories."

None that Susannah wanted to think about, let alone discuss at a restaurant the local gossips loved to frequent.

"Well, I'll be darned," Donna said, her eyes darting to the doorway. "Speak of the devil, look who just walked in."

Russell? Unable to help herself, Susannah glanced over her shoulder. Sure enough, there he stood, as handsome and commanding as she'd last seen him. Their eyes met, and her heart tap-danced to a Shirley Temple beat.

How could the sight of him still draw out such a startling rush? It had been seventeen years, for goodness' sake. Would she ever outgrow the guy who'd once been her teenaged lover?

Donna lifted a hand and waved, motioning, it seemed, for Russell to join them.

Susannah sincerely hoped he was meeting someone else. She was in no mood to sit across the dinner table with the man who still caused her pulse to race, who kept her mentally on her toes. This was supposed to be a quiet, relaxing dinner with her old friend—not a nostalgic evening by the fireside.

Russell grinned and sauntered toward the table. "How's it going?" His words and tone were casual, but his eyes lingered on Susannah's.

"Ooh, that's a nasty bump," Donna said, cocking her head and studying the pink scar over Russell's brow. "Other than that, it looks like you've recovered without a hitch. You had everyone in town worried for a while."

"My bumps and bruises are healing. But don't worry. I'm back to fighting weight." Russell slid Susannah a crooked grin—one that suggested he was ready for another verbal sparring match.

"If you aren't meeting someone else, why don't you join us?"

"Thanks. I'll take you up on that." Russell snagged the chair closest to Susannah.

"Ms. Mason?" the hostess said. "Your table is ready."

"Great." Donna grabbed the purse she'd hung on the back of her chair. "But there will be three of us now."

"Not a problem," the hostess said.

Not a problem? Susannah glanced at her watch. Maybe she should feign a headache and make this evening short. The tension continued to build in her neck.

Russell placed a hand on her back, in a gracious and mannerly way. But heat swirled upon contact, and her heart thudded in her chest. Darn the attraction she continued to feel for an arrogant rich boy who'd once broken her heart.

She'd healed, thank goodness. But she didn't like the constant reminder of what they'd shared. Of what he'd once meant to her.

If she could have thought of a way to excuse herself from dinner, she would have.

As it was, she'd have to pretend he didn't still have such a powerful effect on her senses.

"Can I interest anyone in dessert?" the waiter asked. Russell studied the silver tray laden with an array of chocolate delights, cheesecake, a glazed pear something-or-other, mousse and berries with whipped cream.

"What would you ladies like?"

"I'll pass," Suzy said. "Just a cup of decaf."

No wonder she'd kept her shape over the years. She'd refused to put butter on her bread and had lemon juice on her salad. Didn't the woman enjoy eating anymore?

Russell remembered sharing double-thick milk shakes, French fries, just about everything. The Suzy he remembered liked to nibble. He'd just have to remind her how much she was missing by being so rigid.

Donna pointed to a goblet topped with whipped cream and a drizzle of chocolate sauce. "I'd like that sinful, fudgey thing."

"Give me the strawberry cheesecake and two spoons," Russell said.

Suzy's eyes locked with his. "Why the extra spoon?"

"You love cheesecake." Russell sent her a dazzling smile, meant to disarm her. Miss Susannah McCord had become too stodgy for her own good. She needed to loosen up.

"I don't love cheesecake anymore."

"How can you stop loving something?"

Or *someone*. The unspoken words hung in the

air, and try as he might, Russell couldn't think of a way to backpedal.

Even Donna seemed to take note, because her fork stopped in mid descent, and she glanced first at Suzy, then at Russell.

"I'm focused on my health and my weight. There are a ton of calories in cheesecake, not to mention the cholesterol."

"Good grief, Suzy," Russell said, glad to get the topic moving in a better direction. "You should relax a bit. Take a bite of the cheesecake, then work out an extra thirty minutes tomorrow."

"I don't have an extra thirty minutes tomorrow." She crossed her arms and leaned back in her seat, distancing herself from him. "We have a business meeting scheduled at eight, and I have several reports yet to study."

Candlelight glistened off the gold strands in her fiery hair, and a flush rose to her cheeks. Her eyes flickered with intensity. The woman was beautiful. And too damn business-minded for her own good.

He'd like to see her dressed in a silky pink vintage dress and a pair of sheer dark stockings with a seam up the back. Watch her dance and smile. He shook off the vision from his dream.

An opinionated workaholic was the last thing on

earth Russell wanted in a wife or a lover. But why did Suzy continue to make his blood pump?

Destiny came to mind. She'd come back to Rumor for a reason. And he'd been reminded, through his dream, of how much she'd once meant to him. What they'd both given up when she left town seventeen years ago.

What they had to lose if they ignored Fate.

They'd loved each other once, shared dreams of a life together—marriage, children.

Sure, things had changed. They both had changed.

But the past offered a firm foundation, and the future was still theirs to claim.

Somehow, he had to convince her to loosen up. To take a chance on loving him again.

How hard could that be?

Chapter 3

Montana West Airlines took off from Billings at two-thirty in the afternoon, one week and a day before Christmas.

A varied assortment of holiday travelers stowed colorfully wrapped gifts in the overhead bins or tucked them under the seats. But Susannah wasn't thinking about Christmas, last minute shopping or holiday cheer.

She sat beside Russell in first class, trying hard to keep her mind focused on business, not the man beside her or the two days and one night they would spend together.

This is a business trip, she reminded herself for the tenth time since Russell had picked her up at the house and driven her to the airport.

The engines droned as the Boeing 747 climbed to an altitude high above the clouds. Russell peered out the window like a child who had never flown before. His enthusiastic interest was hard to ignore, particularly since Susannah suspected he traveled a lot on business.

A bell signaled the flight attendants to unbuckle their seat belts and begin service.

"Can I get you something to drink?" a pretty flight attendant asked Susannah.

"Coffee with cream and sugar."

"And you, sir?" the blonde asked. Her eyes lingered on Russell a bit longer than necessary. And although her manners and demeanor were polite and professional, Susannah noted that the attendant had assessed him with a critical and appreciative female eye.

Russell was too darn good-looking for a woman—either happily married or actively single—to ignore. As a teenager, she'd proudly worn his high school ring and his letterman's jacket. Even now, it pleased her to sit beside him, to have his attention.

"I'll have Scotch and water," he told the atten-

dant, flashing her a crooked grin. "And some pretzels or peanuts, if you have them handy."

"I'll bring one of each." She returned his smile,
then proceeded to take the other orders of first class
passengers.

"Why did you order coffee?" Russell asked.
"You had two cups while we waited at the airport."

"And one before I left the house," Susannah
said. "I like coffee."

"Afraid a glass of wine will cause you to put
down your guard?"

That was certainly part of it, but she wasn't about
to admit it to him. "I don't drink alcohol when I'm
on a business trip."

"The meeting is bright and early tomorrow
morning. We're on our own until then."

On our own. That was another reason she intended to stay alert and focused.

Not about to reveal her personal concerns, she
pulled the tray table out of the armrest, preparing
for the coffee she'd ordered. "I plan on looking
over the financial reports one last time this evening,
so it's business as usual for me."

Again, that wasn't entirely true. She'd already
studied the files and reports until she knew them
backward and forward. But it seemed as good a

response as any. And it was certainly the only thing she wanted to reveal to Russell.

She wasn't particularly happy about arriving in Monterey before dinner, especially since she'd always found the coastal city to have a quaint, romantic charm and didn't particularly look forward to sharing it with Russell. But the flight schedules hadn't offered them much choice, if they wanted to make each of the four meetings she had lined up with accountants, corporate officers and attorneys. And with the holidays quickly approaching, everyone's time and availability had been tight.

Russell stretched out his legs, utilizing the extra space in the first class cabin, and studied her profile. "I love to fly. How about you?"

"I don't give it much thought. In my line of work, flying is just a way to get from point A to point B."

He reached over the console that separated them and took her hand, giving it a brief but intimate squeeze that left her wanting more. "The old Suzy was always adventurous."

"I don't have much time for adventures anymore." Business took up most of her time. And no matter how much Russell enjoyed this flight, it was still business to her.

But she was glad he had agreed to make the trip.

When she'd suggested they look over the prospective farming operation and produce brokerage firm MonMart hoped to purchase, Russell told her to set it up. It was the first time they'd actually seen eye to eye on anything during the past two weeks.

At first, she suspected his plan to fly to Monterey had more to do with getting her alone than it had to do with business, but she quickly dismissed the idea. MonMart and its success meant a great deal to the Kingsleys, particularly Russell. And since it was most likely her last consulting job, the success of the venture meant a lot to her, too.

She turned and caught him looking at her. *Again.* But the intensity of his gaze made her heart pound and stirred a longing she hadn't expected and didn't welcome.

He flashed her a wry smile. "You always had such a passion for life. Did I put the flame out?"

A lump swelled in her throat, and she struggled to find the right words. He had, in a sense, rained on her dreams. But his rejection had also strengthened her, toughened her. Made her into the woman she was today.

"My passions run in a different direction these days. I won't lie to you, Russell. When I left Rumor, I was hurt. Crushed. But I rallied. And I'm a better person because of it. In actuality, I should thank you.''

"No,'' Russell said. "I'm sorry. Forgive me for hurting you. I'd make it up to you, if I could.''

By putting them in a position where he could break her heart again? No, thank you. "You don't have any apologies to make. It's over. And long forgotten.''

But when she looked into the warmth of his green eyes, she wasn't so sure.

And the sudden realization scared the liver out of her.

Russell checked them into adjoining rooms at the Pacific Breeze, a small but luxurious hotel on the bluffs overlooking the ocean. According to online sources, it was one of the nicest getaways the Monterey Peninsula had to offer.

And one of the most romantic.

It might have been sly on Russell's part, but he didn't feel the least bit guilty about setting the stage. He wanted some time to get to know the new Suzy. If she suspected he wanted more out of this trip than an agribusiness venture, a great view and a good night's sleep, she didn't mention it.

She hadn't been happy to learn Russell had changed the hotel reservations after she'd given him the itinerary she'd carefully planned, but like any other business consultant on retainer, she kept her mouth shut when the corporate executive insisted he wanted a view of the Pacific on the only night he'd spend in town.

After registering at the front desk, Russell escorted Suzy to the elevator and up to their third-floor rooms. He opened the door for her, then followed her into the spacious accommodations.

''It's lovely,'' Suzy said, placing her briefcase and purse on the king-size bed and making her way to the sliding door that opened onto a balcony.

The intimate patio overlooked a green, rolling hillside and revealed a stone wall that protected sightseers from the craggy edge of a rocky bluff that rose above the vast Pacific. She opened the door and stepped outside.

Russell followed her.

The sea breeze was invigorating. And stimulating—in a romantic sense. He had half a notion to tell the front desk they'd only need the one room. But he knew better than to suggest it.

He might believe Destiny had brought him and Suzy together again, but she obviously remained skeptical.

''How about a glass of wine now?'' he asked. ''Our business day won't start until tomorrow.''

As she turned slowly from the railing, the wind caught a tendril of her hair and blew it across her cheek.

The air was crisp and cool, yet a heat settled in his gut. He had an overwhelming urge to take her in his arms, see if her kisses tasted as sweet as they once had. Instead, he shoved his hands into the pockets of his jeans.

"I don't suppose you're hungry," she said.

He *was* hungry. For her.

"I could use a snack." He picked up the phone and dialed room service, asking for a fruit and cheese plate and a bottle of California wine. When she objected to the bottle of wine with dinnertime nearing, he changed the order to include two single glasses of chardonnay.

All right; so getting Suzy to loosen up wasn't going to be as easy as he'd hoped. Russell was a patient man. When he had to be.

Minutes later, a bellman brought their luggage. "Can I do anything more for you, sir?"

"Will we need reservations for dinner tonight?" Russell asked.

"No, sir. With this being a weeknight and close to Christmas, we aren't too full. You shouldn't have any problem being seated."

Russell thanked the man and gave him a generous tip.

Moments later, another bellman arrived bearing a tray, and Suzy directed him to place it on the balcony.

After Russell signed the bill, he reached for a roll of cash in his front pocket and handed the waiter a ten. Then he joined Suzy outside, where she munched on an apple slice. He handed her a glass of wine, and although he had a feeling she wouldn't take it, she did.

Maybe the romantic ambiance had affected her, too.

They sat quietly, enjoying the view, the cries and antics of two sea gulls swooping through the sky, the sun as it descended like a fiery ball into the Pacific.

"I know you said I don't owe you an apology, Suzy, but I want you to know why I broke up with you."

"I know why." Her voice, soft and wistful, caressed him like a whisper, a revelation. At that moment, he knew he'd touched the heart of the Suzy he once knew.

She turned slowly, her eyes meeting his. Sadness pooled in the depths, but not the kind that threatened teary emotions. The kind that revealed pain.

And acceptance of things that couldn't be helped, or things that couldn't be changed. "Three days before you asked for your class ring, you took me to your house. I hadn't really wanted to go, since your dad had been more grumpy and crotchety the last few times I'd come around. You left me on the patio and went inside to get us something to drink."

He remembered the day well. His dad had been unusually harsh to Suzy. And when Russell had gone inside to get them a couple cans of soda, his dad had cornered him and asked why he was still seeing *that girl*. Hadn't Russell listened to a word he'd said?

"The window in the kitchen was open."

Russell tensed. It hurt—even now—to know Suzy had overheard only a few of the things his dad had said. The actual ultimatum, thank goodness, had come after Russell had taken Suzy home.

"Your dad spoke to you about family loyalty and duty. About honor and blood. He said you had a birthright, a responsibility to your father and your Kingsley roots. It was all very elegant, and obviously, he made his point."

Seventeen years may have passed, but Russell could still recall the sting of his father's words. Had he known Suzy had heard them, too, he would have… Would have what? Done anything differently? Done everything differently?

Probably not. He hadn't had any other choice he could have lived with. "I loved you, Suzy."

"Hey," she said, garnering a smile. "We made love. A woman usually wants to think sex includes an 'I love you.' As a rational adult, I know better."

"It wasn't sex. Making love to you was special, something I'll never forget. And when I told you that I loved you, I meant it."

She smiled, but it didn't reach her eyes. "Russell, you had a change of mind. A change of heart. It was understandable. What kind of bloodlines could I have offered an heir to the Kingsley fortune? I didn't even know who my father was. And at times, I wasn't sure if my mom knew, either."

He reached for her hand and clasped it in his. Her fingers were soft, smooth and cool to the touch. "Suzy, at that time there was a lot more going on in my life than you'll ever know."

She took her hand from his. "And there was a lot more going on in my life, too."

"Then suppose we lay the cards on the table?"

"I think it's best if we let sleeping dogs lie," she said, countering with a metaphor of her own. Then she turned toward the railing and studied the orange-streaked sunset. "Did you ever watch the sun drop into the sea? It's mystical, really."

She had shut him out, so it seemed. But only for the time being. Russell had every intention of setting her straight.

And getting her back into his arms.

The bellman had been right. There had been no need for reservations. Poseidon's, the elegant restaurant within the Pacific Breeze hotel, was nearly empty.

Susannah and Russell sat at a cozy and intimate table for two that boasted an ocean view. From the time they walked through the carved teakwood doorway, the service had gone above and beyond the five-star rating this restaurant and hotel had received.

In spite of her intention of keeping things formal and businesslike, Susannah found herself relaxing into the romantic setting.

The candlelight glistened off crystal wineglasses and sterling silverware, as the soft sounds of a piano hovered softly, filling the intimate dining room with a classical melody.

Russell's gaze snagged hers. "Remember when I told you that there had been more going on in my life than you knew?"

Susannah nodded. She didn't remind him that she'd had a lot going on in her life, too. That she'd left Rumor, pregnant with his baby. That she'd lost the child, as well as lessened her chance to conceive in the future.

"My dad had been diagnosed with lung cancer."

Susannah hadn't known. "You didn't tell me."

"It was my dad's secret. He was scheduled to go in for surgery to remove a portion of his left lung. They were talking radiation, chemo. Getting affairs in order, just in case."

Susannah placed her fork on her plate and gave him her full attention. "Was that after I went to California?"

He shook his head slowly. "No, it was the week before we broke up. My mom fell apart, and my dad was afraid he would die. *Seriously afraid,* for the first time in his life. When he told me, he broke down and cried. He grabbed ahold of me and sobbed, like I was the parent and he was the child. It scared the hell out of me, and I didn't have a clue how to comfort him."

Susannah caught the pain in Russell's eye, the reality of what he'd been going through prior to their breakup.

"I'd never seen my father shed a tear. It was a low blow. A scary blow. And I realized what he was trying to tell me.'' Russell reached across the table and took Susannah's hand. ''If he died, I was going to have to take over, not just step in and help. I was going to have to run the business. Take over the family, actually, because my mom had been so devastated by the fear of his death that she'd fallen apart. Completely.''

''I'm sorry,'' she said, as though the past wasn't over and her sympathy could actually help.

''That day you overheard our conversation, my dad had just come home from the oncologist, who'd laid things on the line, given him some cold hard facts to digest. Dad was hurting. And scared witless.''

Susannah imagined Russell was hurting, too. His family had always been important to him.

''Later,'' Russell said, ''after I took you home, he demanded that I remember who I was, take responsibility for the family. He told me I had no business talking about love and marriage when the Kingsley family and business were on the brink of disaster. And he gave me an ultimatum.''

An ultimatum. The words struck Susannah with heartbreaking clarity. Stratton had forced Russell to give her up.

At the time, she'd thought Stratton was making reference to her bastard status. She'd felt an incredible sense of shame, but had kept it to herself, as she would continue to do. She'd learned the hard way to keep her dreams and fears close to the vest. "Your father was right, Russell. Ultimately. You've done well by the family, particularly in a business sense."

"I'm still sorry about letting you go. It was the worst night of my life."

It had been a chilling night, she supposed. For both of them. Susannah had her own secrets, which she couldn't see any point in revealing now.

The past was over.

Yet knowing the truth and the depth of Stratton's illness made things a bit easier to understand, even if it didn't take away the pain. Susannah had loved Russell with all her heart. Losing him had nearly destroyed her.

"I called you in California," he said. "After the doctors thought my dad's cancer was in remission."

Susannah's breath caught. "I didn't get the message."

"Your aunt was pretty upset when I gave her my name. She asked whether I'd done enough damage to you already. She said that you were doing just fine without me, and that if I wanted you to heal, I should leave you alone."

"And you did," Susannah said. But she didn't

say it in an accusatory way, but rather as fact. A fact that had sealed the fate of their relationship.

"Think whatever you want, but at that point, I thought leaving you alone and not pursuing a reconciliation was an act of love." Russell reached for the water goblet and took a sip. "So I poured all of my energy into making money and running the family business."

"I guess life has taken us both in different directions," Susannah said.

"And brought us back full circle."

She shook her head slowly. "Not full circle. I just came back to Rumor."

Reality seemed to settle on them both, and Russell signed the bill the waiter had left.

"Let's go back to the rooms," she said, eager to have some time alone. Talk of the past was unsettling, particularly when the past was much different than what she'd believed.

But she still couldn't help wondering what life would have been like had Stratton not been stricken with cancer, had Russell not chosen his family over her.

They walked back to their rooms, each quiet and solemn. Twice she thought Russell might grab her hand or slip an arm around her, but he hadn't, which was just as well. She wasn't sure how she would have reacted, wasn't sure whether she would have liked it or not.

When they reached her door, she paused to pull the plastic key from her purse.

"Suzy?"

She glanced up and caught him looking at her, caught the intensity of his gaze, the desire brewing in his eyes. He was going to kiss her, and although she knew she should pull away, tell him no, something far more powerful than reason or good sense took over. And she stepped into his embrace.

She was accosted by the scent of leather and musk, the feel of his arms on her back, her hips. The mouth that fit hers so perfectly, the daring tongue that already knew each nook and cranny of her mouth with such intimacy. Their tongues mated, and time stopped.

Or rather, seventeen years dissipated into the present. She leaned into him, pressing herself against his arousal, willing herself to stop, yet unable to resist the gentle assault on her senses that she'd never been able to withstand.

Damn Russell Kingsley. And damn her pent-up desire that threatened to go berserk. She wanted to pull him into her room, suggest they take the night one moment at a time. But that would be senseless.

Crazy. Irrational. And Susannah didn't do anything without conscious thought.

She slowly pulled away, put a stop to a fiery kiss that had no business occurring in a hotel hallway, an arousing kiss that belonged behind closed doors. "I'm not ready for this, Russell."

"Then I'll wait until you are."

Would he? She wasn't sure if that made her feel better or worse.

What had gotten into her? Her hand that had once held the key was empty. She glanced at the hallway floor, spotting the key on the floral print of the carpet. She stooped to retrieve it, glad to break eye contact, yet feeling anything but in control.

"Thank you," she said, before taking time to consider a different response. What the hell was she thanking him for? The evening? The dinner? The self-disclosure? The apology? The kiss? Quite frankly, she wasn't sure. And she doubted either of them knew.

"Good night," she said, trying to get back on solid ground.

He nodded. "Sleep tight."

His eyes locked on hers, sending her heart into a tailspin. She had to get away from that piercing gaze.

She turned her back, slipped the key into the slot

and stared at the lock until the green light blinked. He continued to stand behind her until she opened the door and stepped over the safety of the threshold.

The door closed, shutting Russell out of her room, but Susannah wouldn't be able to shut him out of her mind. Thoughts of the past, the present and the future tumbled inside like a mishmash of garments in a Laundromat dryer.

There was a lot for her to sort out, and not nearly enough hours before dawn, when the first of many business meetings would begin.

Could she maintain a professional stance until they flew back to Billings?

And could she protect her heart once she returned to Rumor?

She would have to.

Aunt Hazel had once shared a little advice Susannah would never forget. *Hurt me once, shame on you. Hurt me twice, shame on me.*

Chapter 4

Two evenings later, Susannah stood in front of her bathroom mirror and fussed with her hair, trying to decide whether to wear it up or down.

She wore a classically styled black dress and would have preferred to sweep her hair up in a twist, but as the same stubborn strand refused to stay put, the decision was made. She wouldn't fight any longer, especially with fingers that moved like arthritic tin soldiers.

Trying to convince herself she was merely having a bad-hair day, she ignored a bout of adolescent-style jitters that seemed to creep over her.

Why hadn't she told Russell that she would meet him at the Kingsley Ranch where the MonMart Christmas party would take place?

Because, she reiterated to herself, other than the hauntingly arousing kiss they'd shared in the hotel hallway, the rest of the trip to Monterey had—thank goodness—remained business-oriented. And she couldn't seem to find a reason not to ride with him.

Eden Garden Farms would be a major asset to MonMart. And Susannah had felt a surge of pride when, on the return flight, Russell agreed that the first thing on the agenda, after taking control of the farming operation, would be to make some major changes in management. Like Susannah, he believed they could solve the bulk of the labor problems by replacing a few power-hungry supervisors who had self serving agendas and didn't care about the people who worked under them.

"The employee Christmas party is tomorrow night," Russell had reminded her, as they'd pulled into her driveway. "Will you go with me?"

She'd started to search for an excuse, but quite frankly, hadn't been able to find a reasonable one. She was, after all, a consultant working on a major project. Had Russell been any other client, she would have willingly agreed.

Susannah glanced at the cut-crystal clock on the

dresser and realized there wasn't much time left to stress or struggle. Russell would be arriving to pick her up soon. She ran her fingers through the strands, loosening the natural curls, then gave her head a vigorous shake.

The result was a sexy style she'd never felt comfortable wearing. But, she had to admit, it looked good.

Too good.

Susannah was a consultant on her way to a company Christmas party, for goodness' sake. She jerked open the drawer that held her hair clips, in search of something to soften the effect, just as the doorbell rang.

Shoot. Russell. She blew out a sigh and made one last scan of her reflection. So her hair looked a bit too sexy. There wasn't much she could do now, other than maintain a professional demeanor.

She fumbled with the tube of lipstick before making a quick application, then blew out a sigh. This is business, she reminded herself for the tenth time. Yet she couldn't help but fuss with her hair once again, just for a moment. It was cold outside, and she couldn't keep Russell waiting for her on the front porch.

Susannah made her way through the hall and into the small living room that was much too confining for the furniture she'd brought from Los Angeles. Maybe, in the spring, she could have a yard sale and try to get rid of some of the larger, more sophisticated pieces.

When she opened the door, her gaze locked with Russell's, and she stood statue still, warm all over in spite of the crisp, winter chill.

"Ah, Suzy." His voice settled over her like a callused caress, as his green eyes scanned her with masculine appreciation.

"It's Susannah," she reminded him again, but the tone of her voice hadn't been firm or reprimanding. Instead, it held a husky, sultry edge.

"You look great. Stunning."

That wasn't the image she'd wanted to portray, but she had to admit his expression and comments were flattering. "Thank you."

Russell didn't look half-bad himself. Dressed in formal Western attire—black boots and slacks, crisp white shirt, red-and-black bolo tie and a Stetson—he had a handsome cowboy appeal. And for a moment, she found it impossible to speak, difficult to move.

He flashed her a brilliant smile, much like the one he wore when, after scoring the tie-breaking free throw that sent the Rumor Rangers to the league playoffs, his teammates had scooped him onto their shoulders and paraded him through the gym.

"Lucky me," he said. "The rest of the men at the party are going to have a hard time keeping their eyes off you."

Susannah had half a notion to bop him on the head with a pompom, if she'd had one readily available. Russell might think of the Christmas party as a social function, but as far as she was concerned, her attendance was strictly business. "Maybe I should change clothes and put my hair up."

"Don't you dare." He cupped her jaw and brushed a thumb across her cheek.

She swallowed, unable to think of anything to say, anything that would counteract the almost palpable attraction zapping between them as they hung in the silence like two dangling live wires.

"Do you have a jacket?" he asked.

Still afraid the words would stick in her throat, she nodded, then took the black wool coat she'd hung on the antique rack that decorated the entry.

"Allow me." He took the garment from her hands and held it open. As she turned, he slipped it over her shoulders, enveloping her in a warmth of sensual awareness.

Bad idea, she reprimanded herself. *Agreeing to*

*ride to the party with Russell had been just plain
stupid.*

"My Range Rover is still in the shop, since the
mechanic has been waiting on some parts. So I
brought one of my other cars."

"Other cars? How many do you have?"

"More than most folks, I guess. When my
grandpa died, he willed me his three vintage cars
and a truck. I've bought and traded over the years,
but have added quite a few to my collection of
keepers."

Russell's grandfather, Stratton's daddy, had kept
some classic cars, as a hobby of sorts. As a teen,
Russell had appreciated the collection more than the
other grandkids, and she supposed that's why the
old man had given them to him.

Did Russell still have the 1957 Chevy? The car
they'd taken out to the lake? The car in which he'd
proposed, and she'd lovingly given him her virginity?

She refused to reveal her curiosity, afraid he'd
recall the significance of the car and suspect the
poignancy of her memory.

He escorted her onto the porch and waited while
she locked the front door. Then he took her hand
and led her to the driveway, where a white classic
T-Bird was parked.

"I don't remember this one," she said, as he opened the passenger door, revealing a sharp, red interior that looked brand-new.

"I bought it last year at a car show in Billings."

"It's gorgeous." Susannah slipped into the passenger seat. "What year is it?"

"Fifty-seven—a good year for cars."

Again she wondered about the Chevy, but kept her thoughts to herself.

The sooner she forgot what happened in the back seat of his grandpa's old car, the better. She had no intention of revisiting the past, even though she thought Russell might be hell-bent on taking her there.

Carolyn Kingsley thrived as a hostess, which was one reason Russell liked to hold the MonMart Christmas party at the Kingsley ranch house, a châteaulike log structure his East Coast born and bred mother had decorated to perfection. And this year, she'd outdone herself with the holiday decorations.

They drove through the massive iron gates that had been left open for the MonMart employees. White flickering lights glistened in the trees that lined the long driveway, and the house stood in silent welcome, blazing with Christmas splendor. The only thing missing was a thick blanket of snow.

Russell wondered whether Mother Nature would do her part and ensure a White Christmas, in spite of the unusually mild winter that had been forecast.

His father had insisted upon hiring valets to park cars this year. Following the last party, a couple of stock clerks had backed into each other after imbibing more than their share of holiday cheer—a seemingly innocent rum, ice-cream and eggnog concoction Stratton insisted was a Kingsley Christmas tradition.

The valets, members of the Rumor High basketball team, had been instructed to not only park cars, but to drive home anyone who'd had a few too many.

Dustin Evans, a tall, lanky kid who played center, opened Russell's door. ''Good evening, Mr. Kingsley.''

Russell smiled. ''I appreciate the team helping out like this.''

''And we appreciate the work, sir. The money we earn tonight will take us over the top.''

''That's great,'' Russell said, shaking the boy's hand. ''I'm glad you've reached your goal.''

The team had worked all summer long, and on weekends during the fall semester, to earn the money for a camp run by retired NBA players.

A Rumor High alumni who had once played basketball, Russell had considered donating the money himself, but decided the team spirit instilled by working together would be good for the boys. Maybe even spur them on to a league championship.

His brother Reed had been the athletic superstar of the family, but Russell still recalled the thrill of the game, the rush after sinking a winning shot. A congratulatory hug and kiss from his favorite cheerleader.

As a towheaded kid opened the passenger door, allowing Suzy to slide out, Russell circled the car and took her hand. He led her up the steps and through the entry, where clusters of MonMart employees chatted with each other.

Russell and Suzy smiled, and their steps slowed as they greeted those who'd gathered near the twelve-foot Christmas tree in the spacious living room. More than a few drank his father's holiday grog.

"I see my dad is manning his station." Russell nodded toward the massive, carved-oak bar, where Stratton stood near a crystal punch bowl filled to the brim with his white frothy specialty prominently displayed on a linen-covered serving table.

Jim Taylor and Sam Willett, department managers, chuckled at a private joke, while they waited for Stratton to sprinkle a dash of nutmeg on the top of each glass.

"I like his vest," Suzy said, smiling and indicating the expensive, red silky material that covered his father's chest and stuck out like a beacon. "In fact, he looks a bit like Santa."

Russell chuckled. "He really gets into the Christmas spirit, doesn't he? Come on, I want you to try his holiday cheer."

He expected her to put up a fight, to gripe about calories or fat or cholesterol, but she didn't.

"I'd love some. That ice-cream concoction has been the talk of the store ever since I arrived. I'm not leaving without a taste."

"Then let's head that way," Russell said, although moving through the festive crowd wasn't easy.

He made a point of greeting the two women who ran the layaway department, introducing Suzy as Ms. McCord.

"I've been meaning to ask for a tour of your department," Suzy said. "More than one person has told me you two should be commended."

Both women would see an extra check along with their Christmas bonus, but Russell kept that surprise to himself.

"Thank you for being team players," he told the

women. "I really appreciate your hard work, particularly during the busiest shopping days of the year."

The employees beamed with satisfaction, obviously pleased their efforts had been noticed.

Russell excused himself and Suzy, again trying to make his way to the punch bowl.

He managed only three steps when Tom O'Malley, the produce manager, slapped a hand on his back. "Great party, Mr. Kingsley."

"Thanks, Tom," Russell said. "I'm glad you're having a good time."

"Always!" the heavyset, rosy-cheeked Irishman said.

Russell couldn't help but grin when he recalled last St. Patrick's Day. The MonMart produce manager had not only dressed the part, he'd gone so far as to dye his wheat-colored hair a lucky shade of emerald green.

When Tom spotted a friend in the entry, he left Russell and Suzy with a clear path to the punch bowl.

"Mr. Kingsley?" a familiar voice asked.

Russell turned to see Sheree, his teen angel, wearing a bright-eyed smile. He fought the urge to say, "Look who's here" to Suzy. This pretty young teen wasn't their daughter Isabelle, and she and Suzy clearly didn't know each other.

"I sure appreciate you getting me the cashier job." Sheree's smile broadened, revealing two dimples that validated her sincerity. "And the schedule they gave me is perfect. I can work twenty hours without my job interfering with any of my classes at school."

"I'm glad everything worked out," Russell said. He smiled at the girl, who vaguely reminded him of a young Suzy, then added, "Sheree, I'd like to introduce you to Susannah McCord, a business consultant, but also an old high school friend."

"It's nice to meet you." Sheree took the hand Suzy offered in greeting.

"Sheree was the candy striper who played a big part in my recovery," Russell told Suzy, as he placed a gentle hand on the teenager's shoulder. "She's also a poet."

"Really?" Suzy said. "I used to write poetry, too, although I haven't taken time since law school."

"I know how it is to be too busy to write," Sheree said. "My time is taken up with homework, my job and clubs."

"That sounds like my high school days," Suzy

said, eyes glistening with a vivacious sparkle Russell hadn't seen since his senior year.

Suzy had been very social as a teenager, and Russell hoped Sheree would touch the old Suzy, make her remember how things used to be. As he watched, the two redheads warmed to each other and slipped easily into a conversation of pep assemblies, team spirit and homecoming, much like his old Suzy would have done, bolstering him with a renewed sense of hope.

"What clubs do you belong to?" Suzy asked the teen.

"I'm in both Health Careers and Future Teachers, which is probably weird, since I can't very well be a school teacher and a doctor." Sheree shrugged her shoulders. "But I really enjoy working with people, helping them, and I can't decide which field I'd rather work in."

"I'm sure you'll choose just the right career," Suzy said. "Have you considered which college you'll attend?"

"Probably the junior college in Whitehorn. Money is pretty tight right now."

"You might check into financial aid," Suzy suggested.

"I will. But I'm not sure how long I'll have to help out at home. My mom had an accident on the way to work. She ruptured her spleen and had complications after surgery. Her doctor doesn't know when she'll be released to go back to work.''

Sheree was another MonMart employee who would find a second check, along with her bonus. And as far as Russell was concerned, financing college would be the least of her problems. He intended to make sure she could attend any school she wanted.

As the two redheads began to chat about poets they enjoyed, Russell slipped off to get Suzy a cup of Stratton's grog. He had every intention of seeing Ms. McCord loosen up tonight, even if it meant plying her with a bit of alcohol to make sure the festive, holiday spirit touched her heart and allowed him access.

The MonMart Christmas party could only be labeled a success, as far as Susannah was concerned. Laughter, smiles and happy chatter filled the house, convincing her that everyone was having a good time.

The employees, as well as their spouses or significant others, feasted on the impressive buffet Carolyn Kingsley had planned in classic Martha Stewart–style.

Soon, music filled the house, and couples made

their way to the dance floor the Kingsleys had
rented for the occasion. The band played a mix of
country and light rock, but it seemed to Susannah,
they played more nostalgic sets as the evening progressed.

Had love songs from the eighties been Russell's
idea? Or had the warm, festive occasion merely
brought her memories to the forefront?

"Can I have this dance?" Russell stood before
her, a hopeful grin on his angular face.

He'd been a handsome teenager, but she never
would have guessed how the years would enhance
his rugged good looks. It took all she had not to
gape at him like a gawky, enamored preadolescent.

When he reached out a hand, she allowed him to
lead her to the dance floor and pull her into an
intimate embrace. She fell easily into his arms, into
his lead, as the years seemed to slowly peel away,
leaving the past and present blurred.

Or maybe it was Stratton's holiday cheer. The
rum-laced drink packed a powerful zing, and Susannah found herself leaning closer to Russell. For
support, she told herself, but maybe it was just her
body's desire to mold to his familiar form, to feel
his arms wrap around her, stroke her back and pull
her close.

They swayed to the slow, sensual beat of a love

song, straight from the old days—a song they'd danced to on prom night. And in spite of her resolve, she found herself hurtling into the past.

She closed her eyes, falling into the gentle beat of a love song that had been one of her favorites. The original band had been Air Supply, and Susannah found her own air supply infiltrated by Russell's musky, cowboy scent.

"Remember this song?" Russell asked.

The song? "Yes." But she remembered a whole lot more than the heart-stirring words and gentle beat. She remembered an embrace that was all too familiar, the easy way their bodies melded together. How could she not?

There were some things a body and heart didn't ever forget.

Chapter 5

Susannah and Russell waited until the last guest had gone home, then climbed into the T-Bird for the drive back to her place.

It was well after midnight, and although the winter air was crisp and cold, the sky was clear, and a full, silvery moon reigned over a million twinkling stars.

Susannah peered through the windshield, marveling at each sparkle of diamondlike clarity. "I'd forgotten how pretty a Montana sky could be."

"You always could spot more constellations than a seasoned boy scout leader." Russell chuckled, slipped the key into the ignition and flipped the switch.

Nothing happened.

She watched as he tried again, but the engine didn't even choke or whimper in response.

Blowing out a sigh, he tossed her a sheepish grin. "Sorry about that. I'd been having trouble with the starter, but was sure I'd fixed it."

Funny, but the car not starting didn't seem to bother her as it should have. For some reason, Susannah wasn't quite ready for the evening to end.

Maybe it was the magic of a clear winter night that shot her full of vitality. Or it could be the surreal, nostalgic mood that settled over her in Russell's presence.

"Sounds like the battery needs a jump-start," she said.

"It's a new battery." Russell leaned back in his seat. "How do you feel about walking? My place isn't far, and I can use another car to take you home."

Walking? In the cool, night air? Under a canopy of starlight? "Sure. I'm up for a midnight adventure."

Russell climbed from the car and opened the passenger door, allowing Susannah to slip out of her seat. Before closing the door, he reached into the glove box and pulled out a flashlight. "Then let the adventure begin."

As they began the trek to Russell's house, Susannah drew her jacket close and studied the night sky. "Look at that moon. It's so bright, I'll bet we don't even need the flashlight."

"Probably not, but I like to be prepared."

So did Susannah. She'd always made an effort to keep her options open. At least, that had been her game plan, after finding herself pregnant and alone.

"Since the accident, I want to be ready for the unexpected," Russell said.

"From what I hear, there wasn't anything you could have done to prevent it."

"No. But since then, I've reevaluated my life. Facing my mortality did something to me."

She looked at him, realizing he didn't mean a few yellowed bruises or a scab or two. The effect he was talking about had been psychological. Or spiritual.

"The accident gave me a new outlook and made me reconsider some of my past decisions."

She wondered if he was talking about the choice he'd made after Stratton's ultimatum, but kept her curiosity at bay. In a way, she'd had her own recent epiphany. "Something similar happened to me on my thirty-fifth birthday. I had been so busy building a career, that I realized life was passing me by.''

''Is that why you moved back to Rumor?''

''In a way, I suppose it was.'' For the first time in her life, Susannah's focus had shifted to the daughter she would adopt and the home she intended to provide. She, too, had reevaluated her life. She'd considered her friendships, as well as the relationship she'd had with her mother, a woman who blamed her fatherless daughter for all of life's disappointments.

Four years ago, the bitter woman passed away in Alaska. And although she and Suzy had been estranged for years, she'd willed her daughter the small house in which they once lived.

Growing up in Rumor hadn't been especially happy, but the other memories—childhood friendships, a quaint and intimate small-town atmosphere, had called Susannah home. She wasn't sure whether Russell would understand. Lord knew some of her colleagues and clients in California hadn't. ''I wanted to settle in a small town, and this is the one that came to mind.''

She suspected he was waiting for her to go on, but talking about life and family to the man she'd once hoped to marry was tough. Instead, she preferred to relish the sound of their feet on the pavement, the occasional feel of his shoulder against hers, the faint scent of leather and musk.

If she closed her eyes, she could almost imagine being a teenager again. A teenager in love.

Russell had a feeling the old Suzy was just within reach, but he struggled not to take her hand or to pull her close and slip an arm around her.

A couple of times their shoulders had brushed, and he'd wanted to slow her steps, make her face the reality of what he knew she must be feeling.

"Do you ever think about having kids?" he asked, hoping to encourage more of her self-disclosure. "You know, raise a family?"

She paused as though contemplating the question, but he wasn't sure if that was because the thought hadn't crossed her mind, or if she just didn't want to share it with him.

"Yes," she said. "I want a child."

She wanted a child. How about a husband? he wanted to ask. Or were a child and husband connected, like peanut butter and jelly, birthday cake and ice cream?

"When I was in the coma, I had a dream, although it was so vivid, so lifelike that it seemed real."

She didn't say anything, so he continued. "You

came back to Rumor with a sixteen-year-old daughter, a pretty redhead named Isabelle.''

This time, her steps slowed. "Isabelle?"

"Yes." He couldn't help but notice her interest. It was, he decided, more evidence that Destiny had provoked his dream.

"We'd talked about naming our daughter Isabelle, don't you remember?"

Vaguely, he supposed.

"You came over to my house one Saturday afternoon, and we watched an old black-and white movie. I don't remember the name anymore or who starred in it, but Isabelle was one of the characters."

He didn't remember that particular movie, either. But he liked the fact that Isabelle connected them somehow and couldn't help prodding her further. "I sometimes wonder what life would have been like if you and I had married. Had kids."

Again, her silence filled the night air, casting memories and tension in equal doses.

She blew out a soft sigh, her breath fogging in the still night air. "We almost had a child, Russell. And I think of the baby often, wondering what life would have been like, had I become a mother. But I don't include you or fantasies of family life in my thoughts. Seventeen years ago, you made it all too clear that I wasn't the woman for you."

Her words sucker punched him in the gut, and the tension that had bobbed in a sea of memories built to a tsunami crest that threatened to slap him to the ground.

Did he and Suzy have a daughter? A redheaded girl they should have named Isabelle and raised together?

He stopped and took her hand, pulling her face-to-face. "What do you mean, we almost had a child?"

Her blue eyes grew luminous, the lids heavy. "I was pregnant when I left Rumor."

Pregnant. With a daughter, no doubt. This time, Fate waved a sense of irony in Russell's face.

He placed his hands on Suzy's shoulders and gave her a firm but gentle squeeze. "What happened to our baby?"

Her agonized gaze sliced clear to his soul, and whatever words she held back threatened to wound him, too. Had she given the baby up for adoption? Or had she chosen to abort their baby? Sudden, unexpected grief rocked him to the core.

"I lost the baby, Russell." Her voice was soft, filled with pain, the depth of which made his chest ache.

He wrapped her in a bear hug and pulled her

close. "Oh, God, Suzy. I had no idea you were pregnant. I would have never let you go."

Susannah buried her face into the coarse wool of his jacket and closed her eyes, accepting his embrace yet knowing it wouldn't have helped, had he offered the same sympathy and support seventeen years ago.

She wouldn't have married him, not knowing how his father felt about her, because she would have always felt second best, a throwback in the gene pool.

And having a child out of wedlock would have brought either scorn or pity from the entire Rumor community. The baby would have been a bastard, like Susannah had always suspected she'd been. And that wasn't a label she'd slap on a child of hers.

"You shouldn't have had to go through that alone."

She knew he meant the loss of their baby and accepted his sympathy, appreciating the fact that he at least had some kind of idea how terrible it had been. How difficult it had been to face the loss of their baby and an emergency surgery on her own. But for some reason, she wanted to absolve him from guilt. "My aunt Hazel was there for me. I wasn't alone."

"That's not the same."

It wasn't. She'd screamed Russell's name in the hospital, and cried tears of grief for both their child and their star-crossed love as she was wheeled into surgery. But the past was over.

Russell slipped an arm around her and pulled her close. "I can't fix what happened between us. And a lot of time has passed us by. But what we had— what I think we can still have—is strong. Special. I've always thought of you as my soul mate. Maybe even more so now that you're back."

Did soul mates let each other walk away for seventeen years? She doubted it. But she had to admit there was a strong pull between her and Russell, something more than lust or love that drew her to him. As it did now. But she fought the desire to reach out to him, to accept the olive branch he'd offered, to take hold of his hand and hang on tight.

She tucked her hands into the pockets of her coat and balled her fingers into fists.

A porch light burned up ahead, and before the conversation grew too heavy—too laden with guilt and pain, regrets and thwarted dreams—they reached the driveway of Russell's house.

"Will you come inside?"

She nodded. There was so much more that

needed to be said, that needed to be shared, although she didn't think now was the time.

He opened the door, allowing her to enter his home, decorated in a rustic blend of nature and craftsmanship. The house had a masculine appeal, she supposed, with its dark wood, stone and glass.

The Spanish-tiled entry led to a spacious living room with high ceilings and a rugged stone fireplace. She couldn't help but examine the interior, the leather upholstered furniture and more than a few interesting pieces of cowboy art.

She'd studied some interior design books lately, due to her interest in redecorating her house, and truly believed Russell's home held a manly charm.

She spotted a wilted orchid on the coffee table. "You should probably get a new plant."

He followed her gaze, then shook his head. "No way. That's the orchid you brought…I mean, you sent to me when I was in the hospital."

"But it's dying."

"I'm going to revive it," he said simply.

Good luck, she wanted to tell him. That orchid had seen better days.

She scanned the living room until her eyes lit on a godawful lamp made out of a deer antler. It looked like the kind of thing found on the bargain table at a Jeff Foxworthy family garage sale.

In spite of her best efforts, a giggle slipped out and she couldn't help commenting. "Where did you get that tacky thing?"

Russell followed Suzy's gaze and laughed, not at all surprised she'd found the handcrafted lamp disagreeable. "My brother Reed gave that to me as a housewarming joke."

She stepped closer to the end table that supported the lamp and squiggled her nose like a teenage girl looking into a mold-infested petri dish during biology class. "Do you give all of your gag gifts a place of honor?"

"Just this one." Russell crossed his arms and smiled, unable to mask a sense of masculine pride. "The joke turned into a bet."

She arched an auburn brow. "What kind of a bet?"

"Reed bet me a thousand dollars that some woman would talk me into stuffing it in the attic before New Year's Day."

Susannah laughed, the lilt of her voice causing his heart to react in adolescent pleasure. "Well, it looks like you've nearly won. You only have two weeks to go."

"Reed paid up three and a half years ago, but the lamp kind of grew on me. It has a certain amount of charm, don't you think?"

She stepped closer, as though trying to find some kind of merit in the ugly light fixture. "Nope. No charm whatsoever."

He laughed again. She was right, but the lamp would stay put. It was a guy-thing, he supposed, a way of proving a woman couldn't make Russell do anything he wasn't inclined to do. "Want something to drink? Coffee? Tea? Hot cocoa?"

"No, thanks," she said. "I probably should get going. I've got to paint the spare bedroom tomorrow."

"I heard that you plan to do most of your remodeling by yourself." It surprised him a bit, since he figured she could well afford an army of decorators and handymen.

She nodded. "Especially my old bedroom. I'm making it into a nursery."

Her words slammed into his chest, nearly spinning him around. "You're pregnant?"

"No."

A sense of relief settled over him, although he wasn't entirely sure why. He supposed it was because he should be the one to father her baby.

"I'm adopting a little girl." She said it as a matter of fact, as though she'd given it a great deal of thought.

"Why?" he asked, unable to hide his surprise. "Can't you have a baby of your own?"

"I had a tubal pregnancy, which means the baby grew in the fallopian tube, instead of the uterus. The tube burst, and I had emergency surgery. I can still conceive, or so the doctors have said. But I only have one remaining ovary and tube. And," she said, blowing out a weary sigh, "at my age—"

"You're not too old to have a baby. That thirty-fifth birthday of yours must have been a psychological humdinger."

"I don't have a prospective husband, and since romantic relationships take time to develop, my chances of conception are passing me by. Besides," she said, brightening. "There's a little girl in China just waiting for a mom like me."

There was a little girl waiting for her—their daughter Isabelle. Suzy didn't need to adopt a baby. They could have a child of their own—maybe two or three.

Heck, he'd love to have a little Russell Kingsley running around. Of course, he wouldn't push the issue now. It was enough that she was feeling maternal and open to starting a family.

He cupped her jaw and brushed a thumb across the silky skin of her cheek. "You're going to make one heck of a mom, Suzy."

She opened her mouth, as if to object, although he wasn't sure to what. To the high school nickname he insisted upon calling her? Or to his touch?

Her eyes snagged his, pulling them into their blue crystal depths. "Thank you."

Maybe somewhere along the way—from Rumor to Monterey, or from her little house to the Kingsley estate, or along the midnight walk to Russell's place—the old Suzy had surfaced. Or so he hoped.

He brushed a kiss upon her brow and savored her familiar springtime scent. She wore the same French perfume he'd once given her, the same orchid-laced scent that had haunted him for years— even while comatose.

Suzy might want him to think she'd forgotten how things used to be, that the past was long gone. But he didn't buy it. He had a suspicion that she held on to some of the memories, just like he had. The only difference was, he knew how things would play out. Destiny had revealed itself in his dream.

"Let's take time to get to know each other better, Suzy. We might find that what we once had is still there."

"We can't go back, Russell. What we had is in the past." But skepticism crept into her eyes, and her gaze begged him to convince her otherwise.

''Tell me that you don't feel something for me. Tell me that kiss we shared in Monterey didn't have the same heat, the same passion as before.''

''I'd be lying.''

''Then stay here tonight. Let's make love for old time's sake.''

''And then what?'' she asked, her eyes searching his for an answer he didn't have.

''I don't know. Take one day at a time?'' How did he explain his belief that Fate meant for them to be together, that they were soul mates or maybe something better than that? That he hoped taking things day by day would lead to forever?

He'd hurt her years ago, and although they both understood how it had happened, they'd changed along the way. Changed for the better, he hoped. Grown stronger and wiser, a man and woman who would appreciate each other more than before.

And why would it not be better? God knew the passion was still there and, he suspected, blazing hotter than before.

He watched the emotions sweep her face, saw her struggle with the decision. He lifted her chin and brushed her lips with his, sweeping them into the past, into the desire that once threatened to consume them both.

This is crazy, Susannah told herself. But crazy as

it was, she couldn't stop the sensual assault, the mindless desire to feel him inside of her again.

And she didn't want it to stop.

It had been a long time since she'd fallen under Russell's spell, a long time since she'd allowed herself to be swept away by desire. She'd had a few other men in her life, but none of them had ever held the same power over her as Russell once had.

As Russell still did.

She opened her mouth, allowing his tongue to claim hers, as she leaned into him, felt his arousal and shared her own with him.

His hands roamed her back, caressed her derriere and pulled her flush against his erection, enflaming her desire. She couldn't get enough of his touch, his scent. She was on fire for her old lover. And nothing seemed to matter—nothing except making love to him.

She'd had a couple of drinks earlier this evening, but it wasn't the alcohol that warmed her blood, that caused her to whimper into his mouth as his hand sought her breast. It was the gentleman cowboy who held her captive with his touch, his stroke, his kiss.

His mouth broke free of hers, only to blaze along her jaw, her neck, her throat and then back again.

He traced her ear with the tip of his tongue, driving her wild with need.

"I've missed you, Suzy," he whispered in a husky voice laden with desire.

And she'd missed him, too. Missed his hardened body, his skillful caress.

"Come with me. To my bed." His eyes, hooded with passion, begged her to give in to the overwhelming temptation. "Please."

Just this once.

She took his hand, brought it up to her mouth, and brushed a kiss across his knuckles. "I may be sorry for this tomorrow."

"I won't let you be sorry." Then he scooped her into his arms and carried her to his room.

He let her slowly slide down the front of him, until she stood beside his bed. For a moment, they stared, caught in a sensual time warp. Then he cupped her cheeks and brushed an angel-soft kiss across her lips. "You have no idea how badly I want you."

Oh, yes she did. And she wanted him, too. Far more than she cared to admit. So she kept quiet, waited as he unzipped the back of her dress and gently pushed the fabric from her shoulders, revealing a black lace bra.

He blew out an appreciative sigh, then unhooked

the front clasp and slipped a hand inside, cupping her breast and sending her pulse skyrocketing. Her breath caught, as he thumbed her nipple, and she closed her eyes, wondering if her knees would buckle while he expertly took his time, loving her with an easy hand.

Russell didn't know if he could hold back any longer. He knew he should make love to Suzy—slowly—taking his time, savoring each stroke, each taste.

But after seventeen years, the desire to bury himself in her sweetness was too great. Too strong. Yet he feared it was more than lust and passion assaulting his patience.

On prom night, love had swelled in his heart. And now, so many years later, his chest felt like it might burst.

It would be his undoing, if he didn't take her and make her his—and not just for tonight.

Her springtime scent snaked its way into his memories, into his heart. Some things didn't change. Thank goodness. And holding Suzy in his arms only enhanced his memory, strengthened his need.

She seemed to be caught up in the same passionate intensity, because she began to struggle with the buttons of his shirt. He didn't care if she ripped the damn thing off; he wanted to feel her skin to skin.

How they managed to divest themselves of clothing, Russell couldn't be sure. But within moments, they lay on his bed, caught in the throes of passion, oblivious to anything except pleasing each other.

In a sense, Russell didn't give a damn about anything but being inside of her, where he belonged. Yet he paused long enough to reach for the condoms he kept in the drawer of his nightstand.

There would come a time when they wouldn't need contraception, when they would welcome pregnancy. But for now, it was enough that she let him love her again.

When he'd protected them both, Suzy guided his entry.

"It's been too damn long," Russell said. Then he took what should have been his for the past seventeen years.

And as he increased the tempo, she arched up, receiving his thrusts until they reached a mind-spinning, breath-catching climax. He could have sworn he saw a burst of starlight, a fireworks display that wouldn't quit. And as they lay, caught up in what they'd shared, relishing each wave of pleasure, he was too overcome to speak.

Susannah lay wrapped in Russell's arms, a powerful climax still contracting in pleasure and the scent of their lovemaking swirling around them.

He said she wouldn't be sorry. And she wasn't. Not for what they'd done, what they'd shared.

But was he sorry? Was he pleased? Or was he completely sated and as caught up in the heady afterglow as she?

She wasn't about to ask the proverbial was-it-good-for-you? Wasn't about to let her insecurities rise. Because in spite of her best intentions, a small voice surfaced, whispering that she still might not be good enough for Russell Kingsley.

But she struck at the voice, quieting it with reason rather than emotion. Susannah had come a long way since her questionable birth. And she'd proven herself many times over.

As Russell rolled to the side, he took her with him, holding her close and running a hand along her hip. "I hope you're up for a marathon night."

"What do you mean?"

"I've only begun making up for the lost years." Then he kissed the tip of her nose, his eyes glazed with sincerity. "And I'm not sure that one night with you will be enough."

It *had* been good for him. Her heart did a little flip-flop, and she shot him a wobbly smile. "Let's see how we feel in the morning."

''Fair enough.'' Then he kissed her again, letting her know his passion hadn't begun to be quenched.

Of course, that didn't really surprise her, since her desire for him hadn't ebbed in the least.

But morning wasn't far off.

And she hoped they wouldn't wake in a flood of regret.

Chapter 6

Daylight seeped through the bedroom blinds, waking Susannah from a second nearly sleepless night, this one spent in her own bedroom.

She tried to focus on the faded wallpaper that needed to be removed, the nail holes that needed to be puttied, the blinds that needed to be replaced. But it was impossible not to think of the man lying next to her.

Russell held her close, one arm under her head, the other draped across her breast. Making love to her high school sweetheart had been wildly intoxicating, the kind of pleasure that could become habit-forming if one wasn't careful.

It wasn't that Susannah regretted their joining, but she had hoped it would get Russell out of her system.

Unfortunately, once hadn't been enough. And Friday night had merged with Saturday. The next thing she knew, they'd spent the weekend making sensual memories together.

As she rested her back against his chest, her bottom nestled in his lap, she felt him stirring, coming to life. A smile tugged at her lips. Apparently, *three* nights of lovemaking hadn't been enough.

"Good morning." He nuzzled her cheek and ran a hand possessively over her hip. "Sleep well?"

"Not really, but for some reason, I feel pleasantly rested." She arched and stretched. "And that's a good thing, especially with this being Monday morning and a work day."

Russell brushed her hair aside and kissed her shoulder. "Let's call in sick."

"No can do," Susannah said, pulling free from his embrace and climbing from bed. "Reality has set in, Mr. Kingsley."

He grumbled, but threw off the covers and swung his feet to the floor. "What we shared was pretty darn real."

She grabbed her robe from the floral chaise that

had once graced her California bedroom. "I agree."

The sex was great. That much was a given, yet neither of them had discussed the future, and the weekend had passed without a solid commitment. Of course, that was all right with Susannah. She wasn't entirely sure what she and Russell had embarked upon. An affair, maybe. A trial run, so to speak. And she had no idea where they'd go from here.

He'd suggested they take things one day at a time, and she supposed that's what they were doing. But as they went to work this morning, they would take separate cars—something she would insist upon. Because once they drove onto MonMart property, their relationship was back to business.

Susannah wouldn't have it any other way.

She had never liked being the subject of gossip. And she could imagine the whispers of the townsfolk. *Little Suzy McCord returned to snag wealthy Russell Kingsley as her husband.*

While she stood before the linen closet, reaching for a towel and hunting for a bar of soap that was more appropriate for a man than the lavender bath gel she used, he placed a hand upon her shoulder. "Shower with me."

"No. I think it would be a better idea if we start

practicing the Monday morning separation.'' She handed him a white Turkish towel and a bar of glycerin face soap, which she hoped had a manly scent. ''You go first, and I'll start the coffee.''

''You're a hard taskmaster, Ms. McCord.'' He flashed her a smile, took the towel and soap she offered, and padded down the hall to the shower.

When he closed the bathroom door, she went to the kitchen and, rather than starting the coffee, plopped onto a chair and blew out a ragged sigh.

Had she made a mistake in allowing their relationship to get intimate when things were still so cloudy between them?

A lot had happened in seventeen years. She and Russell had both changed, and in spite of his efforts to remind her of the way things used to be, they were no longer teenagers. And they no longer knew each other. Not really.

Just because they'd once been lovers and had recently wandered down the same lover's path didn't mean that their relationship—or whatever it was— would last.

And to top it off, Susannah had a child to consider. Her child. The little girl in China who was waiting for a loving home.

Slow down, she admonished herself. Hand Russell a cup of coffee, then send him on his way. The sooner he went, the better. She had a lot to think about.

Yet she couldn't help wondering what he thought about the surreal lover's weekend they'd spent. What were his intentions? How did he feel about things?

Meanwhile, down the hall, Russell stood under the pulsing shower, letting the water work his muscles, clear his mind.

Making love to Suzy had been better than he'd imagined in his coma-enhanced dream or even in his memories.

It was impossible not to believe that Fate meant them to be together. Of course, he didn't think Suzy was convinced yet, but that was okay. He'd take things slow and easy, give her time to think about things. Get to know him better, if that's what she wanted.

And even though he felt like shouting his happiness from the snowy rooftops of Rumor, he'd agree to keep their relationship quiet—for the time being.

Hell, he could slip into a formal, business mode at work, but he had every intention of spending his nights locked in Suzy's arms.

He turned off the faucet, climbed from the shower and snatched the towel from a wiggly rack that needed a molly or two. He'd pick some up in the hardware section and fix it for her tonight.

Suzy's house was definitely ready for a remodel, and this bathroom needed to be modernized. Maybe he should suggest she get an estimate from Tag. His younger brother was a whiz at construction.

Russell reached for the shaving kit he'd brought over last evening. Would Suzy mind if he brought some personal items to keep here?

Slow down, he told himself. She hadn't actually mentioned anything about tonight. Or the future, for that matter. And if he'd learned anything, it was that the new Suzy didn't like being pushed.

Maybe all he needed to do was wait. Let Fate take things from here.

Susannah tried hard to focus on the work at hand, at the files spread upon her desk. But when the office door creaked and slowly swung open, she looked up.

A little girl with light-brown, shoulder-length hair stood in the doorway and studied Susannah with cocker-spaniel eyes.

Who was she? Had a customer's child wandered upstairs, sparking fear in the mother's heart? The girl couldn't be older than four or five.

"Hi, there," Susannah said, setting the report

she'd been working on to the side. "What's your name?"

The girl lifted her hand from the front pocket of a bright red jacket and gave a little wave. "Samantha Kingsley."

Tag's daughter, Susannah realized. He was the only Kingsley with a child.

"It's nice to meet you. I'm Susannah McCord."

The introduction seemed formal and lacking something, but she wasn't sure what else to say. *I'm a consultant working with MonMart? An old friend of the family? Your uncle's lover?*

None of the comments that came to mind rang true or were appropriate, so she let a further explanation die a merciful death.

"Do you keep candy in your desk drawer?" the child asked. "My grandpa does."

The thought of Stratton as a doting grandfather with a sweet tooth pleased Susannah, made the man seem real and likeable. Worthy of forgiveness.

In the past, she'd always thought of him as an opinionated, cigar-smoking, bourbon-drinking ruler of a dynasty. But apparently, Susannah and Russell weren't the only ones who had changed.

She smiled at the girl. "I'm afraid I don't keep candy in my desk."

In fact, the only thing other than the office supplies that sat in Susannah's drawer was a stress-relief ball and, if she was lucky, a sponge-flavored nonfat protein bar, neither of which sounded more appetizing than the other.

She actually wouldn't mind a candy break, especially with the bright-eyed moppet who had eased into her office. Children had such an interesting view of life. And Susannah couldn't wait to have a little girl of her own.

"Want some of my candies?" Samantha reached into her coat pocket and withdrew a bag of jelly beans. "I have a whole bunch because me and Grandpa are working on our colors."

Before Susannah knew it, the child had pulled up a chair and spread jelly beans across the desk, separating the candy into brightly colored piles.

"See? These ones are red. And these are yellow." She paused, glancing at Susannah with an impish grin. "Wanna see a trick Grandpa taught me?"

Susannah smiled. "Sure."

The child grabbed two black jelly beans, then swirled the chair around. When she swung back, she smiled, revealing two black front teeth. "It's funny, don't you think?"

In spite of herself, Susannah laughed. Stratton Kingsley had definitely mellowed over the years, and she imagined having a granddaughter like Samantha had touched his heart.

"But you can't tell Grandma," Samantha said, hazel eyes growing wide. "It's a secret 'cause she doesn't think black teeth are funny, and she got mad at Grandpa for doing it in front of me. But it's too late. I already learned how to make Bucky Beaver teeth."

Susannah smiled in spite of the urge to take an adult slant on the episode. She supposed every child deserved to be the apple of someone's eye. And clearly, Stratton and Carolyn Kingsley both loved their only grandchild, even if they had a difference of opinion on what was proper grandparent behavior.

But how could they not love Samantha? She was entertaining and sweet, reminding Susannah how much she yearned to have a child of her own. A daughter to love.

Up until Friday night, she had no reason to reconsider adopting a baby girl. But now that she and Russell had...

Now that she and Russell had what?

They'd spent an incredible weekend together, mostly in bed. But they hadn't made any kind of commitment. And Susannah wasn't sure she wanted one.

What would become of them now—after the lovemaking? Would they grow closer? Get married? Have a baby?

But what about the baby she would soon bring home? The little girl who needed her? Would Russell accept a child that wasn't his?

And what about Stratton? The patriarch had always been big on Kingsley bloodlines.

A knock sounded on the doorjamb, and Susannah looked up to see Russell's brother.

"Hi, Daddy!" Samantha smiled, revealing black-stained front teeth.

Susannah hoped the little girl didn't get in trouble for her Bucky Beaver impression. And considering the broad grin her tall, dark-haired father wore, it didn't appear likely.

"I hope she isn't bothering you," Tag said.

"Not at all." Susannah smiled at the man who'd grown taller than his older brothers by an inch or two. "Samantha and I are getting to know one another."

Tag looked at the candy-littered desktop and grinned, his eyes crinkling with mirth. "She likes to work on her colors."

Obviously, Susannah wasn't the only one pleased to see Stratton's soft spot for the child.

"Did Grandpa say he could baby-sit me today?" Samantha asked her daddy.

"No, Sammy. He has a dentist appointment in Whitehorn." Tag furrowed his brow and caught Susannah's eye. "A root canal."

"And Grandma can't watch me because it's Monday, and she has a board meeting, and then she has to get my Christmas present."

"Can I help?" Susannah asked, not at all sure she'd get a minute's worth of work finished, but not really caring. She figured the single dad could use some help.

"I hate to bother you," Tag said. "Besides, it's not critical today. I can take her with me. I just have a couple of estimates to make."

Susannah thought about encouraging him to leave Samantha with her. But the fact was, she had to draw up a proposal, and as delightful as the little girl was, they'd spend the entire day chatting and playing. "Who usually watches her for you?"

"It depends. I take her with me when I can, and my family helps out, but they're all pretty busy, and I can't always find someone to keep an eye on her." Tag leaned against the door. "I could sure use a good nursery school or at least a full-time sitter I can trust."

"It sounds to me like Rumor needs a child care facility."

"I hope someone opens one soon." Tag helped his daughter collect the piles of jelly beans. "Come on, honey. I've got an appointment, and you'll need to come with me."

Susannah told them both goodbye, then sat back in her chair. As soon as she brought her daughter home, she'd need to find child care, too. And Susannah would be as fussy as any parent, maybe even more so.

Her mom had to work two jobs in order to pay the mortgage on their house. And as a kid, Susannah had spent more than her share of time with child care providers, some of whom were kind and loving. Some of whom were not.

Rumor definitely needed a nursery school.

And Susannah was looking to start a business. Before she knew it, the germ of a wild idea began to sprout.

Yet what did she know about children's day care needs? Not a lot. But the more she tried to talk herself out of considering the half-baked scheme, the more it seemed possible. And practical.

If she actually owned the nursery school, ran it herself, she could spend quality time with her own daughter every day, watching her dark-haired little girl grow while supporting her family and providing a much needed service to the community.

And Susannah loved kids.

In spite of a compulsion to turn her seat toward the computer and click on the icon that would send her online and allow her to research the answers to a ton of questions, she returned her attention to the offer she and Russell intended to propose for the Eden Garden Farms purchase.

But soon, in the next few weeks, her job with MonMart would come to an end. And she would be free to open her own business—whatever she chose to do.

As Susannah walked through the MonMart doors on her way home, the rows of Christmas trees she'd passed for the last two weeks caught her eye.

She hadn't really celebrated Christmas in years, other than the annual holiday visits with Aunt Hazel and the office parties she'd practically been required to attend. Besides, she'd been too busy to haul a tree home and decorate it.

As she stopped to feel the green branches and smell the pine scent, something warm and wistful settled on her, and holiday traditions began to dance in her head like sugarplum fairies.

Next Christmas she would have a child.

And stockings on the mantel. Colorfully wrapped presents under the tree. A glass of milk and sugar cookies for Santa. Carrots for Rudolph. A nativity scene. They would attend the Christmas service at the Rumor Community Church, then come home to a turkey baking in the oven.

Susannah had planned to nest in Rumor, planned to make a home. And spending Christmas without a tree or a turkey seemed wrong. Out of whack.

She turned on her heel and returned to the crowded store, bumping past last minute shoppers until she reached the holiday display and found a box of lights. But the other decorations had been picked over.

Could she come up with another idea? Some clever way of decorating her tree until she had time to invest in just the right ornaments?

Last year, at the Walk of Lights, a holiday display sponsored by the Boys and Girls Club, she'd seen a lovely tree a florist had created with fresh flowers and gold garlands of ribbon. She checked her watch. Four-fifteen. How late did the florist stay open?

Twenty minutes later, a tree tied to the roof of her silver Mercedes, she turned on Main and pulled into a parking spot right in front of Jilly's Lilies, where an Open sign was still prominently displayed.

When she walked inside, a bell on the door alerted the florist of a customer's arrival, while a mix of floral scents worked its magic on all who entered. The twenty-something owner of the shop, Jilly Davis, looked up from her work and tossed out a pleasant smile.

From what Susannah understood, the attractive young woman had grown up in Rumor and had a home life similar to her own, or worse. And like Susannah, Jilly had managed to make good in spite of a crummy family background by purchasing her own business and holding her head high, an accomplishment Susannah found admirable.

"Merry Christmas." The slender brunette with vibrant brown eyes made her way from the worktable in the center of the room to the small counter in the front. "What can I do for you?"

"Well," Susannah said, tucking a strand of hair behind her ear, "I've decided to decorate my tree with fresh flowers. What do you suggest?"

A creative spark lit Jilly's eyes, telling Susannah her faith in the young woman was not misplaced.

Moments later, Susannah headed home, a tree on the roof of her car, and a back seat loaded with a variety of red flowers, gold ribbons, pinecones, plastic tubes to keep each stem watered and green floral tape and wires.

She'd almost hired Jilly to help her decorate, but realized she'd be cheating herself. Decorating a tree should be a family affair, a family tradition. And this year, she and Russell could...

She and Russell.

Was that where their relationship was headed? Toward wedding bells and happy-ever-after?

The thought of her and Russell having children, a family, caused her heart to pound, but not in a warm, nostalgic way.

It actually frightened her.

Russell's change of heart had crushed her years ago.

But it was different now. Wasn't it?

As she turned onto State Street, old feelings of insecurity reared their heads. Russell seemed eager to pursue a relationship with her, but how would he feel about the dark-haired daughter she would soon bring home? The little girl who needed a mother's love. Would he pull away then? Change his mind about her again? Decide she wasn't good enough to bear Kingsley heirs?

Dusting off her mental pompoms, she quickly rallied, reminding herself of all she'd accomplished, all she had become. She didn't need Russell Kingsley to make her happy. She'd survived his change of heart years ago and could do it again, if need be.

When she pulled into her driveway and spotted Russell's Range Rover, her tummy did a summersault.

She hadn't given him a key, hadn't even considered it, so she wasn't surprised to see him waiting in the driver's seat with the engine idling.

As soon as Suzy parked, Russell shut off the ignition and climbed from the car. "You should have told me you wanted a tree. I would have gotten it for you."

"We're keeping things low-key, remember?" She reached for one of several boxes in her back seat.

"Let me have that." He took the box from her hands.

"I'm not helpless." She nodded toward the back seat. "There's plenty for you to carry."

Russell peeked inside and scratched his head. "What are you doing with all these flowers?"

"Decorating my tree."

With flowers? He wondered whether that was some kind of California fad, then shrugged it off. As long as they could spend Christmas together, he didn't care how she decorated the tree.

Of course, they'd have to go by his folks' place

for Christmas dinner. He hadn't said anything to
his mother, but he was sure she wouldn't mind putting another china and crystal setting on the table.

Within no time, he and Suzy had the car un-
packed and the tree carried into the living room.

"Where do you want it?" he asked, branches
scratching against his face and tickling his nose.

She paused and scanned the room, then focused
on the corner by a bookcase that seemed too large
for the living room.

Funny, how the place seemed much the same, yet
different. But the Naugahyde couch that had graced
Suzy's house years ago and wheedled its way into
the throes of his comatose dream, was gone, replaced by a cream-colored leather sofa and designer
furniture. Suzy must have had one hell of a place
in California.

Still the walls needed fresh paint. And the carpet
was as ratty and threadbare as he remembered. She
might have aired the house out as best she could,
but he could still pick up the scent of stale cigarette
smoke, a lingering reminder of her grim-faced
mother.

He wondered why Mrs. McCord hadn't sold the
house when she moved to Alaska. Why she hadn't
rented it to anyone. It never had seemed like good

business sense to him, but then again, Suzy's mom had been a strange one.

Since Suzy could obviously afford to purchase a house or lot on Logan Street, in the better part of town, he wondered why she chose to live in the old house where she grew up. Maybe it was her way of reinventing herself. He knew better than to pry, so he held his curiosity at bay. But suffice it to say, the new Suzy confused him.

"Just put it right there," she said, turning to point at the living room window.

Good choice. He'd been afraid she would have him moving the bookcase around to make room for the tree.

It took a few minutes of twisting and turning, but he managed to get the tree placed with the right branches pointing out.

"My family usually gets together about two o'clock on Christmas Day," he said, hoping his invitation would please her. "I'd like you to go with me."

Her movements froze, and he realized she wasn't ready to meet his family in a Russell-and-Suzy-are-lovers way.

"I don't think that's a good idea. Not yet. I'm not up for a family holiday."

Well, he was up for it. "I wish you'd give it some thought."

"I've already got a lot to think about, Russell. And slipping into a Kingsley family Christmas photo isn't one of them." She was a bit more decisive and adamant than he expected.

He strode toward her and took a roll of gold ribbon from her hand. "I didn't mean to push, Suz. And I was serious about taking one day at a time."

"I'm still not sure that we haven't leaped feet first into a mire of quicksand, Russell."

He cupped her cheek and brushed a thumb across her silky skin. "Maybe after the first of the year, you'll feel better about renewing our relationship and better about getting to know my family."

"Maybe so," she said.

But her eyes told him she wasn't convinced.

Chapter 7

The former high school sweethearts continued their discreet love affair well into January, with no one the wiser. Or so it seemed.

In the past few weeks, Suzy had picked up several black-and-white classic movies at the library, a quiet evening activity they'd both enjoyed.

Russell and Suzy had just made popcorn and settled on his family room sofa in front of the widescreen television, ready to watch *Casablanca,* when the phone rang.

"Hello," Russell answered rather brusquely, not appreciating the interruption. The time he and Suzy stole to be together was priceless, especially since she still insisted upon keeping their relationship quiet, and he'd decided not to fight her on the issue.

"Russell, your father and I are having a small, family dinner party on Sunday evening, and we'd like you to come."

He slid a glance at Suzy, caught her gaze and smiled. "Sure, Mom. What time?"

"Cocktails at six and dinner at seven," his mother said. "Oh, and Russell, why don't you bring Susannah?"

His brows shot up. "Susannah?"

"A little bluebird told me you might be seeing her. And I just thought…well, it would be nice if you brought her to dinner, too." Carolyn Kingsley might be the epitome of all that was proper, but she had a Sherlock Holmes intuition that had always kept her three steps ahead of her children.

And Russell suspected his mother knew that he and Suzy had been spending more nights together than apart.

He'd yielded to Suzy's wish to keep things secret and not mentioned anything to his family. But he hadn't made any effort to be sly—like parking his car around the corner from her house, wearing black and slipping through the back door after dark. Nor had he suggested she hide her car in his garage.

As far as he was concerned, it was just as well that they'd been found out. Maybe now Suzy would agree to make their relationship a matter of public knowledge, maybe even agree to make things permanent with a diamond ring.

"I'll have to ask her and let you know, Mom."

"All right, dear. I'll see you tomorrow night."

"Bye." He hung up the telephone, then turned to Suzy. "My folks are having the family over for dinner, and they'd like me to bring you."

"Me?" She tensed, which surprised him. Had she really thought they'd kept some kind of secret in a town where the local newspaper was called *The Rumor Mill?*

Heck, they'd only spent a handful of nights apart in the past month, none of them his idea. "It looks like our secret is out, Suz."

"I don't know how." She worried her lip and shot him a suspicious frown. "Unless you told."

Russell slipped an arm around her shoulder, pulling her close, catching the scent of her floral shampoo. "Rumor is a small town. And whether you want to believe it or not, people have probably been watching us, wondering if we'd start things where we left off."

"But we've been so careful at work and around town." She furrowed her brow and nibbled on the edge of a fingernail, trying, it seemed, to figure out who'd spilled the beans.

"Would it be bad if people knew we cared about each other? You might be the only one in Rumor who would question whether we have a future together."

Was she?

Susannah doubted that Stratton Kingsley had totally forgotten her tainted blood. Sure, he'd been cordial and appreciative at the office. And respectful of her work on the Eden Garden Farms venture. But the words he'd said seventeen years ago had etched an indelible reminder in her brain.

Russell took her open hand, brushed his lips across her palm. "It's just a family dinner. No big deal."

"Let me think about it."

"Why?"

She'd asked herself that same question after spending Christmas afternoon alone. The holiday had never been that special to her, not after countless disappointments as a child. Susannah had been the only kid in elementary school who wasn't looking forward to Santa Claus, because the jolly fellow rarely stopped at her house.

And when he did, she might wake to find a shopping bag filled with new underwear and socks, which was a treat, she supposed, but not the same thing as a Barbie doll or a bicycle. And certainly not the kind of gift to mention at show-and-tell.

She was twelve when she realized that even though there weren't presents under a tree, her mother never failed to get new earrings, a watch or sweater near the holidays.

"A gift for myself," her mother would say. "Since your father bailed out, and I have to work two jobs, I deserve it. Don't you think?"

No, Christmas hadn't been particularly special growing up.

She supposed a person didn't miss what they never had. But for the first time, sitting near the blinking lights of her flower-decorated tree, smelling the aroma of a turkey breast baking in the oven and unable to call Aunt Hazel who'd died last year, Susannah had felt truly alone.

Yet she hadn't had any second thoughts about declining Russell's invitation to spend the holiday with his family. And she wanted to decline this dinner invitation, too.

But why?

Did she fear a confrontation from Stratton, even if it was only a raised eyebrow that indicated his disapproval of her contribution to the Kingsley gene pool?

Or was it because gracious Carolyn might take her under wing, offer kindness and benevolence as she would to the children in the Mexican orphanage she supported?

Susannah suspected the real reason might lie in the fact that she didn't have any idea where this relationship with Russell was going. That was also why she preferred a noncommittal love affair.

She blew out a sigh. A discreet, no-strings-attached relationship might be what her ego preferred, but it wasn't what she wanted for her daughter.

Her children?

The clock was ticking, and her next birthday was closing in on her, minimizing her chance to bear a child.

Their child?

Russell placed a hand on her denim-clad thigh and gave it a gentle squeeze. "Come on, Suz. You'll have a good time. I promise."

The earnestness of his request made her feel guilty for listening to her teenage insecurities. She wasn't the old Suzy anymore and didn't bear much likeness to the young girl in Rumor who wore hand-me-downs and never knew her dad. "Okay, Russell. I'll go to the family dinner with you."

He slipped his arms around her, embracing her with the soft brushed-cotton of his shirt, flooding her with his musky scent, bolstering her with his strength and support.

Yet instead of feeling completely at ease with the decision, she felt much like the wilted orchid that Russell insisted upon keeping as a centerpiece on the glass coffee table, yet she wasn't sure why. Probably because the old Suzy wasn't convinced she'd be accepted as part of the Kingsley family.

Some memories were ingrained in the heart.

And so were some old insecurities.

Sunday evening, Russell thumbed through a magazine while waiting for Suzy to come out of his master bathroom, where, over the past few visits, she'd gradually left her mark.

A pink toothbrush, deodorant and a lady's razor graced his medicine cabinet, and several bottles of pastel-colored, floral-scented lotions and creams feminized the marble countertops.

It felt damn good to walk into his house and smell her lingering scent, feel her presence.

She hadn't exactly moved in—not by a long shot—but her being here one night a week was a start. His relationship with Suzy was blossoming, even if the orchid she'd sent him wasn't.

Russell studied the withered flower, the drooping

stem. He wouldn't give up on either Suzy or the orchid.

As he continued to thumb through the magazine, reading by the muted light of the ugly deer antler lamp, a grin tugged at his lips. Suzy may not know it, but he'd be willing to move the ugly fixture to the attic if she asked him. But he doubted she'd suggest it.

For one reason, they spent far more nights at her house than his. Of course, that was probably because he had no qualms about dropping by her place—invited or not. And she'd been reluctant to have any of his family members see her car parked in his driveway.

Besides, she was too wrapped up in painting her house, tearing up carpet and laying down ceramic tile. She was turning into a cross between Martha Stewart and Tim the Tool Man. And he'd much rather she focus on making a home where they would both live and raise a family—the family they were destined to have.

He wished she'd feel more comfortable about their relationship. He couldn't think of anything better than making Suzy his wife and finishing what they'd started seventeen years ago in the back seat of his granddad's Chevy.

His granddad's Chevy. Russell's lip quirked into

a crooked smile. Maybe Suzy needed another nudge. Another reminder.

"I'm sorry to keep you waiting," she said, entering the living room. She wore a pair of black slacks and a cream-colored cashmere sweater. Casual, yet elegant.

In his coma-enhanced dream, she'd worn pink—like the prom dress he'd slowly peeled from her shoulders that night they parked under the moonlight at Lake Monet.

"I don't mind waiting," he said, meaning far more than the time it took for her to dress. Shoot, he'd waited too damn long to make things right as it was. But he wouldn't rush fate.

Instead of jumping up and grabbing the car keys, he relished her beauty and the things she did to his heart, his body. Like she did now, stirring his blood, making him want to postpone their leaving.

Her auburn hair curled around her shoulders in a loose, natural style. Shades of gold shimmered in the lamplight, drawing his attention, urging his fingers to twine in the silky strands.

He would never grow tired of looking at her—dressed to go out on the town or padding around the house in one of his shirts and a pair of silk panties. He might have thought he'd wait forever, but he was eager to make her his wife and he feared his patience would wear thin.

"Russell," she said, her head cocking to the side and her blue eyes glistening. "Why are you looking at me like that? It makes me think you want to stay home and cuddle."

"I do."

"But it's too late." She reached for her purse, which she'd placed on the recliner in front of the television. "Your mother already has the table set."

"I know." He took her hand. "I have something to show you. Come on. Let me help you with your coat."

"What do you want to show me?" she asked, slipping into the sleeves of her wool jacket.

He merely grinned, then led her outside and around the house, down the snow-lined stone pathway to the showroom garage he'd built to display his collection of hot rods, trucks and classic sedans.

Their feet crunched along the walk, until they reached the garage. He punched in the security code, and the electric door rose to allow them entrance.

He flipped on the light, then ushered her inside. Fifteen vehicles, all antiques or classics, lined up in sparkling vintage perfection.

"Oh, my," Suzy said, her mouth opening into a

kissable little o. "I knew you had a few old cars, but I didn't realize the extent of your collection."

He grinned, glad that she could understand his enthusiasm, his pride in the vehicles. He ushered her through the showroom garage, pointing out each car and what made it a classic. He stopped in front of the 1957 Chevy Belair, the car his granddad had willed to him. The car in which he'd proposed to her seventeen years ago. The car in which they'd first made love. "This one is my favorite."

Her steps froze, and it seemed that she was swept up in time, carted off to the place where memories were stored. But she didn't speak. Didn't utter a word.

Yet the memory of prom night and Lake Monet hovered around them, thick and heavy. Inviting a revisit.

"Let's take this car tonight," he suggested.

She still didn't speak, yet stepped forward, placed a hand softly on the glossy sheen of the turquoise paint, as though caressing the vehicle.

He opened the driver's door. "Why don't you slide in."

He expected her to say something, although he wasn't sure what, but she merely climbed into the car and waited.

Then without any further ado, he slid into the

driver's seat and started the engine. The pistons and rods came to life, purring their satisfaction at his choice of rides.

Russell fiddled with the radio dial, catching the station out of Billings that played soft rock and hits from the eighties. After turning on the heater, he backed out of the garage and headed toward the paved road that would lead them to the Kingsley ranch house.

He didn't encourage Suzy to speak, preferring to let the memories of steamed windows and hot kisses do the talking.

When they reached the ranch house where he'd grown up, he parked along his mother's now dormant flower garden, then reached across the seat and took Suzy's hand. "You're not nervous, are you?"

"Not really." She slid him a crooked grin. "I'm just not sure what they're expecting from me."

"They just expect you to be yourself." Russell threaded his fingers through hers. "Things have changed, darlin'."

"Isn't that my line?" she asked. "You're supposed to be spouting off about Destiny and Fate, aren't you?"

"Yep. Time may have passed and things may have changed, but I still believe we're meant to be together and raise a family." *Maybe even have a daughter named Isabelle someday.*

"Maybe so," she said, taking her hand from his. "Let's go inside before we stir up more curiosity than is necessary."

"Relax, Suz. I doubt my parents have given you and me much thought. And they're certainly not hovering around the window, watching to see when we drive up." He brushed a kiss across her lips, then climbed from the car and escorted her toward the house.

Russell was more than ready to let his family get to know the woman he hoped to marry, the woman with whom he planned to have children and spend the rest of his life. He just wished Suzy felt the same way, and it bothered him that she seemed so reluctant.

Nerves swarmed in Susannah's stomach like angry hornets desperate to find who or what had disturbed their nest. She should have taken an antacid. Or maybe had a glass of wine before leaving Russell's house.

Good grief, this was just a quiet family dinner, she reminded herself.

Yet it felt like much more than that to her.

As Russell led her to the front door, she gazed up at the sprawling Kingsley ranch house, a châteaulike log structure that was elegant, even with a wood and stone exterior. The building stood three stories high, with rooftops boasting steeples.

Inside the estate, Carolyn's East Coast charm had left its refined and tasteful mark.

Susannah had been here for the MonMart Christmas party, but with the throng of festive employees, it had been hard to really take in the graceful décor of the ranch. She'd seen enough to know that Carolyn favored a classy combination of cream and beige in her basic color scheme.

And now, Susannah would get a chance to see how the upper dyad of the Kingsléy family lived.

As they stepped into the marble-tiled entryway, Russell took her jacket and hung it in the coat closet before removing his own.

"Is that you, Russell?" Carolyn asked from the living room.

Could the woman recognize her firstborn son's footsteps in the entry? Or had she been peering through the light oak shutters, in spite of Russell's belief to the contrary?

"Yes, Mom. It's us."

Get a grip, Susannah told herself. This was just a casual family dinner party. No big deal. She quickly rallied, shaking off the worry and illogical apprehension.

They'd no more than entered the living room when tall, auburn-haired Carolyn greeted them. "I'm so glad you could join us for dinner, Susannah."

"Thank you for inviting me."

"Well, hello there," Stratton called from the den. "Can I get you something to drink?"

"I'll have a beer," Russell said, then he looked at Susannah. "How about you?"

"A glass of white wine, please."

Within moments, Maura—the baby of the family and the only girl—entered the den. The pretty redhead was a petite version of her mother, at least in appearance.

Russell greeted Maura with a warm hug, clearly indicating his little sister held a special place in his heart—and he in hers. It made Susannah wish that she had a big brother of her own.

Tag and little Samantha arrived next. And as Susannah had suspected, both Carolyn and Stratton fairly glowed when the girl lovingly wrapped her arms around each grandparent and gave them a loving squeeze.

"Did you have a good week with the new sitter, sweetheart?" Carolyn asked.

Samantha scrunched her nose. "It's not very fun,

and she didn't have any toys. We just watched cartoons all day.''

Parking a child in front of the television didn't seem like the kind of activity to encourage learning or stimulate a young imagination, as far as Susannah was concerned. She didn't have a problem with occasional cartoons, but this was just one more reminder that Rumor needed a preschool—a place that nurtured the whole child, with healthy snacks and meals, educational toys and games. A safe playground. And most important, loving supervision.

''Sorry I'm late,'' a male voice said from the entry.

''That's okay, son. We're still in the den having cocktails.''

Reed, the middle Kingsley brother and Rumor Fire Chief, wore his black hair in a buzz cut and was every bit as good looking as Russell and Tag. ''One of my crew was late showing up for the third time in a row, and I had to formally reprimand him.''

''Well, at least you're all here now.'' Stratton placed a hand on his son's broad back. ''It's good to have everyone home.''

''The only one missing is Jeff,'' Maura said, referring to Carolyn's nephew who came to live with the Kingsleys when he was six. Since that was about the time Susannah left town, she hardly knew him then and wouldn't recognize him now if he passed her on the street.

Carolyn clicked her tongue and sighed. "I wish that boy would come around more often."

"He's busy, but happy," Russell said. "Jeff never has been one to let moss grow under his feet. He likes the travel and excitement of working with the forest service."

"Yes," Maura said, "but I think it's the flying that he loves."

"That's for sure. All he can do is talk about planes." Stratton laughed. "It's almost like he's bi-lingual."

Susannah found herself drawn into the conversation, the camaraderie, and as much as she'd dreaded the Kingsley family dinner, it turned out to be quite pleasant.

The rest of the evening progressed without a hitch. Both Stratton and Carolyn had welcomed her with grace and charm. And she'd truly enjoyed chatting with Russell's siblings.

And when it was time to leave, she actually felt a slight pang of regret that the evening had passed so quickly.

* * *

After thanking Carolyn and Stratton for dinner, Susannah and Russell said their goodbyes then climbed into the 1957 Chevy and headed home.

Susannah settled back in her seat and scanned the interior of the vintage car. It was obvious that Russell had taken care of the vehicle his granddad had given him. She didn't pay attention to the road until Russell passed his hilltop house and turned onto Kingsley Avenue.

He was heading toward town and her house, which really shouldn't have surprised her since they hadn't discussed whether they would spend the night together. But she wasn't ready for the night to end. "Are you taking me home?"

"I hadn't planned on it. But I've got to tell you, Suz, this bouncing around from house to house is a pain."

Had their relationship become a pain? Or just the stipulations she'd placed upon it? "Would you rather we backed off a bit? Slowed things down?"

"I'm not complaining."

Yes, he was. In a way. But she wasn't ready for them to move in together. She still feared that Russell would grow tired of her. Change his mind—as he had before. And she wanted to make sure renewing their relationship hadn't been some kind of nostalgic lark on his part.

Shoot, he'd had a major head injury. Who knew what had been shaken loose.

She blew out a sigh. It all boiled down to trust. She flat-out didn't trust Russell not to hurt her again. To bare his heart and propose, then jerk the professions of love out from under her.

He turned left onto Main, and her curiosity piqued. "Where are we going?"

"Just for a ride," he told her, although she figured he knew exactly where he was heading.

He flipped on the blinker, then swung left onto State, instead of right, which would have led to her house. It didn't take long for her to realize what he had in mind. "You're taking me out to the lake."

"Remember the last time you and I rode out there in this car?"

How could she ever forget? Prom night. He'd taken her out to the lake and told her he loved her. Proposed. And she'd given him her heart, as well as her virginity. "Yes, I remember."

The heater hummed inside the car, warming the interior, yet the air fairly glistened with memories of youthful desire.

"So let's make a new memory," Russell said. "In the back seat."

Her eyes widened, and she shot a glance at him. "You've got to be kidding. We can't do that."

"Why not?"

"Well, because...we're adults and we have beds to make love in, homes to provide privacy."

"It could get boring if we only make love in a bed." He slid a hand across the seat and caressed her thigh, sending a quiver of heat to stoke a fire that pooled in her belly. "And besides, what does being adults have to do with it?"

"It's against the law to make love in public."

"In public? No one in their right mind is going out to the lake tonight."

"You've got that right, Russell. We'd have to be crazy to do something so wild and reckless."

"I am crazy, Suz." He took her hand in his and gave it a gentle squeeze. "Crazy about you."

When his heated gaze locked on hers, stirring her heart as well as her soul, she nearly believed him. God knew she wanted to believe him.

They drove along the paved road, then pulled off to the side, not far from where they'd parked that long ago night in early May.

"I've dreamed about being here with you again, kissing you senseless, fogging the windows. Making love to you." He pulled the Chevy to a stop and let the engine idle. "We'll have to make a few adjustments, though."

She laughed. "Like keeping the heater on."

"Unless you want to freeze your sweet bottom off."

Susannah glanced into the back seat. "I'm not sure there's much more room back there than up here. We could end up looking like permanent pretzels."

"Then we'll use my cell phone and call an understanding chiropractor with a romantic streak."

Susannah couldn't help but laugh. "Are you sure about this?"

"I'm sure about wanting you. About wanting to get my hands under that sweater and unhook your bra. I want to rub against you and let you decide how serious I am."

Then he pulled her into his arms and took her mouth with his, kissing her with youthful abandon, while sliding his hands under her sweater and unsnapping the front hook of her bra to release her breasts.

She savored each kiss, each caress that stoked a fire she couldn't contain. The intensity drove Susannah wild with need, and she slipped the sweater off, revealing breasts that ached to be touched, kissed. Laved.

"Back seat or front?" he asked.

"I don't care," she said, her breaths coming in short little pants. Her need was too great, and her core ached with an emptiness only Russell could fill. She began to unbutton her pants. She wanted him now and didn't think she could wait long enough to reposition themselves in the back seat. "Love me right here and now."

"Then to heck with the steering column," Russell said. "I'm more than happy to oblige."

And beneath a Montana winter sky, in the front seat of his granddad's old Chevy, the former high school lovers made a new memory, this one better than the last.

Chapter 8

The Montana days warmed, as winter turned to spring, and so did the intensity and passion of Susannah and Russell's affair.

Susannah pushed a cart through the aisles at MonMart, her mind on everything but the list she'd made.

She still wasn't ready to make a commitment to Russell, still wasn't ready to lay her heart and dreams on the line, especially when she didn't trust him not to hurt her again.

Seventeen years ago, when she'd been young, innocent and idealistic, she'd fallen deeply in love with Russell, given him her heart, her body and her soul. And he'd tossed them back at her.

Sure, she understood the complexity of the situation, Russell's youth and Stratton's illness. But that didn't mean she was willing to throw caution to the wind, open up and share her heart and dreams, reveal her innermost fears and insecurities.

Yet her resolve faltered each time Russell hinted at white lace, diamonds and promises, each time he smiled and pointed out babies riding in strollers or being cuddled in their mothers' arms.

The problem was, he had Susannah thinking about them, too. Babies with his dark hair and her blue eyes. Little girls with pudgy cheeks and boys with impish grins.

Maybe there was something to his claims of Destiny and Fate. Being together felt right.

That January night in the 1957 Chevy, they'd thrown caution to the wind, making love without protection. And although she voiced her concerns about being careless, Susannah nurtured a tiny hope that they'd conceived another baby in that car.

Maybe it would have forced her hand, caused her to relinquish those things she hid protectively in her heart. It was, she supposed, the coward's way out.

But they hadn't conceived a baby. And when her period came, she was actually disappointed. Of course, she didn't mention a word about it to Russell. Still, that didn't mean she hadn't thought long and hard about having his children.

But there was no reason why she couldn't mother both children—natural-born and adopted. A pregnancy wouldn't cause her to give up the baby girl waiting in China.

When all the paperwork for the adoption had been completed, Susannah had received a Dossier To China date, which marked the beginning of her long wait. And each month the China Council on Adoption Affairs took the next batch of documents off the stack, reviewed them and matched parents with babies.

Once a month the CCAA sent out a group of matches called referrals, slowly working their way through the piles and piles of applications from all over the world.

An adoption listserv that Susannah belonged to reported that the CCAA was currently working on applications with dates four to five weeks before Susannah's. Which meant, God willing, she'd be matched with her baby in just over a month.

It was time to ready the nursery.

Susannah stopped the cart, long enough to make sure she'd picked up everything on her list. Groceries for the week, coffee filters, vacuum cleaner bags. Baby lotion, powder and oil. Little white undershirts, a pink-and-white-striped sleeper. And a daisy-shaped pacifier.

On each shopping trip, she would gather more and more items, making her baby seem all that more real. As she placed a bottle of liquid pain reliever for infants—grape flavored—in her cart, she made one last scan of her list. Yep, she had it all.

MonMart was a one-stop wonder, and she was proud to have been part of the company's recent economic growth spurt. Yet she was thankful when her consulting job had ended. Now, she could focus on putting the finishing touches on her remodeled house, starting her own business and, most important, bringing her baby girl home.

As she proceeded to the checkout aisles, she spotted Sheree working on register three. And even though the teenager's line was longer than the others, Susannah chose to wait her turn and speak to the young girl Russell admired and mentioned affectionately.

A matronly brunette stood in line ahead of Susannah, tapping her foot and grumbling under her breath. And when her turn finally came, the woman thrust a small, brown paper bag in front of Sheree. "I want to return this. It's defective."

Sheree looked inside, then without removing the contents, scrunched her nose. "I'm sorry, but this has already been used."

"Of course, it's been used." The brunette crossed her arms. "That's how come I know it doesn't work."

"But it's a home pregnancy test," Sheree said.

"And it said that I'm not pregnant. And I'm certain that I am. I want my money back."

Susannah watched the ridiculous conversation unfold. Was the woman nuts? Who returned a used pregnancy test?

"Ma'am," Sheree said, her voice kind and respectful. "I can't take this back."

"I'm pregnant," the woman said, her voice rising several octaves. "I just know it. I *have* to be. And that stupid test didn't work."

"Have you been to the doctor?" Sheree asked.

"That's none of your business, young lady." Then the woman lashed out with a stream of obscenities the teenager didn't deserve.

Susannah donned her legal side. "Excuse me, but I'm sure the public health department won't allow this cashier to take back a used pregnancy test. Maybe you should talk to a manager and try to browbeat him into giving your money back."

The woman shot Susannah an angry glare, then

scooped up her brown bag and headed for the customer service desk.

When Sheree's eyes met Susannah's, they glistened with unshed tears. "Some people are really nice. But others, like that woman, can be rude."

"Tough job?"

"Sometimes it's the worst. At least on days like this." The redheaded teen sighed heavily. "If I didn't need the money, I'd quit and go back to my candy striper position. I'm not cut out for this kind of thing. Some of the other cashiers are great with the public. They can coax a happy face from the most difficult customers. But I'm not that good at it."

She was also young, and the burden of helping to support her family while struggling to keep up her grades had to be tough. Russell thought the world of the girl, and Susannah did, too.

Deciding to offer Sheree a lifeline—of sorts—Susannah made a confession she hadn't shared with anyone else. "I'm seriously thinking about opening up a preschool in Rumor. If I do, would you be interested in working for me?"

"Oh my gosh," the teen said. "In a heartbeat. I love kids. And I've even had a child development class at school."

Susannah smiled. "Hang in there, Sheree. I'll let

you know as soon as I'm in need of a teacher's aid."

It was probably against standard cashier procedure, but Sheree left her register, came around to the customer side and gave Susannah a hug. "Thank you so much for thinking of me. I'd love to work with you. And I'll even be happy to pull weeds in the playground or scrub the bathrooms."

The warmth of the embrace and the sincerity of the teenager's affection touched Susannah to the bone, drawing out maternal feelings that had long sat dormant. "I'm happy that you'll be working with me, Sheree."

"You are too cool, Ms. McCord. It will be so neat working with you and the kids. I'd do it for free, if I could."

Susannah laughed, understanding the teenager's excitement. "This isn't a volunteer position. You'll earn your paycheck, Sheree."

"Yeah, but I really like kids. Especially three-and four-year-olds. You must love kids, too."

She did. More than she'd allowed herself to contemplate in the past.

If she'd had any qualms about establishing a child care facility, they'd flown by the wayside with each step she took toward opening the doors for business.

Susannah was going to open a first-class pre-school, the likes of which this town had never seen.

Later that afternoon, Susannah drove the streets of Rumor, looking for suitable sites.

On the corner of Logan and Main, across the street from the police department and catty-corner to the Rumor Community Church, she spotted a For Sale sign in front of a vacant house sitting in the middle of a neglected lot. It needed a fence, not to mention a lot of work, but the location was great—under the watchful eye of God *and* the men in blue.

A parent couldn't feel any more comforted than that.

And now that Susannah had garnered her share of experience in remodeling a house, she had no reason to believe she couldn't tackle a project of this sort. In fact, she was eager to get started, to make it all come together.

She parked along the curb in front of the house and climbed from her car. Sure, she'd take down the information on the sign and contact Ralph Bennett at Rumor Realty, but first, she wanted to peek in the windows, see what she might be up against.

And she wanted to dream about what could be.

Some people might look at the house and see chipped paint, a cracked window, stained carpet.

They might stroll to the back, as Susannah did, and notice the weeds that had lain dormant through the Montana winter, poking up their green heads, ready to run rampant throughout the yard.

But Susannah saw a picket fence, a yard that boasted fresh green sod, a white house with children's artwork displayed in the front windows. A warm and inviting entry, where parents could check in their children and kiss them goodbye, knowing they'd be happy, healthy and safe.

She closed her eyes and smelled the scent of finger paint and school glue wafting through the room, while a batch of Aunt Hazel-the-health-nut's yummy oatmeal cookies baked in the oven, evidence of a nutritious, after-nap snack.

She saw a swing set in the backyard, a slide and a colorful climbing structure. A sandbox.

And she heard the happy sounds of children laughing.

She'd found the perfect site.

Now all she had to do was make an appointment to see the inside and bring along a contractor to make sure the building was structurally sound.

And then she'd make a fair offer.

The place needed a name, she supposed. And she thought about the high school mascot. A Ranger. The Rumor Rangers. She liked the alliteration.

How about the Rumor Rangerettes?

Nope. Sounded like a high school flag and drill team. Well, she'd think of something.

A slow smile crept to her face. Excitement like she'd never known bubbled inside, making Russell's ideas of Destiny and Fate ring true.

And speaking of Russell, maybe she should give him a call. Let him know of her good fortune.

Did she dare open up? Share her heart? See if he would be as supportive as she hoped?

Calling Russell might be the first step in making their relationship open and honest. Making it real.

She dug into her purse, pulled out her cell phone and dialed the number she knew by heart.

The intercom buzzed, and Mahnita's voice sounded over the line. "Mr. Kingsley, Ms. McCord on line two."

Russell picked up the phone. "Hey, Suz. What's up?"

"I've got some great news."

She'd decided to move in with him? Permanently? At least that was the first thing that crossed his mind. "What's your good news?"

"I've decided on a business." Her voice was light and girlish, like that of the cheerleader he remembered.

"That's terrific." He leaned back in his leather seat and dropped the ballpoint pen he'd been using onto the desk. "What kind of business?"

"I'm going to open a nursery school."

"What did you say?" He furrowed his brow, thinking the cell phone reception was acting up or something.

"I've decided on the business I want to start. Rumor needs a preschool and day care facility. And I've found the perfect place."

Her news struck him as a bit odd. "What do you know about kids?"

The minute the question left his mouth, he regretted it. And when she didn't answer, he realized it hadn't come across the way he'd intended. "I mean Ralph Bennett is talking about retiring and Rumor Realty is for sale. A real estate agency seems like something you could do while utilizing your skills."

More silence.

Okay, Russell. Regroup. Why did men have a tendency to upset women with perfectly innocent, well-intentioned comments?

"Well," she said, her voice losing all signs of the old Suzy. "Maybe I don't want to spend the rest of my life dealing with mergers, acquisitions, escrows or mortgages."

"You shouldn't have to do anything you don't want to do."

"Thank you," she said, yet her voice remained stilted. Strained.

"You know, if you feel this need to be around kids all day, maybe you could be a stay-at-home wife. I'd like to have a whole minivan full of kids, Suz. *With you.* You'd make the perfect mom. Can't you see us having a little redheaded girl? We can name her Isabelle."

"Russell, you're not listening to me. You don't even care about my dream of starting my own business."

Okay. So this was more complex than he thought. He needed to get back on track, on even keel. On her side of the fence.

"Suz, I'm sure Rumor could use a nursery school. Tag would give his right arm to find a place for Samantha to stay, a place where he knew she was being taken care of." He glanced at the ceiling, looking for a script to magically appear and give him a hint at how to fix things, how to make her tone lighthearted and happy again. "And I'm sure you'll do a great job. Maybe make a fortune."

"I'm not in it for the money, Russell."

Why would someone open a business and not care whether it made money or not? But he knew better than to say any more. There was just so far a foot could wedge into a guy's throat, and he had a feeling his had reached a world record mark. "How about dinner at the Rooftop tonight? We can celebrate."

"No," she said. "I'm going to be busy."

He raked a hand through his hair. Maybe a stop at Jilly's Lilies was in order. A bouquet of roses might help. But he supposed an apology was in order, as well.

Yet he wasn't entirely sure what he should apologize for. Not being thrilled at her announcement? It just surprised him, that's all. "Suz, I'm glad you found a business and a perfect site. When you're finished being busy, how about we toast your good news?"

"All right," she said. Yet he noticed the happy tone was still undeniably absent. "I'll talk to you later."

You can bet on it, Russell thought. *And he'd bring roses, a bottle of champagne and a better apology.*

On the other end of the line, Susannah jabbed at the End button on her phone before giving Russell a chance to say goodbye.

What did she know about kids?

More than she'd realized when the preschool idea sprouted.

Seventeen years ago, when she'd moved in with Aunt Hazel and come to grips with her pregnancy, she'd signed up at the local junior college and registered for a full semester of child development courses, hoping to give her an idea of what to expect when her baby was born.

But she'd lost the baby in August, just after classes started. During the first dark days, she'd toyed with the idea of dropping out of school, of holing up in her bedroom for the rest of her life.

Aunt Hazel, bless her heart, encouraged Susannah to get her mind on something other than the miscarriage and surgery. She was right, so Susannah returned to class the following Monday morning.

But she had no idea how difficult it would be to focus on kids and babies, when she'd so recently lost her own. One day, Aunt Hazel had found her crying over her books and suggested she drop the classes or file incompletes.

"You can return to school next semester," her mother's kindhearted sister had said.

But Susannah had refused to consider the suggestion. She was determined to finish what she'd started and succeed in spite of the odds—a new attitude that was her first step in personal growth.

Emotionally battered by the loss her baby, the classes had tormented her, so from the second semester on, she'd thrown herself into courses that required high academic standards and tons of studying. It was, she supposed, a way of sheltering her heart, of hiding her pain.

In an effort to protect herself from the psychological effects of the tubal pregnancy and surgery, she turned her heart away from home, hearth and family.

But maybe, deep inside, she'd always wanted to work with kids. Only the timing had been wrong.

And now the opportunity had presented itself.

What did she know about kids?

She might not have all the units needed to please the state requirements, but she knew enough. And she'd take online courses or go back to college in order to become a certified preschool teacher.

Susannah McCord would do whatever it took to make her dream come true—in spite of Russell's lack of support and enthusiasm.

On the verge of tears, her feelings too raw and unpredictable, Susannah put off making the call to the real estate office. Instead, she aimlessly drove around town until she felt more in control.

Still, she'd come to grips with her goals and wanted to share her news with someone who would be excited and eager to hear her plans. The only one who came to mind was Donna, so she steered her car toward The Getaway Spa, hoping her old friend had some time on her hands.

Donna looked up from her desk in the back office. "Hi, Suzy! What are you doing here? Need a massage? Things are pretty slow today, so I can squeeze you in."

Susannah shook her head. "I could use a friend. Do I need an appointment?"

"Not to talk to me." Donna stood and led her outside onto the patio, where a fountain bubbled and a flower garden thrived, painting the grounds with splashes of color.

Susannah sat in the shade of an umbrella tree, while Donna went to get iced herbal tea.

"Here we go," Donna said, placing two glasses on the table and taking a seat.

Susannah relished the cool liquid as it quenched her thirst. "It's quiet and peaceful here."

"Yeah. I love it. I try hard to keep this place serene so people can relax. That's why they come here, to get away." Donna reached across the mosaic-tiled, wrought-iron table and took Susannah's hand. "So what's on your mind?"

Susannah merely shrugged, unable to rustle up the enthusiasm she'd had prior to the call to Russell. "I finally decided on a business."

Donna cocked her head. "So why do I detect an overwhelming sense of sadness?"

Because Russell didn't offer the support she'd hoped, and in spite of her independence, his support mattered far more than it should have.

She kept that secret to herself and tried to push the disappointment out of her eyes and voice. "It may seem weird to you, Donna, but I want to open a preschool. Rumor needs one, and when I bring my daughter home, I'll have need of day care, too."

"Suzy, if that's what you want to do, go for it."

"You don't think it's out of…character for me?"

"Heck, no. You always used to love kids. Remember the hours of baby-sitting you used to do?" Donna laughed. "We all took the sitting jobs that came our way so that we could earn spending money, but I swear, you used to thrive on being around the little rugrats."

The little rugrats. A smile crept to Suzy's face. She had loved watching over the kids, playing with them, reading stories. And Donna had always referred to kids as rugrats, a term that some might find negative in connotation.

But rugrats didn't remind Susannah of ragamuffins or naughty, unruly children. The term reminded her of the cute little cartoon characters who had personalities of their own and saw the world through a kid's eyes.

Kids with a vision.

Rumor Rugrats.

It had a nice ring, and Susannah felt a renewed rush. "What do you think of me calling it Rumor Rugrats?"

"Cute. I like it." Donna smiled. "Have you told Russell?"

The zip that had only momentarily returned to her heart sputtered and died. "Sort of. He doesn't think it's the right business for me."

"So that's what has you so glum."

Susannah managed a smile. "But not for long. I'm not going to let his negativity get me down."

"Good for you."

Susannah took a long sip of her tea, hoping to wash away the lump in her throat, hoping to put the zip back in her heart.

What did it matter what Russell thought?

It mattered because Susannah had hoped that he

really loved her, that he would support her dreams, share her fears.

She didn't mention that to Donna, didn't share the one thing she feared most—that she might have fallen in love with Russell again, a man with the power to break her heart for a second time.

And what was worse, Russell might never understand her inner desires, her determination to follow through on the adoption, to make a home for a little girl who needed a mother.

Russell had been a father to a redheaded girl during his coma-based vision, but that was his dream. Susannah wanted the baby who waited for her across the ocean.

Would Russell understand her love for a child she had yet to see?

Or would he refuse to father a child who wasn't his?

The Kingsleys, or at least Stratton, put a big emphasis on bloodlines.

She hoped that wasn't the case for Russell. She preferred to think that Isabelle represented Russell's idea of life with the old Suzy.

But Susannah had evolved from the old Suzy, becoming so much more. And in spite of Russell's hopes to the contrary, she couldn't give him Isabelle. Whether Russell liked it or not, she couldn't live up to his dream.

And she didn't want to.

She had dreams of her own.

Chapter 9

The flowers, champagne and apology hadn't worked as well as Russell intended, although Suzy seemed appreciative.

Something had changed between them, and Russell wasn't sure what.

He tried to tell himself it was because she was so busy and intent upon her plans. Hell, she'd thrown herself into the purchase of the rundown house on Main, rolled up her sleeves and begun cleaning up the place.

She'd hired his brother to help, and it seemed the only enthusiasm she could spare was when talking to Tag about knocking out a wall or putting in pint-size toilets. Unfortunately, the glimmer in her eye didn't transfer to her conversations with Russell.

The effervescence that had finally returned to Suzy's personality had gone flat, and she'd become withdrawn, more pensive than before.

Their lovemaking continued to be great—thank goodness—but more often than not, she was too tired or too busy to spend the night with him.

But not to worry.

Russell had an ace in the hole.

He glanced across the seat of the 1963 Corvette, where Suzy sat primly, her eyes on the road, her thoughts somewhere else. She wore a simple, peach-colored sundress and strappy sandals that revealed pretty toes and a new pedicure. Hair the color of New England autumn hung in natural curls that graced her shoulders.

"You look lovely tonight."

She turned and caught his eye, a slow smile settling on kissable lips. "Thanks. You look rather dashing yourself."

"We make a good couple, then." Russell shot her a crooked grin, hoping that things between them would ease up. That the new Suzy and the old Suzy would merge, and she would realize he'd fallen in love with her for the second time in his life.

He hadn't said the words, in part because he was afraid she wasn't ready to hear them. But in a way, he figured the words weren't necessary. She had to know how he felt. He certainly hadn't made any secrets about wanting a commitment, wanting marriage. A family.

And he planned to use her birthday to further his case.

As they drove into the parking lot of the Rooftop Café, he noticed Donna Mason slip quickly inside the restaurant. Another glance across the seat told him Suzy hadn't noticed.

She expected a quiet, celebratory dinner for two. And why not? That's what he'd told her this was. But actually, he'd reserved the entire rooftop and sent invitations to a few close friends and family members.

Since Suzy had told him her thirty-fifth birthday had brought on an epiphany of sorts and jump-started her biological clock, Russell hoped tonight's surprise party would bring another jolt to her internal timepiece.

It was time for a commitment. A marriage. And quite frankly, his patience had run out.

Now, more than ever, he wanted his old Suzy back. And he hoped the birthday party would set things in motion for the rest of their lives.

He parked the car, then opened the door for her and led her to the entrance.

"Hello, Mr. Kingsley," the blond hostess said, a broad, lipstick-enhanced grin threatening to burst with the news that his guests had secretly arrived.

"I have reservations for a table on the roof," he said, hoping Suzy hadn't noticed the woman's goofy smile.

"Yes, sir. Your table is ready." She pointed to the stairway. "You can go on up. And your server will be right with you."

"Thanks." Russell placed a hand on Suzy's back and guided her to the stairs, allowing her to go first.

When she reached the top of the landing, she paused, and a chorus of voices shouted, "Surprise!"

"Oh, my gosh," she uttered, before turning toward him. "Who did this?"

He shot her a crooked grin. "Happy Birthday, darlin'."

Susannah didn't know quite what to say. She'd never expected a party. But before she could respond, a crowd surrounded her.

"Hey, birthday girl!" Donna made her way through the throng and gave her a hug. "Were you surprised?"

Susannah nodded. "Absolutely."

Reed Kingsley, obviously off duty at the firehouse, meandered forward and tossed her a grin. "Can I get you something to drink? Wine maybe?"

She nodded, still stunned that so many people had turned up to celebrate with her. "White wine would be great. Thank you."

"I hope you're here as a guest," Donna said to Reed. "I'd hate to think the restaurant called in the fire chief because of all the candles that will be going up in flames."

"Very funny," Susannah said, cuffing her friend on the arm. "You're going to be over the hill before you know it."

"I've always liked mature women." Russell placed a kiss on Susannah's cheek, staking a claim, so it seemed.

But she didn't care. The fact that he'd taken time to plan a party and pull off a surprise, made her feel all warm and mushy inside. Made her feel as though she'd always belonged in Rumor, on Russell's arm. In his life.

After he'd shown so little initial excitement about her plans for Rumor Rugrats, she'd pulled away from him. He'd tried hard to make up for it, though. Maybe she'd overreacted. Life was, she supposed, a matter of giving and taking.

Somehow, Reed managed to place a wineglass in

her hand and a beer in Russell's, then he slipped away to make room for the others who wanted to greet Susannah and offer their wishes for a happy birthday.

As the band began to play, Russell slipped behind her and placed a hand on her shoulder. "Want to dance?"

"I'd love to."

He led her onto the portable dance floor that had been set up in the corner and drew her into his arms. The embrace was warm, comfortable. Familiar. As though they'd been born to hold each other and sway to a romantic beat.

Underneath a full moon and a canopy of stars, while the partygoers mingled with each other, laughing and enjoying the easy camaraderie, Susannah closed her eyes and relished Russell's scent. The easy rise and fall of his chest offered her a comfort she found hard to explain, a physical and emotional solace she could easily lay claim to.

She loved this man. No doubt about it.

Maybe the problems she'd imagined had been her own insecurities mounting a campaign to discredit Russell and the Kingsleys.

She glanced at the happy faces of Maura, Reed and Tag, spotted Carolyn and Stratton chatting with

Donna Mason. The Kingsleys, she realized, were not her enemies. They were friends.

Were they more than that? Would they someday be family members?

Susannah had a lot to think about, a lot to reconsider.

Russell led her off the dance floor and pulled out a chair at the head table.

"Thank you," she said, taking a seat. "I've never had a surprise party."

He grinned, his eyes glistening with sincerity. "I wanted this birthday to be special."

She cupped his cheek, stroked the light bristle of his skin. "The party is lovely."

And it was. Everyone seemed to be having a great time, even Carolyn and Stratton.

"Look at them cut the rug," Russell said, nodding to his parents as they jitterbugged on the dance floor.

It pleased Susannah to see the older couple joining in the fun, obviously enjoying themselves at a party in her honor.

Yes, maybe her reservations about a permanent relationship with Russell had been brought on by old fears she needed to let go.

As the party progressed, Susannah received more than her share of compliments on the preschool and

questions about the grand opening she had scheduled in the next few weeks. Apparently, Tag Kingsley hadn't been the only one in Rumor who'd had
a tough time finding dependable day care.

For the first time in years, she felt like a part of
the Rumor community.

After the goodbyes were said and the last guests
left, Russell escorted her downstairs and out the
front door.

Home.

To his house.

To *their* house?

Let go, Susannah told herself, as she gazed into
the diamond-studded Montana sky. Let go of the
past and embrace the future.

A baby cried in a slow, mournful wail that tore
at Susannah's heart.

Her movements slowed by a long, bulky evening
gown, she swept through cobblestone streets,
searching for the waiflike cries before the cold, dark
of night consumed the sound.

Her shoes clicked upon the stone surface and
echoed in her ears. As she reached the wharf, the
water splashed upon the hulls of a hundred ships,
each wave slapping harder.

But the infant cries only grew louder.

Susannah tried to hurry, but her feet caught in the hem. She fought to kick free of the yards of material that bound her feet, determined to continue her frantic search. The baby was calling her, crying out in need.

Her heart raced and she fought to outrun the darkness, to find the child before it was too late.

"Suzy."

Russell?

His hand gripped her shoulder, gentle but firm, and slowed her flight.

She fought him off. *I've got to find the baby,* she screamed with a voice that refused to speak. *Help me, Russell.*

"Suzy, you're having a nightmare."

She opened her eyes, caught the concern in Russell's expression. Felt her heart pounding in her ears. She sat upright in bed, reached for his arms and fell into his embrace, hoping to warm the clammy chill of her bones.

Her face nuzzled into his bare chest, she breathed in the scent of him, held tight to his solid form, waiting for her pulse to slow, the thud of her heart to quiet, her frayed nerves to still. "God, Russell, it was so real."

"You were talking about a baby."

Susannah nodded, trying to shake off the pangs

of fear. The frustration. The mournful cry of the baby. "She needed me, and I couldn't find her."

"It was only a dream, darlin'."

Was it?

Or had it been a premonition? A warning?

Was her baby all right? She wasn't one to believe in that sort of thing, preferring to think dreams were a tired psyche's way of figuring out one's lot in life. But this nightmare had startled her and certainly jerked her to attention.

"Maybe it's time we think about having babies, Suz."

"Maybe so." But she couldn't bring herself to tell him that her first priority was the baby girl in China.

Russell was the one who was always talking about Destiny and Fate and suggesting a redheaded daughter named Isabelle was in their future. Well, the dark-haired baby girl—whether that precious child fit into Russell's plans or not—was in Susannah's future.

She'd mentioned the baby to him, but he'd seemed to shrug off her dream as unnecessary, now that they could have children of their own. But the baby, even if Susannah hadn't yet seen her face or held her, had become a part of Susannah, and she didn't think Russell understood that.

Of course, she would have to tell him soon, face the inevitable day of reckoning. But not tonight. Not while her heart pounded in her ears, while her skin still felt clammy to the touch.

Within the next few days, they would have to sit down and discuss the future. In fact, they would have to decide whether they would have a future together or not.

Susannah closed her eyes and held tight to Russell, hoping this wouldn't be their last embrace.

Her daughter had cried out to her across the Pacific, but Susannah's hands were bound until she received word that it was time to travel.

The news would come soon; she was sure of it.

Her passport was in order and her shots were up to date. It was just a matter of weeks, and Susannah would fly to China.

And she wouldn't rest easy until she'd brought her baby home.

Each year, on Susannah's birthday, she made an appointment for a regular gynecological checkup and Pap smear. It had been an easy way to remember an important and potentially lifesaving exam.

Three days before her surprise party, she'd called the Rumor Family Clinic and scheduled an appointment.

The clinic was actually a renovated white clapboard house at the end of the main strip of town, located near the general store and across the street from The Getaway, Donna's spa. Maybe, when Susannah had finished here, she'd drop in on Donna, share a glass of iced tea and chat, if her friend had some time to spare.

Susannah signed in with the receptionist. She'd arrived early, but didn't expect to be called right away. She wandered to the magazine rack, picked up a recent issue of *Working Mothers* magazine, then took a seat and waited to be called.

In spite of what appeared to be a full house, a nurse announced her name in short order, then led her down the hall. They stopped at the scale.

Uh-oh. She'd gained five pounds since she'd arrived in Rumor. Russell might complain about her watching carbs and fat, but it was back to the basics, as far as she was concerned.

Her blood pressure and temperature were normal, as she expected.

After leaving a white gown for Susannah to put on, the nurse left her alone to contemplate the exam women didn't look forward to, but couldn't afford to ignore.

Moments later, a light knock sounded at the door, and a tall, attractive woman wearing a white lab coat entered the room. "Hello. I'm Dr. Brynna Holmes."

"It's nice to meet you." Susannah tugged at the back of her gown, trying to close the gap that revealed more skin than she would have liked.

As Dr. Holmes glanced over the forms Susannah had filled out, noting prior health problems and family history, Susannah couldn't help but study the woman with golden blond hair, brown eyes and a serious manner.

"You've been relatively healthy," Dr. Holmes said, laying the chart on the counter. "Tell me about the tubal pregnancy."

The question didn't surprise Susannah, since this was her first visit to the clinic. "There's not much to tell, I guess. The fallopian tube burst, and I had surgery."

The doctor merely nodded, then glanced back at the chart.

"I've lost an ovary and a tube," Susannah added. "But I want to discuss my chances of having a baby. I'm thinking about getting married and starting a family."

Sheesh. The idea had been building ever since she and Russell started seeing each other, but it felt weird saying the words out loud.

She'd put him off whenever he wanted to discuss

the subject, but the time had come for a heart-to-heart. Perhaps today or tomorrow. She still had a feeling the adoption issue would stand in their way, and she hadn't been ready for a confrontation that might end the relationship they had.

"Conception with only one ovary shouldn't be a problem," Dr. Holmes said. "Let's get on with the exam, and then we can talk about it."

As Susannah laid back on the table and focused on the ceiling, Dr. Holmes went to work. When she'd finished, she helped Susannah sit up, then removed the glove and washed up.

"Well," Susannah began. "Did everything look okay?"

"For the most part," Dr. Holmes said. "But I've noticed an abnormality. Your left ovary seems to be enlarged, although not tender to the touch."

"What does that mean?"

"It might not be anything to worry about, but I'd like to schedule an ultrasound and see if that shows us what—if anything—is going on. Since we're not able to do an ultrasound here in Rumor, I'll have to send you into Whitehorn. And I'd also like to see some lab work, which you can have done down the hall."

The weight of her words slammed Susannah in

the chest. "And if there's something wrong with the ovary?"

"We may have to remove it. But let's not worry until we see the ultrasound and get the lab results back."

Not worry?

That was impossible. If there was something wrong with her remaining ovary, she would never have a baby.

And all she could think to do was rush home to Russell. Have him wrap his arms around her and offer his support.

Because the diagnosis—whatever it turned out to be—would affect them both.

At least, it would if Russell had meant what he said about them getting married, making a home and having children together.

After the lab technician withdrew her blood and taped a cotton ball on her arm, Susannah headed for the clinic door that led to the parking lot.

Outside, the sun shone brightly and birds chirped from springtime green treetops. Life, it seemed, had renewed itself.

So why did Susannah feel so dried up and withered inside?

Because her life had taken an unexpected turn.

Once in her car, she dialed Russell at his

MonMart office and waited for Mahnita to pass the call to him.

"Can you come by my house after work?" she asked.

"Sure. What's the matter?"

I need you to hold me, tell me it doesn't matter that I might not be able to bear your children. "Nothing. I just need to talk to you."

Chapter 10

When Russell walked into Suzy's house, tension hovered in the air, like a thunderstorm brewing.

He found her sitting on the sofa, a closed paperback novel resting in her lap like a prop. Something told him she hadn't been reading. "What's the matter?"

She looked at him with red-rimmed eyes. "I went to the doctor today."

"And?" He was beside her in a minute. "Are you sick?"

"No."

Well, that part was good. He waited for her to

speak, to share what was bothering her. Something more than the doctor's appointment had burdened her heart, something she refused to share with him.

Ever since the day she'd found the property for the preschool, she'd been acting strangely. Withdrawn. Touchy.

She'd accepted his apology, but he'd been careful to think before speaking. He wondered whether her hormones were acting up. Or maybe...

Could she be pregnant?

His heart did a flip-flop, skipped a gear then accelerated. He couldn't seem to wipe the sappy grin from his face. "Are we going to have a baby?"

If her serious expression hadn't been bad enough, her face fell, and he knew she wasn't pleased. For some reason, she preferred to think of adoption rather than pregnancy. But she'd get used to the idea. He'd make the best expectant dad in the world.

"It's okay, honey." He took her hand. "I'd love to have a baby. And if it's a girl—"

"It's not a girl." Tears spiked her lashes. "It's not even a boy, Russell. I can't have a baby. There's something wrong with my remaining ovary."

Her remaining ovary. The ovary she had left after the tubal pregnancy he'd caused. Guilt lanced his heart, and he didn't know what to say. What to offer. How to make things better.

He'd been so sure that they were meant to be together, to have the babies they'd once planned on having, a daughter named Isabelle.

God, in his dream, it had all been so real. Joy like he had never known had flooded his soul when he learned that Isabelle was his child. And now he felt so cold, so empty.

He'd tried to convince Susannah they were meant to be together, to have children and be a family.

Where had Destiny and Fate slipped off to?

Had he been wrong?

A sense of betrayal swept over him, Fate's as well as Susannah's.

Maybe she'd known all along that she couldn't have kids. Was that why she hadn't wanted to discuss it with him?

Had she held back, unwilling to tell him she couldn't give him the kids that he wanted?

Was that why she got excited about opening a preschool where she could care for other people's children? And why she'd been angry at him for not sharing her enthusiasm?

Fate, it seemed, had played a cruel joke, and his emotions spun out of control. His disappointment was palpable, and he was choking on the words that tumbled inside his mouth. ''I don't know what to say, Suz. I was so convinced that we were going to have a family together that I hadn't considered I might be wrong. I guess I'll have to form a new game plan.''

She turned her face away, hiding her pain and tears, he supposed.

He reached out to embrace her, give her a hug that offered his love and support, but feared it wouldn't be enough.

It hadn't been. Before he could take her in his arms, she pulled away, stiff as a mannequin. Then she stood. ''I think you'd better leave. I want some time alone.''

She'd shut him out again, and he wasn't sure why. But it was more than the baby thing. She'd pulled away from him the moment she'd found the preschool property and began to nurture her own goals.

He didn't feel as though he understood this woman at all. There was so much she held back, kept private. Was she just trying to end things between them? ''How can I make this better?''

''You can't. Please, just go.''

Maybe she needed some space, some time to deal with her disappointment. Hell, he had some re-grouping to do, as well. All he'd been doing over these past few months was pushing her into believing their relationship was right. Pointing out babies, trying to force her to think about the children they would have.

"All right, honey. I'll go. Maybe I've been pushing you too hard. Maybe we've rushed into something that needs more time."

"Yeah," she said, walking to the door and indicating it was time for him to leave with the toss of her head, the cross of her arms. "Maybe we need to think about our future together."

"I love you," he said, meaning the words from the bottom of his heart.

She didn't respond. Didn't act as though she'd even heard him.

He stood at the door, not sure what he was expecting her to say. "Call me later, okay?"

"Yeah," she said. But he had a feeling she wouldn't call. And he was scared to death of pushing her further away.

He'd counseled enough of his buddies in the past to know the score. When a woman told a man she needed some space and time, it was just a kind way of saying, "Get the hell out of my life. It's over. This isn't working."

Some guys couldn't leave it be; they had to chase after the woman, buy her gifts, trinkets. Call daily.

Apologize and make promises as a means of grasping at frayed straws of hope.

It had been his experience, as an observer, that those last-ditch, desperation-driven chases made a guy look like a wuss and only sealed a floundering relationship's fate.

Backing off and giving the woman time was the only possible recourse. The only chance of her missing him badly enough to change her mind.

So Russell would give her time.

Hell, he'd give them both time.

He'd been clinging to the past, trying to make Susannah McCord remember the old Suzy, to become the old Suzy. But she'd been right. The past was over and couldn't be relived.

And his coma-enhanced dream had been merely a fantasy, not a surreal glimpse at the future.

He'd had a head injury for God's sake. Not a Fate-filled message of what was meant to be.

For the first time since his accident, he didn't know what he wanted.

And he didn't know what the future held.

When Russell quietly shut the front door, Susannah gave way to the tears she'd been holding at bay since Dr. Holmes had told her she might not be able to bear Russell's child.

She cried for the children she wouldn't have, but

that wasn't the bulk of her grief. Before coming to Rumor, she hadn't expected to conceive a baby. And in a matter of weeks, maybe even days, she *would* be a mother—to a precious, dark-haired daughter who needed a loving home.

But she wouldn't share a life with Russell, wouldn't mother his children.

The tears that wrenched her heart came from deep in her chest, deep in her core.

Russell wanted a family of his own. A redheaded dream child he called Isabelle, a child Susannah couldn't give him.

She could see the disappointment, the sense of betrayal in his eyes.

I'd been so convinced that we were going to have a family together that I hadn't considered I might be wrong. I guess I'll have to form a new game plan.

Yeah, he needed a new game plan. And so did she. There would be no Russell Kingsley in her future, no husband, no father to her baby.

How can I make this better? he'd asked.

She'd wanted to tell him he could love her for who she really was. Accept her faults and limitations. Love the baby she would bring home.

Maybe I've been pushing you too hard. Maybe we've rushed something that needs more time.

He had that right. She hadn't wanted to get involved with him in the first place. She'd certainly known better. The past should have been lesson enough.

The firstborn golden-boy of the Kingsley family had changed his mind, fallen out of love with her seventeen years ago—if he'd loved her at all.

Sure, he could use Stratton's cancer as an excuse—and his own youth—but the fact of the matter was Susannah wanted a man who would stand beside her, through thick and thin. She didn't want to worry about her husband having a change of heart just because life wasn't going the way he intended.

She wanted a man for the long haul. For richer, for poorer, in sickness and in health.

Forever, and all that blather, which is exactly what it seemed like to her.

Blather.

Where was a knight in shining armor when a woman needed him? He certainly wasn't holed up at the Kingsley Ranch.

I love you, Russell had said. *Call me later.*

Yeah. Right.

Russell had abandoned her yet again.

And she had no one to blame but herself.

*   *   *

The time had finally come. Rumor Rugrats was on its way to becoming a reality.

On Saturday afternoon, Susannah stood in the middle of the spacious preschool, amazed at the transformation she'd orchestrated. Boasting new carpet and a fresh coat of paint, each room glistened in welcome for the children who would soon walk through the front door.

Sheree, who had far more artistic talent than she'd previously admitted, designed a couple of darling murals to grace the walls.

In the library corner, she'd painted a tree with five little monkeys swinging through the branches. And in the nap room, Rip Van Winkle snored lazily on a grassy slope. On the front door, in colorful balloon letters, Sheree spelled out Rumor Rugrats.

Susannah had been thrilled with the teenager's work, and even more so when the young artist agreed to help with art projects several afternoons a week.

Scanning the room she'd never grow tired of looking at, Susannah couldn't help but marvel at the way her dream had come to life.

The furniture she'd ordered—little tables and chairs, a miniature kitchen where the children would play house during free time, a bookcase for the library corner—would arrive any day. And then the facility would be ready for business, ready to welcome children into the loving arms of the teachers who would nurture and care for them as their own.

Tag had estimated it would take them two months to get the building ready for the Rumor Rugrats grand opening, but he hadn't realized how much of the work Susannah would do herself. The grand opening celebration was set for Wednesday evening.

A knock sounded at the door, and Susannah answered. She was surprised to find Dee Dee Reingard on the stoop. Susannah had met the middle-aged woman at The Getaway Spa on her first day back in town.

Dee Dee smiled. ''I heard about you opening a preschool and wanted to come by, maybe get a job application.''

''Sure,'' Susannah said, stepping away from the door and allowing the woman inside. ''Do you have any experience? Or have you ever taken any child development classes?''

''I sure have,'' Dee Dee said. ''I'm even a state certified preschool teacher, although I've never actually worked in a preschool. I was too busy raising my own kids, baking cookies, volunteering for the P.T.A. and orchestrating my quilting circle.''

"Sounds like you've got plenty of experience. Why don't you come with me to my office."

Susannah hadn't been in town long before the local gossips had shared the unfortunate news. Dee Dee's husband, the former sheriff of Rumor, had killed the woman with whom he'd been having an affair. The man was doing time, but he'd left an embarrassing mess for his wife and children to live down.

With Dee Dee's kids getting older and her husband in prison, Susannah figured a job might help the woman in more ways than one. And if Dee Dee had the necessary education, it would be a win-win situation for them both.

"You've done wonders with this place." Dee Dee craned her neck, checking each nook and cranny of the preschool. "It looks great."

"Thanks." Susannah handed her an application. "Would you like to take it home and fill it out?"

"Sure," Dee Dee said, "unless you have a bunch of other applications to choose from. I'd really like this job, especially after seeing what you've done here. I'm getting excited already. And I love small children. Big ones, too," she said with a laugh. "But they're not nearly as sweet and cuddly."

"You've got that right," Susannah said, although she thought Sheree was about the neatest teenager she'd ever met.

"Well, if it's all right with you, I'll bring this back on Monday morning."

"Great," Susannah said. "I'll look forward to seeing you again."

As Dee Dee opened the door to leave, Sheree called from the playground where she'd been working. "Hey, Ms. McCord. I have the sandbox filled. What do you want me to do next?"

"I'll be right there," Susannah said, making her way outside.

Sheree had worked tirelessly to help get Rumor Rugrats up and running. And her enthusiasm was appreciated.

"I could try to put together the play structure," the helpful teen said.

"Tag is coming by this afternoon. I think we'd better leave that project to him." She scanned the yard and noted the sod that covered the ground. "How about watering the grass? We haven't had the usual rainfall this spring, and the new lawn looks a little limp and dry."

Sheree headed for the hose and sprinkler. "Yesterday, at MonMart, I saw Mr. Kingsley and his brother. You know, the fire chief?"

"Reed," Susannah said, yet her thoughts were

on Russell. Crushed by his emotional betrayal, she'd focused her efforts on making her dream come true. But as much as she wanted to pretend he didn't exist, that he hadn't broken her heart, shutting him out only helped when she was elbow-deep in work.

The moment she went home and fell into bed, exhausted, his image returned to haunt her. The crooked smile that took her breath away. The way he kissed her senseless. The leathery-cowboy scent that stole into her dreams and left her aching with need.

She closed her eyes, willing the memory away. Yet her efforts didn't work. Russell, she feared, would haunt her for years to come.

"Yeah, that's right," Sheree said. "The fire chief's name is Reed. Well, anyway, they were talking about the upcoming fire season. I guess, since we had a mild winter and not much rain this spring, we're having drought conditions. I'd hate to have the new sod dry up and die on us."

Susannah felt as though her heart was in the midst of a drought that had left her dry and shriveled.

Yet one thing gave her hope.

The China Council on Adoption Affairs was most likely looking over her application now. Any day, she could receive the news. Mother and daughter would be matched.

Susannah watched as the sprinkler spun water onto the fresh-laid sod, her own thoughts swirling and spinning like mad. Soon, her heart would be full again. Warm and happy, with hope for the future replenished.

''Well,'' Sheree said. ''Is there anything else we can do? Maybe bake cookies for the Grand Opening?''

The girl, bless her heart, had been a great help, coming in after school and on weekends to paint and work on bulletin boards.

''Let's take a break,'' Susannah said. ''I've got lemonade in the fridge.''

As they headed inside, the doorbell rang.

''I'll get it,'' Sheree said.

When the girl opened the door, a dark-haired teenage boy stood on the porch, a bouquet of roses in his arms. His mouth seemed to drop, and blue eyes widened as he admired the redheaded young woman in front of him.

Susannah wondered whether he'd forgotten the flowers he held. ''Can I help you?''

''Uh…'' The kid glanced up, cheeks flushed. ''Yes. I have a delivery for…'' He paused long enough to double-check the card poked into the bouquet. "Susannah McCord."

"Cool," Sheree said, taking the crystal vase that held the bouquet. "Someone sent you flowers."

The good-looking kid on the porch seemed to take note of the pretty girl's interest in the roses, and Susannah couldn't help but smile. Spring was in the air, she supposed. And it looked as though the young man was twitterpated, to quote Thumper, Bambi's bunny friend.

"They're gorgeous." Sheree took a deep whiff. "And they're so fragrant. I wonder who they're from?"

Susannah took the flowers, then placed them on the table that held a sign-in book parents would be required to fill out each day. She opened the small envelope that bore a Jilly's Lilies logo and pulled out the card.

Susannah,
Good luck and best wishes for a wonderful grand opening. May your future be everything you hoped for and more.

Russell

Tears filled Susannah's eyes, as she read the words and tried to search the subtext and decipher a hidden meaning.

"Who are they from?" Sheree asked, as eager and enthusiastic as ever.

"Russell." Susannah's voice cracked, and she rued the emotional reaction.

He'd written the card himself, which meant he had to drive over to Jilly's Lilies and make the purchase, rather than make a quick, impersonal call over the phone.

Red roses meant love. Or did men even know that kind of sentimental stuff? Maybe Jilly had a special on red roses today.

And he'd called her Susannah, not Suzy. Was that his way of respecting her wishes, of acknowledging she was so much more than his memory of Suzy McCord?

Or was he merely letting the old Suzy go and saying goodbye?

He'd signed it simply Russell. No love, no fondly, no hint of what he was feeling.

Maybe that's because he wasn't feeling anything other than cordial.

May your future be all that you wish for and more.

What in the hell did that mean?

She swiped at her eyes with the back of her hand. Dammit. She wouldn't read anything into the gesture.

Russell had merely sent her flowers as a token of goodwill from one businessman to another.

Her heart couldn't take any other explanation.

"Mr. Kingsley is so nice, don't you think?"

Susannah caught the young girl's eye and tried to smile. "Yes. He's a nice man."

"I think he likes you."

"We're just friends," Susannah said. "Nothing more."

And probably a whole lot less than that, if truth be told.

The teenager continued to stand in the doorway. Susannah doubted he was waiting for a tip, because he still seemed to gawk at Sheree as though he hadn't seen a pretty girl on the threshold of womanhood before.

She found her purse where she'd stashed it early this morning, then pulled out a five and handed it to the kid. "Thank you."

"Huh?" the delivery boy said, as though just noticing Susannah for the first time. He glanced at the five. "Oh. Thanks."

She watched as he struggled to find something witty to say to Sheree, and it reminded her of young love, sending a bittersweet dagger through the heart.

"I'm new in town," the teen said. "Do you go to Rumor High?"

Sheree flashed him a pretty smile. "Yes."

"Well..." He grinned sheepishly, as though the girl had agreed to wear his ring. "I guess I'll see you around."

"Probably," Sheree said.

"Uh. My name is Blake Cameron. I live in the apartments on State."

"Me, too. My name is Sheree."

The boy lit up like a Fourth of July night, then slowly backed away from the door. "Then I guess I really will see you around."

Susannah wondered if the boy would get into Jilly's delivery van and curse himself for repeating the inane comment, and the whole scene brought a wistful smile to her face.

"Bye." He turned at the gate and strode toward the vehicle.

Sheree gave him a little wave.

Yep. The young man was clearly twitterpated.

As Susannah had once been.

"I think Blake likes you," she told Sheree.

The girl smiled. "He was kind of cute, huh?"

Susannah nodded.

"Did I act okay? You know, kind of interested but not?"

"Trying to play hard to get?"

"Well, not overly so," Sheree said with a smile. "I just might want to get caught."

Susannah laughed and shook her head. "Come on, let's have that glass of lemonade."

Was this any indication of the future that lay in store for her? Would she one day share life's ups and downs with her own daughter?

She hoped so. Being a mom would be a lot of fun.

And a lot safer, since she intended to look at love as an outsider from now on.

Russell Kingsley had seen to that.

Chapter 11

Russell stood at his office window and gazed at the parking lot, where a hundred or more cars had parked, indicating another successful shopping day at MonMart.

In the past, steady sales had pleased him, bolstered his pride in the superstore he'd created. But it didn't do a damn thing to him these days, not since Suzy had asked him to leave her house.

Maybe he shouldn't have been so quick to go, but he'd needed time to think, needed a new game plan. For months he'd tried to convince Suzy that they were meant to have a future together, but she'd held back, refusing to make any kind of formal commitment or long-term promises.

And the moment she began to put her own dreams into play, she began to pull away from him.

He'd hoped that his dreams and his destiny would be enough for her. But obviously, that wasn't the case. And he wasn't sure there was anything he could do to alter that fact.

In spite of his hope that she would call him, she hadn't. And now, three weeks later, he doubted she would.

He could always chase after her, of course, like other brokenhearted guys he'd known. But he held on to the advice he'd offered those other sorry saps who'd been dumped by women wanting more space and time.

Let the lady go. If she really loves you, she'll come back.

You wouldn't want her any other way.

And dammit, Russell wouldn't want Suzy any other way—her arms open wide and her heart on the line, ready to go the distance.

Since climbing into his Range Rover and driving away from her house for the last time, he'd had to reevaluate a lot of things, especially his past, present and future.

He loved Suzy McCord, both the young cheerleader he'd once dated and the cashier dream girl who'd given birth to his daughter, a child that didn't exist.

But times had changed. And like it or not, he really didn't know Susannah McCord.

He longed to start over, to try and understand who Susannah was and where she was going, but she'd let him know their relationship was over each time his phone didn't ring, each time he climbed into an empty bed.

Sending flowers for her grand opening seemed like a good idea.

Had she received them? Set them aside as an unwelcome reminder of what she and Russell once had? Or had she understood his intent? A simple peace offering that came from the heart.

For some reason, a dozen red roses didn't seem to be enough.

He glanced at the phone, but fought the urge to pick up the receiver and dial her number.

What would he tell her? "I love you, darlin'. Life doesn't mean squat without you in my life."

Hell, he loved the girl he remembered, but did he love the woman she'd become?

He shoved his hands into the front pockets of his jeans, willing them to stay put and not reach for the phone.

What would he say?

Should he grovel like a lovesick fool? "Being without you is killing me. I miss you so bad I can't think, can't work, can't…" He blew out a sigh.

Russell Kingsley didn't grovel, especially to a woman he hardly knew.

In his dream he'd proposed in front of a full gymnasium, getting down on bended knee to make his point. It had embarrassed him, yet he'd had no other way to let Suzy know how he felt about her.

And it had worked. The old Suzy— the dream Suzy—had succumbed to his heartfelt pleas.

But Susannah?

She was strong and self-sufficient. And too damn tough to read. He wondered whether the old Suzy had ever existed, because she sure didn't seem to be a part of the business woman who'd moved back into the once cold and lonely clapboard house on State Street and made it a warm, stylish home. The woman who gave up a career in corporate law to work with preschoolers.

Nope. Russell didn't know Susannah McCord. He'd been in love with a memory, in love with a dream.

Yet he'd held a flesh and bone woman in his arms, relished her springtime scent, brought fire to her eyes, watched as she reached a peak of desire and collapsed in waves of pleasure in his arms.

What did he want? The woman or the dream?

He scoffed at himself. What did it matter?

Russell Kingsley, MonMart magnate and first-born son, had always gotten what he wanted in life—one way or another. But this was the first time he felt cheated. Lacking. Missing out on something special and meaningful.

Too bad he didn't know just exactly what that something was.

Again, he glanced at the phone that waited silently, mocking his one-time belief in Fate, Destiny and a future with the cheerleader he'd married in his heart.

He grimaced and wedged his hands deeper into his pockets.

On Friday, Susannah sat in her office and studied the list of children she would welcome on Monday morning—just three days away.

According to her budget, she was right on track—thanks to a successful grand opening and word of mouth. She held twelve completed application packets and had sent out at least that many more to parents who wanted to complete the paperwork at home and get the forms back within the next few days.

She glanced across the desk, where Russell's roses—fully bloomed—gaped at her, reminding her that he'd sent flowers but hadn't attended her grand opening.

But why had she expected him to?

He didn't have any children to enroll.

Yet.

She wondered whether he was setting his sights on the perfect mother, a woman who would bear him bright-eyed Kingsley heirs. The thought tweaked her already damaged heart, and when the telephone rang, she nearly jumped out of her shoes.

"Rumor Rugrats," she answered, still getting used to the name of her new business.

"Ms. McCord?"

She didn't recognize the voice. "Yes."

"This is Mary Hsu with CCAA."

China Council for Adoption Affairs. Susannah could hardly catch her breath or find her voice. "Hello."

"I called to tell you we've matched you with a daughter."

Tears welled in Susannah's eyes, and clogged her throat. "That's…wonderful."

"She's about five months old and a bit small for

her age. But the doctors have deemed her healthy. We've been calling her Mei.''

Mei. Mei McCord. Her baby, her daughter. ''When can I come and get her?''

''I'm going to overnight a packet, which should reach you by Monday morning, since that will be the next business day. It'll contain further instructions and more information about your baby.''

''Can you tell me anything? Anything at all?'' *Something that will make her seem more real, more a part of my life?*

''Let me see. Hmmm. Yes. Mei is a bright-eyed little thing, cute as a button. She'd been abandoned on the waterfront of a small seaside village. Two fishermen heard her cries and found her in a hand-crafted basket.''

Goose bumps shimmied up and down Susannah's arms. Her baby had been crying on the wharf.

And Susannah had heard her.

''I'll also include some other things in the packet,'' Ms. Hsu said. ''Her medical records, instructions for you and paperwork to take to China. A photograph.''

A picture of her little girl. ''I can't wait to see her and bring her home.''

''Things will happen fast, now,'' Ms. Hsu said. ''You'll need to wait for travel approval, which is something the agency will have to get for you. And once your trip has been approved, you'll need a visa. The written instructions are pretty clear, but if after receiving the packet you have any further questions, please give me a call."

"Certainly. Thank you so very much."

"The pleasure is mine, Ms. McCord. I receive a great deal of joy in finding loving homes for these precious children."

When the call ended and Susannah hung up the phone, she stared at the receiver for the longest time, wondering if the conversation had indeed taken place. Wondering if Mei—her baby daughter—was truly waiting in China.

She had so much to do, according to the listserv she belonged to, packing clothing and supplies not only for herself, but for her child.

Excitement bubbled inside, and Susannah wanted to share her happiness with someone. But Dee Dee wouldn't arrive for another hour, and Sheree was home getting ready for school.

Russell came to mind, then she shook her head. He wouldn't give a hoot about her baby, and the thought brought a lump to her throat, an ache to her heart, tears to her eyes.

But she refused to let thoughts of Russell tarnish her happiness.

She picked up the phone and called Donna at home.

"My baby's name is Mei," Susannah told her friend. "I can change it, of course. Americanize it. But I like Mei. And it keeps her connected to her culture. It's a beautiful name, don't you think?"

"It sure is," Donna said. "I like the sound of it. Mei McCord has a nice ring."

Susannah smiled. "And the nicest thing of all, is that I can raise her at the preschool. I can keep her near me all day long."

"I'm so happy for you. It sounds as though everything you've ever wanted is falling into place."

Not everything. Susannah didn't have a husband to share her thrill, a father for her baby.

She scolded herself for letting her single parent status bother her. For goodness' sake, she'd applied to adopt as a single parent and hadn't given a darn about raising a child alone.

But that was before Russell had waltzed into her life, turning her dreams and memories on end and giving her a glimpse of what would never be.

A sense of sadness swept over her, but she didn't mention it to Donna. The disappointment and betrayal was something she'd carry alone. It was, she supposed, the penance she paid for trusting Russell, for believing in him and falling in love all over again.

Her heart had mended once, but this time Susannah feared it had been damaged for good—at least the part of her heart a woman shared with a lover.

But the maternal part was alive and beating strong.

"When will you go to China?" Donna asked.

"Within several weeks or so, I suppose. There's still a lot I need to do, stuff I couldn't do until the referral came though." In the midst of Susannah's excitement, nervous energy began to brew. "A packet is going to arrive on Monday morning, which will give me a better idea."

Monday. Three more days.

She donned her best Scarlett O'Hara smile and lifted her chin. Her hope was in the future, not in Russell Kingsley.

The man couldn't offer her anything but disappointment and pain.

So why did she feel so utterly empty with him out of her life?

The more Russell thought about missing Susannah's open house, the worse he felt. He'd told himself that giving her space, staying out of the picture was the right thing to do.

Hell, she wouldn't want to see him there anyway. Besides, he'd sent roses from one business owner to another.

But there was more to it than that.

He missed holding her in his arms, missed the way she whimpered when he took her mouth in his. He missed waking to her smile, seeing her face light up when she greedily drank that first morning cup of coffee loaded with cream and sugar.

Hell, he even missed cuddling on the sofa and watching those old black-and-white movies that she enjoyed and he pretended didn't have enough action for him.

But *who* did he miss? The girl he remembered? Or the woman who'd always held a part of herself back?

The walls of his office seemed to close in on him, boxing him in like a death row inmate. He had to get out of here, maybe take a drive to Lake Monet in one of the vintage convertibles he owned, relax while the fresh air blew in his face.

As he strode out the door, intending to escape the office, he met Tag and Samantha standing near Mahnita's desk.

His niece was a cutie pie, and he sometimes wondered how his brother managed to ever tell the child no.

Samantha wiggled her hand in a little wave, and Russell smiled. "Hey there, munchkin. Here to loot Grandpa's candy drawer?"

The pretty child giggled. What was it about little girls that touched Russell's heart?

"What are you two up to?" he asked Tag.

"We're looking for Dad, but he's gone to inspect some property in Billings."

"And he can't take me to see my new teacher," Samantha added with a pout.

Russell ran a hand along the soft, silky strands of his niece's brown hair, then looked at his brother, hoping to get a better explanation.

"Her first day of school is on Monday, and I promised to take her to check out the playground and visit with her new teacher, especially since we missed the open house." Tag sighed. "But I've got to go to Whitehorn to meet with a building inspector at the job site. He's leaving town this afternoon, and the meeting can't be postponed. I was hoping Dad could—"

"I'll take her," Russell said.

Tag arched a dark brow. "You?"

Yeah, him. Russell thought the world of his niece. Besides, it would give him a believable excuse for stopping by the preschool so he could check it out, too. And so he could see Susannah again.

It was a perfect excuse. He wouldn't have to feel like a spineless wuss, and Susannah wouldn't think he was chasing after her. Hell, he was just being a decent uncle.

"What's wrong with me taking her, Tag?"

"I don't know. It's fine, I guess. But I didn't expect you to make an offer like that."

"Why not? Don't you think I can handle baby-sitting Samantha for a few hours?"

"You've never really taken her anywhere before."

"I've been a busy man, but I've got some free time today." Russell flashed a smile at his niece. "Want me to take you to see your teacher?"

Samantha nodded eagerly, her hazel eyes growing wide. "Can we take the race car?"

"My race car?"

"You know, the red-and-white one."

The 1963 Corvette. "Sure, if you don't mind me running home to get it."

Samantha clapped her hands. "Goody!"

And for the first time in weeks, Russell felt much the same way.

Excited.

Expectant.

Nervous anticipation kicked his pulse up a notch. He'd always felt confident around Suzy, but this meeting was with Susannah. And he didn't feel nearly as sure of himself.

For the first time, he would put his dreams and memories behind, facing her on her own turf.

And Russell had no idea what to expect.

Susannah stood before her office window, a mug of coffee in her hands. As she savored the taste, she scanned the playground that would soon be full of happy children.

"Excuse me," Dee Dee said softly. "Russell Kingsley is here to see you."

Susannah nearly dropped the mug in her hands. "I'll be right there." *As soon as my heart stops pounding in my ears.*

She entered the main classroom, which had once been the living and dining rooms before Tag knocked out a wall. She found Russell standing before her, a happy Samantha holding his hand.

"Tag had promised to bring Samantha to visit and see the playground, but he was called to a business meeting in Whitehorn." Russell shot her a crooked grin that sent her heart soaring, in spite of her resolve not to let him have any kind of hold on her again. "Is it okay if we look around?"

"Certainly," Susannah said, trying to regroup and gain some control over her body's reaction.

She knelt before the child. "I'm so glad you came to visit us today. And I'm especially glad that you'll be coming to school here. We've worked hard to make this a fun place for you to be."

"I can't wait until Monday."

Susannah laughed, then led Russell and his niece back to the entry, where all of her tours began.

She pointed to the sign-in table. "Each morning, your daddy will bring you to school and write your name in our book. If you have a jacket or sweater, you'll hang them on the hooks against the wall."

Samantha watched intently, taking in every word Susannah said.

"You see these big round tables?" Susannah asked.

The child nodded.

"They're empty today. But on Monday morning, we'll have four different activities for you to choose from: puzzles, Play-Doh, coloring sheets and paper cutting projects."

"I'm not allowed to play with scissors," Samantha said.

"That's a very good rule, but at school we have specially made scissors that are safe for children to use."

Russell found himself listening with profound interest, watching a part of Susannah open up. A part of her he hadn't seen before. She glowed while talking to Samantha and patiently answered all the child's questions.

"What's circle time?" Samantha asked, hazel eyes trying to absorb everything about the room— the shelves of books, the play kitchen, the colorful bulletin boards.

"It's storytime," Susannah said, "but we'll also talk about all kinds of interesting things."

Samantha brightened. "What do we get to do after that?"

"We'll have a snack, then go outside and play."

"My daddy showed me the playground when we were driving by one day," Samantha said, "but I didn't get to see it very good."

Susannah looked at Russell. "Do you have time to let her play for a while?"

Time? To hang around and see where Susannah would spend her days? Maybe get to watch her at work? Talk to her some more? Heck, yes.

But he glanced at his wristwatch, just so she wouldn't think he'd come to spy on her. Or worse yet, pine over her. "Sure. I've got some time."

"Great." Susannah took Samantha by the hand and led her outside.

Russell followed, taking in the shapely, denim-clad backside he hadn't had the pleasure of watching in weeks. A part of him wanted to reach out and take her hand, pull her close, whisper words of apology and promises to make things right. But he kept his hands and his thoughts to himself.

As Samantha ran to the slide, he leaned against the side of the house, his eyes on his niece, his mind on the pretty preschool director.

"You've done a great job getting this place in shape," he said. "I can't imagine any kid not loving it here."

She slid him an appreciative grin, but their eyes locked. And something—he wasn't entirely sure what—passed between them, making his heart skip and stammer. He feared his words would do the same, so he kept his mouth shut.

"Thanks," she said. "It means a lot to hear you say that."

He merely nodded as though understanding. He supposed their separation bothered her. Or maybe it was just the way in which they had separated.

The memories of what they'd shared over the last six months hovered around him until he couldn't shake them, couldn't ignore them much longer. "I'm sorry that things didn't work out for us." *Far more sorry than you'll know.*

"Me, too," she said, her voice soft and wistful.

What did she mean?

Again, he tempered his thoughts, held them close, as he did the questions that tumbled around in his chest. *Do you miss me? Do you lie awake at night in an empty bed and think about what we had, what we shared? And like me, do you wonder what—exactly—went wrong?*

He slid a glance her way, trying to read something in her expression, something that would indicate she was just as heavy-hearted and befuddled as he was.

She nodded toward the playground. "Samantha is a beautiful child."

Russell looked at his niece, watched as she slid down the shiny new slide and landed in the sand at the bottom. "Yes. Tag's a lucky man."

Susannah nodded. "Children are truly a gift from God. I wish all people understood that."

Was she talking about her own mother?

Or people in general?

In the past, as their relationship had seemed to blossom, he'd found himself wondering what she meant many different times. He supposed he'd been waiting for her to explain or for things to fall into place.

He should have flat-out asked. Then, maybe he would have had a better handle on the woman Suzy

had become, and maybe they would still be together.

"You're right about kids being special," he said.
"And I imagine a lot of people consider them bur-
dens. Are you thinking about your mom?"

"Not exactly, although she'd definitely fall in
line with those people who see kids as an unfortunate obligation." She tucked a strand of hair behind
her ear, then glanced down at her feet. "I was actually making a general statement about people who
have kids and don't appreciate them."

He supposed she was feeling badly about not being able to have kids of her own. "Do you still
plan to adopt?"

She turned to face him, her expression growing
soft and maternal. "I doubt that I can explain it to
you, Russell, but I'd never give up my plan to adopt
that child."

He nodded, trying to understand. "Is it because
you can't have a child of your own?" He didn't
mean anything at all by the question. Her feelings
suddenly mattered a great deal, and he wanted to
understand where she was coming from.

"No," she said. "It might be hard for you to
comprehend, Russell, but I began falling in love
with my daughter the day I filled out the first of a
million forms. She has no one else but me."

For the first time, he began to understand the heart of Susannah McCord. There was so much more to her than he'd anticipated. It actually deepened his sense of loss.

He caught her gaze, and relished the short time he spent connected to her. ''I'm glad things are working out the way you want them to.''

''Thank you,'' she said.

But something told him things weren't as perfect as she wanted him to believe.

Chapter 12

On Monday morning, Susannah waited for the children to arrive and wondered who would be the first one placed in her care.

She had studied the file of each child, carefully going over the family information the parents had provided and memorizing many of the details that would make her job easier. Since she and Dee Dee had set up the classroom with the utmost care, she was more than ready to welcome each of the fifteen children who would walk through the Rumor Rug-rats door.

It was just too bad that she didn't have something

more to do, some last minute preparations to keep her mind focused on the day at hand or even on the promising future before her. Instead, her mind insisted upon rehashing the recent past.

She blew out a sigh. As much as she hated to admit it, thoughts of Russell had plagued her long after he and Samantha left on Friday. And they'd continued throughout the weekend, taunting her with a new side of him.

He'd seemed different to her, although she couldn't put her finger on why.

Seeing him again had triggered all kinds of crazy thoughts and feelings, each one reminding her how much she'd missed him, how much she'd missed the nights spent nestled in his arms.

But missing him had also brought back a fresh memory, a painful reminder of the day she'd come back from the Rumor Clinic in hopes of finding Russell's understanding and support.

Instead, he'd pulled away, apparently focusing on his own disappointment.

Sure, she'd asked him to leave her house, but only because it was clear he didn't care about her feelings. In fact, he'd never really understood her or taken time to ask whether she had any hopes or dreams of her own.

He'd been too concerned about recreating the past. Or at least his memory of the past.

She'd felt very much alone when he walked out her door claiming he had some thinking to do. Well, let him think away.

Their lives were no longer connected, which, she reminded herself, was a good thing. Her heart couldn't take any more rejection, certainly not the kind Russell managed to deal out each time he abandoned her when she needed him most.

The past couple weeks had been a perfect example. She'd had the ultrasound Dr. Holmes had ordered. The abnormality of her ovary appeared to be genetic, rather than an indication of disease, but the results were inconclusive, at least as far as her chances of conception went.

"Time will tell whether you can conceive a baby or not," Dr. Holmes had said.

But Susannah was no longer concerned about bearing a child. She already had a daughter.

A car pulled into the driveway, interrupting her musing, and she peered out the window, grateful to see Dawn Winters escort her four-year-old son, Joey, up the walk.

Thank goodness Susannah could finally sweep aside all the unwelcome thoughts of Russell.

"Good morning, Joey," she told the boy who had a glimmer of mischief in his bright blue eyes.

"I brought a car," he said, tugging a little Matchbox racer from the cramped confines of his jeans' pocket.

Susannah smiled and brushed a hand along his short, dark hair, caressing a bold cowlick with a mind of its own. "That's a neat car, Joey. I have a special marker we can use to put your name on the bottom, just in case it gets lost."

Minutes later, Josh Holbrook dropped off his daughter Bonnie Sue, a cute little girl dressed in a crisp white blouse and denim jeans that sported a patch on one knee.

In no time at all, the classroom had filled with children, some apprehensive and clingy, but most of them eager to explore their new surroundings and make friends.

Susannah's heart soared as she watched the preschool in full operation. It pleased her to know that Rumor Rugrats would provide an important service to the children and families of the community.

A few minutes before eight, just as Dee Dee took charge of the activity tables, Stratton Kingsley arrived with his smiling granddaughter in tow.

After a quick greeting, Tag's daughter zipped off

to the miniature kitchen, where several youngsters prepared a feast out of plastic groceries.

Susannah expected Stratton to quietly slip away, as the other adults had, but he stayed, obviously watching the morning activity with a great deal of grandfatherly interest.

"It's amazing what you've done with this place." The patriarch shook his nearly gray head. "Who would have guessed?"

Guessed what? she wanted to know. Who would have guessed that poor little Suzy McCord could have pulled off something of this magnitude?

"I mean," the older man said, "after all you've accomplished in the business world, you've chosen to open a preschool."

She stiffened, ready to defend her decision, but Stratton chuckled. "And a damn fine preschool at that. It appears that everything you touch turns into gold, Susannah."

His compliment took her by complete surprise, but she managed to utter a "thank you."

"Rumor has needed a day care facility for years, and you zeroed in on that need." Stratton slowly shook his head in amazement. "But look at this place."

Susannah couldn't help but scan the room and try to imagine what had caught Stratton's attention.

The contented children? The flurry of quiet activity? The freshly painted building itself?

"You took a community eyesore and turned it into a state-of-the-art facility."

She found herself standing taller, felt a smile play on her lips. It wasn't every day that the Kingsley patriarch took the time to share his admiration.

"Thank you, Stratton."

"You know," he said. "I owe you an apology, Susannah."

She slowly turned her head to find him gazing at her. "An apology? For what?"

He wasn't going to dig up the past, was he? It didn't seem within his character, or at least in keeping with the image she'd always had of him.

"Seventeen years ago, I was pretty tough on Russell. He told me that he loved you, but I didn't take him seriously. I mean, you two were just kids."

She doubted Stratton knew she'd overheard the cruel things he'd told Russell years ago, so she didn't think he would apologize for that. But back then, he'd been tough on her, too, oftentimes acting cold and aloof.

Not once had she felt the least bit welcome at the Kingsley Ranch, but that was water under the bridge, as far as she was concerned. Ever since she'd come back to town, Russell's father had treated her with respect.

"There's no need for an apology, Stratton. That was a long time ago."

"Not too long to tell you I'm sorry that I wasn't more accepting of Russell's choice in girls. He obviously saw a lot more in you than I did. And I'm glad to say I was the one who was wrong."

"Apology accepted," she said. "Russell explained that you were suffering from cancer at that time. I'm sure you had a lot on your mind."

He nodded slowly, his gaze focused on the pointed toes of his polished boots. "For what it's worth, my wife and I would be happy to have you in our family."

His acceptance was a day late and a dollar short, but Susannah appreciated his candor. "Thank you."

She didn't, however, mention that whatever she and Russell once had was over. He would figure it out soon enough.

Stratton looked up and caught her eye. "Carolyn just mentioned the other day that it was time to have the family over for dinner again. We're thinking about next weekend. I hope you'll be able to join us."

Apparently, Russell hadn't mentioned their

breakup. Well, she wouldn't mention it, either. She still wanted to keep their relationship—or the lack of one—discreet. "I'm afraid I won't be able to join you, Stratton. I'll be leaving the country soon and expect to be gone for several weeks."

Stratton arched a brow. "Where are you going?"

"To China. I've adopted a daughter and need to bring her home."

"You're adopting a child?"

"As a single parent," she said, hoping he didn't think she'd roped his son into anything the Kingsleys weren't prepared for.

Stratton shook his head, as though understanding, although she wasn't sure he had. "Children enrich a person's life. I never really understood that until Samantha was born. I suppose I was too busy in the early years to fully appreciate my own kids. But I wish you the best of luck with your travel and in bringing your daughter home."

"Thank you," she said, this time truly meaning the words. Stratton Kingsley was the first member of the community, other than Donna Mason, who indicated an approval of her endeavors to adopt a baby and create a family.

"Well, I'd better get going." Stratton took one last look at his happy granddaughter. "It's nice to see her laugh and play with kids her own age."

"I'll take good care of her."

"I know you will." Then the older man offered her a smile and slipped out the door.

Better late than never, Susannah supposed.

But she couldn't shake the sense of bittersweet remorse that washed over her.

Just before lunch, Susannah stood to the side of the classroom, watching as an animated Dee Dee read the children a story. The kids giggled as they heard the antics of a baby elephant who thought he was a hoot owl.

So far the day had progressed without a hitch, if she didn't count a scuffle by the water fountain.

Eager to quench his thirst, Joey Winter had jumped in front of Bonnie Sue Holbrook, a little girl who had learned to hold her own with a house full of older brothers. Not about to be taken advantage of, Bonnie Sue pushed Joey out of the way, resulting in angry words and tears.

Both children were reprimanded, then made to sit by the wall for a few minutes of time-out, which seemed to do the trick.

Those were the things, Susannah supposed, she could expect to deal with as preschoolers learned to socialize, take turns and share.

A knock sounded, pulling Susannah from her

classroom observation. She strode toward the front door and answered, hoping to keep voices down so as not to interrupt Dee Dee's story time.

When she opened the door she spotted a deliveryman on the porch. "Susannah McCord?"

"Yes."

He handed her a large, bulky envelope and thrust a clipboard at her. "Sign here, please."

She scribbled her name, then took the package addressed to her.

China Council on Adoption Affairs.

Her heart spun out of control, and she swore the blood had nowhere to flow. This was it, what she'd been waiting for. A real connection to her child.

She carried the treasured packet to the privacy of her office and slid into the chair. Her fingers fumbled to open the brown, travel-worn envelope and pull out the secrets held inside.

As a black-and-white photograph fell into her hands, her breath caught.

"Mei," she whispered.

Her daughter was a tiny thing, with tufts of black hair, almond-shaped eyes and pudgy cheeks. She looked so precious, so small.

And heartbreakingly lonely.

Susannah stared at the photo, hoping to see some sign of a smile, a glimmer of recognition in those little brown eyes. But the precious baby merely stared back at Susannah, searching, it seemed, to find a mother's love.

"I *do* love you, sweetheart, and I'll make everything all right, as soon as I get there. And the minute I arrive at the orphanage," Susannah said, making them both a solemn promise, "I'll coax a smile from you and try my best to make sure you experience a happy future."

And like magic, a glimmer of hope and recognition peered back from the black-and-white photograph.

A rush of love swept across Susannah's barren heart, warming Susannah to the bone. Her dream had a name, a face.

She couldn't wait to hold her baby in her arms and kiss away the sadness little Mei had suffered while living an ocean away.

For what seemed a long time, Susannah sat behind the desk, studying the photograph of the child who had been placed in a basket, abandoned on the wharf and left prey to the elements and any number of unsavory characters.

Thank God the honorable fishermen came along when they did.

Susannah closed her eyes and whispered a prayer for Mei, thanking God for her safety and asking

Him to bless the families of the men who'd found her child.

Mei McCord had become a real, flesh-and-blood person today. Susannah pressed a soft kiss to the priceless photo. "Mommy is coming, Mei. It won't be much longer, then I can bring you home."

Never had the decision to adopt felt so right. This little girl who'd been left alone would soon have a mother to care for her. A mother who would shower her with all the love she had to offer.

No one deserved Susannah's heart and soul more than the child who had been abandoned by the people who should have loved her dearly.

By Monday afternoon, Russell was going nuts.

He hadn't been able to get a damn thing done all day. And for no reason at all, he'd snapped at Mahnita, a real godsend to MonMart and the entire Kingsley family.

He'd apologized to the kindhearted woman, but that didn't make him feel any less of an ogre. Or any less touchy and ready to burst.

It wasn't until the sun had descended in the Montana sky, that he began to sort through his feelings. Susannah McCord—not Suzy—had a real hold on him.

He'd reluctantly left the preschool on Friday afternoon, since there was so much he didn't get to see, to ask, to learn.

Rather than appeasing his curiosity, seeing Susannah had only made matters worse. He wanted more time with her; he needed more time.

All weekend, off and on, he'd fought the urge to call her at home and ask her out to dinner. In a sense, he supposed he'd won the battle. He hadn't chased after her, made promises or begged her to give him another chance, to give *them* another chance.

For the most part, he'd let go of the old memories. And interestingly enough, it wasn't the old Suzy he'd been hell-bent to call or see.

There was something new and exciting about Susannah, something he hadn't noticed before.

Yet he had hoped the attractive businesswoman would make the first move by picking up the phone and calling him, which would certainly save his pride. But apparently, Susannah was just as stubborn and prideful as he.

The intercom buzzed, drawing his attention.

"Yes, Mahnita?"

"It's five-thirty, Russell. If you don't have anything else for me to do, I'm going to head home."

"No, that's all for today." He couldn't very well give her another job when he hadn't gotten a damn thing done all day. "I'll be leaving soon, too. Have a nice evening, Mahnita."

"You, too."

Yeah, right. Another night eating takeout from the Calico Diner in front of the television.

Unless you call Susannah. Ask her to have dinner with you.

Oh yeah? he questioned the weird voice in his mind. And what if she says no?

She might surprise you.

That was for sure. Everything about Susannah surprised him. And intrigued him, he realized, once he'd put his memories of Suzy aside.

And once he'd put away his dreams of having a daughter named Isabelle.

Russell, is this all about Isabelle? Or is it more than that?

More than that? Had his imagination—rather than Destiny—manifested Isabelle for some other reason? Or had she merely been a dream-enhanced vision, a figment of his brain injury?

He glanced out the window, watched another miserable day pass away.

What the hell do you want out of life? the voice asked, louder and more insistent. *Marriage? A family?*

Yeah. He wanted a wife and kids, and it was about time he settled down. So what?

The closest you got to having a family was when Susannah was a part of your life.

That was a fact. And Russell hadn't appreciated her.

He hadn't appreciated the changes that had evolved over the years or the way her eyes lit up when she challenged him, the way she set his blood on fire with a smile and the toss of her head.

Susannah might not have been the same girl he'd loved in high school or the woman in his fantasy, but she'd enriched his life in a way he couldn't explain.

And having her gone was killing him.

Suddenly, groveling at her feet didn't seem like such a bad idea, not if it was the only hope he had of apologizing and setting things straight.

God, why had it taken him so long to see the full picture?

His dream of being with Suzy and Isabelle wasn't just a desire to have a child of his own—it was a desire to no longer live alone. To settle down and start a family.

A family that included Susannah McCord.

Chapter 13

As the last child left the preschool, waving happily from the car seat in back of his mother's minivan, Susannah blew out a sigh.

It had been a good day—busy but rewarding.

As she prepared to turn off the lights and lock up the classroom, a car drove up.

Had someone forgotten something?

She glanced out the window, and when she spotted Russell's Range Rover, her pulse skipped a beat, then surged. Why had he come by?

She lifted her hand to her hair, feeling for loose strands that had escaped the big brass clip she'd used to hold her curls out of the way, then swore under her breath.

What did it matter? There was no reason to care about her appearance. Russell Kingsley meant nothing to her. Not anymore.

Still she watched as he climbed from the late-model SUV, watched as he sauntered along the sidewalk to the door. Cowboy and businessman rolled in one.

He adjusted his Stetson, revealing a head of black hair that glistened in the late-afternoon sunlight. He wore faded jeans, a white cotton shirt, a lightweight black jacket and a hard-edged look of determination on his face.

Because he hadn't noticed her through the window, she continued to observe him. It had been weeks since she'd had the opportunity to admire his form, his physique.

When he stepped inside, as handsome and alluring as he'd ever been, their gazes locked.

"I need to talk to you, Susannah."

Her heart continued to race, in spite of her efforts to remain detached and unaffected. "What do you want to talk about?"

"Us."

She crossed her arms and placed her weight on one foot. "There's nothing to say."

"Yes, there is." He removed his hat and set it on the sign-in table, as though he meant to stay awhile. "I have some explaining to do."

Two Kingsley apologies in one day? That had to be some kind of record.

He closed the gap between them, making her painfully aware of his musky scent, aware that he was merely an arm's length away. His hair appeared mussed, not just compressed by the Stetson. It looked as though he'd run his hands instead of a comb through it—more than once.

She realized he'd had something weighing on his mind, and for some reason needed to share it with her.

"It's my fault things didn't work out between us."

That much she could agree with. "You don't need to explain."

"Yes, I do. You may have figured out what went wrong ages ago, but it's something that just became clear to me."

Curiosity wouldn't allow her to interrupt. Did he truly understand why their relationship had ended?

"After my accident, I was intent upon making things right in my life, in making things right with you."

If he went into that stupid, prophetic dream he'd

had, she just might pick up one of the wooden
building blocks in the corner and chuck it at him.
She'd had her fill of the old Suzy, how things used
to be and a redheaded daughter named Isabelle,
who'd been named after someone in an old movie
neither of them could remember.

Russell sighed, then raked a hand through his
hair, validating her belief that he'd been repeating
the nervous gesture a lot today. "I'd been trying to
recreate that past and build a future based upon a
fantasy. But I've found out what's important in
life."

So had she.

"You're the best thing that ever happened to me,
Susannah." His gaze lanced her with sincerity.

She opened her mouth to object, but the words
wouldn't form. So she remained standing, silent and
apprehensive.

"I'm not talking about the old Suzy," he said,
"but *you,* Susannah McCord."

"You don't even know me, Russell. Not really."
She turned her back, wishing she'd left some task
undone, something with which she could dismiss
him.

He placed a hand on her shoulder and stepped
closer. Dangerously close.

She could smell the lingering scent of his cologne and detect a hint of peppermint. He slowly turned her around, to face him, to listen to his explanation. "You're right. I was so determined to make you into the Suzy I remembered that I didn't acknowledge the woman you are, the woman you've become."

Her heart thudded in her chest, clamoring to get out and echoing with the truth of his words.

"I love you, Susannah."

He'd said the same thing each time he abandoned her.

Did Russell Kingsley know the meaning of the word love? Or was he just so used to getting whatever he wanted that he used those words as a platitude he hoped would change her mind?

It would take more than words to break through the protective barrier she'd erected. "You said it yourself, Russell. You don't know me. So how can you possibly love me?"

"I don't know a man alive who can explain love, darlin'. But I love you, Susannah. And I want to marry you, whether we have children together or not."

She desperately wanted to believe him, but her battered pride looked for evidence of a lie. "What about Isabelle?"

"She was merely a figment of my imagination,

triggered by a vision of Sheree and the sound of her voice." Sincerity glistened in his eyes, shaking Susannah's resolve not to trust him again.

"You don't want a redheaded daughter?" she asked.

"I don't need kids to make me happy. I only need you. And I'll support your dreams, whatever they are."

"This school is part of my dream."

"That's great. If you want to pour your love and affection on the kids here, that's fine with me. I'll come read them stories at lunchtime. I'll chaperon field trips. I'll even dress up like Santa and come visit on Christmas. If there's something I can do to help, just let me know."

His enthusiasm was contagious, and she found it hard not to collapse in his arms. But there was more to her dream than the school. "What about adopting a baby?"

"That's great. And I'll be the best father you've ever seen." Russell's hand brushed a lock of hair from her face. "But me loving you has nothing to do with children. If you want them, we'll have them. If not? Then I'll be content to be your husband."

"I want the baby I'm adopting."

"Then I want that baby, too. Your dreams are my dreams. And we'll make our own destiny."

"Are you sure about this?" she asked. "I don't want my daughter disappointed. She deserves a loving family, a mom and dad who think the world of her."

"I'm in this for the long haul, Susannah." He cupped her jaw, his thumb softly stroking her cheek. "I love you, and if you bring a daughter into our family, by any means, I'll love her, too."

God help her, Susannah wanted to believe him. But could she risk not only her own heart, but Mei's heart, as well? The decision she would make would affect them both, and she had to start thinking like a mother, not just a woman in love.

She drew away from him. "Excuse me for a minute, Russell. I'll be right back."

When she returned with Mei's photograph and handed it to him, he studied the black-and-white image, then looked up at her. "Is this our baby?"

Our baby? Was he accepting her daughter as his own? "This is Mei. And she was found abandoned near the wharf in a small Chinese fishing village. She has no one but me."

"No one but *us*," he corrected.

Tears welled in her eyes, and she bit her tongue, held back the words. She didn't know what to say or how to respond, so she merely watched him. Waited.

Russell looked at the photograph again and studied the delicate features of a baby who looked like a solemn-faced China doll.

She was a beautiful child, but her expression haunted him, drawing his sympathy. How could someone abandon a baby? Leave her on the wharf by the sea?

A fiercely overwhelming need to protect the little girl swept over him, touching his heart. He suddenly understood why Susannah would go to such lengths for a child she hadn't met. And he wanted to go the same distance.

He looked up at the woman he loved, caught her gaze as she tried to read his mind. "Do you want to be this little girl's mommy?"

She lifted her chin in that decisive manner he'd come to love and respect. "I *am* this little girl's mommy."

Russell cupped her cheek and smiled. "Then can I be her daddy?"

Susannah swallowed hard, choking back her emotion, but tears welled in those pretty blue eyes, giving away her secret.

"Do you want to be?" she asked, her voice soft yet husky.

"I want to be a part of your family, Susannah. I want to curl up on the sofa with Mei and watch those goofy puppets on TV that Samantha likes. And I want to stand in line for an hour, just to get a picture with Santa. I want to buy a camcorder and hover by the stage to film school programs and dance recitals." He pulled her close and relished the faint whiff of springtime perfume that mingled with finger paint and paste. "I want to be a daddy to Mei. And I want to come home at night and find you and her waiting for me, with smiles on your faces and love in your eyes."

Susannah wrapped her arms around his neck, squeezing him tight, drawing him closer—so it seemed—than she ever had before.

He lowered his mouth to hers, kissing her as he'd never done before, loving her with a gentle tongue. Their bodies melded in a new way. A better way.

When they came up for air, still holding each other tight, he whispered against her ear. "Marry me, Susannah. Be my wife."

She pulled away, her eyes wide. "I can't."

Her words and the apprehension in her voice sucker-punched him in the gut. "What do you mean, you can't? Don't you love me?"

"Yes," she said, "I love you, Russell. More than you'll ever know. But I can't marry you. Not yet."

Not yet? Hell, he was ready to fly to Vegas and get married tonight. As far as he was concerned, there was no need to even pack a bag. They could buy what they needed in a hotel gift shop.

"Why won't you marry me now? I can't see any logical reason to wait. Shoot, Susannah, we're getting married seventeen years too late as it is."

"I'd lose Mei." Her eyes searched his, as though desperately wanting him to understand.

"How would our getting married cause you to lose Mei?"

"I've been approved to adopt as a single parent. But you haven't gone through the process. If we married before the adoption is final, we'd have to start the lengthy process all over again. And…"

Russell kissed the furrow in her brow. "I understand, darlin'. We won't do anything to jeopardize the adoption. Will you marry me as soon as we get home?"

As the worry left her face, her expression softened. "What do you mean, as soon as *we* get home?"

"You're not going to China alone, Susannah. There's no rule about you taking an escort, is there? An old friend?"

"Of course not. You can go with me. We just

can't get married until we bring Mei home and the paperwork is complete.''

"How soon can we leave?" he asked.

"Well, there're a few steps we need to take yet. And you'll need to get a visa." Her eyes widened. "Oh my gosh, you have a passport, don't you?"

"I sure do."

She blew out a sigh, and he wanted to wrap his arms around her and never let go. He loved this woman, more than he ever imagined possible. But he waited, watched as her voice caught up with her mind.

"Well, then, as I was saying, we need to get our visas." She tried to rake a hand through her hair, only to find her fingers hampered by a brass clip.

Russell laughed and removed the barrette, freeing her hair and allowing the silky red tresses to fall loose around her shoulders and down her back. He ran his fingers through the strands, feeling the softness.

"I love you, Susannah. And I can't wait to tell the world how much." Then he took her mouth with his, sealing his words the only way he knew how.

He held her close for a while, then stroked her back. "Let's go home, darlin'. We have some celebrating to do."

"Which home?" she asked. "Yours or mine?"

"Either. As far as I'm concerned, we're sharing everything from now on—houses, cars, dreams and destinies."

"Desire?" she asked, her eyes twinkling with mirth.

"That, too."

Then they turned off the lights and locked up the classroom until tomorrow morning.

For the rest of the night, Russell intended to show her just how much he loved her.

Russell could hardly believe his good fortune. Susannah McCord had agreed to be his wife.

And in a week or two, they would be going to China to bring home their new daughter, a pretty baby girl who would be given more love than she knew what to do with.

As they entered his house—their house—he smiled. Susannah had done wonders with her mother's rundown place on State Street, and he wondered what touches she'd add to the home where he hung his hat.

He slipped off his watch, meaning to lay it on the glass coffee table, but his movements froze. "Look at the orchid."

It stood as tall and healthy as the day it had arrived at the hospital.

"Who would have guessed," Susannah said. "You've got a green thumb."

"I don't know about that. I didn't do anything except cross my fingers and hope."

Yet Russell couldn't shake the feeling it was more than that. Destiny had pulled something off, but he wasn't sure what it was. It was enough that he could bask in the warmth of Susannah's love.

He laid the watch on the glass tabletop, then glanced up. His eyes lit on the tacky deer antler lamp that Reed had given him, the lamp he'd refused to hide in the attic. "I guess it's time to unplug that thing and haul it away."

"What thing?" Susannah asked. She dropped her purse onto the sofa and kicked off her shoes.

"The Bambi lamp."

She made her way to the table that displayed the monstrosity and smiled. "You know, Russell, it really isn't that bad."

"You're kidding, right?"

"It was a gift from your brother. I suppose it will grow on me."

"It was a gag gift, Susannah. Reed never intended me to give it a place of honor."

She broke into a smile, and he realized she was playing with him. And it felt good. Damn good.

"This is your place to decorate as you want, darlin'. The Bambi lamp can stay or go. Your call."

She offered him a playful grin. "Let's see how the fixture looks in the morning."

"Then let's go to bed." Russell made his way toward the woman he loved, the woman with whom he would share the rest of his life, and took her in his arms. "I have a hankering to get the happily-ever-after stuff started."

Susannah laughed. "So do I."

Then he drew her into the bedroom—their bedroom—and brushed a kiss on her lips.

"We might have to wait until we return from China to get married, but I plan on hosting the biggest engagement party Rumor has ever seen. I want everyone to know my intentions."

"I don't know about that," Susannah said, wrinkling her brow.

"Humor me, darlin'. This is going to be the biggest, most successful merger either of us have ever put together. And I want everyone to know how much I love you." Then he kissed her. Slowly at first, savoring each moment he held her close.

As the kiss deepened, the fire in them grew, and

so did his determination to make their marriage and their family work.

He loved her with his body, giving and taking until he thought he'd die of wanting her. He savored each stroke, each thrust, until a soul-touching climax gave him a glimpse of forever.

"I'm going to make love to you all night long," Russell whispered, as he rolled to the side, taking her with him.

"I've got an early day tomorrow," she said. But she kissed his chest, taking a nipple into her mouth and biting it softly, stirring his passion to new heights.

Then he loved her again, a joining that brought on a powerful climax that caused her to cry out in pleasure and rake her nails on his back. Unable to hold back any longer, he released his seed and held her close until the last wave passed, until the past no longer mattered and the only thing they had to cling to was each other and hope for the future.

She smiled, giving him a glimpse of all the love in her heart.

How could one man be so lucky? He stroked the downy soft skin on her cheek. "The preschool and Mei have put a light back in your eyes."

"Maybe so," she said, "but you've put a light back in my heart."

Russell pulled her close, his own heart swelling in his chest. "We've been given a second chance, darlin'. And I intend to do everything right this time around."

"Me, too. I love you, Russell."

"I love you, too," he said. "And I promise to be a good husband and father."

For the rest of the night, they lay in each other's arms, amidst tangled sheets and promises they both intended to keep.

Epilogue

Russell and Susannah stood on the sprawling Spanish-tiled patio and surveyed the vast backyard of the Kingsley Ranch, where their engagement party would be held.

The verdant grounds sported an Italian water fountain, imported stone-crafted benches and a colorful array of artistically planted flowers, which made it one of the most impressive gardens in all of Montana.

At first, Carolyn had told Russell he hadn't given her enough time to plan the kind of party he and Susannah deserved, but when his mother learned of their impending trip to China, she quickly went to work.

Russell held Susannah's hand, as they strolled the grounds, making sure everything was ready for the first guest to arrive. Nearly all of Rumor had been invited.

A party rental company had set up linen-covered tables decorated with floral bouquets, and the caterer had prepared a feast.

"I'm amazed at how your family pulled together for this," Susannah said.

"They've been real troupers."

Maura, Tag and Reed had been working since early morning, just to make sure Russell and Susannah's special day would be perfect.

"Aunt Susannah," Samantha called from the patio. The little girl skipped out onto the lawn to greet them, her father following a few steps behind.

Susannah stooped to give the child a hug. "Well, if it isn't my soon-to-be favorite niece. Hi, sweetheart."

Tag's daughter had been thrilled to know her preschool teacher would become part of the family. She twirled around, showing off her clothes. "I have a new party dress, see? And new party shoes. Grandma took me shopping."

"You look so pretty." Susannah smiled warmly,

and Russell imagined she was dreaming of the day she could take her own daughter shopping.

"Sammy," Tag said to his daughter. "Grandma needs your help. She'd like you and Aunt Maura to greet people as they enter and have them sign the guest book."

"Oh, goody. I get to help with the party, too." Then she skipped off to find her grandmother, passing her uncle Reed in the process.

"Jeff's on the line, Russell." Reed lifted the portable phone in his hand. "He wants to talk to you."

Russell took the receiver and spoke to the cousin his parents had raised. "Hey, Jeff."

"Listen, Russell, I'd planned on coming home for the party, but MAFFS has been called out to fight that forest fire in California. A call with my best wishes will have to do for now."

"I understand." Russell glanced at Susannah and smiled. "You'll have to come see us after we return from China."

"You got it. I've got some vacation time coming, so I'll make an effort to come home soon. It's been too long. Anyway, congratulations, Russell."

"Thanks, Jeff. Mom will be glad to hear you'll be coming home to visit. Take care." He pushed the power button, ending the connection, then looked at Reed. "The Modular Airborne Firefighting System has called him to Colorado this time.

With the drought, his unit will be pretty busy this summer.''

"Fire season is right around the corner. I imagine, as fire chief, I'll be busy, too," Reed said. "Well, I guess I'd better help man the bar. That's the job I've been given."

Tag laughed and placed a hand on his brother's shoulder. "I'll help you set up, Reed—before Mom and Dad think I'm too idle and give me cleanup detail."

As the two younger men headed toward the house, they passed Carolyn who walked across the lawn, a large silver frame held close to her heart.

She turned the frame around, revealing an 11x14 enlargement of Mei's photo. "What do you think? I had it blown up at the MonMart photo department. I thought our new granddaughter should be represented today."

Russell took the picture and kissed his mother's cheek. "It's beautiful. I wish the baby could be here to help us celebrate. But this is the next best thing."

"Thank you, Carolyn," Susannah added, her voice soft and full of emotion. "It's a beautiful touch. And very much appreciated."

"Mom," Maura called from the open sliding door. "The caterer needs you."

"You'll have to excuse me." Carolyn turned and

hurried to the house, leaving Russell and Susannah with the photograph of their daughter.

"I'm not sure we needed a party of this size, Russell. I still think a quiet family dinner would have been enough."

Russell kissed Susannah's brow. "I wanted a wedding, but this engagement party is the next best thing." Then he reached into the lapel pocket of his black suede jacket and withdrew a small velvet box and handed it to the woman he loved.

Susannah caressed the velvet edges for a moment, then lifted the lid, revealing a huge, heart-shaped diamond. "Oh, Russell, it's beautiful."

"So are you." Russell slipped the ring on her left hand. "Susannah, I promise to love you forever. In sickness and health, for richer for poorer, until hell freezes over and the fat lady sings."

Susannah laughed. "That's not how it goes."

"I haven't been to many weddings and couldn't remember all the words, but I want you to know I'm going to love you for the rest of our lives and then some."

Susannah wrapped her arms around his neck. "I love you, Russell Kingsley. And I'm glad you convinced me to give us a second chance."

"I'm glad I took time to get to know the real Susannah." He brushed a kiss across her lips.

"You've taught me to how to seize the day and quit living in the past."

"Excuse me."

Russell turned to see Sheree, her red hair pulled back in a customary ponytail, cheeks flushed and eyes glowing.

The teenager offered a bright-eyed smile. "I wanted to tell you both how happy I am for you and how glad I am that you invited me."

"In a way," Russell said, "you brought this all together, Sheree."

"Gosh, Mr. Kingsley. I'm not sure that I did anything at all, but it's kind of cool that you think so."

"I can't explain it, either. But you did." Russell tugged lightly on her ponytail. "Don't be a stranger, Sheree. I hope you'll drop by and visit us sometime. Maybe you and I can shoot some hoops in the backyard."

The teenager laughed. "I don't know about that. I'm a little clumsy in the athletic department. But I'll come by and see you guys." Sheree looked at Susannah. "And I'll help Dee Dee while you're in China. You don't have to worry about the preschool."

"I know you will. I've also hired a second certified teacher. Between the three of you, I know the children will be in good hands." Susannah gave the teen a hug.

Russell glanced at the photo of Mei, feeling like a family. And it seemed especially nice to have Sheree with them. She was, in a way, a reminder of Isabelle and would always hold a special place in his heart.

As the young girl walked away to greet a neighbor she spotted on the patio, Russell slipped an arm around Susannah and pulled her close.

Some people thought the firstborn Kingsley heir and MonMart magnate had always led a charmed life. But he hadn't, up until now.

It wasn't until Susannah McCord agreed to marry him that Russell Kingsley realized how truly blessed he was.

Second chances didn't get any better than this.

* * * * *

Don't miss the continuation of
MONTANA MAVERICKS:
THE KINGSLEYS,
where nothing is as it seems beneath the big skies of Montana.

MOON OVER MONTANA
by Jackie Merritt
Silhouette Special Edition #1550
Available Now!

MARRY ME...AGAIN
by Cheryl St. John
Silhouette Special Edition #1558
Available August 2003

BIG SKY BABY
by Judy Duarte
Silhouette Special Edition #1563
Available September 2003

THE RANCHER'S DAUGHTER
by Jodi O'Donnell
Silhouette Special Edition #1568
Available October 2003

HER MONTANA MILLIONAIRE
by Crystal Green
Silhouette Special Edition #1574
Available November 2003

SWEET TALK
by Jackie Merritt
Silhouette Special Edition #1580
Available December 2003

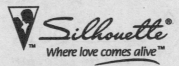

A **brand-new** *Maitland Maternity* story!

MAITLAND MATERNITY

Baby 101

by
Marisa Carroll

The first in a quartet of Maitland Maternity novels connected by a mother's legacy of love.

Lana Lord denies any interest when she receives a letter from the mother who gave her up for adoption twenty-five years ago. But when she sees single dad Dylan Van Zandt struggling to raise a child on his own, Lana realizes that love's choices aren't always easy.

Look for BABY 101, available in August 2003 at your favorite retail outlet.

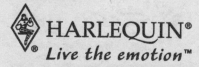

HARLEQUIN®
Live the emotion™

Visit us at www.eHarlequin.com

CPB101

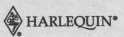

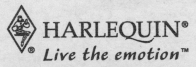

Is your man too good to be true?

Hot, gorgeous AND romantic?
If so, he could be a Harlequin® Blaze™ series cover model!

Our grand-prize winners will receive a trip for two to New York City to shoot the cover of a Blaze novel, and will stay at the luxurious Plaza Hotel. Plus, they'll receive $500 U.S. spending money! The runner-up winners will receive $200 U.S. to spend on a romantic dinner for two.

It's easy to enter!

In 100 words or less, tell us what makes your boyfriend or spouse a true romantic and the perfect candidate for the cover of a Blaze novel, and include in your submission two photos of this potential cover model.

All entries must include the written submission of the contest entrant, two photographs of the model candidate and the Official Entry Form and Publicity Release forms completed in full and signed by both the model candidate and the contest entrant. Harlequin, along with the experts at Elite Model Management, will select a winner.

For photo and complete Contest details, please refer to the Official Rules on the next page. All entries will become the property of Harlequin Enterprises Ltd. and are not returnable.

Please visit www.blazecovermodel.com to download a copy of the Official Entry Form and Publicity Release Form or send a request to one of the addresses below.

Please mail your entry to: **Harlequin Blaze Cover Model Search**

In U.S.A.
P.O. Box 9069
Buffalo, NY
14269-9069

In Canada
P.O. Box 637
Fort Erie, ON
L2A 5X3

No purchase necessary. Contest open to Canadian and U.S. residents who are 18 and over. Void where prohibited. Contest closes September 30, 2003.

HBCVRMODEL1